"I am completely at fault," Fanny choked between inhales.

"Not completely, no." Jonathon's deep voice poured warmth over her cold heart. "We share the blame and will face the consequences together, no matter how dire or life-altering."

He did not mention marriage, but he was thinking it. The evidence was there, in the grim twist of his lips and the stern set of his shoulders.

"Come." He tugged her toward the ballroom, toward their moment of reckoning. "Time to face the good people of Denver."

He guided her to the very edge of the French doors. A few more steps and they would cross over the threshold, into a future neither of them truly wanted. Jonathon for his reasons.

Fanny for hers.

She shot a glance at Jonathon from beneath her lashes. Even in the dense, flickering shadows, she recognized the resolve in his eyes, the willingness to do whatever was necessary to protect her from another scandal.

She could not let him compromise his future for hers.

Renee Ryan
and
Danica Favorite

The Marriage Agreement
&
Shotgun Marriage

LOVE INSPIRED
INSPIRATIONAL ROMANCE

LOVE INSPIRED®

INSPIRATIONAL ROMANCE

ISBN-13: 978-1-335-45672-4

The Marriage Agreement and Shotgun Marriage

Copyright © 2021 by Harlequin Books S.A.

The Marriage Agreement
First published in 2015. This edition published in 2021.
Copyright © 2015 by Renee Halverson

Shotgun Marriage
First published in 2016. This edition published in 2021.
Copyright © 2016 by Danica Favorite

Recycling programs
for this product may
not exist in your area.

Love Inspired
22 Adelaide St. West, 40th Floor
Toronto, Ontario M5H 4E3, Canada
www.Harlequin.com

Printed in U.S.A.

CONTENTS

Renee Ryan grew up in a Florida beach town where she learned to surf, sort of. With a degree from FSU, she explored career opportunities at a Florida theme park and a modeling agency and even taught high school economics. She currently lives with her husband in Wisconsin, and many have mistaken their overweight cat for a small bear. You may contact Renee at reneeryan.com, on Facebook or on Twitter, @reneeryanbooks.

Visit the Author Profile page
at Harlequin.com for more titles.

THE MARRIAGE AGREEMENT

Renee Ryan

For You formed my inward parts; You covered me in my mother's womb. I will praise You, for I am fearfully and wonderfully made; Marvelous are Your works, And that my soul knows very well.
—*Psalms* 139:13–14

For Cindy Kirk and Nancy Robards Thompson, the best plotting partners on the planet. Thank you for walking beside me throughout the process of writing this book and being willing to help me plot myself out of a corner far too many times to admit. I love you both!

Chapter One

The Hotel Dupree, Denver, Colorado 1896

Shadows sculpted the darkened ballroom as Fanny Mitchell awaited her employer's arrival. A happy sigh leaked out of her, echoing off the ornate walls. She loved this cavernous, oft overlooked room, loved it above all others in the hotel.

An expectant, almost dreamy silence hung in the air, as if Fanny was on the brink of something new and wonderful. Arms outstretched, she executed an uninhibited spin across the dance floor. Then stopped abruptly, frowning at her whimsy.

A quick tug on her sleeves, a readjustment of her skirt, and she was back to being the oh-so-proper guest-services manager of the finest hotel in Denver, Colorado.

Decorum restored, she continued her inspection at a more sedate pace. In four days, Mrs. Beatrix Singletary would hold her annual charity ball in this very room. Three hundred of Denver's most important residents were invited to attend, including most of Fanny's family. It would be the first time the widow held the event outside her home. Fanny suspected this change in venue was because Mrs. Singletary now owned one quarter of the Hotel Dupree.

As owner of the other three quarters, Fanny's employer wished to impress his new business partner with the efficiency of their hotel staff. Fanny would not let him down.

She would not let herself down. This was her chance to prove she was more than the gossips claimed, more than the labels others had attached to her since childhood.

By organizing this particular function, the largest and most anticipated of the year, Fanny would finally show the good people of Denver that she was worthy of their respect. That she hadn't jilted one of the most highly respected men in town on impulse, or because of some hidden flaw in her character.

Her decision had been well thought out and for all the right reasons.

Fanny moved to a nearby wall and pressed a switch on the raised panel. The recently installed Maria Theresa chandelier came alive with light.

The absurd fee to ship the exquisite fixture from Europe had been well worth the cost. Airy and delicate, the handblown glass and crystal rosettes twisted around the metal frame in such a way as to give the illusion of a floating waterfall.

Continuing her inspection, she made mental notes where to put tables, chairs and the myriad of flower arrangements she'd personally designed.

This was what she was born to do, taking an annual event people talked about for months and turning it into an even more spectacular occasion.

Why, then, did she experience a sudden burst of melancholy? Why this strange bout of dissatisfaction?

Fanny knew, of course.

She would soon celebrate her twenty-fifth birthday. Unlike her four married siblings, Fanny had no one special in her life.

There was still time for her own happily-ever-after. For now, she would focus on the many blessings the Lord had bestowed on her. She had siblings who adored her, parents who supported her unconditionally and a job she loved, working beside a man she greatly admired.

"Fanny," a deep, masculine voice called from behind her, the tone a mix of amusement and lazy drawl. "You've arrived ahead of me as usual."

She ignored a rush of anticipation and slowly pivoted around to face her employer. For one dreadful, wonderful moment, her heart lifted.

There he stood, framed in the doorway. Jonathon Hawkins. The intensely private, overly serious, wildly successful hotelier, whose rags to riches story inspired everyone he met, Fanny most of all.

He was so competent, so handsome. Tall, broad-shouldered, with a head of glossy, dark brown hair, he attracted more than his fair share of female attention.

He seemed oblivious to his effect on women. His mantra was business first, business always. Though she felt a sad heart tug over his resolve to remain unattached and childless, Fanny appreciated his single-minded focus.

That was, at any rate, her official stand on the matter.

His mouth curved in an easy half smile and a sudden dizziness struck her.

"Mr. Hawkins." She ordered her heartbeat to slow to a normal rate. "You'll be pleased to know I've secured—"

He lifted a hand to stop her. "You agreed to call me Jonathon."

Her breath snagged on a skittering rush of air. Of course. They'd been on a first-name basis for over a year. She'd nearly forgotten in his absence, though he'd been gone but a week.

"I…yes, I…" *Get control of yourself, Fanny.* "Are you ready for our final walk-through, Jonathon?"

"I am, indeed." He pushed away from the door frame.

Here we go, she thought, silently bracing for the impact of his nearness.

As his long, purposeful strides ate up the distance between them, she noted how he moved with predatory grace. Jonathon Hawkins was a study in contradictions, a man who could be sophisticated and mannerly, or cunning and shrewd, depending on the situation.

He stopped, leaving a perfectly appropriate amount of space between them. *Always the gentleman*, she thought. She knew enough about his past to find that especially intriguing. And there went that sad little heart tug again.

"Shall we begin?" Under the bright glow of the chandelier, his eyes seemed to hold a thousand shades of blue.

She swallowed back a sigh. "Yes."

"After you." He gestured for her to take the lead.

For a dangerous moment, she couldn't make her feet work properly. Jonathon seemed different today, more intent, more focused. His silvery-blue eyes gleamed with intelligence and something else, something she knew better than to define.

Quickly breaking eye contact, she directed him to the far right corner of the ballroom. Their heels struck the freshly polished floor in perfect rhythm with one another.

"We'll set up banquet tables here and…over there."

She made a sweeping gesture toward the opposite corner. "This will allow easy access to the food without obstructing the general flow of traffic to and from the dance floor."

He studied the two spaces. His eyes narrowed slightly, as if picturing the setup in his mind. "Excellent."

Pleased by his approval, she continued guiding him through the room, stopping at various points along the way to explain her ideas in greater detail. When they were once again standing in the spot where they'd begun, she drew in a deep breath. "Do you have any questions or concerns?"

"Not at the moment." He smiled down at her. "Thank you, Fanny. As always, you've thought of everything."

Had she? She turned in a slow circle, attempting to determine if there'd been a forgotten detail, something they were both missing. When nothing came to mind, she returned his smile. "I think we're ready."

"So it would seem."

A moment of silent understanding passed between them. His expression was so full of meaning, so unexpectedly affectionate, she thought he might lean in closer and…and…

She quickly looked away. "I hope Mrs. Singletary agrees."

That earned her a soft chuckle. "You've left nothing to chance. I'm confident your efforts will find favor with the illustrious Beatrix Singletary."

"Did I hear someone mention my name?" As if she'd been waiting for her cue, the widow materialized in the doorway, one hand on her hip, the other poised against her chin.

On anyone else, the pose would look ridiculous. Not

on Mrs. Singletary. She was a woman with flair, always dressed impeccably in the latest fashion. A renowned beauty in her day, the widow had golden-brown hair that was a perfect foil for her fair complexion. Her face showed few signs that nearly four and a half decades had passed since her birth.

Fanny liked the woman. She especially appreciated the way she ran her vast fortune, and hoped to learn much from her now that she'd joined forces with Jonathon.

As was his custom, he stepped forward and greeted the widow by placing a light kiss to her extended hand. "It's always a pleasure to see you in the hotel, Mrs. Singletary."

"It's always a pleasure to be in the hotel, Mr. Hawkins."

Mouth tilted at an amused angle, he released her hand. "Would you prefer a walk-through of the ballroom now, or after we review the final guest list?"

"Now, of course. We did, after all, come here first."

One dark eyebrow shot up. "We?"

"My companion and I. Do come along, Philomena." A slight crease marred the widow's forehead as she glanced over her shoulder. "Lurking in the shadows is quite unseemly."

The young woman hurried forward.

Philomena Ferguson was, to Fanny's thinking, the most likable of the seven Ferguson sisters. With her remarkable hazel eyes, golden-brown hair and flawless complexion, she was also the most beautiful. Her pale green shirtwaist dress, cut in an A-line silhouette, only served to enhance her extraordinary looks.

Wondering if Jonathon noticed Philomena's undeniable charms, Fanny slid a glance at him. He was still looking at her. Not Philomena, *her*.

Fanny knew better than to read too much into his attentiveness. The one occasion she'd thought he might actually kiss her, or perhaps profess a personal interest in her, he'd taken the opportunity to explain the motivation behind his refusal to marry. Ever.

This time, when the heart tug came, she shoved it aside with a fast, determined swallow.

"Mr. Hawkins." Mrs. Singletary tapped his arm, the gesture sufficiently pulling his attention away from Fanny. "I believe you've met my companion."

"We are acquainted. Miss Ferguson." He cast a pleasant, if somewhat distant smile in Philomena's direction. "Lovely to see you again."

An attractive blush spread across her cheeks. "Thank you, Mr. Hawkins, and you as well."

As she bounced her gaze between the two, a speculative gleam lit Mrs. Singletary's eye.

That look put Fanny instantly on guard. It was no secret the widow considered herself an accomplished matchmaker. For good reason. Mrs. Singletary had proved herself quite skilled at ferreting out potential love matches. One of her most recent successes involved Fanny's childhood friend Molly Taylor Scott, who was now married to Fanny's brother, Garrett.

Thanks, also, to the widow's efforts, her sister was happily settled, as well—to Fanny's former fiancé. She was glad Callie and Reese had found one another. They'd married for love, which was the only reason for pledging lifelong vows, to Fanny's way of thinking. Marrying for anything less than an all-consuming love would be tantamount to imprisonment.

Mrs. Singletary's eyes sharpened over Jonathon and

Philomena. Oh, no. Did the widow have her next match in mind?

"Well, then, Mr. Hawkins." A sly smile spread across the widow's lips. "Since you and my companion are already acquainted, I trust you have no objection to attending the opera with us tomorrow evening."

Fanny made a soft sound of protest in her throat, barely audible, but Jonathon must have caught it because he asked, "You have a concern?"

Think, Fanny, think.

"We're scheduled to, ah, review next month's bookings tomorrow afternoon." An endeavor that almost always went late. She started to say as much but stopped when she glanced at Mrs. Singletary's raised eyebrow. "However, we can certainly reschedule."

Jonathon frowned at her. "Reschedule? But we always—"

"Oh, excellent," Mrs. Singletary declared, cutting him off midsentence. "This is most excellent, indeed. You, Mr. Hawkins, are now perfectly free to join Philomena and me tomorrow evening."

His frown deepened. "Mrs. Singletary, I cannot attend the opera when I have a prior commitment here at the hotel."

"Miss Mitchell." Mrs. Singletary gave Fanny a pointed stare. "You don't mind, do you, dear, if Philomena and I steal your employer away for one evening?"

Actually, she minded a great deal. "Certainly not."

Jonathon opened his mouth, then shut it again as he considered the widow through narrowed eyes. "You seem very determined I join you."

"I am quite determined."

"Why?"

Undaunted by his suspicious tone, Mrs. Singletary gave a jaunty wave of her hand. "Considering the nature of our business relationship, I am determined we get to know one another on a more personal level. The opera is an excellent place to start."

Fanny shook her head at the widow's flimsy excuse. Surely Mrs. Singletary had figured out by now that *no one* knew Jonathon Hawkins on a personal level. He always held a portion of himself back, never letting anyone past the polished facade. It was that mysterious air that made him so attractive to women, and so confounding to Fanny.

"I appreciate the invitation," he said at last. "But I must decline."

He did not expand on his reasons.

A brief battle of wills ensued, but Mrs. Singletary gave in graciously after only a few seconds. "I suppose we will have to try for another time."

He smiled. Or maybe he didn't. Fanny wasn't sure what that twist of his lips meant. "Indeed we will," he said.

"Well, now." The widow clapped her hands together. "Shall we begin our tour of this lovely ballroom?"

Before anyone could respond, she linked her arm with Fanny's. "You will show me around, Miss Mitchell, seeing as the majority of the preparations have fallen upon your capable shoulders."

The widow all but dragged Fanny deeper into the ballroom, leaving Jonathon and Philomena together. Convenient.

At least neither of them seemed overly pleased to be in the other's company. Fanny found far more comfort in their mutual uneasiness than she should.

Did Jonathon have any idea what his business partner was plotting? Would it matter if he did? It was a well-known fact that once the widow set her sights on a particular match, there was no changing her mind.

Perhaps Fanny should warn him. Or…perhaps not. She was merely his employee. He'd made it painfully clear there would be nothing more than business between them. She had no claims on him, and she certainly wasn't interested in him romantically.

That was, at any rate, her official stand on the matter.

Jonathon had heard his share of disturbing tales concerning Mrs. Singletary's penchant for matchmaking. He'd dismissed them out of hand. Beatrix Singletary was eccentric to be sure, but he'd never found cause to think her the meddling sort.

Until now.

The woman was actually pushing her companion on him, and she wasn't even attempting to be subtle. When next he had Mrs. Singletary's ear, he would inform her that her efforts were wasted on him.

Jonathon would never marry, nor father any children. He came from bad blood, from a long line of selfish men who'd destroyed the women in their lives.

He would not perpetuate the cycle. His newest project would become his legacy, a tangible way to help women rather than hurt them.

He clasped his hands behind his back and looked up at the ceiling, then across the ballroom, over to the doors leading to the terrace, anywhere but at the pretty young woman standing beside him.

Miss Ferguson was likable enough. She was perfectly suitable—for some other man.

"Mr. Hawkins, I apologize for my employer." Philomena shifted uncomfortably beside him. "She means well, I'm sure. But when Mrs. Singletary gets an idea in her head, she can be unrelenting in her desire to see it through to the end."

Pleased by the young woman's directness, Jonathon decided to be equally forthright in return. "Tenacity is an admirable trait. However, in this instance, Mrs. Singletary will be disappointed if she continues to push you and me together."

Relief filled the young woman's gaze. "I concur completely. You and I would never suit. A match between us would be the very worst of bad ideas."

Jonathon offered a sardonic tilt of his lips.

Her hand flew to her mouth. "Oh, Mr. Hawkins, please forgive my wayward tongue. I did not mean to insult you."

"I'm not offended, Miss Ferguson. I find your candor refreshing."

"Praise the Lord." She sighed. Then, clearly eager to move away from their discussion as quickly as possible, she looked out across the ballroom.

Jonathon followed the direction of her gaze and felt his gut take a slow, curling roll. Fanny was working her charms on Mrs. Singletary, directing the widow through the ballroom. Even dressed simply in a black, high-collared dress, Fanny exuded grace and elegance. Rather than detract, the lack of color in her clothing emphasized her natural beauty.

He watched, fascinated, as she pointed to the chandelier he'd had recently installed. Beneath the glow of a thousand flickering electric lights, her blue-green eyes sparkled with pleasure.

Jonathon blinked, unable to tear his gaze free of all that joy, all that beauty. He'd spent too many years surrounded by ugliness not to appreciate the way she'd scooped her silky blond curls in some sort of fancy twist atop her head. A few errant strands tumbled free, framing her exquisite oval face.

Fanny Mitchell was one of the Lord's greatest works of art.

She captivated him. In truth, she'd intrigued him from their first meeting. If any woman could entice him to reconsider his opinion on marriage, it would be Fanny Mitchell.

And yet, because he admired her so much, liked her even, she was the last woman he would consider pursuing romantically.

She'd become indispensable to him. *Here*, at the hotel. Her personal touches were everywhere. From the elegant yet inviting furniture in the lobby, to the specialty chocolates hand-delivered to the rooms each evening, to the list of Denver attractions provided to each guest at check-in.

As if sensing his gaze on her, she shot him a wink from over her shoulder. His mind emptied of all thought.

Footsteps sounded from the outer hallway, heralding someone's approach. Jonathon jerked his attention toward the doorway.

His assistant, Burke Galloway, hastened into the ballroom, a scowl on his face. Recognizing the look, Jonathon addressed Miss Ferguson directly. "Will you excuse me a moment?"

"Of course."

He approached his assistant, a tall, lean young man with dark hair and startling, pale blue eyes. "Is there a problem?"

Burke's mouth pressed into a grim line. "Joshua Greene is here to see you. I put him in your private office."

Everything in him went cold. "Which Joshua Greene, father or son?"

Neither man was welcome in the hotel.

"Son." Burke spoke in a hushed, hurried tone. "He refuses to leave the premises until he's spoken with you personally."

What business did his half brother have with him? Jaw tight, Jonathon returned to Miss Ferguson.

"I must bid you good-day, but I leave you in capable hands." He motioned Burke over. "Miss Ferguson, this is Mr. Galloway. Burke, please show the young woman around the ballroom while I address this other matter."

Burke's eyes filled with quiet appreciation. "With pleasure, sir."

Jonathon adopted a clipped, purposeful pace. He caught Fanny's eye before exiting the ballroom. She gave him a brief nod. The gesture confirmed that he'd left Mrs. Singletary in capable hands, as well.

Whatever he discovered during his meeting with Josh Greene, Jonathon knew one thing for certain. He had good men and women in his employ, people far more faithful to him than the father and half brother who'd dismissed him the one time he'd reached out for their help.

He'd come a long way since those dark, hopeless days of surviving alone on the backstreets of Denver by any means possible. He was a success in his own right now, on his own terms. He owed his family nothing.

After a final nod in Fanny's direction, Jonathon headed out of the ballroom, prepared for the confrontation ahead.

Chapter Two

Jonathon stood near the door, feet spread, hands clasped behind his back. He'd held the position for some time now, waiting for his half brother to stop pacing and state his business.

At seven years his senior, and their father's sole legitimate heir, Josh had been given all the advantages of a privileged birthright, including an education from the finest schools in the country. Yet the man had nothing to show for his life, other than a string of gambling debts and a miserable marriage.

Always the outward picture of propriety, Josh wore one of his hand-tailored suits. The tall, leanly muscled build, the dark, windswept hair and classically handsome features fooled many.

But Jonathon knew the truth. The outer trappings did not match the inner man.

Like recognizes like, he thought, a harsh reminder of the things he'd done to drag himself out of poverty. Though his choices had been about survival, at least at first, he would still have much to answer for when he faced the Lord. Sobering thought.

His brother finally paused, turned and studied him intently. Jonathon matched the rude regard with unflinching patience, a strategy he often adopted to ferret out a business opponent's underlying agenda.

Far stronger men than his brother had buckled under the calculated silence. Josh proved no more immune to the tactic than others before him.

"I need money," he blurted out.

With slow, deliberate movements, Jonathon unclasped his hands and balanced evenly on both feet. The irony of the situation was almost laughable.

I need money. Those were the exact same words Jonathon had uttered to his father twenty years ago in a final, desperate attempt to save his dying mother's life.

Resentment flared.

Jonathon struggled to contain the emotion, reminding himself he was no longer that helpless boy facing an uncertain future. He had power and wealth now.

He answered to no one but God.

"How much did you lose at the faro tables this time?"

Josh's mouth went flat. "I don't need the money for a gambling debt, I need it for—"

He broke off midsentence. His gaze darted around the room, landing nowhere in particular. "Do you mind if I sit?"

Not wanting to extend this conversation longer than necessary, Jonathon frowned at the request.

Without waiting for a response, Josh sat.

After settling in one of the wingback chairs facing away from the door, he rubbed an unsteady hand across his face. "Lily is with child."

Every muscle in Jonathon's back coiled and tightened. "Your wife's name is Amanda."

The other man sighed heavily. "Lily is my mistress."

Jonathon went very still. The son had followed in the father's footsteps. Inevitable, he supposed.

And he walked in all the sins of his father, which he had done before him...

Throat tight, Jonathon tried to empty his mind, but a distant memory shimmered to life. His mother, sitting in a tattered dress falling apart at the seams, tears running down her cheeks as she anxiously waited for the tall, distinguished man to return as he'd promised.

Even in her darkest days, when money had been scarce and she'd been forced to turn to prostitution to feed them both, Amelia Hawkins had continued hoping her lover would finally leave his wife.

That day had never come.

Jonathon had been too young back then, barely five, to remember much about the man whose visits had stopped so abruptly and left his mother in permanent despair. Only later, when he'd been sixteen, had he discovered that the venerable Judge Joshua Greene had been his mother's paramour. And Jonathon's father.

Josh's voice cut into his thoughts. "I need money to set Lily up in a small house of her own. I'll repay you, of course, when I'm able."

A spurt of anger ignited in Jonathon's chest. He moved to a spot behind his desk. Rather than sit, he remained standing, mostly to prove to himself he was still in control of his emotions. "Why come to me? Why not go to your father?"

Josh shook his head. "I can't. He warned me Lily would try to trap me with a child."

Trap him with a child? Jonathon had the presence of mind to pull out his chair before his legs collapsed beneath him. As if in a dream, he was transported back in time, to the terrifying nights he'd been banished to the alleyway behind the brothel.

Blinking rapidly, he heard his brother speaking, explaining his desire to keep his secret from his family. A part of Jonathon listened, taking it all in. The other part was unable to forget that he and this man shared the same blood. They came from the same, contemptible father.

He surfaced at the word *mistake*. "What did you say?"

"Father will never forgive me for making the same mistake he did."

Mistake. Jonathon had been Joshua Greene's greatest mistake. That's what the good, upstanding judge had told him on their first meeting.

"I'm not like Father. I won't turn my back on Lily. I won't let her fall into…" Josh glanced down. "You know."

"Do I?"

His brother's head snapped back up. "I should have known you wouldn't make this easy for me."

"And yet you came to me, anyway."

"All right, I'll say it." He rolled his shoulders as if trying to dislodge a heavy weight. "I don't want Lily to become a prostitute like…like your…mother."

Jonathon barely contained his rage. "And you think that makes you a good man?"

"It makes me better than our father."

Jonathon cleared his expression of all emotion. Inside, he burned. He briefly glanced at the small picture on his desk of his mother as a young woman. He knew a moment of pain, and the hollow feeling of remembered sorrow he'd tucked inside a dark corner of his soul.

Amelia Hawkins hadn't turned to prostitution lightly. She'd held out as long as she could, but had finally admitted defeat and taken a position in Mattie Silks's brothel. Jonathon had been seven at the time. The infamous madam had only agreed to take him in, as well, with the understanding that the customers must never find out about his existence.

Whenever his mother "entertained" he'd been locked outside, no matter the weather, left to run the streets. Out of necessity, he'd learned to take care of himself. He'd become a master at picking pockets and winning fights.

He would have continued down a similar path the rest of his life had it not been for Laney O'Connor, now Laney Dupree. She'd offered Jonathon a home at Charity House. She'd built the orphanage for kids like him, kids who weren't really orphans, whose mothers worked in brothels.

Jonathon shuddered, thinking of the things he'd done to survive prior to Laney's rescue, and the things he'd done after leaving Charity House to make his fortune.

Could God forgive so much sin? A preacher friend of his said yes. Like waves crashing to shore, the Lord's forgiveness was infinite and never ending. Jonathon had his doubts. The world was rarely fair.

And now, another woman had been lied to and compromised. Left to her own resources, she could very well travel the same path as Jonathon's mother. Joshua Greene's despicable legacy would live on into the next generation, and possibly the next. A never ending cycle.

Was it any wonder Jonathon never wanted to marry? Never wanted to bear children?

"I'll give you the money."

Saying nothing more, he opened the safe nestled beneath his desk, and pulled out a bundle of neatly stacked bills. The amount was more than enough to purchase a small, comfortable home for Josh's mistress and her innocent, unborn child.

Once the money was in his brother's hands, Jonathon rose. "If you'll excuse me, I have a hotel to run."

"Of course."

In silence, he escorted his brother to the exit. "I bid you good-day."

Josh started to speak.

Jonathon shut the door on his words with a resounding click. For several moments, he stared straight ahead, his gut roiling. In the unnatural stillness, he made a silent promise to himself. No woman would suffer because of his selfish actions.

The cycle of sin that ran in his family ended with him.

With their walk-through complete, Fanny escorted Mrs. Singletary and her companion back to the main lobby of the hotel. As they entered the skinny hallway leading out of the ballroom, Philomena fell back a step. The move put her directly beside Burke Galloway. Their footsteps slowed to match one another's, and their voices mingled in hushed tones.

Fanny wondered if the widow noticed the two were so obviously attracted to each other. She looked over at Mrs. Singletary, but the sight of Jonathon's office distracted her.

He rarely shut his door. The fact that he'd done so today warned Fanny something wasn't quite right. A terrible foreboding slipped through her.

Mrs. Singletary glanced at the closed door as well, a delicate frown knitting her brow. "It would appear Mr.

Hawkins is still occupied with whatever concern called him away."

"I believe you are correct." Fanny's heart beat faster. She fought a sudden urge to go to Jonathon, to make sure he was all right.

But that would be overstepping her bounds. She continued leading Mrs. Singletary and the others down the hallway.

Once they were in the main lobby, Mrs. Singletary dug inside her sizable reticule and pulled out a stack of papers.

She handed them to Fanny. "Since it appears Mr. Hawkins will not be available for our meeting today, I am entrusting you with my final guest list for the ball."

Fanny scanned the top page, not really expecting any surprises. But when her gaze landed on a particular set of guests, her breath hitched in her throat. Judge and Mrs. Joshua Greene.

Joshua. Greene.

The man wasn't welcome in the Hotel Dupree. Short of exposing Jonathon's personal connection to the prominent judge, Fanny could say nothing to Mrs. Singletary.

She coerced air into her lungs, and adopted a breezy, nonchalant tone. "I will deliver your list to Mr. Hawkins as soon as possible. If he has any questions or concerns I'm certain he will contact you at once."

"That will be fine." Mrs. Singletary's gaze narrowed over her companion conversing softly with Mr. Galloway.

The widow sniffed in mild disapproval. Philomena didn't appear to notice her employer's reaction. She was entirely too absorbed in whatever Burke had pointed out to her in the lobby.

"Mr. Galloway, do come here." The widow spoke in a fast, impatient tone. "And you, as well, Philomena."

The two walked over as a single unit and faced Mrs. Singletary shoulder to shoulder.

Philomena spoke for them both. "Yes, Mrs. Singletary?"

The widow's gaze bounced between the two, a look of vexation in her eyes. "Mr. Galloway, would you please see that my carriage and driver are waiting for me out front?"

He gave her a pleasant smile. "I would be delighted."

"Yes, yes, off you go." She sent him away with a distracted flick of her wrist.

Philomena gazed after him with a wistful expression.

Mrs. Singletary studied the young woman closely, then pressed her lips into a tight, determined line. Fanny feared the widow still planned to push a match between Jonathon and Philomena.

"Hopeless," Fanny muttered under her breath.

"Did you say something, my dear?"

"No, Mrs. Singletary." Fanny lifted her chin. "Is there anything else I can do for you today?"

"Not a thing. Your commitment to detail is much appreciated, Miss Mitchell. I predict this year's ball will be spoken about long after the evening comes to a close."

"That is the plan."

"Yes, yes." The widow patted her hand. "I wish to raise quite a sizable amount of money for the new kitchen at Charity House."

Excitement spread through Fanny. "It's a worthy cause."

"Oh, indeed, it is."

They shared a smile. Fanny volunteered much of her free time at Charity House. She was even contemplating starting a program at the hotel to provide work experience for the older children. She wished she could do more. The orphanage had molded some of her favorite people into men and women of strong, moral character.

The widow continued speaking. "I understand the majority of your family will be in attendance at my ball."

Fanny's smile widened. It had been years since so many Mitchells were in one place at the same time. "I've reserved rooms for them here in the hotel. My parents will be staying in the bridal suite."

A gift from Jonathon. The dear, dear man.

Mrs. Singletary's expression turned somber and she reached out to touch Fanny's arm. "How is your mother managing these days?"

"Her asthma is much better." Or so her father had claimed the last time he'd come to town. The worry in his eyes had told a different story.

Her mother, always so full of life and energy, had contracted asthma recently, a chronic disease that usually showed up in childhood, but was not uncommon to reveal itself later in life. Although the doctor said Mary Mitchell's illness was manageable, Fanny still feared the worst.

Asthma was incurable. People had been known to die from a severe attack. Her mother suffered bouts regularly. Though hers were usually moderate in nature, stress brought on more severe symptoms. Fanny prayed the party didn't cause her any additional strain.

"I look forward to catching up with her while she's in town," Mrs. Singletary said. "Your mother has always been one of my very special friends."

"And you, hers."

"Walk us out, Miss Mitchell."

"Of course." Fanny led Mrs. Singletary and Philomena to the front steps of the hotel, then bade them farewell. Back in the lobby, she fingered the guest list. *This needs addressing immediately.* She cast a surreptitious glance toward Jonathon's office.

The door swung open and out walked the man himself.

Never one to put off an unpleasant situation, Fanny hurried over to meet him. Something in the way he held his shoulders caused her unspeakable concern.

Judge Greene forgotten, she touched her employer's arm. It was barely a whisper of fingertips to sleeve, yet had the intended effect. Jonathon slowly looked down at her.

The moment their gazes merged, Fanny's breath backed up in her throat. His face was like a stone, but his eyes were hot with anguish.

She tightened her grip. "What's happened? Is something wrong with the hotel?"

"No, it's my…" His words trailed off and his gaze fastened on a spot somewhere far off in the distance.

Her hand fell away from his arm. However, her resolve to ease his distress remained firmly in place. "Perhaps you would care to take a short walk with me?"

She spoke in a mild tone, the way she would when making the same suggestion any other time. They often took walks together, mostly when Jonathon required her opinion about some issue in one of his hotels.

"A light snowfall has begun," she added, knowing it was his favorite time to be outdoors.

Hers, as well. There was nothing more wonderful than those precious moments when the world fell quiet beneath a blanket of fluffy white flakes.

Jonathon remained silent, his gaze unblinking.

"Come with me." She took his hand and pulled him toward the exit.

For several steps he obliged her. Just when she thought she had him agreeable to the idea of a brief stroll, he drew his hand free.

"Not right now, Fanny." His voice was hoarse and gravelly, not at all the smooth baritone she was used to hearing from him. "I have another matter that requires my immediate attention."

His deliberate vagueness put a wedge between them. She bit back a sigh. "I understand."

In truth, she understood far too well. He'd shut her out. It wasn't the first time and probably wouldn't be the last. Nevertheless, it stung to realize he didn't trust her, at least not enough to share what had put him in such a dark mood.

Without a word of explanation, he turned to go, then just as quickly pivoted back around to face her. "I'm not certain how long I'll be gone. I need you to see to any issues that may arise in my absence."

"You can count on me."

She didn't attempt to pry for additional information. He would reveal whatever was on his mind when he was ready. Or he wouldn't. It was a reminder of how little he trusted her concerning his life outside the hotel.

He's not for you.

But there was someone out there who was; she sensed it as surely as she knew her own name. She simply had to trust the Lord would lead her to her one true love in His time. Patience, faith—those were her greatest tools.

"I'll be here when you return," she said when Jonathon made no move to leave.

He reached up and touched her cheek. The gesture was brief, yet so full of tenderness she thought she might cry. Did the man realize how good he was beneath that polished, unflappable exterior he presented to the world?

He would make a wonderful husband, and an exceptional father, if only he would allow someone—anyone—to squeeze through the cracks and into his heart. She wanted that for him, desperately.

"I count on you always being here when I return, Fanny." His expression softened. "More than you can possibly know."

With relief, she heard the message beneath his words. Jonathon relied on her above all others.

The thought should have made her happy, but instead produced a small stab of pain in the vicinity of her heart. The sensation felt a lot like loss.

Chapter Three

Later that same afternoon, Fanny found one excuse after another to return to the hotel lobby. If she was called away, she took care of the matter quickly and then hurried back to her post behind the registration desk. She was probably overreacting, but she couldn't shake the notion that Jonathon needed her.

She knew the exact moment he reentered the hotel. Even if she hadn't been watching for him, the air actually changed. The atrium felt somehow smaller, his presence was that large and compelling. Everyone else in the building faded in comparison.

Or maybe that was Fanny's singular reaction to the man. None of the guests milling about seemed quite as captivated by Jonathon Hawkins as she.

Of course, she'd been watching for his return. Her concern had grown exponentially with each passing hour. Catching a glimpse of his face and the way he held his shoulders, she knew she'd been right to worry. He was still as distraught as when he'd left.

He hadn't seen her yet.

She took the opportunity to study him without interruption.

His steps were clipped, purposeful, a man in complete control of his domain. But his eyes. Oh, his eyes. Fanny had never seen that look of raw emotion in his gaze before.

Hurrying out from behind the registration desk, she cut into his direct line of vision.

His feet ground to a halt.

"Jonathon." Unable to mask her concern, Fanny spoke his name in a rush. *No good, no good.* That would only entice him to put up his guard.

She adopted a breezy, businesslike tone and began again. "Tell me what you need. Name it and it's done."

He looked at her oddly, then cracked a half smile. "I appreciate the offer, but everything's under control."

She frowned at the rasp in his voice. "Why don't I believe you?"

"Go back to work, Fanny." He shifted around her and continued on toward his office. Not sure why she couldn't leave him alone, she grabbed her coat from behind the registration desk and then hurried to catch up with him again.

His pace slowed.

She easily fell into step beside him.

He cast her a sidelong glance but didn't tell her to go away. *Progress.*

"You do realize, Jonathon, that you have *the look.*"

His footsteps stopped altogether. "What look?"

"Whenever something goes wrong in the hotel, a groove shows up right…there." She pointed to a spot in the middle of his forehead.

A strangled laugh rumbled out of his chest. "You know me well."

Not really. A mild glumness took hold of her. She didn't know him nearly as well as she wished, but enough to know how to lighten his mood.

She took his arm and steered him back in the direction he'd just come. "The snow is falling and you owe me a walk. I'm even prepared."

She gestured with her coat.

He stared down at her for an endless moment, so long, in fact, that she thought he might turn down her offer a second time in one day. But then he nodded and started for the exit with quick, even strides.

She had to break into a trot to keep up with him. Much to her relief, he slowed once they were outside.

They walked at a reasonable pace, falling into a companionable silence as they headed toward the heart of downtown Denver. The afternoon air was scented with fresh snow and a hint of pine. Fat, languid flakes floated softly around them, creating a surreal, almost wistful feel to the moment.

Fanny treasured these brisk walks with Jonathon, when it was just the two of them working out an issue in the hotel.

Although today she sensed the problem was more personal in nature. Something from his past?

She thought of what little she knew of his difficult childhood, so very different from her own. One of seven siblings, Fanny had been raised in a large, gregarious family on a ranch ten miles north of Denver. There'd always been plenty of food on the Mitchell table. Love and laughter had been abundant, as well, with the added bonus of parents who lived out their faith daily.

Fanny couldn't imagine the hardships Jonathon had endured. The thought made her stumble. He caught hold of her elbow, letting go only when she regained her balance.

"I failed to ask you earlier," he said, resuming his quick pace. "Did Mrs. Singletary have any questions about or concerns over the setup for her ball?"

"None. She seemed quite pleased with the preparations."

"Good to know." He drew to a stop.

Fanny followed suit.

Something quite wonderful passed between them.

"I appreciate you taking over in my absence with Mrs. Singletary." He plucked a snowflake off Fanny's shoulder, tossed it away with a flick of his fingers. "You always manage to make me look good. Thank you, Fanny."

"It's I who should thank you," she countered, meaning it with all her heart.

Prior to working at the hotel, she'd been caught up in the various roles others had assigned to her. The dutiful daughter. The adored sister. The accomplished beauty. She'd found favor wherever she went, had never taken a misstep and certainly never let anyone down.

Perhaps that was why her family had been confused and deeply concerned when she'd broken her engagement to Reese Bennett Jr., a man they had deemed her perfect match. Though her parents had been quick to support her decision, her behavior had set tongues wagging all over Denver. The ensuing scandal had been nearly impossible to bear.

Jonathon had come to her rescue, offering her the opportunity to manage the registration desk at his Chicago hotel. She'd leaped at the chance to leave town. Or rather, to escape the gossip.

Fanny wasn't particularly proud of her cowardice, but some good had come from her attempt to run away from the problem. She'd spent a lot of hours in her rented room in Chicago. After much prayer and soul-searching, she'd come to the realization that she was more than a pretty face, more than what others expected her to be.

Now, back in Denver once again, she would like to think she'd found where she belonged. At the Hotel Dupree. She knew better, of course. She loved her job, but...

Something was missing. Her very own happy-ever-after that four of her six siblings had already found and were living out on a daily basis.

Gazing up into Jonathon's remarkable blue eyes, she felt a hopeless sense of longing spread through her. *He's not for you*, she reminded herself. *He doesn't want what you want.*

If only...

She knew better than to finish that thought.

As an uncharacteristic awkwardness spread between them, Fanny tried to think of something to say. She blurted out the first thing that came to mind. "Philomena looked rather lovely today, don't you agree?"

He cocked his head in a look of masculine confusion. "Mrs. Singletary always ensures her companion looks lovely."

So, he hadn't been especially taken by Philomena's considerable charms. Inappropriately pleased by the revelation, Fanny resumed walking, her steps considerably lighter.

They turned at the end of the block and retraced their

route. In the past, this was usually when Jonathon revealed whatever was bothering him.

True to form, he blew out a slow hiss of air. "It confounds me how someone can just show up, unannounced, and expect to be given whatever he wants without consequences."

At the fire in his words, Fanny belatedly remembered the additional name on Mrs. Singletary's guest list. "Did Judge Greene contact you directly?"

Jonathon's face tightened at the question. "Are you saying he showed up at the hotel today, too?"

"No, I just assumed…" She shot a covert glance in his direction. "It's obvious something is troubling you. I thought it might be because Mrs. Singletary added your father to the guest list."

Jonathon stopped abruptly. "She what?"

Fanny sighed. "You didn't know."

"I did not."

She sighed again. She knew about Jonathon's personal connection to Joshua Greene only because the judge himself had told her. He'd misunderstood their relationship. Thinking they were more than business associates, he'd approached Fanny about setting up a meeting with his *son.* When Fanny had gotten over her shock and told Jonathon about the brazen request, he'd been furious. Not with her, with his father.

Her stomach dipped at the memory. "Would you like me to speak with Mrs. Singletary? I could explain the situation, you know, without actually explaining it."

For a moment, Jonathon's guard dropped and she saw the vulnerability that belonged to the boy he'd once been—the one who'd been summarily dismissed by his own father.

She thought he might share some of his pain with her, but his eyes became cool and distant. "Leave it alone," he said at last. "Mrs. Singletary is allowed to invite whomever she pleases to her charity ball."

They finished the rest of their walk in silence.

At the hotel entrance, Jonathon stopped Fanny from entering by moving directly in front of her. "Before we go in, I have a request."

She blinked up at him. "You know you can ask me anything."

"Have you secured an escort for Mrs. Singletary's ball?"

"I…no." She shook her head in confusion. "I have not."

"Good, don't."

"Is…" She cleared her throat, twice. "Is there a reason you wish for me to attend the ball alone?"

His lips curved into a sweet, almost tender smile. "You misunderstand. I don't wish for you to attend alone."

Oh. *Oh, my.* Her breath backed up in her lungs. "No?"

"I would like for you to attend with me." The intensity in his eyes made her legs wobble. "What do you say, Fanny? Will you allow me to escort you to the ball Friday evening?"

Her head told her to refuse. This man was her employer. He'd vowed never to marry. He didn't want children. No good would come from forgetting those very significant points of contention between them.

But then he took her hand.

She felt dizzy, too dizzy to think clearly. Surely that explained why she ignored caution. "Yes, Jonathon, I would very much like to attend the ball with you."

The following morning, Jonathon stood outside his office and tracked his gaze over the crowded hotel lobby.

No matter what tactic he employed, he couldn't seem to concentrate on the scene in front of him. His mind kept returning to his conversation with Fanny after their walk.

He should *not* have asked her to Mrs. Singletary's ball. He knew that, but couldn't seem to regret doing so.

He enjoyed Fanny's company. Probably more than he should. Certainly more than their business association warranted. From very early on in their acquaintance, she'd made it clear what she wanted out of life—a satisfying job, marriage, children, a home of her own. Jonathon could give her only one of those things, the job.

But there were plenty of men who could give her the rest, some of whom would be in attendance at the ball tomorrow evening.

Fanny, with her luminous smile and stunning face, would enchant each and every one of those potential suitors. She was unique. Special. The kind of woman a man wanted to cherish and protect, always.

Something unpleasant unfurled in Jonathon's chest at the thought of her sharing even one dance with someone, *anyone*, other than him.

Shifting his stance, he ground his back molars together so hard his neck ached. He forcibly relaxed his jaw and once again attempted to focus his attention on the hotel.

Again, his mind wandered back to Fanny and how badly he wanted her by his side tomorrow night. Facing his father would be…well, if not easier, certainly less challenging.

Guilt immediately reared up, producing a dull, burning pain in the back of his throat. Jonathon would not use Fanny as a shield between him and his father.

He should let her attend the ball alone. Yet he could

not withdraw his invitation at this late date. He'd gotten himself in quite the quandary, with no simple way out.

He was spared from further reflection when his assistant, Burke Galloway, shouldered his way through the milling crowd.

"Mr. Hawkins, you'll be pleased to know we're nearly at 100 percent occupancy."

Jonathon pulled out his watch and checked the time. Not yet noon. He allowed himself a small smile of satisfaction. "Mrs. Singletary will be delighted so many of her party guests have taken rooms in the hotel."

"The discounted rate was a strong incentive."

"Indeed." The cut in price had been Fanny's idea, a way to show off the newly renovated hotel to the locals. He made a mental note to increase her wages yet again.

"I have a few items we need to discuss." Burke eyed him with a questioning glance. "I trust now is a good time."

Jonathon nodded.

Burke retrieved a small notepad from an inside pocket of his jacket and proceeded to run through a series of problems that had arisen. When he'd finished, and Jonathon had given his decision on each matter, Burke flipped the page and addressed the final item scribbled in his book.

"As per your request, I've prepared the conference room on the second floor for your meeting with the Mitchell brothers this afternoon." He tapped the page absently with his fingertip. "Your attorney has already sent over five copies of the agreement, one for each person involved in the transaction and an additional copy to file with the county clerk's office once the sale goes through."

If the sale goes through.

Hunter, Logan and Garrett Mitchell still had to agree to sell Jonathon the parcel of land they jointly owned north of their family's ranch. He would pay whatever they asked, no matter how outrageous the price.

Turning the run-down train depot into a premier stop on the busy Union Pacific line wasn't just another business venture for him. It was a chance to set a new course for his future, a sort of redemption for the mistakes of his past.

Operating on the notion that the Mitchell brothers would be tough negotiators, he made one last request of his assistant. "Clear my calendar for the rest of the day, in case our meeting runs long."

"Of course." Burke made a notation on his notepad, then looked up. "We've covered everything on my list. Is there anything else you wish to review?"

"That's all for now."

"Very good." Burke left a few seconds later.

Jonathon returned his gaze to the lobby, his thoughts as disordered as the scene in front of him.

People came and went. Some hurried, others meandered. There was no pattern to their movement, yet the scene was a familiar one, replicated in every one of Jonathon's hotels, on any given day of the week.

After years of traveling from hotel to hotel, room to room, living out of a trunk or suitcase, Jonathon was ready to put down roots, deep and strong and lasting. His family would be the men and women he hired to work at the train depot, their changed lives his legacy.

If he happened to find himself lonely at times, it was the price he was willing to pay to break the chain of sin that plagued his family.

As if to test his resolve, he caught sight of Fanny out of the corner of his eye. *Beautiful.* That was the first thought that came to mind as Jonathon watched her move out from behind the registration desk.

She scanned the immediate area with a slightly narrowed gaze, probably looking for something out of place. Her earnest, blue-green eyes, starred with heavy, dark lashes, swept across the lobby, over the marble flooring, up to the glass atrium above her head.

The sunlight streaming through the windows slid over her in washes of yellow and gold, highlighting the variegated strands of blond hair piled atop her head.

Jonathon remembered the first time he'd seen her, standing in much the same place as she was now. He'd sensed the moment their gazes met that she was going to pose a problem for him. Not on a business level, but on a personal one.

He hadn't been wrong.

She caught him watching her. Smiling, she immediately changed direction. When she stopped beside him, his heart actually stuttered.

Up close, she was even more spectacular.

Her skin was flawless, her features almost doll-like. Pieces of hair had fallen free from her tidy coiffure. Since Jonathon rather liked the effect, he deemed it best not to point this out. No doubt she would reach up and tuck the wayward curls back in place.

"We have a busy few days ahead of us." She'd barely uttered the statement before a bellman, juggling several large pieces of luggage, staggered toward her. Deftly moving aside to let him pass, she added, "We're booked solid through Monday morning."

Not sure what he heard in her voice—worry, tension,

mild agitation?—Jonathon raked his gaze over her face. She was definitely anxious about something. "Any concerns I should know about?"

She answered without hesitation. "No, of course not."

Highly unlikely, with every room booked for the next four nights. "None?" He lifted a single eyebrow. "Not one?"

Laughing softly, she shook her head. "Let me rephrase. Have problems presented themselves this morning? Yes, absolutely. Anything I, or my staff, can't handle? No."

"Good answer."

She flashed a smug grin. "I know."

He chuckled. She joined in.

A moment later her smile slipped, just a little, but enough that Jonathon noticed. He wondered at the cause but thought he probably knew. Her mother and father had arrived earlier this morning. "I trust your parents are settled in their room?"

"They are, yes." She angled her head to gaze up at him. "Thank you, Jonathon, for giving them the finest suite in the hotel. You have no idea how much I appreciate your thoughtfulness and generosity."

Something about her expression, so grateful, so overcome with emotion, made him stand a bit taller. He had a sudden urge to shield this woman from all the evil in this world, to slay every one of her dragons, real or perceived.

The need to protect Fanny, stronger than he'd felt for anyone before, wasn't entirely unexpected. Nor was it new. The sensation had been with him from the start of their association.

If she were a different woman, he a different man...

He shoved the thought aside. Fanny wanted marriage, children. Family. Jonathon knew nothing of those things.

But he wanted her to have them. He wanted her to find happiness. With some other man?

No.

His mouth went dry as dust. He cleared his throat with a low growl. "How is your mother feeling?"

"She seemed well enough when I left her. Her color was good and she was breathing easily, but…"

Fanny's words trailed off and she snapped her mouth firmly shut.

"But…?" he prompted.

"But the ten-mile journey into town wore her out. She's putting up a brave front. I'm not in the least fooled by her false smiles. Thankfully, Dr. Shane is upstairs with her now, administering a breathing treatment." Gratitude returned to Fanny's gaze. "Thank you for making sure he was already here when she arrived."

Something that looked like affection, perhaps even admiration, replaced the gratitude.

How he wanted to be the man he saw in her eyes right now.

He cleared his throat again.

"I was happy to send for the doctor." Of course, Shane Bartlett wasn't just any doctor. He was the best in Denver. His connection to Charity House and his willingness to see patients regardless of their past—or current—lifestyles made him one of the few men Jonathon trusted. "I know how much your mother means to you."

Another, heavier sigh leaked out of Fanny's very pretty mouth. "I don't know what I'd do if one of her attacks becomes so severe she isn't able to recover."

The anguish in Fanny's voice was a sharp, tangible thing.

Jonathon was reminded of the day his own mother

had taken ill. How well he understood the fear and pain Fanny fought to control.

Wanting to comfort her, he opened his mouth to say something, not precisely sure what, but a minor event playing out at the hotel's entrance captured his attention.

An expectant hush fell over the lobby as a stunning couple walked in with their sizable brood, plus one former, notorious madam Jonathon knew a bit too well. After all, she'd once owned the brothel where his mother had worked.

He had a lot of memories connected to Mattie Silks, not all of them good. But her appearance in his hotel wasn't the reason every muscle in his back knotted with tension.

Hunter Mitchell, the oldest of the Mitchell siblings, had arrived ahead of his brothers.

One down, two more yet to show.

Jonathon managed, just barely, to keep the anticipation from showing on his face. Unfortunately, none of his outward calm could temper his impatience to begin negotiations with the Mitchell brothers.

Soon, he told himself. If all went according to plan, his future would take a dramatic turn *very soon*.

Chapter Four

Fanny knew a moment of quiet desperation as she watched her brother herd his family deeper into the hotel lobby. *That's what I want, Lord. That joy, that sense of belonging, a family of my own.*

She had to believe her time would come. For now, she would take a moment to enjoy the show. Hunter had brought his entire household to town, including his wife, all four of their children and, of course, his wife's mother, the incomparable Mattie Silks.

Laughter abounded among the group, while an entire team of bellmen wrestled the family's luggage onto a cart. Fanny's sister-in-law, Annabeth, attempted to oversee the process. Unfortunately, her mother added her own, very vocal "suggestions" on how to speed along the process. Mattie's input caused more mayhem, not less.

Hunter's oldest daughter, Sarah, skillfully pulled her younger siblings out of the fray. Unfortunately, Mattie added her assistance there as well, and pandemonium soon followed. The children quite literally ran circles around their grandmother.

Fanny thought she saw a brief twinkle of amusement dance in her brother's eyes before he quickly restored order with the gentle strength that had always defined him. Hunter looked good, she decided. His hair was a sun-kissed, sandy blond from the hours he spent outdoors on his ranch. His long-legged, leanly muscular cowboy swagger was replicated in all the Mitchell men.

Hunter had experienced some difficult years, including two spent in prison for manslaughter, but he'd overcome his past and was stronger for the challenges he'd once faced. She was proud to call him brother.

"Now, that's what I call an entrance," Jonathon muttered.

The look of amused horror on his face made her smile. "I should have warned you, the Mitchells never do anything by half measure."

"I was speaking about Mattie." His voice was infused with a touch of irony. "Watch. She's about to strike a pose. Ah, yes, there she goes."

As predicted, Mattie sauntered to a spot in the middle of the hotel lobby. With exaggerated slowness, she lifted her chin, thrust out a hip and then planted a fist on her waist.

The pose was so…completely Mattie. A snort of laughter erupted before Fanny could call it back. "You know the woman well."

"Too well," Jonathon muttered, his mouth now a little grim. "She's managed to draw almost every eye to her."

Gazes were, indeed, riveted in Mattie's direction. But Fanny suspected much of the interest was for the extraordinary-looking group as a whole. Even Hunter's children were beautiful.

A range of emotions swept through her. Fanny was excited to spend time with her family, but also determined to make the next few days count. When Mrs. Singletary's ball was over, all of Denver would see her differently. She would no longer be defined as that pretty Mitchell girl. Or that poor, misguided woman who'd jilted a prominent man in town.

She would prove she was a competent woman, capable of handling great responsibilities. When she walked through town next week, the whispers following in her wake would be not only accurate, but also complimentary.

Catching sight of her from across the room, Annabeth squealed in delight and waved enthusiastically.

The entire group changed direction, Annabeth leading the way with a waddle that bespoke her current condition. Judging by the size of her belly, Hunter's fifth child would be making an appearance in a few short months.

As Annabeth approached, smiling broadly, Fanny noticed that her sister-in-law glowed with good health and happiness. She was so very beautiful. The rich, caramel-colored skin and sleek dark hair she'd inherited from her Mexican father were the perfect foil for the pale blue eyes she'd gotten from Mattie.

Oddly, as Hunter and his family drew closer, Jonathon seemed to grow tenser. He shifted his stance slightly, then repositioned himself once again.

Interesting that while he appeared outwardly loose-limbed and relaxed, the lines around his mouth gave him away.

Fanny was given no more time to contemplate his strange behavior before she was hauled into her brother's strong arms and swung in fast, dizzying circles.

"Put me down, you big oaf."

He obliged, but only after two more heart-pounding spins.

Then, hands on her shoulders, Hunter studied her face with the narrow-eyed focus that had kept him alive during his rebellious years. She tried not to fidget under the inspection.

At last, he gave a quick nod of approval. "You look well, Fanny. Happy."

"I am well and happy." *Mostly.*

Angling his head, he paused, as if about to say something, then abruptly refocused his attention onto Jonathon.

They shook hands in a very businesslike manner.

"Have my brothers arrived?" Hunter asked.

"Not yet."

As Fanny watched the formal exchange between the two men, she had the distinct impression she'd missed something, something important. She opened her mouth to inquire, but they moved a few steps away and began speaking in low, hushed tones.

She couldn't quite make out what they said. She stepped closer. At the mention of a meeting—*what meeting?*—she leaned in a smidgen closer. She thought she caught Jonathon say her brother Garrett's name, but then Annabeth swooped in for a hug and that was the end of Fanny's eavesdropping.

She spent the next few minutes greeting the rest of Hunter's family. "Mattie, I do believe you look ten years younger than the last time I saw you."

The former madam responded to the compliment with a nonchalant wave of her hand. "It's all that fresh air."

The harried tone implied that fresh air was something to be avoided at all costs. Fanny wasn't fooled. The former madam was delighted with her decision to sell her brothel and move onto the ranch with her daughter, son-in-law and grandchildren.

Who would have thought Mattie Silks would turn into a doting grandmother?

"Hello, Aunt Fanny."

Fanny spun around at the sound of her name. "Sarah, look at you. You're all grown up."

The girl beamed. "I turn sixteen in four months, one week and five days. But who's counting?"

Fanny laughed. The sweet, pretty child with the dark hair and tawny eyes had become a confident, striking young woman. "Tell me how you've been."

Sarah did, in great detail, barely taking a breath. When she finally paused, Fanny took the opportunity to steer the conversation in a slightly different direction than the latest fashion for hats. "Are you excited about attending school in Boston next year?"

"I am. Very much. I thought Pa would never agree to let me go." She rolled her eyes in her father's direction. "He only relented when I promised to carry on your legacy at Miss Sinclair's Prestigious School for Girls."

Though she was flattered, and really quite touched, the last thing Fanny wanted was for her niece to follow in her footsteps. She'd been a model student at Miss Sinclair's, uncommonly obedient. That had been a mistake. When a young girl went away to school, she was supposed to spread her wings a little, to test her boundaries, to make mistakes and then learn from them.

Wanting to offer what advice she could on the matter, she touched her niece's arm, then decided it wasn't her place. Sarah should be allowed to find her own way, on her own terms. But still. "Let's talk more later, just the two of us."

Sarah's smile turned radiant. "I'd like that."

Fanny switched her attention to her sister-in-law's rounded belly. "How are you feeling?"

"Excited, impatient." Annabeth leaned in close. "Your brother hovers like an old woman. Honestly, you'd think I'd never birthed a child before."

Despite her slightly miffed tone, Annabeth glanced over at Hunter. The way she looked at him, all dreamy-eyed and in love, told Fanny her sister-in-law adored every bit of the attention her husband bestowed on her.

A tinge of melancholy struck without warning. Would Fanny ever find that kind of love?

She certainly hoped so. And yet she wondered…

Was she even capable of having deep feelings for a man? She certainly hadn't felt anything more than friendship for Reese. What did that say about her?

Breaking away from the group, Hunter's youngest child toddled toward her. Happy for the distraction, she reached down to pick up her nephew. But the eighteen-month-old miniature copy of his father had a different plan in mind.

The little boy bypassed Fanny and went straight to Jonathon. "Up." He yanked on the crisp pant leg. "Up!"

Pausing midsentence, Jonathon looked down.

Christopher lifted his arms high in the air. "Up, up, up."

Chuckling, Jonathon obliged the child. The move was so natural, so casual, Fanny found herself staring at them in stunned silence. Christopher babbled away, while Jonathon responded as if he completely understood.

Fanny's heart gave a hard tug. Jonathon was so comfortable with the child, so patient and kind.

I will never father children.

His reasons for avoiding fatherhood made sense—at least to him. Not to Fanny. Yes, the Bible warned of the sins of the father, but Scripture also promised victory to those who broke the cycle.

Watching Jonathon with her nephew, knowing he'd make a great father, she couldn't understand why he was so determined to avoid having children.

Releasing a heartfelt sigh, Annabeth linked her arm through Fanny's. "Johnny's very good with Christopher. Of course, I'm not surprised. He was the best big brother."

Fanny blinked at her sister-in-law in confusion. Then she remembered that Jonathon—or rather, *Johnny*—had lived in Mattie's brothel as a child. His path must have crossed Annabeth's often, probably even daily.

What else did she know about him?

Curiosity drove Fanny to pry. "What was he like as a boy?"

"Loyal, caring, a bit wild, but also protective of the other children. He…" Annabeth paused a moment, as if gathering her thoughts. "I guess you could say he kept a part of himself separate. He was friendly, but he didn't have a lot of friends."

He must have been so lonely, always watching out for others. *Oh, Jonathon, who watched out for you?* Fanny's heart hurt for the little boy he'd once been.

"That's not to say the other children didn't adore him. They did. Everyone looked up to him, even the girls." Annabeth laughed as if caught in a happy memory. *"Especially* the girls."

The boy Annabeth just described was much like the

man he was today. Good. Kind. Distant. Fanny had more questions, lots more, but another commotion broke out at the hotel's entrance.

Her second oldest brother pushed into the lobby, his wife and three children in tow.

Her smile returned full force.

Logan and his family had arrived.

Later that afternoon, Jonathon stood in the conference room, impatiently biding his time. He wanted to begin negotiations at once, but the remaining Mitchell brother had only just arrived at the hotel. Coming straight off the train from Saint Louis, Garrett had promised to join them as soon as he helped his young wife get settled in their room.

That had been over thirty minutes ago.

Since Garrett's wife was with child as well, Jonathon figured getting her settled meant more than merely helping with the luggage. If the man was anything like his older brother, there was bound to be a good deal of husbandly smothering.

Jonathon felt a jolt of…something churn in his gut. Jealousy? Regret? Neither emotion had any place in today's meeting. He shoved the futile thoughts aside and attempted to get down to business.

Hunter stopped him midsentence. "We'll wait for Garrett. We make decisions as a family, or not at all."

Considering the nature of his relationship with own brother, Jonathon was both intrigued and baffled by the united front. He knew Hunter and Logan hadn't always been close. They'd actually been on opposite sides of the law for years and, according to some accounts, even enemies.

But now they were as close as any brothers Jonathon had run across. They even owned neighboring ranches connected to their parents' larger spread, which said a lot about their commitment to family.

At last, the door swung open and Garrett Mitchell entered the conference room in a rush.

"Sorry I'm late." The besotted smile on his face said otherwise. "Molly needed me to help her switch hats, and then we somehow got tangled up. The laughing began next, and well, here I am at last, better late than never."

"Save the excuses, little brother." Logan lifted his hand in the air. "We all know you just wanted to spend extra time with Molly."

Garrett's grin widened. "Jealous?"

Logan snorted. "Have you seen my wife? She's always the most beautiful woman in the room."

"Unless, of course," Garrett countered, "*my wife* is in the room."

"Or mine," Hunter added.

Since Jonathon had known all three women in question before they'd met and married the Mitchell men, he kept his mouth shut on the matter. Each of their wives was special in her own way. Beautiful, smart, the very essence of goodness.

Jonathon nodded to Burke. His assistant shut the outer door to the conference room.

The brothers fell silent.

"Gentleman, if you will have a seat." Jonathon motioned them to the table in the middle of the room. "We'll begin."

They remained where they were, standing shoulder to shoulder. Three against one. Not the worst odds Jonathon had ever faced.

Normally, he enjoyed a tough negotiation, especially if pitted against a worthy opponent or, as in this particular case, several worthy opponents. However, the outcome of today's meeting was too important to indulge in the thrill that came from a proper battle.

Jonathon got straight to the point. "I recently acquired the property that runs along your northern border and—"

"So you're the anonymous Denver businessman who purchased Ebenezer Foley's ranch," Logan said, with the barest hint of bitterness.

Jonathon understood the man's frustration. It was no secret the Mitchell brothers had wanted the land. But Ebenezer Foley had nursed a lifelong hatred for the entire family. He'd carried that animosity to the grave. On his deathbed, he'd instructed his son to sell his ranch to anyone but a Mitchell.

Mouth set in a grim line, Hunter crossed his arms over his chest. "You didn't ask us here merely to tell us you bought the land directly north of ours."

"No. I want to make an offer on the three hundred acres you jointly own that run along my southern border, including the dilapidated train depot. I'm willing to pay 10 percent above the going rate, as you will see in the offer my attorney drew up. Take a look."

He pointed to the files laid out on the conference table in a tidy row.

A silent message passed between the brothers before they stepped forward and opened the files with identical flicks of their wrists.

Hunter and Logan skimmed their gazes across the top page. Garrett Mitchell actually picked up the sale agreement and read through the legal document, page by page. It made sense he would take the time to consider the offer in its entirety, being an attorney who specialized in sales and acquisitions.

After a moment, Garrett looked up. "The asking price is more than fair, as are the other terms."

"Nevertheless." Hunter took a step back from the table. "We have one rule in our family when it comes to business. Mitchell land stays in Mitchell hands. We can't sell you the property."

Every muscle in Jonathon's back tightened and coiled. He forcibly relaxed his shoulders, then felt them bunch again. "Can't or won't?"

"Does it matter?"

No. He supposed it didn't.

Jonathon showed none of his reaction on his face, but inside he burned with frustration. To come so far…

"I'll pay an additional 10 percent per acre."

"Still no." Hunter said the words, but the other two men nodded in silent agreement.

And that, Jonathon realized, was the end of the negotiations. Five minutes, that's all it had taken.

The worst part, the very worst part, was that he respected the Mitchell brothers' reasons for not selling. *Mitchell land stays in Mitchell hands.*

There were other comparable properties near Denver. Two even had run-down train depots similar to the one on the Mitchell property. But none of the available parcels had a river running through the land. The natural water source made the Mitchell parcel ideal.

"You're a busy man," Hunter said. "Our decision is final. We won't take up any more of your time."

"I appreciate you hearing me out." Jonathon shook hands with each man. The oldest two brothers left the room almost immediately after that.

While Burke gathered up the files and followed them out, Garrett Mitchell hung back. "I'd like a quick word with you."

Eyebrows lifted, Jonathon gave a brief nod. "All right."

"Tell me your plan for the train depot. I know you have one or you wouldn't have mentioned it specifically in the contract."

Having worked with the young attorney before, Jonathon sensed the man's interest was genuine. Garrett Mitchell had a keen mind for business and a penchant for taking risks.

What harm could there be in sharing the basics of his idea? "My ultimate goal is to turn the stop into a premiere destination, with restaurants, shops, lodging and more."

Garrett rubbed his chin in thoughtful silence. "Entire towns have been built on less."

The other man's insight was spot on. "My hope is to create a community, not precisely a town, not at first, anyway. Rather a safe haven for my employees and their children."

He paused, thinking of his mother, of the desperation that had led her to make bad decisions out of terrible choices. "Each position will include a fair wage, on-the-job training, as well as room and board."

"If done right," Garrett mused, "the venture could bring you a great fortune."

"Money isn't the driving force behind the project." He went on to explain about the types of employees he would hire, mostly women like his mother.

"Ah, now I understand."

Jonathon believed Garrett Mitchell did, indeed, comprehend his motives. After all, the man was married to Molly, a woman whose mother had worked in Mattie's brothel, and whose older sister had adopted her when she was five.

"Let me speak to my brothers. Perhaps we can come to an arrangement."

Jonathon appreciated the gesture, but he needed to make one point perfectly clear. "I won't accept a lease, no matter how agreeable the terms."

"Understood." Now that their business was concluded, Jonathon expected the other man to take his leave.

Once again, this younger Mitchell brother surprised him. "Now that that's settled, tell me how my sister is faring in her new position here at the hotel."

Jonathon hesitated. He didn't feel right discussing Fanny with her brother. It felt like a betrayal to their friendship. "Why not ask her yourself?"

The other man shrugged. "I could. But she'll merely tell me she's doing fine."

True enough. "I can't speak for Fanny, but I can tell you she's doing an exceptional job. In truth, she's become indispensable to me." At her brother's lifted eyebrow, Jonathon added, "I mean, of course, *here*, at the hotel."

"Have a care, Hawkins." Garrett's eyes took on a hard edge. "Fanny has brothers who'll take on any man who tries to take advantage of her."

The warning was unnecessary. Jonathon would never hurt Fanny. If anyone dared to harm her or threaten her well-being, he would be first in line to deal with the rogue.

A knock came at the door and the very woman they were discussing appeared in the room. "Jonathon, we have a situation and…oh." Her eyes widened. "Garrett. I didn't realize you were involved in this afternoon's meeting."

"Didn't you?"

"No. I…" She tugged her bottom lip between her teeth. "I'm sorry, but I need to steal my boss away for a few minutes. We have a…situation." She gave Jonathon an apologetic grimace. "It's somewhat urgent."

"We'll talk out in the hall."

Before leaving the room, she tossed a sweet smile at her brother. "Good to see you, Garrett."

"You, too, Fanny. Been too long." He gave her a wry twist of his lips. "Great talking with you."

She laughed at his teasing tone. "Sorry I have to rush off. We'll catch up later?"

"Count on it."

The affection between the two was obvious. Clearly, the bond Jonathon had witnessed among the Mitchell brothers included the sisters, as well. For a brief period in his life he'd felt something similar with the other kids at Charity House, but that was a long time ago.

He followed Fanny out of the room, shut the door behind them. "You mentioned a situation?"

She puffed out a frustrated breath. "Mrs. Singletary has asked for extensive changes to the menu for tomorrow night."

"How extensive?"

"Ridiculously so, but before I send Philomena back with my carefully worded reply, I thought I'd better run it by you first."

She handed him a slip of paper with her neat handwriting scrolled across the page. The firm, yet oh-so-polite explanation as to why the hotel could not accommodate the widow's request was so perfectly phrased that Jonathon felt something move through him.

Admiration, to be sure, but something else, as well.

Not quite affection, something stronger, something with an edge. "Fanny Mitchell, you are a marvel."

"You're not…" she took back the note "…upset that I'm holding firm against the widow's request?"

"On the contrary." He subdued the urge to kiss the top of her head. And then her temple. Perhaps even the tip of her nose. "I completely and thoroughly approve."

Chapter Five

The next morning, Fanny woke before dawn and went straight to work. Preparations for Mrs. Singletary's ball kept her busy all day, making it impossible to find a spare moment for herself. There hadn't even been time for a cup of tea with her mother.

Tonight, she promised herself, as she hurried back to the room she called home in the wing reserved for hotel staff. She would seek out both her parents later tonight, as well as visit with each of her siblings and their spouses. For now, she had to dress for the ball.

She slipped into her gown, buttoned up the bodice, tied the ribbons on her sleeves, then secured the last pin in her hair. Turning her attention to the writing desk, where she'd laid out her lists in a neat, tidy row, she couldn't help but think she'd forgotten something important.

Why did she have this nagging sense of doom, this foreboding that something terrible was going to happen at the ball this evening?

Nerves, she told herself, a simple case of nerves. Perfectly understandable, considering the importance of tonight's event.

The clock on her nightstand told her she had nearly two hours before the first guests arrived. Plenty of time for another run-through of the ballroom, as long as she didn't fuss over her appearance.

Ironic, really, since most of her life she'd been lauded solely for her looks. Far too often she'd been touted as that lovely, charming Mitchell girl. Not a terrible reputation to have—quite pleasant, actually—but Fanny wanted to be seen as more than a pretty face.

Tonight the good people of Denver would meet a new Fanny Mitchell. A woman with substance and depth and a complex brain beneath the doll-like features.

With that in mind, she moved closer to her writing desk and reviewed her notes again. Working from top to bottom, left to right, she considered each item, one list at a time. Only after repeating the process twice over did she let out a sigh of relief.

The hotel was ready.

Was she?

Giving in to a moment of vanity—she *was* representing the Hotel Dupree, after all—she checked her reflection in the standing mirror by the window. The woman staring back at her looked refined and cultured, not frivolous and shallow. She supposed she looked pretty as well, not as striking as she had in the past, but not bland, either. The modern cut of her gown set off her trim figure, while the silvery-blue satin served as a perfect accompaniment to her pale blond hair. Best of all, the color of her dress was Jonathon's favorite.

A stirring of fascinated wonder settled Fanny's nerves, calming her ever so slightly. She still didn't know what had motivated his request to escort her to the ball. And yet hope surged. Why not use her time by his side to get to know him on a more personal level?

Her mood lighter than it had been in days, she gathered up her lists—all five of them—rushed out of the room and sped down the back stairwell. The noise level increased as she conquered each step. By the time she reached the first floor of the hotel she could no longer hear her footsteps.

The kitchen was a hive of activity. A sea of staff members hurried this way and that, carrying trays laden with food, moving with purpose and efficiency.

Fanny nodded in approval.

She entered the ballroom and paused a moment to catch her breath. Light blazed from the chandelier, wall sconces and candelabras placed strategically throughout the empty space. The floors gleamed. The gilded walls shone bright.

For days, Fanny had worried her decision to go with a simple color palette of green, gold and white was a mistake. Not so. Instead of overshadowing the crystal chandelier hanging from the high ceiling, the decorations enhanced the structure's unique artfulness.

Pleased by the overall effect, she floated through the room, her slippered feet soundless on the parquet flooring. A few mistakes caught her notice, mostly minor details, certainly nothing major. But still.

She could only hope Mrs. Singletary didn't notice that the ribbons on the candelabras were closer to ivory than gold. And that the cloths on the buffet tables had only three inches of lace hanging over the edge, instead of the requested four.

The stillness on the air was both soothing and yet

disconcerting. A room this grand was meant to be full of laughter. Soon, hundreds of voices would clamor for supremacy, each trying to be heard above the loud din. Fanny would probably miss the quiet then.

She turned. And froze.

Her heart took an extra hard thump as she caught sight of the man standing just inside the ballroom. One shoulder propped against the wall, Jonathon watched her in silence, an unreadable expression in his gaze. A sense of déjà vu rocked her to the core. He'd stared at her like this once before, only a few days ago, and she'd found the experience just as unnerving now as then.

She scanned his face, seeing something quite wonderful in his eyes, something soft and approachable and solely for her. She was staring, she knew, but couldn't help herself. He'd never looked more handsome, or more accessible.

Her heart took a quick tumble.

She searched her mind for something to say. Anything would do, anything at all. "Jonathon, you haven't changed into your evening clothes."

Oh, excellent, Fanny, stating the obvious is always a marvelous way to show off your intelligence.

A slow smile spread across his lips. "Not to worry. The ball isn't for several hours yet, still plenty of time for me to transform into a suitable escort for a woman of your class and style."

What a kind thing to say, and spoken with such sincerity, too. Really, could the man be any more charming? Could she be any more touched by his compliment?

"You look perfectly fine just as you are," she whispered.

It was no empty remark. Even in ordinary, everyday

business attire, Jonathon Hawkins exuded refined elegance.

Chuckling softly, he pushed away from the wall.

Now her heart raced so hard she worried one of her ribs would crack as a result.

Jonathon's eyes roamed her face, then lowered over her gown. Appreciation filled his gaze. "You're wearing my favorite color."

"I…know." She swallowed back the catch in her throat. "I chose this dress specifically with you in mind."

Too late, she realized how her admission sounded, as if her sole purpose was to please him. She had not meant to reveal so much of herself.

He took a step forward. "I'm flattered."

He took another step.

And then *another*.

Fanny held steady, unmoving, anxious to see just how close he would come to her.

He stopped his approach.

For the span of three rib-cracking heartbeats they stared into each other's eyes.

She sighed. The sound came out far too tremulous.

"Relax, Fanny. You've checked and rechecked every item on your lists at least three times, probably more. Go and spend a moment with your—"

"How do you know I checked and rechecked my lists that often?"

"Because…" his expression softened "…I know you."

She fought off another sigh. There was a look of such tenderness about him that for a moment, a mere heartbeat, she ached for what they might have accomplished, together, were they two different people. What they could have been to one another if past circumstances weren't entered into the equation.

"We're ready for tonight, Fanny. *You're* ready."

She drew in a slow, slightly uneven breath. "I suppose you're right."

He took one more step. He stood so close now she could smell his scent, a pleasant mix of bergamot, masculine spice and…him.

Something unspoken hovered in the air between them, communicated in a language she should know but couldn't quite comprehend. If he lowered his head just a bit more…

"Go. Spend a few moments with your mother and father before the guests begin to arrive. I'll come get you there, once I've changed my clothes."

"I'd like that." She'd very much enjoy the chance to show him off to her parents.

He leaned in closer, closer. Fanny let her eyelids flutter shut. But then the sound of determined footsteps commandeering the hallway had her opening them again.

"That will be Mrs. Singletary," she said with a rush of air. The widow's purposeful gait was easy enough to decipher.

"No doubt you are correct." His lips tilted at an ironic angle, Jonathon shifted to face the doorway.

Mrs. Singletary materialized two seconds later, Philomena a full step behind her. Like Fanny, both women were already dressed for the ball. The widow looked quite striking in a gown made of black and glittering gold satin that spoke of her wealth and status in town.

Philomena's dress was slightly less elegant, but the pale green silk complemented her smooth complexion and pretty hazel eyes. She looked beautiful, excited.

"Ah, Mr. Hawkins, Miss Mitchell. The very people I wish to see." The widow moved to a spot directly between Jonathon and Fanny, forcing them to step back. "I have a concern about the timing of our request for donations."

She paused, eyed them both expectantly, as if waiting for one of them to respond.

Jonathon took the cue. "You foresee a problem?"

"Not a problem per se, I merely wish to switch the order of the night's events. In the past, I have presented the goodwill baskets at the end of the party. However, this evening I would prefer to do so earlier."

Though Fanny didn't think the timing truly mattered—the guests understood this was a charity event—Mrs. Singletary seemed to think this change was necessary. Important, even.

Jonathon inclined his head. "We'd be happy to accommodate your request."

Taking his lead, Fanny added, "I'll let the staff know of the change."

"Excellent." The widow glanced over her shoulder, clucked her tongue in frustration. "Whatever is that man doing here, when I specifically sent him on an errand outside the hotel?"

Curious as to the identity of *that man*, Fanny followed the direction of the widow's gaze. Burke Galloway stood in the doorway, conversing quietly with Philomena. Both looked caught in the moment, as if they were the only two people in the room.

"That girl is proving a most difficult challenge." Mrs. Singletary shook her head. "Most difficult, indeed."

Fanny bit back a smile, even as a quote from her favorite poet, Emily Dickinson, came to mind. *The heart wants what the heart wants—or else it does not care.*

It was clearly evident that a match between Philomena and Jonathon would not come to pass.

Surely, Jonathon was relieved.

Fanny cast a covert glance in his direction. His gaze was locked on her and that was *not* business in his eyes.

Something far more personal stared back at her. She had but one thought in response.

Oh, my.

Barely two hours after the first guests arrived, the ballroom overflowed with at least three hundred of Denver's finest citizens. With the strains of a waltz floating on the air, and a rainbow of dancers whirling past, Jonathon stood away from the main traffic area, Fanny by his side.

He liked having her close, liked knowing they were here, together, presenting a united front as representatives of the hotel.

It seemed the entire female population of Denver had gone all out for tonight's event. Dressed in formal gowns made of colorful silks or satins, the women wore long, white gloves, and jeweled adornments in their hair that matched the stones glittering around their necks.

Fanny outshone every one of them, including the women in her own family.

He watched her siblings laughing, joking with one another and generally having a good time. Their interaction spoke of affection and easy familiarity. There was an unmistakable connection between them, one that went beyond words.

The Mitchells represented the very essence of family.

An icy numbness spread through Jonathon's chest.

What did he know of family? Nothing. No, that wasn't

entirely true. His mother had tried to give him a sense of belonging. And, of course, Marc and Laney Dupree had created a home for him at Charity House.

For nearly five years, they'd shown him unconditional love. They'd stood by him, even when he'd made terrible mistakes. It was Marc who'd retrieved him from jail the night Jonathon had confronted Judge Greene at his home, Laney who'd hugged away his pain and sense of betrayal.

Jonathon made a promise to seek them out tonight and thank them for their love and acceptance.

He searched for them now, but was distracted when a shrill, high-pitched female giggle sounded from the center of the dance floor.

One of the two oldest Ferguson sisters was making a spectacle of herself. Jonathon wasn't certain of her name. He always found it difficult to tell them apart. Unlike their younger sister, Philomena, the two oldest tended to behave in an inappropriate manner more often than not. Yet somehow they always managed to stay just on the right side of propriety.

Fanny released a chagrined sound from deep in her throat. "Penelope is in high spirits this evening. As is Phoebe, I'm afraid. I can't decide which of them is worse."

Jonathon divided his gaze between the two women in question. Both were shamelessly flirting with their dance partners. The sisters were so similar in appearance and behavior they were practically interchangeable.

"How do you tell them apart?" he wondered aloud.

"Years of practice." Fanny sighed again, then pointedly lifted her attention away from the Ferguson girls and to her own family. "My brothers are especially handsome this evening, their wives beyond beautiful. And Callie, oh, how she shines tonight. She's practically glowing."

Jonathon didn't disagree. "Your siblings seem happy."

"Marriage suits them." Fanny smiled. "Garrett once told me that when Mitchells fall in love they fall fast, hard and for keeps."

Emotion flashed in her eyes as she spoke. For a moment, she seemed very far away and very, very sad. As Jonathon watched Fanny, while she watched her siblings, a pang of remorse shot through him.

Was he making the correct decision about marriage? With the right woman, perhaps he *could* be a good husband. Perhaps, unlike his father and half brother, he wouldn't let down his wife. Perhaps the risk was worth the reward.

Another louder, shriller giggle rent the air.

"Poor Philomena," Fanny said, shaking her head. "To have such sisters."

Jonathon opened his mouth to agree when an older couple twirled past them. He studied the pair, the woman in particular. Fanny's resemblance to her mother was uncanny. They had the same tilt to their beautiful eyes, the same classic features, the same regal bearing.

"Your mother is quite lovely."

Fanny's eyes grew misty. "I'm so relieved to see her breathing easily."

He reached down to take Fanny's hand, and laced their fingers together. The connection was light, and was meant to offer her comfort. Yet it was Jonathon who experienced a moment of peace, of rightness.

This woman meant much to him, too much. He never wanted to lose her.

However, lose her he would.

Maybe not tomorrow, or next week, but one day, when

some wise man offered her marriage, for all the right reasons.

As much as it would pain Jonathon to watch her fall in love with another man, he wouldn't stand in her way. Thankfully, the prospect of her leaving him—or rather, the hotel—was a problem for another day.

Tonight, Fanny was all his.

He gave her hand a gentle squeeze.

She returned the gesture, then angled her head to peer into his eyes. A small, secretive smile slid along her lips. His throat seized on a breath. Fanny Mitchell was the most beautiful woman he'd ever known.

For the rest of the evening, he promised himself, he would avoid thinking of the future, forget memories of the past. All that mattered was this moment. This night. This woman.

"Fanny, would you do me the honor of—"

Her sharp intake of air cut off the rest of his request.

He attempted to search her gaze for the cause of her distress, but she was no longer looking at him, rather at a spot just over his right shoulder.

A cold, deadening sensation filled his lungs.

Jonathon knew who stood behind him.

His father. He felt the man's presence in his gut, in the kick of antagonism that hit Jonathon square in the heart.

His grip on Fanny's hand tightened. He was probably squeezing a bit too hard. He couldn't help himself. She was his only lifeline in a sea of uncertain emotion.

Let her go, he told himself. Let. Her. Go.

He couldn't make his fingers cooperate, couldn't seem to distance himself from her.

Let her go.

Fanny was the one who pulled her hand free. The absence of their physical connection was like a punch, the pain that sharp and unexpected.

Instead of stepping away, she moved closer and secured her fingers around his arm. Her eyes filled with understanding and something even more disturbing. Sympathy.

He didn't want her sympathy. *Anything but that.*

He began to step away from her, to distance himself from what he saw in her eyes. She tightened her grip and smiled sweetly. "You know, Jonathon, it's long past time we took a turn around the dance floor."

Her voice came at him as if from a great distance, sounding tinny in his ears, waking a favorite memory he'd tucked deep in the back of his mind. Another evening. Another one of Mrs. Singletary's charity balls.

Fanny had stood at the edge of a similar dance floor, on the very night of her return from Chicago. Gossip had erupted the moment she'd stepped into the room. Speculation about her reasons for leaving town had been voiced in barely concealed whispers.

She'd held firm under the censure, alone, her posture unmoving, chin lifted in defiance, as courageous as a warrior. She'd been magnificent. Beautiful. Yet Jonathon had seen past the false bravado. He'd seen the nerves and vulnerability living beneath the calm facade.

He'd asked her to dance.

Later, when the waltz had come to an end, she'd thanked him for rescuing her from an uncomfortable moment.

Now *she* was rescuing *him.*

It seemed somehow fitting.

"I'd like nothing more than to dance with you, Fanny."

Taking charge of the moment, he directed her onto the floor and then pulled her into his arms.

Chapter Six

Although Fanny had initially suggested she and Jonathon join the flurry of dancers, she was pleased he'd taken the lead and guided her into the waltz. His father's hold on him was lessening, or so she hoped.

With the music vibrant around them, she settled into his embrace. They fitted well together, their feet gliding across the parquet floor in seamless harmony.

She'd known a moment of terrible distress when Judge Greene entered the ballroom. She'd recovered quickly, and had immediately taken charge of the situation.

Fanny was good at anticipating problems at the hotel, even better at dealing with situations before they became, well…problems. It was one of the reasons Jonathon valued her, why he kept giving her more and more responsibility.

Tonight, she'd been happy to put her skills to use for his sake.

Step by step, spin by spin, she could feel the tension draining out of him.

Beneath the flickering light of the chandelier, and the

glow of a thousand candles, his features gradually lost their dark, turbulent edge. Jonathon was a man with many secrets and hidden pain harvested from a past no child should have to have suffered.

His present was proving no less harrowing, all because his father wished to acknowledge him publically. Not out of remorse for years lost, or guilt, or even sorrow for the harm he'd caused his son, but because Jonathon was a success now. His rags-to-riches story was legendary in Denver, almost mythical, and thus he was now worthy of Judge Greene's notice.

What a vile, hideous man.

Fanny caught a glimpse of him out of the corner of her eye. Tall and fit, with a shock of thick, white hair, he stood near the buffet table with his wife and family. The judge's features were distinguished and classically handsome, his face almost pretty. It seemed unfair that the man should look twenty years younger than his age.

His sins were supposed to show in his appearance, weren't they?

"He doesn't matter," she muttered.

To his credit, Jonathon didn't pretend to misunderstand who she meant. "No, he doesn't, not tonight."

Not ever, Fanny wanted to add, but Jonathon's hold around her waist tightened ever so slightly and he twirled her in a series of smooth, sure-footed spins.

The man was incredibly light on his feet.

"Where did you learn to dance so beautifully?"

"My mother taught me." His gaze darkened, filling with the shadows of some private memory. "She believed every gentleman should know how to waltz, her son most of all."

Proving his expertise went beyond the basics, he spun

Fanny in a collection of complicated steps that had her gasping for air. "She instructed you well."

"Indeed."

They smiled at each other. More than a few interested gazes followed them through the next series of twirls. Fanny frowned at the words she caught from a gaggle of ladies on her left. *That's the girl who jilted Reese Bennett Jr.*

Whatever was she thinking?

Fanny could tell them, if they condescended to ask her directly. She would gladly explain that her worst fear was marrying a man she didn't love, or worse, who didn't love her. She couldn't imagine anything more awful than being trapped in a miserable, unhappy marriage.

Jonathon changed direction, backpedaling once, twice, spinning her around. And around. Her head whirled in the most delightful way, leaving her pleasantly breathless.

The whispers traveling in their wake were all but forgotten. She ignored everything—everyone—and focused solely on enjoying this moment, in this man's arms.

A man she admired above all others.

A man who'd made it perfectly clear he didn't want to marry, because of the paternal example he'd been given. The thought left her feeling glum. No. She refused to allow anything to ruin this waltz, this night.

Fanny's parents twirled past, catching her notice. She allowed their joy to fill her. They were both so beautiful, the handsome rancher and his stunning wife. Her mother was dressed in a midnight-blue gown several shades darker than her steel-blue eyes. Her entire being glowed as she smiled up at her husband.

Cyrus Mitchell's expression was incredibly tender as he gazed into his wife's eyes. The fear and worry was still there, but not as apparent tonight. Gone was the gruff rancher, and in his place, dressed in formal attire, was a besotted husband.

Fanny sighed. She adored her parents, and desperately wanted what they had—a blessed, godly marriage filled with laughter, loyalty and, of course, love.

As if sensing her gaze on him, her father smiled over at her and winked. Fanny barely had time to return the gesture before Jonathon whirled her in the opposite direction.

Her heart lifted and sighed with pleasure.

He took her through another spin, then slowed their pace. The smile he gave her nearly buckled her knees. "Have I told you how beautiful you are tonight?"

"Yes, several times."

"It bears repeating."

She swallowed a nervous laugh. "You look quite handsome this evening yourself. Very elegant, very refined. I thoroughly approve of your attire."

The tension in his shoulders immediately returned.

What had she said to put him on guard once again?

"Clothing can change a man's appearance, but it cannot change his character."

What an odd thing to say. Surely he wasn't referring to himself. "I don't quite know what you mean."

His gaze connected with his father, who now stood just on the edge of the dance floor, watching them intently. "The inner man doesn't always match the outer trappings."

Ah, now she understood. "Don't compare yourself to your father," she ordered in a low, fierce tone. "You're nothing like him."

"You don't know that, Fanny."

"I know *you*. You're kind and generous and—"

"You wouldn't say that if you were privy to the things I've done in the past." Pain and self-recrimination inhabited his eyes as he spoke.

She wanted to weep for the little boy who'd done whatever necessary to survive, for the young man who'd made questionable choices to pull himself out of poverty. "The past should be left in the past where it belongs."

"Such innocence." The tenderness in his smile nearly broke her heart. "There are some things that can't be undone, Fanny, mistakes that can't be forgotten."

"You're wrong, Jonathon. That's the wonder of God's grace. He knows what we've done and loves us anyway."

Her partner opened his mouth to speak, probably to argue with her, but the music stopped.

Their steps slowly drew to a halt. By some unspoken agreement, they stayed linked in each other's arms, neither moving, neither speaking. One heartbeat passed, then another, by the third Jonathon took a deliberate step back and offered her his arm.

She accepted the silent invitation without question.

In strained silence, he escorted her off the dance floor. Fanny hated the sudden shift in the mood between them. A sense of awkwardness had returned to their relationship.

Experiencing a desperate urge to put matters right, she made a bold request. "Would you care to join me outside on the terrace for some fresh air?"

For several endless seconds, he simply stared at her. She could see the silent battle waging within him. "That would be unwise."

"Not if we stay in plain sight." She spoke in a rush, then forced herself to slow down, to speak calmly. "We

won't be fully alone. People have been coming and going
through the French doors all evening."

He glanced at the wall of glass doors lining the balcony. He drew in a slow, steady breath and then nodded
in agreement.

They made their way across the ballroom without
speaking.

He paused at the exit, dropped his gaze over her silk
gown. "You aren't dressed for the weather."

"I can tolerate a few moments in the cold."

"That," he said, shaking his head, "I won't allow."

He shrugged out of his jacket and placed it around her
shoulders. The gesture was so thoughtful, so... Jonathon.

Tears burned in her throat. He was such a good man,
down to his very core, generous in both deed and spirit.
If only he would see himself the way she did.

Blinking back a wave of emotion, she pulled the jacket's lapels together. Jonathon's warmth instantly envel-
oped her.

She walked with him onto the terrace, then lifted her
gaze to the heavens. The air was cool on her face, refreshing after the stifling atmosphere of the ballroom.

Several other couples meandered past them. Others
leaned on the balcony's railing. Caught up in their own
conversations, none seemed to pay Fanny and Jonathon
any notice.

She maneuvered past the bulk of the crowd, stopping
at the edge of a tiny alcove at the end of the walkway.
Though not completely hidden from sight, the small space
afforded relative privacy.

Still, Jonathon took up a position at the railing.

Of course he would refuse to put her in a compromising position. Was it any wonder she admired this man?

Accepting the wisdom of the move, she joined him in the light, in full view of the ballroom, and anyone who cared to look. People *always* cared to look.

Something Fanny must keep in mind if she was to change the way society saw her.

Hard to do, when all she wanted was to be alone with the handsome, thoughtful, interesting man by her side.

Too late, Jonathon realized he'd made an error in judgment. He should never have agreed to escort Fanny outside. The intimacy of the moment was nearly too much to bear. Looking at her wrapped inside his jacket gave him all sorts of thoughts he shouldn't be entertaining.

She was a beautiful woman and he a man just hitting his prime, a man with a tainted past and a host of bad choices behind him.

He'd like to think he'd grown wiser in the past few years. Clearly, he hadn't. As evidenced by the fact that he was out on the terrace with Fanny.

Even if they stayed in the open, her reputation was at risk by simply being in his company. "Time to head back inside."

He reached for her hand.

She skillfully sidestepped him. "I have something to say."

Impatience slid through him. If they stayed away from the ballroom much longer, someone would come looking for them. "We can speak inside."

"Please, Jonathon. I'll be brief."

"All right." He made a grand show of putting a large amount of space between them. "I'm listening."

She gave him a mildly scolding look. "How am I supposed to talk to you when you've put a giant chasm between us?"

"Three feet is not a giant chasm."

"You're missing the point."

No, actually, *she* was missing the point. She, of all people, should know what was at stake if someone chose to misinterpret their little meeting out here on the terrace.

"Fanny, we can't stay out here much longer. Our absence will soon be noticed, if it hasn't been already."

"You're right, of course." She handed him back his coat but made no move to return to the ballroom. "I'm sorry Judge Greene showed up tonight."

Her words were steady, but her eyes spoke of her distress. So much sorrow, sorrow for him.

Had anyone ever cared for him that much? His mother, of course. Marc and Laney. A piteously small number of people, to be sure. "It's not your fault, Fanny. You didn't invite him."

"I didn't try to uninvite him, either."

She truly cared about him. The selfish part of Jonathon longed to bask in such favor. A dangerous prospect.

He had nothing to give her beyond material things. Fanny deserved more than pretty trinkets. And Jonathon wanted to give her more. But if he let down his guard, enough to explore the feelings he already had for her, there was no guarantee he wouldn't ultimately hurt her.

He couldn't risk causing her harm.

"You shouldn't be out here with me."

"Why not?"

"Your reputation—"

She cut him off with a delicate sniff. "My reputation was put into question long before you and I…"

Her words trail off, as if she wasn't sure what they were to one another.

He wasn't sure, either.

"Let's go back inside."

She remained rooted to the spot. "I haven't had my say."

"Then by all means carry on, but quickly."

"You aren't your father, nor are you going to turn out like him. I have faith in you. You should have faith in yourself."

Her conviction shook Jonathon to the core. He hadn't expected this unwavering defense of his character. "What if you're wrong about me?"

"What if I'm right?"

For a dangerous moment, he allowed her certainty to sink past his cynicism, to permeate all the reasons he'd kept his distance from her.

"Yes, Jonathon, you started out life with the odds stacked against you. Of course you made mistakes, and a few bad choices. Haven't we all? What matters is who you are today, not who you once were."

She pulled his hand to her face, sighed into his palm.

Mesmerized, he could only stare. The smooth skin of her cheek felt like silk against his roughened hand.

He might not be able to give her what she wanted, what she needed, but he couldn't seem to walk away. He couldn't even pull his hand away from her face.

He stared at her, thinking…maybe. Maybe…

"Fanny." He said her name in a low growl. The sound came from deep within his soul, dangerous and full of warning. "Don't romanticize who I am beneath the fancy evening attire. You're looking at me from the goodness of your heart, not the reality of mine."

"You're wrong." She lifted her head. Her eyes were filled with warmth and affection.

His heart soared.

This woman could rescue me. He shoved away the reckless thought. "Don't look at me like that."

"I could make you happy."

Yes, he thought, she could. But he might very well destroy her in the process. She mattered too much to take the chance. "You want a conventional marriage. You want a happy, normal home full of children. And I want those things for you, too."

"But not with you."

The look of shattered dreams swimming in her eyes nearly brought him to his knees. "You know why."

"Why must you persist in thinking you'll become your father?" She practically hissed out the words, her tone fierce, her face a little ruthless. "Why? When evidence to the contrary is in everything you do?"

"Joshua Greene and I share the same blood."

"There are other examples in your life. Men who've mentored you. Marc Dupree, for instance. And, of course, there's the best example of all, our Heavenly Father."

There it was again, that unfailing faith in him. She couldn't know how badly he wanted to be the man she deserved.

In that instant, he allowed himself to believe in the impossible. "I like the man I see in your eyes."

He closed the distance between them, but still had the sense not to take her into his arms. A slight movement on his part, a shift on hers, and their lips would meet. He shouldn't kiss her. It would be the same as making a promise.

A promise he couldn't keep.

When clouds covered the moon, casting them in shadow, he didn't have the strength to push her away. The inevitability of this moment had been coming on for months.

There was still one small hope left. "Go back inside, Fanny, before I do something you'll regret."

Showing the stubborn streak he'd once admired, she stayed firmly rooted to the spot. "I'm perfectly happy right where I am."

A man could take only so much temptation.

Jonathon placed his hands on her shoulders, prayed for the strength to set her away from him.

"Leave me, Fanny." He gritted out the order through clenched teeth.

"Oh, Jonathon."

The way she said his name, so soft, so full of affection, he wanted to—

Suddenly, she cupped his face and pulled his head down to hers. At the same instant, he drew her against him. *Inevitable.* The word echoed in his mind.

The moment their lips touched, he was lost.

Inevitable.

By sheer willpower, he kept the kiss light, still on the edge of friendly, but barely. He tore his mouth free and lifted his head to stare into her eyes.

She blinked up at him in wonder. He'd done that to her. He'd put that dreamy look in her gaze. He was too much of a man not find satisfaction in that.

With his hands still on her shoulders, his breathing as unsteady as hers, he said, "We must get back."

She didn't argue the point. "Yes."

At the same time she lowered her hands from his face, he attempted to release his hold on her shoulders.

Only one of his hands came away. The other, or rather, his cuff link, was caught in her hair. He tugged as gently as possible. They remained connected.

He tugged again.

"Oh!" she cried out. "You…your sleeve…it's—"

"—stuck in your hair."

He reached up with his free hand.

Her instinctive flinch only managed to twine her hair more securely around his cuff link. "Hold still."

"I'm trying."

Additional clouds moved in, swallowing what was left of the already meager light. Jonathon leaned in for a better look.

With his forehead practically pressed against Fanny's ear, he was finally able to discern that her hair had curled around his cuff link in a counterclockwise fashion. "I see the problem."

He slowly, carefully, unraveled each strand.

Just as he managed to pull his hand away, a female gasp sounded from behind him—followed by a distressingly familiar giggle.

He knew that sound. One of the silly Ferguson sisters stood at his back. The question was, how much had she seen?

The giggle turned into two, interspersed with titters, followed by overexcited, feverish whispering.

Both Ferguson sisters had come upon him and Fanny.

Jonathon told himself to remain calm. The shadows may have sufficiently hidden them from sight, or at least covered their identities.

Bracing himself for the worst, he gave Fanny an apologetic grimace, then pivoted to face the consequences of his actions.

His gaze fell on empty air.

Whoever had come upon them was now gone.

He turned back to Fanny. "I'm sorry."

Her lips quivered. "We are both to blame, I more than you, since I initiated our kiss."

Wishing he could take back the last half hour—not for his benefit but for hers—he refused to let her feel a moment of guilt.

"No, Fanny, the blame falls solely on my shoulders. I should not have escorted you outside. I should have at least insisted we return to the ballroom sooner."

She didn't immediately respond. With her finger tapping her chin in thoughtful reflection, she glanced to her right, then to her left. "You know, the Ferguson sisters may not have any idea who it was they interrupted. We may yet be safe."

"Perhaps," he agreed, although he didn't hold out much hope for that, especially since he and Fanny would be returning to the ballroom together. He would not allow her to face alone whatever censure awaited them. He would stand by her side and assume the bulk of the blame.

He feared his efforts wouldn't be enough. Fanny's reputation would soon be in tatters. At a time when she'd nearly broken free of the previous scandal, she would once again be the center of ugly gossip.

Mere days ago, Jonathon had promised himself his legacy would be different from his father's. He'd vowed no woman would suffer because of his actions. Now, because of his actions, the one woman he most wanted to protect was good and truly ruined.

As far as he was concerned, that didn't make him as bad as his father.

It made him worse.

Chapter Seven

Fanny held Jonathon's unwavering gaze with one of her own. As a matter of honor, she refused to be the first to look away. Because she watched him so attentively, she knew the precise moment their relationship took another critical turn. There was an invisible link between them now.

The anxiety roiling in her stomach calmed, then returned full force when Fanny thought of her mother. Mary Mitchell was just beginning to manage her devastating illness. Would another scandal attached to her daughter's name stifle her efforts? The doctor had warned that stress worsened the asthma attacks.

Something dark moved through Fanny, something that felt like guilt, or perhaps even shame. It appalled her to feel tears gathering in her eyes. She hadn't once thought of her mother when she'd convinced Jonathon to leave the ballroom, nor when she'd coaxed him farther along the terrace, and certainly not when she'd kissed him.

Jonathon had tried to send her back into the safety of the ballroom. Instead of heeding his warning, she'd dragged his head down to hers and melded their mouths together.

She was not innocent. She was not good. She'd earned every bit of the censure awaiting her in the ballroom.

To think, but a few hours ago, Fanny had convinced herself tonight would change the way people in town saw her. She'd certainly accomplished her objective. Clearly, she'd learned nothing from her past mistakes. Now others would suffer the consequences of her actions. Her mother. Jonathon. The rest of her family.

What have I done?

Another spurt of guilt squeezed the breath from her lungs. "I am completely at fault," she choked out between inhalations.

"Not completely, no." Jonathon's deep voice poured warmth over her cold heart. "We share the blame, and will face the consequences together, no matter how dire or life-altering."

He did not say marriage, but he was thinking it. The evidence was there, in the grim twist of his lips and the stern set of his shoulders.

She'd dragged this man to a place he'd vowed never to go.

What have I done?

"Come." He tugged her toward the ballroom. "Time to face the good people of Denver."

He guided her to the very edge of the French doors. A few more steps and they would cross over the threshold, into a future neither of them truly wanted.

The faint strains of a waltz floated out of the ballroom. One, two, three. One, two, three. The notes were simple in structure, but a mockery of the complex emotions pulling at her composure.

What have I done?

She shot a glance at Jonathon from beneath her lashes. Even in the dense, flickering shadows, she recognized the resolve in his eyes, the willingness to do whatever was necessary to protect her from another scandal.

She could not let him compromise his future for hers. "We should enter at separate times. Give the gossips less fodder to build their stories upon."

He lowered his gaze to meet hers.

"No, Fanny. We are in this together."

We are in this together. Jonathon Hawkins was proving to be a man of integrity—honorable, upright, noble. Was there any wonder she'd kissed him? And wanted to do so again?

For his sake, she once again grasped at a single thread of hope. "Perhaps Penelope and Phoebe didn't see us kiss. Perhaps they will only tell the tale of my hair stuck in your cuff."

The shake of his head said he didn't believe that any more than Fanny did. "More likely they will embellish what they saw with a decided lack of decorum. We'll find out soon enough."

He released her hand, moved in beside her, then offered her his arm in a gentlemanly gesture. Her throat seized shut.

What have I done?

If she walked inside the ballroom so thoroughly allied with him, there would be no turning back. For either of them.

"Take my arm, Fanny."

The request was kindness itself. Still, she hesitated. "I have weathered gossip before. I am not afraid to do so again."

"You are a strong woman, there is no doubt. However, you were not alone in the kiss we shared." His tone was resolute, but when he touched a fingertip to her cheek, the contact was gentle, a mere whisper of skin to skin. "I was thoroughly present then, and I will not abandon you now."

Without pause, with one single, fluid motion, he scooped up her hand and placed it in the crook of his elbow.

They entered the ballroom side by side.

Every head turned in their direction. Significant glances were exchanged as people separated off into groups and began whispering over the music.

So the Ferguson sisters had done their worst.

Mrs. Singletary bustled through the crowd, her stride full of purpose. She met Fanny and Jonathon at the edge of the dance floor just as the final notes of the waltz played out.

"Ah, Mr. Hawkins, Miss Mitchell, there you are." She gave them each a pointed look, silently urging them to follow her lead. "I thank you for ensuring all is ready for the next portion of our evening."

Before either Jonathon or Fanny could respond, the widow positioned herself between them. The move was full of easy familiarity, as if they'd rehearsed this moment a thousand times over.

"Smile," she ordered under her breath.

Fanny managed a tentative smile, but feared she failed in her attempt to fully hide her nerves. A quick glance to her left and she saw that Jonathon had no such problem. His smile actually looked genuine.

Mrs. Singletary nodded to the staff lined up against

the walls. With wicker baskets in hand, they took up strategic positions throughout the room.

The widow drew in a slow, dramatic breath, pulling every eye to her. An expectant hush fell over the room. "Mr. Hawkins, would you do the honor of calling for donations?"

"It would be my pleasure."

He asked for the crowd's attention. A ridiculously wasted effort, as all eyes were already on him. "As most of you know, Mrs. Singletary hosts her annual charity event to raise funds for one of her favorite causes in town."

As he spoke, he leveled a gaze over the assembled group, silently daring anyone to interrupt him.

No one dared.

Not even Fanny's brothers, who glared at Jonathon with the kind of disgust they reserved for poachers and horse thieves. Their wives held on to them with white-knuckle grips, as if holding them in place.

Ice lifted from Fanny's stomach, setting up residence in her lungs, stealing her ability to take a decent breath.

Jonathon continued his speech. "Tonight's proceeds will fund a long overdue remodel of the new kitchen at Charity House."

He went on to explain why the orphanage needed the upgrade, but Fanny was only half listening now. She circled her gaze around the room, stopping at various clusters of wide-eyed guests staring back at her.

She soon found Penelope and Phoebe. They stood among a group of their friends, looking smug, triumphant even, and completely unrepentant of the gossip they'd already spread.

Fanny leaned forward, counted to five silently in her

head, putting a number to each second, then pointedly moved her gaze away from the troublemaking sisters.

She searched for her parents next, found them almost immediately.

No. *No!* Her father appeared to be supporting the bulk of her mother's weight. The once active, vibrant woman looked so small, so pale and vulnerable. Her breathing was coming too fast. Any moment she could suffer an asthma attack.

Fanny was the cause of her mother's distress. She'd given her reason to worry, the very thing Dr. Shane had warned against. Right then, in that moment, Fanny vowed to do anything, *everything*, to ensure Mary Mitchell suffered no setbacks because of her.

Jonathon's speech came to an end. "We thank you for your contributions to such a worthy cause."

Moderate applause broke out among the guests.

A single lift of Mrs. Singletary's chin and the hotel staff moved through the crowd, baskets extended. Despite the tension in the room, donations flowed in quickly.

The orchestra struck up a lively country reel. Some of the assembled men and women took to the dance floor, others resumed their private conversations.

Fanny didn't have to guess at the topic of their discussions.

She sighed. "Thank you, Mrs. Singletary. You quite literally saved the day."

"No, dear, I merely forestalled the inescapable." She patted Fanny's hand sympathetically, leveled a speculative glance over Jonathon. "The rest is up to the two of you."

She made to leave.

Fanny forestalled her departure a moment longer. "I'm sorry we ruined your ball."

"On the contrary." The widow fluttered her fingers. "I'm quite delighted with this turn of events. Tonight's ball will be talked about for months to come."

While that *had* been the intended goal, Fanny had hoped the talk would be for far different reasons than her scandalous behavior.

What have I done?

Her head grew light. Little spots played before her eyes. She swayed. Jonathon was by her side in an instant, hand at the small of her back, supporting her.

She lifted her gaze up to his. His attention was no longer on her, but trained at the back of the ballroom. Fanny swiveled her head in that direction, connected her gaze with Judge Greene. The odious man had the nerve to smile at her, the look far from polite.

Feeling suddenly unclean, she tore her gaze away.

Rising onto her toes, she caught sight of her father leading her mother to a chair. "I must go to my mother."

"I'll escort you." Jonathon shifted his hold to her arm.

They'd barely taken a step when Mrs. Singletary's voice halted their progress. "Brace yourself, Mr. Hawkins. Your moment of judgment is fast approaching."

Fanny nearly groaned aloud. Her brothers strode through the crowd, seemingly oblivious of the stares following them. Hunter led the charge, his menacing gait reminiscent of the ruthless gunslinger he'd once been.

Jonathon met the silent challenge with his own personal brand of grit. Not a blink. Not even a twitch. His eyes were as hard as Hunter's, and an equally threatening smile curved his lips.

Both men's dark pasts were evident in every fiber of their being. The two would be formidable foes under normal circumstances. These were *not* normal circumstances, Fanny realized with a jolt of terror. They must not fight over her.

She would not allow them to come to blows. With swift, sure steps, she hurried forward, slapped her palm on Hunter's chest. His feet pounded to a stop.

"Out of my way, Fanny." He glared hard at her hand. "This doesn't concern you."

She held her ground. "On the contrary, this is completely about me."

Logan and Garrett stood beside Hunter, flanking him, their eyes trained on Jonathon. He held their stares without flinching.

"You will not hurt Jonathon." She included all three of her brothers in the warning. "I will not allow it."

"Step aside, Fanny." This from Jonathon, spoken in a flat, unemotional tone. "Your brothers will have their say, and then I will have mine."

Jonathon's face was calm, almost stoic. She recognized that look, had seen it several times in the past year while working closely by his side. He would not tolerate her interference.

She would give him no other choice.

Just as she opened her mouth to explain her position, he shifted to stand in front of her, shielding her body with his, literally protecting her from her own brothers.

A sweet gesture, but unnecessary, especially when he was the one at the greatest risk.

She scrambled back around him. Again, he put himself between her and her brothers.

"This is ridiculous," she said. "You cannot think that I—"

She broke off, realizing the crowd was pressing in on their unhappy little group. Switching tactics, she carefully modulated her breathing and aligned her shoulders with Jonathon's.

"I can count on you to be reasonable?" She directed the question at her brothers. When none of them responded, she repeated herself.

They nodded, with very little enthusiasm. Nevertheless, she took them at their word. "I will hold you to your promise."

The next few moments passed in a blur.

Hunter officially requested to speak with Jonathon in private. Jonathon agreed, then suggested they continue their discussion in his office.

Fanny barely had time to blink after their retreating backs when Mrs. Singletary came up beside her. "Well, well, well, what I wouldn't give to be a witness to *that* conversation."

Fanny could not say the same.

The moment the men left the ballroom, Fanny was surrounded by her brothers' wives. They huddled around her, their physical presence and sympathetic smiles evidence of their unconditional love.

Each woman took a turn pulling Fanny into her arms. Annabeth spoke for the group, her words of encouragement reminding Fanny that she was not alone, never would be alone, and could turn to any of them in the next few weeks for whatever she needed.

"You can even move out to the ranch with Hunter and me," Annabeth assured her. "If it comes to that."

Fanny would never allow it to come to that.

More promises of a place to call home came from the others, then, at last, Fanny stood before her parents. Renewed panic stole her ability to take a decent breath. Her mother's face had gone white as the moon, her breathing labored, but not a full wheeze. Yet. "I'm so sorry, I didn't mean to—"

"Not now, Fanny." Her father laid a hand on her shoulder, cutting off the rest of her words. "Not here."

He was right, of course. Too many people closed in around them, prepared to spread pieces of conversation they overheard.

"Let's get you upstairs, Mary, my love." Her father helped her mother stand.

Fanny twisted her hands together. Oh, how she hated seeing her mother so dependent on assistance.

Proving she still had some spunk left in her, Mary Mitchell swatted at her husband's hand. "Cyrus, stop hovering like an old bird. I can walk on my own."

"Never said otherwise." Though he stepped back and let his wife leave the ballroom on her own steam, Fanny's father stayed close, hands poised to reach out if she lost her balance.

Lips pressed tightly together, Fanny trailed in her parents' wake.

At the elevator, her mother pulled to a stop. "Cyrus, you will join our sons and Mr. Hawkins, and ensure order is kept. Logic and good sense must rule the day."

"Now, Mary, you are my primary concern, I will see you settled in our room before—"

"I wish to speak to our daughter alone." She spoke with the no-nonsense tone that had kept her seven rambunctious children in line.

After a brief argument, Fanny's father admitted defeat. He turned to go, paused, then spun back around. His gaze was not unkind as it settled on Fanny. "You rarely take a misstep, my dear, but when you do, you make it a big one."

She could not argue the point. "Pa, please don't let the boys hurt Jonathon."

Her father looked at her steadily, with an ironic lift of his eyebrows. "I suspect the man can take care of himself."

"Please."

"Yes, yes, I will be the voice of reason."

"Thank you." As she watched her father disappear around the corner, a flood of helplessness washed over her. Jonathon had promised to take his share of the blame.

What if he claimed all of it?

She would not put it past him. Her brothers would force his hand then, which must never happen. If only she knew what was being said behind that shut door. Perhaps she should—

The elevator whooshed open, reminding her of a far greater concern. She ushered her mother inside and told the attendant to take them to the ninth floor of the hotel.

By mutual agreement, Fanny and her mother kept silent on the journey to her parents' suite. Once inside, with her heart drumming wildly against her ribs, Fanny shouldered the door closed and then helped her mother to a small sofa.

The milky glow of the moon spilled in from the windows, creating a long, pale beacon across the blue-and-gold rug. Additional light from strategically placed lamps chased shadows into the far corners of the room.

Fanny sat beside her mother and took her hands.

For a moment, she simply studied the beloved face of the woman who'd raised her. There were new, deeper lines around her eyes and mouth, additional grooves across her forehead. But—Praise the Lord—her breathing sounded regular.

Relief had Fanny's eyes filling with tears. "Oh, Mother, I'm so sorry, I—"

"Hush, child, no apologies are necessary." Her mother pulled her into her arms and rocked her gently, in the same way she'd done when Fanny was a child.

The lack of condemnation was nearly her undoing. Several tears slipped free before she could call them back. She clung to her mother, praying for a composure she didn't feel.

In the next heartbeat, she squeezed her eyes tightly shut. A picture of Jonathon's face loomed in her mind. She shoved away the image. Enough stalling.

Sighing heavily, she set her mother back against the brocade cushions and said, "Pa was right. I've taken another misstep, far worse than the one before."

A broken engagement was nothing compared to kissing a man of some renown in the shadows. Her reputation was most definitely ruined. Her life would never be the same.

Jonathon's had permanently changed, as well.

"You know, Fanny." Her mother took her hand. "I have never put much stock in gossip. Why don't you tell me what really happened between you and your Mr. Hawkins?"

Fanny lifted her hands in a helpless gesture. "I don't know where to start."

"At the beginning, of course."

Yes, but where was the beginning? Long before tonight's kiss, she realized. Thus, Fanny told her mother about her relationship with Jonathon over the past year, highlighting how well they worked together. How much he trusted her, and she him. She spoke of their many walks, and felt a smile playing at her lips. "Jonathon and I prefer to stroll in the snow most often."

"You like him."

"I do. Oh, Mother, I do like him, so very much."

"He clearly likes you, as evidenced by his behavior this evening. He did, after all, kiss you under the moon and stars."

Fanny's heart sank, both at the romantic image her mother painted and the realization that the Ferguson sisters had witnessed everything.

"Jonathon behaved like a perfect gentleman. It was only at my suggestion he escorted me out onto the terrace."

"I see."

"No, you don't." Why did her mother have to be so understanding, so accepting, so *wrong*? "Jonathon didn't take advantage of the situation, I did. *I* kissed *him*."

There, the truth was out at last. Unfortunately, she felt no better. Wasn't confession supposed to be the first step toward healing her soul?

Fanny felt only worse.

"You claim you initiated your kiss, yet Mr. Hawkins stood by your side during the call for donations, as if he'd been equally culpable."

"He is a kind, generous man. The very best I know."

"Perhaps marriage is the answer."

"No. Do not say such a thing." Fanny's pulse hammered in her ears. "Jonathon must not be forced to marry me."

"Perhaps he will want to marry you. The relationship you just described sounds far stronger than most marriages."

Fanny refused to allow a single spark of hope to flare into life. She liked Jonathon too much to trap him in an unwanted union. She would honor his reasons for remaining unattached. She owed him that. "I will never marry him."

"You may not have a choice, Fanny. The scandal may be too big for any other solution."

Fanny refused to despair. There were other ways to avoid scandal. She could return to the Chicago Hotel Dupree, or the one in Saint Louis, or even move to San Francisco. Except...

What if she moved away and her mother's asthma became worse? What if she had a severe, life-threatening attack? Fanny couldn't bear the thought of being so far away.

Besides, running away didn't solve anything. She'd learned that lesson well enough after the first scandal attached to her name. No matter how ugly the whispers became, no matter how hard her life grew, Fanny would not run again.

She would face whatever ugly gossip was thrown her way. She would stand sure, with courage and conviction. She would not, under any inducement or threat, force Jonathon into marriage.

Chapter Eight

When Jonathon was eight years old, and still new to the survival game, he'd picked the pocket of a man three times his size. To this day, he still remembered the fury in his quarry's eyes.

That same look was replicated in all but one of the four Mitchell men. Fanny's father simply observed the scene in cold, stark silence, arms crossed over his chest, expression inscrutable. With his back propped against the door, Cyrus Mitchell was either blocking the exit or allowing his sons to have their say before he intervened.

The three brothers stood shoulder to shoulder facing Jonathon. Their dark scowls and rigid stances indicated their mood. Even dressed in formal attire, each man projected intense, unyielding resolve to get answers.

Jonathon got straight to the point. "I will make this right for Fanny."

Unfortunately, the right thing by society's standards might very well be the wrong thing for her. A hard rock of remorse settled in the pit of his stomach. There could be no happy ending for Fanny. She wanted more than

Jonathon had to offer. He wondered if she would grow to resent him one day.

How could she not?

She was all that was light and good and true. Jonathon was a mix of dark layers and murky complexities. He would ultimately let Fanny down.

Eyes hard, Hunter stalked up to him, going toe-to-toe, a move meant to antagonize. Jonathon strained to keep his hands loose by his sides. He no longer solved problems with his fists. He would not be induced into forgetting that he knew how to keep his temper in check.

"Tell me this, Hawkins." Hunter spat out his name as if tasting something foul. "Did you intentionally set out to ruin our sister? Was it part of some devious plan to get your hands on our land?"

A deep red haze fell over Jonathon's vision, momentarily blinding him. Of all the evils that could be laid at his feet, Hunter's indictment was the most insulting of all.

In a precise, cold tempo Jonathon ground out his response. "I would never use Fanny, or any woman, for my own personal gain."

The idea made him sick, a sensation that turned to a hot ball of revulsion in his gut. Using women was his father's modus operandi. Jonathon had thought himself better than the man who'd sired him.

Yet he'd followed in his father's footsteps and caused a woman's downfall. Not just any woman, either, but one he cared about above all others. Dark emotions pulled at him.

He clasped his hands behind his back.

"I'll marry Fanny as soon as we can make the arrangements." The instant the words left his mouth, he realized he'd made the decision long before this moment. He'd known what he would do even before he'd escorted her back inside the ballroom.

No turning back for either of them now.

Fanny would be trapped with him the rest of her life. Knowing she wanted things he couldn't give her, he felt his throat burn with self-recrimination. He wished there was another way, but there could be no other solution to save her reputation at this point.

The Ferguson sisters had made sure of that.

"Not so fast, Hawkins." Taking over for his brother, Logan shoved his face inches close to Jonathon's. "We haven't yet decided if you're worthy of marrying our sister."

Voice low and rough, Jonathon pointed out the obvious. "You would rather she face ruin?"

"That's not what I said."

"You would have her denied access to public businesses, her favorite shops, perhaps even her friends' parlors? You would have her whispered about on the streets, pointed out as a cautionary tale by mothers of young girls?"

"Of course that's not what we want." Logan bellowed louder this time. "But even you must agree. Marriage to a man such as yourself may be an equally devastating fate as the one you just described."

The insult hit home, a solid punch to his gut.

Jonathon blinked hard, his guilt a tangible thing, gnawing at him like tiny little rat claws. He'd made a terrible mistake out on that terrace, and now Fanny would suffer.

Still, resentment formed in the depths of his soul. All three of Fanny's brothers were married to women with similar backgrounds as his. "The circumstances of my birth—"

"Are not in question." Garrett dragged his older brother a few steps back, then took his place in front of Jonathon. "Our concern has nothing to do with who your mother was, or the childhood you endured. That sort of bias would make us hypocrites."

Indeed.

"It is the way you earned your fortune that gives us cause for concern," Hunter added, his mouth as flat and hard as before. "Your past is not exactly that of a godly man."

"Interesting argument," Jonathon said, leveling an ironic gaze over the other man, "coming from you."

Hunter inclined his head. "Point taken. However, my wife has suffered because of her connection to me. If she marries you, Fanny will also face unnecessary censure simply because she carries your name."

It was Jonathon's turn to incline his head. Fanny claimed she didn't care about his past, but polite society was not so forgiving. Oh, the good people of Denver loved his rags-to-riches story. That didn't mean they considered him one of them.

Beneath his outward control, Jonathon burned with regret. He'd had several opportunities to walk away from Fanny tonight. Instead, he'd given in to temptation. A single moment's indiscretion had brought life-altering consequences. Yet he wasn't sorry he'd kissed Fanny. He was only sorry she would have to marry a man such as him.

Her brothers flung more questions at him, most concerning his motives for throwing Fanny in the middle of another scandal. When the land deal came up once again,

Jonathon chose his words very carefully. There could be no misunderstanding on this matter.

"For the entire time I was out on the terrace with Fanny, your land never once crossed my mind."

"And yet here we are, one day after turning down your offer, all but forced to welcome you into the family." Logan curled his lip. "Rather convenient, wouldn't you agree?"

"I would not."

More questions came at him, most about his motives, some concerning his intentions, his plans for the future.

Jonathon kept his responses clear and concise, even as his mind circled back to the same reality. If he acquired the piece of property from the Mitchell brothers now, his legacy would be forever tainted. And still he wanted to build something out of nothing. He wanted to create jobs for women like his mother, women with few choices available to them in the untamed West.

He did what he could now, gave many of them jobs at the hotel when a position came open, but it wasn't enough. Not nearly.

Cyrus Mitchell shoved away from the door and held up his hand to stop the questions.

Silence fell over the room.

"Boys, you have made your positions clear. I would now like a word with Mr. Hawkins alone."

The three brothers made no move to leave the room. *"Out."*

His sons headed for the door. Before exiting, they each tossed a silent warning in Jonathon's direction. He acknowledged them with a single nod of his head.

Once just the two of them were left in the room, Jonathon focused his full attention on the older man. Cyrus

Mitchell stared back at him with the eyes of a concerned father.

Jonathon cleared his throat. "I meant what I said, sir. I will do right by your daughter."

He wouldn't rest easy until Fanny's reputation was restored, if not completely, then as much as possible given the situation.

"I appreciate that." The other man shifted his stance. "This is your chance, Mr. Hawkins, to tell me what really happened out on that terrace between you and my daughter."

Jonathon hadn't expected an opportunity to explain himself. He kept his gaze as neutral as his tone. "We walked outside for some fresh air. We talked for several minutes. We kissed. We came back inside."

For several beats, the other man stared at him in stony silence, his face a landscape of hard planes and angles. "I sense you have glossed over several of the important details."

Perceptive man. "I provided the relevant information."

"Save for one key point. Do you care about my daughter?"

"I do."

The man's entire body seemed to relax, and Jonathon felt as though he'd passed a difficult test. But he knew that Cyrus Mitchell was not yet through with him. "Did you intentionally set out to ruin my daughter's reputation for a piece of land?"

"I did not."

Jonathon held steady while Fanny's father took his measure. "I believe you."

Unexpected relief nearly buckled his knees. The rest of the conversation would go easier now that this man knew where Jonathon stood. Or so he hoped. "Mr. Mitchell, I would like your permission to ask Fanny for her hand in marriage."

"You are asking for my blessing?"

"I am," Jonathon said without hesitation. "I would consider it an honor to call you my father-in-law."

A look of respect came and went in the older man's eyes. "Don't get ahead of yourself, son. My daughter hasn't said yes yet."

With the faintest trace of amusement shadowing his mouth, Fanny's father opened the door and waited for Jonathon to join him on the threshold. "Fanny has a mind of her own and can be as stubborn as they come. You may be up against a tougher opponent than my sons."

Jonathon couldn't argue with the truth. "But if she does accept my proposal?"

"Then I will happily welcome you into the family."

By the time Fanny returned to the ballroom, the majority of the guests had left. A spattering of hangers-on milled about, perhaps hoping to see how the latest scandal would play out.

Fanny would like to know that herself.

She caught sight of Jonathon standing in the far corner of the room near the buffet tables, talking to Callie and Reese.

For a moment, Fanny studied her sister and brother-in-law. Marriage suited them both, but Callie positively glowed with happiness. Dressed in a delicate gown a lovely shade of green that matched her eyes, she kept smiling up at her husband, who seemed equally mesmerized with her.

The two were so obviously in love, Fanny's heart sighed with pleasure.

She wondered what people saw when they looked at her and Jonathon. Did they see two friends? Amicable business associates? Or something else entirely?

He caught her watching him and slowly, with casual effort, reached out his hand to her, as if asking her to join him while also giving her the opportunity to make the decision on her own.

She heeded his silent call and set out in his direction.

Whispers followed her as she made her way across the ballroom floor. She ignored them. Or rather, she *tried* to ignore them. Hard to do when speculation about her was so…profoundly…*vocal*.

She wanted to pretend she and Jonathon had done nothing wrong. But they *had* behaved inappropriately. The resulting scandal would not disappear easily. Fanny would give it her best effort, anyway.

Marriage was the obvious option, and one Fanny refused to entertain, even in the privacy of her own mind. Unfortunately, her mother's words came back to haunt her. *You may not have a choice.*

There was always a choice.

Finally, she arrived at her destination.

Jonathon took her hand, then laced their fingers together. The simple gesture gave her renewed strength.

She turned to her sister. Callie smiled at her, as did Reese, their unconditional support evident in their sympathetic gazes. Fanny was reminded of Mrs. Singletary's ball a year ago. They'd looked at her much the same way when she'd shown up unannounced, with no warning of her return to Denver.

Fanny still remembered her sister's shock at seeing

her from across the room. She still remembered her own shock at seeing Callie with Reese.

Reese had taken Callie's hand and, together, they'd approached Fanny. By then, Jonathon had come to stand by her side. The four of them had exchanged awkward glances.

Just as she'd done that night a year ago, Callie broke the silence. "Well, here we are again."

It was the perfect thing to say to alleviate the tension, and Fanny finally found her smile.

She dared a glance in Jonathon's direction.

He stood silently beside her. He was so tall, strong and vigilant, ever watchful and protective of her. A little flutter took flight in her stomach.

Callie seized control of the moment, speaking of nothing in particular. Fanny was grateful for the easy conversation. Reese and Jonathon fell into their own side discussion, something about a contract negotiation that had gone bad. Apparently Reese had drawn up the initial agreement that had been summarily turned down.

The two men were of an equal height and build, their hair nearly the same color. Why had Fanny not noticed the similarities before?

Jonathon took advantage of a conversation lull. "Fanny, I'm afraid I have a handful of duties yet to tackle before the night is through. Will you join me?"

His gaze was so intense, so full of hidden meaning that she drew in a sharp breath. "Yes, of course."

They said their farewells to Callie and Reese.

As they strolled along the perimeter of the room an expectant hush fell over the remaining party guests. It was as if the entire room was poised in anticipation, eager to witness firsthand what she and Jonathon would do next.

Suddenly fatigued of the entire business of scandal, Fanny wanted nothing more than to retreat to her room and sleep for a solid week. There was still a very large issue that needed addressing first. "I hope my brothers weren't too hard on you."

"We'll talk about it later." He smiled at a cluster of guests passing by on their right.

Fanny waited until they were alone again, then asked, "Will you at least tell me if they were reasonable?"

"As reasonable as the situation warranted."

She opened her mouth to ask him to clarify. At the same moment Mrs. Singletary hurried over to them, her skirts making a soft whooshing sound as she came to an abrupt halt. "I officially declare the evening a success."

Fanny nearly choked on her own breath.

Jonathon gave the widow a sardonic smirk. "I believe your definition of success, Mrs. Singletary, is at odds with mine."

"Now, Mr. Hawkins, there's no need to be distressed over tonight's doings. You simply need to reframe the evening's events from the proper perspective."

"And what perspective would you suggest?"

"The positive one, of course." She tapped him on the arm, as if scolding him for asking such a ridiculous question. "Not only did we raise a considerable amount of money for a very worthy cause, but tonight's ball will be remembered for a good long time to come."

"This is a true statement." Jonathon shot Fanny an apologetic grimace. "But for all the wrong reasons."

"On the contrary." The widow blessed them both with a self-satisfied smile. "The Lord has once again used me as His vessel to bring together two worthy people. My reputation as a successful matchmaker has been confirmed once again."

The woman certainly had nerve, Fanny thought, unable to hold silent any longer. "Mrs. Singletary, you cannot seriously think to take credit for…for our…our…"

She didn't quite know how to put the events of the evening into words.

"But of course I can take credit." The widow twirled her hand in the air. "You and Mr. Hawkins are well suited, and, I dare say, perfect for one another. I knew it all along."

Fanny shared a baffled look with Jonathon. "Might I remind you," she said, "that just three days ago you attempted to match Jonathon with your companion, Philomena."

The widow lifted a silk clad shoulder. "All part of the bigger plan, my dear. I am very good, am I not?"

"*Good* is not the first word that comes immediately to mind," Jonathon muttered.

She laughed, clearly delighted by his grumbled remark. "I believe, Mr. Hawkins, you have something important to ask Miss Mitchell. I shall leave you to it."

In a whirl of skirts, the widow exited the ballroom.

Fanny gaped after her. Surely she didn't mean what Fanny thought she meant.

Shaking his head, Jonathon pulled out his watch from his vest pocket and frowned. "It's later than I realized. The sun will be up soon."

"Very soon," Fanny agreed, glancing outside the wall of windows. The gray light of dawn had replaced the deep purple of night. Heavy mist rolled in off the mountains, slinking across the terrace floor.

"Come with me." Jonathon took her hand and towed

her to the west corner of the room, where no one could see them. They might as well be completely alone. That wasn't what bothered her, though. He was entirely too serious for her peace of mind.

"Take a seat."

She reluctantly lowered herself onto the padded, straight-back chair nearest the terrace doors.

Fearful of what was to come, she kept her gaze averted. She smoothed out her skirts with surprisingly shaky fingers.

"Fanny." He said her name in a whisper, the word a sweet caress. "You have no cause for nerves around me."

"I… I know." She balled her hands into fists to still their trembling. This man was so familiar, and yet a complete stranger in so many ways.

He sat beside her. "We are in this together, you and I, and will face the future *together*."

Not daring to look him in the eyes, Fanny kept her gaze trained on the toes of her slippers. She didn't like where this was going, not one bit.

Jonathon closed his hand over hers. "There is only one option at our disposal."

Her heart dipped at the gravity in his tone. When she looked up, she went hot all over. "No, Jonathon, don't say anything else. Please," she pleaded. "Not another word."

He stood, then dropped to one knee.

"Fanny Mitchell. Will you…" His shoulders shifted, flexed, then went perfectly still. "Will you marry me?"

Chapter Nine

Jonathon's pulse roared in his ears. He told himself to remain coolheaded, as he would in the middle of any business transaction. Except this wasn't a business transaction. He'd just asked Fanny to marry him and she had yet to respond.

She simply stared at him in utter stillness, her hands balled into fists atop her lap.

The endless moment stretched into two. He ticked off the seconds in his head, willed her to give him an answer. Any response would do: *yes, no, could you repeat the question?*

She said nothing. She did, however, lower her head. The gesture caused a loose strand of hair to fall across her cheek. Absently, he reached up and tucked it behind her ear.

From his position on the floor, Jonathon had only a partial view of her face. He dipped his head for a better angle, immediately regretted the move. Her lovely features projected a loneliness and vulnerability he recognized. At the moment, the same emotions waged a war within his own soul.

In the halting silence that stretched from one minute into two, he thought about the feel of her in his arms, not only when they'd been out on the dance floor but again on the terrace. He thought about their kiss, and the way she'd fitted perfectly in his arms, about what his life might be like with her as his wife.

Jonathon wasn't much of a dreamer. But right now, he let himself consider the impossible. Things he'd stopped believing in when he was still a boy. Things such as stability, a house of his own, someone to come home to every night. He could have all of that with Fanny, but only if she agreed to marry him.

"Fanny." He rested his palms on her knees, compelled her to look at him. "Will you marry me?" he asked again.

She lifted her head and considered him in the gray light of dawn. He worked at not reacting under her careful scrutiny.

Looking incredibly sad—an ominous sign of things to come—she scooted to her left and patted the chair beside her, a wordless invitation for him to join her.

He remained on bended knee, continued staring into her troubled eyes, waiting, watching, longing for a dream he'd relinquished years ago.

Her eyelashes fluttered and finally, *finall*y, she spoke. "We both know you don't really want to marry me."

The words were wrapped inside a rough whisper. The tortured sound reminded him of sandpaper rubbing against splinters.

"Of course I want to marry you," he said, praying he sounded as sincere as he felt. "I wouldn't have asked otherwise."

Sorrow filled her face. And then—*Dear Lord, please, no*—tears gathered in her eyes. He climbed to his feet, drew her into his arms. "Don't cry. Fanny, please don't cry."

She stood stiffly in his embrace, her entire body taut with tension. He pressed her head gently to his shoulder and simply held her to him for several heartbeats.

Setting her away from him a moment later, he touched her cheek, wiped away the dampness with the pad of his thumb. "We can make a go of this, I know we can. I like you, and I believe you like me. We've conquered half the battle already."

She snuffled, swiped at her eyes, spoke again in that stark, hollow tone. "Marriage requires more than two people liking one another."

Considering her family dynamics, she would know better than he. After all, her parents had been happily married for over thirty years.

He switched tactics. "Let me protect you from ruin. Let me give you my name and shut down the gossip concerning your character."

"Oh, Jonathon." The sadness dug deeper in her gaze, sounded heavier in her voice. "I appreciate what you're trying to do. It's very noble of you to make me an offer of marriage. But you know as well as I that we will never work as a couple, not in the long run. We want different things."

Helpless in the face of her logic, he felt everything in him ache. He actually hurt from the inside out. "We may be able to come to a compromise that will satisfy us both."

She seemed to consider his suggestion. "What sort of marriage do you see us having? Be honest."

His first instinct was to tell her what she wanted to hear. But that wouldn't be fair to either of them. "We would have a marriage built on friendship, mutual admiration, loyalty and, of course, trust."

"You mean a marriage in name only."

"That's right."

He gave her a moment to process the meaning behind his words. Apparently, she needed more than one.

She simply gaped at him in stone cold silence.

"A marriage in name only." Utter disappointment threaded through her voice. "That is what you are proposing?"

He nodded, the muscles in his neck tensing. He knew what she was thinking. Yet she was forgetting an important factor. Him. Who his father was, the corrupted blood they shared. "I will not risk fathering a child."

She held his gaze for three endless seconds. Then slowly, carefully, she raised her chin a fraction higher. "Will you tell me why?"

"The men who share my blood have a history of hurting women. My father is especially guilty of this."

"That's not to say you will follow in his footsteps."

He shook his head at her innocence. "My half brother already has."

"You're not like either man. You are you, Jonathon."

"Precisely." She'd just made his argument for him. "I'm a prime example that mistakes happen."

Color drained from her face. "You are *not* a mistake," she all but growled at him. "You are a precious child of God. The Lord knew you before you were born. He knit you together in your mother's womb. Never believe otherwise, never."

He started to respond, but she wasn't finished making her point.

"Don't take my word for it, search Scripture yourself. Start at Psalm 139 and then move on to the first chapter of Jeremiah."

Jonathon blinked, not sure what to say to the fierce woman standing before him. Normally, he appreciated her keeping her opinions about God to herself. But for reasons Jonathon couldn't explain, her unshakable belief that he was something more than what he himself saw, spread warmth to the darkest places of his heart.

Cradling her face in his hands, he pressed their foreheads together and simply held on.

"You are a good man, Jonathon Hawkins." Her words grabbed something inside his chest and squeezed. "Don't ever let anyone make you believe otherwise, especially not that horrid man who fathered you."

Her words made Jonathon feel strong, keen on conquering the world and slaying her dragons with his bare hands.

Shrugging away the fanciful thought, he stuffed his hands in his pockets and rolled back on his heels. "We're not going to talk about me. You are my primary focus. I don't want to see you hurt, Fanny. Not when I have the power to prevent you from enduring another scandal."

"I'm afraid it's already done." She still sounded sad, as if she wanted something that could never be fully realized.

He knew the feeling.

That didn't mean he wasn't willing to try to make a marriage between them a success. "You haven't answered my question. Will you do me the honor of becoming my wife?"

Her eyes filled with tears once again.

He brushed them aside with his fingertips. The gesture seemed to make her even sadder.

"I cannot accept the type of union you are offering." She rose onto her toes and planted a tender kiss to his cheek. "No, Jonathon, I will not marry you."

Although he wasn't surprised by her answer, his heart took a hit. A part of him actually wanted her to say yes. Not for propriety's sake, not to silence gossip, but simply because he wanted her in his life, wanted to face the future with her by his side.

This isn't about you, he reminded himself. If Fanny wouldn't accept his marriage proposal, then he would give her another option. "Then I'd like you to run my San Francisco hotel."

"You want me to…you wish to send me away?"

"No, I am offering you a job, a chance to start over in a new city, where no one knows you or has knowledge of your past."

She gathered in a sharp breath of air. "The San Francisco Hotel Dupree is still under construction."

"You would oversee the final building phase, and then take over operations once the hotel is up and running." He waited for his words to sink in, for her to understand what he was suggesting. "You would be the first female manager in the company."

"I'm flattered." She didn't sound flattered. She sounded insulted.

Somehow, he'd insulted her. That hadn't been his goal.

"It's a very generous offer. But one I can't accept."

"Why not?"

"If I run away again, I may never stop running. I must stand and face the consequences of my actions. Besides—" she gave a shrug "—a little gossip never killed anyone."

"Fanny, it's not *a little gossip*. Your very reputation is in question. Because of me, because of what I—"

"No, Jonathon. No more assigning blame, on either of our parts."

"If you will not go to San Francisco, then only one solution remains. Marry me, Fanny. It's the only way."

"I can't. Please don't ask me again." Choking on a gasp, she spun around and bolted from the room.

He called after her.

She didn't pause, didn't glance over her shoulder, didn't acknowledge him in any way.

With clipped strides, he set out after her, then stopped when she picked up her pace and disappeared around the corner.

Perhaps he should leave her alone with her thoughts for a while. She needed time to think, to process the situation before he proposed again. And, yes, despite her request, he would propose again, as many times as it took to convince her marrying him was the only way to save her reputation.

Still blinking after her, he caught the sound of masculine footsteps approaching from behind.

Instinct had his hands closing into fists. Forcing his fingers to relax, Jonathon exhaled slowly, turned and saw Hunter Mitchell.

Standing in the shadows of the empty ballroom, Fanny's brother looked as formidable as Jonathon had ever seen him. A very large, very lethal outlaw.

Jonathon remained unmoved. "I'm not in the mood for another lecture from one of Fanny's brothers."

"Good to know, since that's not why I'm here." Hunter

shifted his stance. "I have a few things I'd like to say to you without my brothers or my father interrupting."

"All right."

"Not here, not where we can be overheard. Let's go outside." He cocked his head toward the hotel's exit.

Jonathon eyed the other man, considered, then decided what could it hurt to hear him out? "Follow me."

They left through the terrace doors and fell into step with one another. Neither spoke as they worked their way through the shadows of the back alley.

The air was cool at this early hour, the streets all but empty of activity when they strode onto the main street beside the hotel.

Hunter broke his silence halfway down the block. "I can't understand why Fanny refused your marriage proposal."

Frustration washed over Jonathon. "How much of our conversation did you overhear?"

"Enough to know that Fanny turned you down."

Jonathon stopped walking, waited for Hunter to do the same. "I can't tolerate the thought of your sister weathering this scandal on her own."

"Nor can I." Hunter ran a hand over his face, the scratch of stubble rough against his palm. "The gossips will be harder on her than they will be on you. I don't think she understands what awaits her if she chooses to stay in town without the protection of your name."

"We live in an unfair world."

Hunter's mouth thinned to a line sharp as a blade. "My sister will be ostracized, denied access to most of the businesses in town. She'll be alone in this world but for our family."

"She'll also have me," Jonathon said. "I will not abandon her, I promise you that."

The other man acknowledged this with a solemn nod. "I know what it feels like to be shunned in this town."

So did Jonathon.

Throat tight, he glanced at the millinery shop on his left, one of the establishments that Fanny would be prevented from entering if she didn't accept his proposal. "I don't want her to suffer the humiliation of exclusion and unjust banishment."

"Nor do I."

"The only answer is marriage."

Hunter nodded. "We are full in agreement."

"Any ideas how I can convince Fanny to accept my proposal?"

"Just one." Hunter flashed a grin, his teeth a white slash against his tan face. "Woo her."

Fanny tossed and turned, and eventually gave up any thought of sleeping after an hour of trying. She had work to do, anyway. There were countless tasks that needed her attention. She welcomed the distraction from her thoughts, from the fact that Jonathon had asked her to marry him, and she'd said no.

Of course she'd said no.

The seemingly obvious solution to their problem— *marriage*—was no solution at all. She and Jonathon didn't want the same things out of life.

Regardless of his proposal, he didn't want to be married.

Fanny did.

He didn't want children.

She did.

The biggest tragedy was that she knew—*she knew!*—she would be good for him, and he for her. But without a true marriage, they would never build a lasting connection, one that would help them navigate the ups and downs of life.

Such a shame, really.

Frowning, she flopped onto her back, then kicked off the covers with a jerk of her foot.

Tears of misery formed in her eyes. She refused to give in to them. She must remember that Jonathon had made no declarations. He'd given no promises. He wanted to marry her only to protect her from scandal.

Did he not see how *good* he was, at the core? If only he would allow himself to let down his guard, he could be a loving husband. A wonderful father. A—

This line of thinking was getting her nowhere. She rolled out of bed and dressed for the day. Her movements were slow, her eyes gritty, her heart heavy. Streaks of morning sunlight filtered through the seams in the shut curtains. Considering her gray mood, Fanny kept them closed. She preferred the semidarkness.

She'd made quite a mess of her life. She would have to decide what to do next. Her mother would have wisdom to impart, but Fanny didn't want to risk upsetting her. No, she must come up with a solution on her own. Whenever she found herself indecisive, she turned to her Bible.

Proverbs especially had a way of putting matters into perspective, but nothing caught her eye this morning. She replaced her Bible on the nightstand and went to work.

She made her way directly to her office, avoiding the main hallways and staffing areas.

Stepping inside the tiny room where she spent most of her time, she shut the door, and found she wasn't alone.

"Mrs. Singletary?"

The widow looked up from her position behind Fanny's desk. "Ah, Miss Mitchell, I knew I could count on you to show up to work despite the events of last evening."

Fanny blinked in confusion. Mrs. Singletary was a partial owner of the hotel, but she'd never come to Fanny's office before today. She had to be making some point by sitting at Fanny's desk. Or perhaps the bold move was Mrs. Singletary being, well, Mrs. Singletary.

What was the widow up to now? "Did we have an appointment this morning?"

"No, dear, I merely stopped by to see how you were faring before I head upstairs to visit with your mother."

Fanny smoothed a hand over her hair. "I am well, thank you for asking."

Eyebrows raised, Mrs. Singletary stood and then began a slow perusal of Fanny's office. She moved through the room with a relaxed gait, idly touching random books on the shelving to her left, the stack of ledgers on her right. "Have you no news to share with me, Miss Mitchell?"

Affecting a bland expression, Fanny concentrated on the task of setting the ledgers on her desk in neat, organized rows. "I'm not sure I understand the question."

Mrs. Singletary paused in her inspection of an ink blotter, her eyes sparkling with a shrewd light. "Don't you, dear?"

"I'm afraid not." Fanny went to work on the pencils next, setting them side by side, their tips in a nice straight line.

"I see I'm going to have to be blunt." The widow sounded quite pleased with the prospect. "Did Mr.

Hawkins propose to you after I left the ballroom last night?"

A sound of surprise slipped past Fanny's lips. She nearly said her relationship with Jonathon was none of Mrs. Singletary's business, but she didn't want to be rude. Besides, she rather liked the widow, when she wasn't being intrusive. "Yes, as a matter of fact, he did propose, and I told him—"

"Oh, excellent, this is most excellent news indeed." The woman clapped her hands together in a show of absolute pleasure. "Congratulations, Miss Mitchell. You must be over the moon with happiness."

"You don't understand, Mrs. Singletary. He asked, but I—"

The widow spoke right over her. "I'm assuming you will want a short engagement. There will be very little time to plan your wedding. Let me be the first to offer you my assistance."

Speaking so fast Fanny couldn't keep up with half of what she said, the widow continued making plans without her.

"Of course, I will throw you and Mr. Hawkins an engagement party at my home next week, seeing as how I played such an important role in your romance." She winked. "We will invite everyone who is anyone in town, give them a good show."

The widow was like a runaway train. She had to be stopped. Fanny raised her voice. "Mrs. Singletary, I need you to listen to me before you say another word."

"Oh, well." She blinked, surprise evident in her wide-eyed gaze. "Yes, all right."

"An engagement party won't be necessary."

"Why ever not?"

"Because there is no engagement. I told Jonathon no."

Silence filled the room, a somber, dark curtain of gloom.

"Oh, dear." The widow fluttered a hand in front of her face, as if to fan away her distress. "I am quite confounded. Why would you turn the man down?"

Fanny could give many reasons, but decided to stick to the most simple, straightforward answer of the bunch. "He doesn't love me."

That, she realized, was not only the truth, but also a direct blow to the heart. If Fanny believed Jonathon loved her, really loved her, she might have accepted his proposal and hoped his stand on children would change in time.

"Of course Mr. Hawkins loves you. I have seen the truth of his feelings for you with my own eyes."

Fanny quelled the tinkle of hope that whispered through her battered heart. No good would come of wishing for something that would never come to pass. "I'm not sure what you saw in Jonathon, but I can assure you, Mrs. Singletary, it wasn't love. Affection, perhaps, but not love."

"Now, Miss Mitchell, when it comes to romance I am quite the expert." She gestured to herself with her thumb. "If I had to guess, I'd say Mr. Hawkins fell for you well over a year ago."

That couldn't be right. Just as Fanny opened her mouth to challenge the widow, a knock sounded on her door.

"Enter," she called out, with no small amount of relief.

The front desk manager stuck her head in the room. "Oh, forgive me, Miss Mitchell. I thought you were alone."

"No problem. What can I do for you, Rose?"

"A guest has made a special request I'm not authorized to grant on my own." She cut a glance at Mrs. Single-tary. "But I can consult you on the matter another time."

"That won't be necessary. I'll come take care of it now."

With a smile she hoped registered a sincere apology, she said farewell to the widow and then hustled out of the room before Mrs. Singletary could protest.

Chapter Ten

Two days after Mrs. Singletary's ball, Jonathon sat at his desk, reviewing the latest report on the San Francisco project. A sense of accomplishment brought a smile to his face. Expenses were well within budget and construction was proceeding on schedule.

At this rate, the newest Hotel Dupree would welcome its first guest by midspring of next year. Jonathon calculated the months between now and then. He would attend the grand opening a married man, with his wife by his side, the two of them sharing in the ribbon cutting. It would be a good day, full of laughter and—

His smile slipped.

There was one large hitch in that plan. Her name was Fanny Mitchell. The woman was proving as stubborn as her father warned. She absolutely refused to allow Jonathon to court her, either by ensuring other people were always around her, or by avoiding him altogether.

How was he supposed to win Fanny over to the idea of marriage if he couldn't even get her alone?

Clearly, he needed to rethink his approach. Time was

of the essence. The longer Fanny resisted his suit, the more her reputation would suffer. It was unacceptable.

He shoved away from his desk and got to his feet. Drumming his fingers against his thigh, he contemplated his next move. Now that he'd had time to consider spending the rest of his life with Fanny, he rather liked the idea. They were well suited in nearly every way that mattered.

They had a similar sense of humor, tackled problems with equal amounts of intellect and reason. In fact, they were so compatible they often finished each other's sentences.

They could—no, *they would*—have a satisfying marriage, once Jonathon convinced Fanny to say yes to his proposal.

Impatient to settle the matter, he left his office and strode toward the main lobby of the hotel. Fanny would be at the registration desk, supervising check-in and checkout.

Jonathon rounded the corner, stepped into the open-air atrium and came to a dead stop. The scene before him was worse than he'd imagined, and everything he'd hoped to avoid.

A chill navigated along the base of his spine.

In the four years he'd owned the Denver Hotel Dupree, he'd rarely seen a maddening crush like this one. By his calculation, only half the men and women were actually registered guests. The rest were here for a show, with him and Fanny in the starring roles.

Keeping his expression blank, his movements careful and controlled, he continued toward the registration desk.

The crowd didn't actually fall silent, yet there was a definite lull. He paused once again, reached up and pinched the bridge of his nose.

Conversations slowly resumed. From the bits he caught, Fanny's character was being put into far greater question than Jonathon's. Just as her brother had predicted, and Jonathon had feared.

A proper courtship was no longer an option.

At least Fanny seemed too absorbed in her work to notice the speculation thrown her way.

Eyebrows drawn together, she ran a fingertip along the registration book—top to bottom, left to right—her hand stopping at various points along the way to make marks and notations. Half her face was in shadow, the other half illuminated by a ray of sunlight streaming in from the skylight above her head.

She's so lovely, Jonathon thought, allowing himself a moment to watch her work. Head bent, she shoved a loose strand of hair off her face. She repeated the process twice more before giving up.

Jonathon couldn't look away, didn't want to look away. This wasn't the first time he'd stood in this exact spot, riveted. From nearly the first day of their acquaintance, he'd been irresistibly drawn to Fanny. Over the years, that fascination hadn't faded.

As though sensing his eyes on her, she lifted her head and looked over at him.

Their gazes locked, held.

The chattering grew frantic, a fast staccato of high-pitched whispers and suppositions. Every move Jonathon and Fanny made from this point forward would be discussed over pots of tea later that afternoon. In a few cases, the events would be reported truthfully. In most, they would be expanded upon, while in others, embellished to disastrous proportions.

He should not give the gossips additional fodder. Yet

he couldn't seem to pry his gaze free of Fanny, nor did she seem to be able to look away from him. Seconds ticked by. Everything inside Jonathon settled. Doubt disappeared. He knew exactly what he wanted. Fanny. He wanted Fanny.

The woman understood him better than anyone else. She anticipated his preferences and made suggestions accordingly.

She must become his wife as soon as possible. Jonathon would allow no other outcome to prevail.

Just as he set out in her direction, she abandoned the registration desk and headed toward him. She moved purposely. She hadn't looked that willing to speak with him since the ball.

He paused in his own pursuit, overwhelmed by her fierce beauty. She'd arranged her hair loosely atop her head, with several strands cascading free. The tousled effect captivated him.

He swallowed, forced back a wave of attraction that went far beyond friendship. He'd meant what he'd told her. Their marriage would be in name only. It was the only way to ensure another generation escaped tragedy.

But he was getting ahead of himself.

Fanny still had to accept his proposal.

She closed the distance between them, careful to leave a respectable gap, proving she was fully aware of their audience.

They stared at one another. She looked unusually tired. Exhaustion etched across her features and there were purple bruises under her eyes, a visible sign she hadn't slept much since Mrs. Singletary's ball.

He desperately wanted to soothe away all her worries,

to spirit her off and protect her from the cruel world. If only she would allow him that privilege.

"Good afternoon, Miss Mitchell."

"Good afternoon, Mr. Hawkins." She gave him a perfectly polite smile. It was a valiant effort to remain detached, but Jonathon recognized the nerves beneath her flat expression.

"As you may have noticed," she said, sighing, "the hotel is at full capacity, plus a wee bit more."

"The atrium has always been a favorite gathering spot for our guests." He glanced to his left, then his right, dropping a quelling look on the closest men and women in the process. "Plus a wee bit more."

Her lips twitched. Ah, now they were getting somewhere. He almost had her smiling.

Finished giving the nosy onlookers something to see, he extended his hand.

"It's a beautiful afternoon." He had no idea if this was true. He'd been inside all day. Nevertheless… "Come for a walk with me, Miss Mitchell."

Looking slightly caged, she took a step back, shook her head decisively. "That's a lovely offer, Mr. Hawkins, but I'm afraid I must decline. Duty calls."

"Duty can wait." Before she could protest yet again, he took her hand and guided her toward the exit.

For several steps she obliged him. But then she stopped and drew her hand free. "You do realize it's snowing."

Was it? He looked out the windows and saw that she was right. "So it is."

"We aren't dressed for the weather."

A problem easily remedied. "Get your coat and meet me back here in five minutes."

She hesitated, clearly pondering the wisdom of spending time alone with him.

Her reticence hit a nerve. He'd had enough of her avoidance.

"Get your coat, Fanny." He leaned in, his voice for her ears only. "You'll put me off no longer."

She opened her mouth, an argument clearly on the tip of her tongue, but the crowd pressed in and she simply sighed. "I'll be back shortly."

"As will I." Jonathon went to retrieve his own coat. He found his assistant waiting for him outside his office, shifting from foot to foot, his expression bleak.

"Is there a problem, Mr. Galloway?"

"Possibly." Eyes hooded, Burke consulted his notebook. "Judge Greene has asked for a private meeting with you as soon as possible."

Jonathon lifted his eyebrows. The timing of the request could not be by chance. "Did he mention the nature of his business?"

"No, sir."

Jonathon considered the request, his annoyance tempered by a jolt of curiosity.

"Tell Judge Greene I will see him this afternoon." Jonathon had resisted meeting with his father long enough.

Burke made a notation in his book. "What time should I tell him to arrive?"

"I'll meet with him in my office in one hour."

Jonathon would have preferred to spend the entire afternoon with Fanny, but until she accepted his marriage proposal, it was best to keep their public interactions to a minimum.

"I'll inform Judge Greene of your decision." Burke spared him one last glance before dashing off.

Precisely five minutes later, Jonathon joined Fanny at the bronze-encased glass doors leading to Stout Street.

Keeping silent, he ushered her out onto the sidewalk.

A blast of cold air slammed into them. Fanny burrowed deeper inside her coat, while he turned up his collar. They fell into step with one another, as they did on all their walks.

Rather than taking their usual route, Jonathon directed her down a side street, around the corner, along another street and finally into a small park.

Snowflakes fluttered from the sky, landing soundlessly at their feet. Jonathon brushed powdery crystals off a nearby wrought-iron bench. "Let's sit a minute."

He indicated the now snow-free seat angled beneath a large tree, its bare branches coated in ice. Sunlight danced off the white blanket around them in glittering sparks.

Fanny took her time lowering herself to the bench and then smoothing out her skirts. Once she was settled, Jonathon sat beside her. Her scent wrapped around him, a pleasant mix of wild orchid and mint. The air was clear enough that he easily heard the muffled slam of a door, the yapping of a dog. He tuned out the rest.

Turning slightly in his seat, he took Fanny's hand again and protectively cupped it within his. "You're so beautiful."

Pain flashed in her eyes. Instead of smiling at the compliment, she looked sadder than he'd ever seen her. For the first time in months, he couldn't interpret her thoughts.

Her expression suddenly changed. "My answer is no, Jonathon. I won't marry you."

Sweet, delightful woman. He should have known she

wouldn't make this easy on him. Fair enough. Adopting a relaxed posture, he let go of her hand, leaned back against the bench and smiled. "I don't recall asking you to marry me."

"Oh." Her eyes widened. "You... I...*oh*."

What a wife she would make him. Unpredictable at times, bold at others, sweet. She was so familiar and yet there was still so much he didn't know about her.

A dull ache swirled in the pit of his stomach, a sensation that felt like longing, perhaps even yearning.

He would have liked more time to become better acquainted with her. It would have been pleasant to take his time learning her likes and dislikes, her favorite color and time of day. Was she a morning person or a night owl? Did she prefer chocolate or vanilla?

So much to uncover, so many layers to peel away.

"I want to know everything about you," he said in complete and total honesty.

Suddenly wary, she stared at him through narrowed eyes. "Why?"

He chuckled softly. "Because you're a fascinating woman. Let's start at the beginning. What was it like growing up on one of the largest cattle ranches north of Texas?"

She gave him an odd look, as if she didn't quite know what to make of him. "There was nothing really unique about my childhood." She shrugged. "It was like most others, I suppose."

Certainly not like his. "I can't speak to that. I've not been exposed to many families like yours."

"Oh, Jonathon." Everything about her softened, her eyes, her shoulders, her voice. "I'm sorry. I didn't mean to sound dismissive. I just... I don't understand why we're out here, sitting under a snow-covered tree, talking about my childhood."

He pulled her hand to his lips, letting go after making the briefest of contacts.

"We're getting to know one another outside our relationship at work." He gestured for her to continue. "You were telling me about your family."

"Oh, yes." She chewed on the fingertip of her glove, thought a moment, then smiled. "My parents raised the seven of us to pull our own weight. We worked hard, played harder, laughed a lot. When life got tough, we turned to God, and when things were good we praised Him for our blessings."

Jonathon nodded. None of what she said surprised him.

"With five brothers and one sister running around, I was never alone, never without someone to play with or talk to, or," she said with a laugh, "fight with. Somehow, everything seemed easier, better, because I had so many siblings."

"Sounds pretty incredible."

Her smile widened, while her eyes became wistful, a little distant, as if she'd gotten lost in her memories. "I had a happy childhood. I never questioned whether I was safe or cared for or loved."

"I take it you're an accomplished horsewoman."

"My father wouldn't have it any other way. I learned how to ride around the same time I learned to walk." As she tossed out amusing anecdotes, Jonathon was reminded of his time at Charity House with Marc and Laney Dupree.

He'd been happy and safe in their care. Although he hadn't been with them long, only four years, in that short amount of time Jonathon had enjoyed having a family, siblings included.

Perhaps he knew more about marriage and family than he realized.

But did he know enough to make Fanny a good husband, the kind she deserved?

Or would he eventually let her down, as the men who shared his blood did over and over again with the women in their lives?

The answer was painfully obvious. Fanny wanted a happy marriage like that of her parents. She also wanted a family of her own.

Jonathon could give only bits of those things, never the whole.

In the end, he would disappoint her. What was worse, he wondered. A ruined reputation that Fanny might never recover from fully? Or a childless marriage with a man who could give her only fragments of the life she wanted?

Neither was ideal.

He waited for her stories to end, then took her hand and walked with her back to the hotel. He didn't speak, but used the silence to organize his thoughts, to think through their options.

The things Jonathon wanted for himself must not be factored into his decision. He must act in Fanny's best interest.

It was the one gift he could still give her.

With their walk officially over, Fanny watched helplessly as Jonathon disappeared inside his office. She continued staring at his shut door, trying to pinpoint exactly when things had gone from bad to worse between them.

For a small portion of their time together in the park,

she'd felt closer to him than ever before. As she'd talked about her childhood, she'd watched him visibly relax. He'd been approachable and attentive, until suddenly, he was neither.

One minute he was listening to her stories, smiling, eyes laughing, then, abruptly, his guard was up again.

A sigh leaked out of her. What had she done to change his behavior so dramatically?

As she thought back through the various stories she'd told, someone bumped into her, knocking her slightly off balance. She shifted to regain her balance. At the same moment, a pair of strong hands settled on her shoulders.

She looked up, sighed again. "Garrett, I didn't realize you were standing there."

He gave her a wry smile. "That's probably because you were staring at your boss's door so hard you practically bored a hole in the wood."

"I was just…that is, I was—"

"You don't have to explain yourself to me."

No, she didn't. When he continued watching her, his gaze running quickly over her face, she redirected the conversation in his direction. "How's Molly feeling this afternoon?"

"Exhausted and queasy. I left her resting in our room." He shook his head in wonder and awe. "I still can't believe we'll be welcoming our first child in less than five months."

The look of utter contentment in her brother's eyes sent a wave of yearning through Fanny. Garrett was going to be a father. She would soon have another niece or nephew to spoil.

Fanny had always believed children were a blessing

straight from God. If she married Jonathon, she would never know that joy.

She sighed again.

"Fanny." Garrett took her arm and drew her toward a tiny alcove decorated with potted plants. "Tell me what I can do to make things easier for you. Name it and it's done."

Her brother meant well, she knew, but his soft voice and concerned expression only managed to annoy her.

She blew a wayward strand of hair off her face. "I love you for worrying about me. But, Garrett, I've suffered through gossip before."

"Not like this."

She shoved at the stubborn lock of hair. Why wouldn't it stay tucked behind her ear? "The speculation and whispers certainly feel the same."

"The gossip is much worse and you know it."

She resisted another sigh. "Phoebe and Penelope Ferguson are prone to exaggeration. What happened between Jonathon and me was really quite innocent."

Garrett flicked his gaze over the crowded lobby, then shook his head in disgust. "In situations such as these, the truth hardly matters. The perception is that you and Hawkins—"

"I know what the gossips are saying."

He nodded. "Have you thought about your next step?"

In truth, she hadn't, not really. She'd been too busy pretending the problem would simply fade away. The interested stares from the men and women still milling about in the lobby dispelled that notion. She was going to have to make a decision about her future.

Garrett touched her arm, dragging her attention back to him. "Come live with Molly and me in Saint Louis."

The offer was so Garrett. Fanny wanted to hug him for his concern, for his readiness to rescue her. "I want to stick close to home, near Mother."

"Saint Louis is a train ride away."

"Still too far," she said, shaking her head. "Besides, running away isn't the answer, not this time."

"Was it the answer last time?"

"I believe so, yes." Closing her eyes, she drew in a careful breath, thought about the woman she'd once been. "I needed to go away and work out my convictions on my own. I had to find out who I was beneath the facade I presented to the world."

"Did you discover what you were looking for?"

"I'd like to think I did." She stared off into the distance, tapped her finger against her chin. "I know more about what I want out of life and, consequently, what I don't."

"How does Hawkins play into your future?"

Sometimes Garrett could be such a lawyer. Well, she wasn't a witness in a courtroom he could intimidate with his pointed questions. "That's between Jonathon and me."

"In other words, mind my own business?"

She managed a weak smile. "Something like that."

"For what it's worth, I believe Jonathon Hawkins is a good man."

"I agree." The very best of her acquaintance. If only he would embrace the person she knew him to be.

"Fanny." Garrett touched her arm again. "Tell me what I can do to make your sadness go away."

"I'm fine, really. I just have a lot on my mind."

"Then I'll leave you to your thoughts." He turned, then swung back around and tugged her into his arms. "I hate seeing you unhappy."

"I'm not unhappy." Chin lifted, eyes dry, she stepped out of his embrace. "I trust everything will work out eventually. The Lord already has the solution in place and will reveal the answer in His time."

"My offer still stands. You can come to Saint Louis anytime. The door is always open."

Though she knew she wouldn't accept his generosity, she appreciated the invitation. "Thank you, Garrett. I'll let you know what I plan to do about my future."

He glanced back at the crowd, scowled. "Make a decision soon, Fanny. Time is running out."

"I know."

He kissed her on the cheek and then was gone.

Alone again, she returned her attention to Jonathon's door, and she saw Judge Greene knock once and then enter a second later.

Fanny frowned.

What sort of business did Jonathon have with his father? Or was it the other way around? Was the judge the one who'd called for a meeting?

A protective instinct stole through her. She moved a step closer to Jonathon's office, thinking maybe she could catch part of their conversation.

Perhaps if she pressed her ear to the door—

She froze, horrified at the direction of her thoughts. Oh, the depths to which she'd sunk. Eavesdropping and lurking in shadows was completely, utterly beneath her.

Still, what could it hurt to move a step closer to Jonathon's office?

Chapter Eleven

Standing behind his desk, Jonathon stared in stunned silence at Joshua Greene, not quite believing the conversation he'd had thus far with the man who'd fathered him. Jonathon didn't know whether to laugh at the irony of the man's gall or slam his fist into that sanctimonious square jaw that looked entirely too much like his own.

Jonathon grasped for a calm that hovered just out of reach.

"Let me see if I understand you correctly." He chose his words carefully, keeping his expression blank. Greene didn't deserve a single reaction from him, not even a sneer. "You have come to congratulate me on ruining a young woman's reputation."

Two dark eyebrows lifted, haughty, arrogant arches over feral, ice-blue eyes. "You are intentionally twisting my words."

Maintaining his relaxed posture proved impossible. Jonathon stalked around his desk, stopping several feet from the cold statue who'd fathered him.

The other man stood his ground, unmoving, his gaze so direct it felt like a physical assault.

Jonathon couldn't hold back his sneer a moment longer. "By all means, Judge Greene, please, clarify your earlier statement."

"There's no need to use that antagonistic tone. I simply came here to commend you on your success. You have linked yourself with one of the most well-respected, prominent families in Colorado."

Anger and insult warred within him. Jonathon shoved down the volcanic emotions with a hard swallow. "You think I put a woman's entire future at risk for the sake of an alliance with her family? You think me that calculating?"

"Not calculating." The judge gave a nod of approval. "Merely shrewd."

"Shrewd." Jonathon repeated the word, hardly able to speak through his gritted teeth. This man, so distinguished on the outside, had a black heart, far uglier than he'd realized.

"I'm actually quite proud of your ingenuity," the judge continued. "And now, I believe the time has come for me to publically acknowledge our connection. If worded properly, the voters will find my honesty refreshing. They are already enamored with your climb out of poverty. Add in my heartfelt sorrow over a youthful indiscretion and I'll win over the hardest of hearts."

"Ah, now I understand. This is about your run for the United States Senate."

The man cocked his head in silent acknowledgment, completely unrepentant of his scheming agenda. "Cyrus Mitchell has withheld his support of my candidacy up to this point. However, if you step up and marry his daughter, and I then acknowledge you as my son, he will be forced to reconsider his position."

It was over, Jonathon thought. The last shred of hope for reconciliation with the man who'd fathered him was good and truly gone.

Not once in his childhood had this man acknowledged his existence. Only now, when it served his own purpose, was the venerable judge willing to claim Jonathon as his son.

Casting a brittle, bitter grin in the judge's direction, he paced to the bookshelf, ran his finger along the binding of his Bible. Just this morning, he'd followed Fanny's suggestion and had read Psalm 139, specifically verse 13, a bold reminder that he had a Heavenly Father who loved him. Jonathon didn't need an earthly father's public acknowledgment.

Dropping his hand, he gave a nonchalant tug on his waistcoat, then faced Judge Greene once again.

"This conversation is over." He'd given the man too much of his time already, not only today, but in all the years he'd allowed him to take up residence in his thoughts. "You know the way out."

The judge made no move to leave the room. "You won't do better in a wife than Fanny Mitchell. Your tactic was really quite brilliant. You would have never secured her interest by conventional means."

The barb hit its mark, the message clear. He, the illegitimate son of a callous, calculating man and his prostitute mistress, didn't deserve a woman like Fanny.

"Consider yourself fortunate you are in a position to marry the girl."

"You mean," Jonathon scoffed, his blood icing over

in his veins, "unlike the position you found yourself in when you ruined my mother's reputation?"

"Our situations are vastly different." The judge sniffed in disgust. "I already had a wife when I met Amelia Hawkins."

Jonathon knew better than to ask, yet he couldn't help himself. The words spilled out of his mouth before he could stop them. "Would you have married my mother had you been a free man?"

Greene held his stare, a hard, ruthless look in his eyes now. The world seemed to stop on its axis.

"I would not have married your mother under any circumstances. She was already compromised when I met her. She would never have made a man such as me a proper wife."

Jonathon thought of his half brother, the son so much like the father. The legitimate spawn of this self-serving man and his *proper* wife was, at this very minute, in the process of setting up his mistress in her own little house with Jonathon's money.

Did Judge Greene know what his heir was up to?

Would it matter if he did?

As if from a great distance, Jonathon heard the rest of Greene's words, heard him expanding on his mother's lack of pedigree. A part of him listened, taking it all in, realizing the true condition of this man's soul.

He is my father. I come from this ugliness.

But he also came from Amelia Hawkins.

He thought of the woman who'd given birth to him. Somewhere, deep down, he'd known she wasn't educated or refined or even proper. But she'd been unspeakably beautiful. Men of quality had sought her out over the other girls in Mattie's brothel. Looking back with the wisdom of age, Jonathon realized why. Amelia Hawkins's ethereal beauty had been her greatest attribute.

"…and so my advice would be to secure Miss Mitchell's hand in marriage as soon as possible."

Jonathon felt his jaw clench so hard he feared his back teeth would crack from the pressure. He didn't need advice from this man.

Yet one truth could not be denied. If Jonathon didn't marry Fanny, if he abandoned her to her fate, he would be no better than the man who'd fathered him.

Though he couldn't give Fanny what she wanted—family, children—he could give her other things. Comfort, security, his complete devotion.

"We're through here." Jonathon laced finality in his words. "You will leave my office and my hotel at once."

"I'll go." His eyes full of the cunning he'd wrongfully attributed to Jonathon, Greene headed toward the door, then paused halfway through the room. "You should know I plan to release a statement in the *Denver Chronicle* about our connection, once you do the smart thing and marry the girl."

"I can't stop you from going to the newspaper." Jonathon maneuvered around the other man and set his hand on the doorknob. "But *you* should know that if asked about our connection, I will respond with complete and brutal honesty."

"Is that a threat?"

"It's a promise." Jonathon yanked open the door.

Fanny all but tumbled into his arms.

"Oh." She fought for balance, stumbled a step to her left before righting herself. "I was just about to knock, but I see you anticipated my arrival."

Jonathon eyed her closely, wondering why her gaze

seemed unable to find a place to land. "Was there something you needed that couldn't wait?"

Her hands fluttered by her sides, then gripped one another at her waist.

"There's a…a problem with one of the guests. The situation must be addressed immediately." She cut a quick, furious glance at the other man in the room. "Judge Greene, I'm sure you understand."

"Indeed, Miss Mitchell, I understand perfectly." He gave her a charming smile, with a hint of smugness around the edges. "It's lovely to see you again."

Her scowl deepened. "I'm sorry I can't say the—"

"Fanny." Forestalling the rest of her response, Jonathon put a protective hand on her shoulder. "The judge was just leaving."

She turned her gaze to Jonathon, nodded slowly, then made a grand show of stepping aside to let the other man pass. "Please, Judge Greene, don't let us keep you."

Affection filled Jonathon's heart, warming him from the inside out. Righteous anger suited Fanny. Her face glowed.

Judge Greene paused at the threshold to stare into Fanny's eyes. "I'm sure we will see more of each other in the coming weeks, Miss Mitchell."

"I doubt that very much." Her smile was all teeth. "We rarely run in the same circles."

"An oversight I plan to remedy immediately." Having given his opinion on the matter, he ambled past her without another word.

As she gaped after his retreating back, Fanny's shoulders lifted in a noiseless sigh. "I don't like that man."

"That makes two of us."

Overcome with an emotion he couldn't name, Jonathon wanted to pull Fanny into his arms and kiss her soundly on the mouth. With the gentlest of touches, he instead reached up and tamed a stray wisp of hair behind her ear. "You mentioned a problem with a guest?"

"Oh, yes. It's…not precisely a problem. Just something I failed to mention earlier."

"Go on."

Her expression turned sheepish. "My parents have requested you dine with us this evening. They would like to eat somewhere other than here in the hotel."

"Any particular reason why? When we have a perfectly respectable restaurant on the first floor?"

She gave him a slow, appealing smile. "I believe my father mentioned something about the four of us needing a change of scenery."

Jonathon felt his own smile show itself at last.

"Well?" That stubborn strand of hair escaped once again. "Are you available to dine with my parents and me tonight?"

"My dear, sweet, beautiful Fanny." He tucked the curling wisp back in place. "Tonight, I'm all yours."

Not only tonight, he thought, but if he had his way, every night to come.

Fanny paused briefly at the entrance of the restaurant, her arm looped through Jonathon's. Her parents were a few steps ahead of them, suspended in a similar pose. All gazes turned in their direction and as soon as the whispering began, her mother let out a long, weary sigh.

Fanny's sentiments exactly.

Tonight was supposed to have been a break from the melodrama of the past few days. Apparently there was nowhere she and Jonathon could go in Denver to avoid the gossip. Now, her parents were at the center of the firestorm with them.

Would the stress be too much for her mother?

Fanny's heart endured a tight, panicky squeeze at the thought. But then she noted that her mother's breathing seemed to be coming at a normal rate.

Relieved, Fanny glanced around the restaurant. Rivaled only by the Hotel Dupree, the Brown Palace's rich, expensive decor was considered the height of fashion. The dining room was no exception. Bone china adorned every table. Engraved silverware and crystal goblets completed the elegant place settings.

Wondering what he thought of his competition, Fanny glanced up at Jonathon. His gaze gave nothing away.

Her first inclination was to ask him to escort her out of here, away from the whispers and pointed stares. But her mother seemed to be handling the situation with her usual grace and poise. Fanny would attempt to do the same.

Besides, if she was going to remain in Denver, then she had better get used to the unwanted attention.

At least tonight she didn't have to suffer alone. Jonathon and her parents stood with her. People continued watching them—especially the women—and by the look of their pinched, sour faces, directed mostly at Fanny, many would like to see her brought low.

"Is this a stupendously bad idea?" she asked in the barest of whispers.

Jonathon leaned his head a discreet inch closer. "We will know soon enough, perhaps even before the first course is served."

His response did nothing to dispel her concerns. But then he smiled. And the prospect of spending a few hours under the watchful stares of their fellow diners seemed slightly less awful.

"Smile, Fanny." Jonathon pulled her a shade closer. "I am certain we have nothing but a delightful evening ahead."

She wasn't nearly so confident, but managed a slight lift of her lips.

"Since you agree, let us enjoy ourselves fully." His soft tone and gentle expression instantly lightened her mood. "I have it from a reliable source that the food in this restaurant is of the highest quality."

Since Fanny was the so-called reliable source, she could only laugh and shake her head. His responding wink made her think of happy futures and sweet kisses under the stars.

Out of the corner of her eye she watched her father pat her mother's arm, and the tender gesture spoke of their years together. Watching their easy intimacy, Fanny felt something move in her heart, a desire to have what they had. A bond that withstood life's hardships and grew stronger with time.

If only—

The maître d'hôtel appeared and directed them to their table. They were settled in their chairs with little fanfare, their orders taken quickly and efficiently.

To Fanny's surprise—and tremendous relief—the other diners lost interest in them halfway through the first course of their meal.

Jonathon and her father fell into an amiable discussion over the various investments they'd recently acquired. Fanny and her mother discussed far more important matters, specifically, the latest hat and clothing styles from Paris.

"You can never go wrong with the acquisition of property," she heard her father say. "Land is a finite commodity."

Jonathon agreed. And so began a lengthy discussion of their various individual real estate holdings.

As the evening progressed, the four of them fell into an easy rhythm. Conversation flowed effortlessly, skipping from one topic to the next, sometimes including everyone at the table, sometimes only two or three.

Fanny found herself falling silent more often than not, preferring to watch Jonathon interact with her parents. He seemed perfectly at ease. Everything about the man appealed to her. She admired his sense of honor, his devotion to his employees, his patience while her father grilled him about his finances.

Personally, Fanny didn't care how much money Jonathon had made in recent years. She was more impressed with his work ethic and how he hired people other employers shunned. She really adored his face. Strong and handsome, each feature boldly sculpted. The overall impact was very masculine, very appealing.

She couldn't seem to take her eyes off him.

He looked in her direction and their gazes locked. Her breath caught in her throat. Her mind emptied of all coherent thought.

When he returned his attention to her father, the truth roared through her like a violent summer storm. Quick, fierce, life-changing.

She was lost, completely, hopelessly, irrevocably lost. Her brother Garrett had warned this would happen. His words came back to her with excruciating clarity. *When Mitchells fall in love, we fall fast, hard and forever.*

Fanny's heart twisted. She was in love with Jonathon.

How could she have let this happen?

"Fanny?" Her mother's gaze grew serious. "Is something the matter? Are you feeling unwell?"

"No, I—I'm perfectly fine." But, of course, she wasn't fine.

Too much emotion spilled through her. Her arms felt unnaturally heavy and her pulse grew uneven.

"I just need to—" she touched her head, grateful to find that several stubborn locks had escaped their pins "—readjust my hair."

With her hands surprisingly steady, she set her napkin on the table and stood.

Jonathon was on his feet a half second later. "Let me escort you—"

"No. Stay." She managed a wan smile. "I'll only be a moment."

He reached for her.

Evading his touch, she forced her attention onto her parents. "Please, continue eating. I won't be long."

It took every ounce of control to walk through the dining room at a calm, sedate pace. She could feel countless eyes following her progress, Jonathon's most of all, but she kept her gaze trained on the ladies' washroom. Refuge was but a few feet away.

Slipping quickly inside, she shut the door and looked around for a place to sit. Several plush, navy blue stools stood in a row before individual mirrors encased in gilded frames. The room had an elegant, luxurious ambience that left her feeling empty.

Fanny took a seat before her legs gave way beneath her.

Needing something to do with her hands, she let down her hair and rearranged the loose curls in an easy, simple style. As she worked, she noted her drawn expression. She looked unusually fragile.

Why wouldn't she look fragile? She was in love with a man who wanted to marry her for all the wrong reasons.

There were worse fates, she knew. Yet, for a moment, she allowed herself to mourn what might have been, to regret what could never come to pass.

She would survive this. *She would.* All she had to do was hold firm to the reasons she must not marry Jonathon. Tears of regret pooled in her eyes. She ruthlessly blinked them away.

With stiff fingers, she stuck the last pin into her hair. Composure somewhat restored, she managed to stand.

And then, naturally, one of Denver's most determined gossips entered the ladies' washroom.

Fanny nearly groaned aloud.

Dressed in a pale pink evening gown, with yards upon yards of lace and too many ruffles for her plump figure, Mrs. Doris Goodwin strolled deeper into the room.

"Ah, Miss Mitchell, I see I have caught you alone."

Fanny tried not to bristle at the sugary-sweet tone. Clearly, catching her *alone* had been the woman's intention. "Good evening, Mrs. Goodwin. You are looking well."

"Why, thank you, dear. That is very kind of you to say."

The woman bustled past her, then made an elaborate show of checking her salt-and-pepper hair in the mirror. A ruse, no doubt, since she spent more time studying Fanny out of the corner of her eye than focusing on her own reflection.

Gaze narrowed, Fanny calculated how quickly she could slip out of the room without offending the other woman. All hope of a hasty retreat vanished when Mrs. Goodwin spun around and pinned her with a pointed gaze. "How are you faring since the scandal broke?"

Fanny searched for an appropriate answer but was unable to give one, so she simply shrugged.

"Oh, my, I've upset you." Looking unrepentant, she grasped Fanny's hands in a display of false concern. "Not to worry, dear, your shameful behavior will be forgotten once you are safely married. When should I expect an invitation to the wedding?"

"I… We haven't…" With great care, she withdrew her hands from the woman's clammy hold. "My parents will be wondering where I am. I must return to the dining room before they begin to worry."

Fanny tried very hard to escape, but the detestable woman called after her. "Your mother will never say this, so I will. It's time you faced some hard truths."

Despite knowing better than to engage the woman in conversation, Fanny turned back around. "Hard truths?"

"You must realize your attempt to snag a husband reeks of desperation. I'm afraid your reputation will never fully recover." She patted Fanny's arm in a patronizing manner. "For your mother's sake, I do hope you marry Mr. Hawkins very soon. It is your only hope of regaining a measure of respectability."

Fanny opened her mouth to say something scathing—really, the woman had overstepped her bounds—but then she remembered one of her mother's favorite Bible verses. *Let your conversation always be full of grace.*

She pressed her lips tightly together and boldly held the woman's stare. Mrs. Goodwin shifted uncomfortably from one foot to the other. Fanny felt as if she'd won the battle, but then the odious woman's gaze hooked on a spot just over her right shoulder.

"Oh, Mary, there you are. I was just having a nice conversation with your daughter."

"So I heard."

Her mother's labored breathing sent a jolt of fear through Fanny. She spun around and the panic dug deeper at the sight of Mary Mitchell's unnaturally pale face.

Fanny rushed forward, but her mother shrugged away her assistance.

"You've done your worst, Doris, now I'll ask you to leave."

Face pinched, the notorious gossip sniffed inelegantly, and then stormed out of the room with a hard slam of the door.

The loud bang seemed to steal her mother's last breath, and she was forced to sit down.

Fanny sank to her knees. "Breathe, Mother. Yes, that's it. Slowly now. In and out. In…out."

When her mother's breathing failed to return to normal, Fanny jumped to her feet. "I'll get Father."

Her mother pressed trembling fingers to her throat. "I believe," she wheezed, "that would be…wise."

Chapter Twelve

Jonathon fetched the doctor himself. He escorted Shane through the back entrance of the Brown Palace, ignoring the curious stares from the hotel staff. Fortunately, management had been concerned enough over Mrs. Mitchell's health crisis to provide a room. Unfortunately, that room was on the fifth floor.

Neither man spoke as they entered the stairwell and commandeered the first of the five flights, far quicker than waiting for the elevator. The sound of their heels striking wood reverberated off the walls like hammers to nails.

Shane carried a medical bag in one hand, a breathing apparatus in the other. He wore what Jonathon thought of as his uniform—black pants, a crisp, white linen shirt and an intense expression. Jonathon had seen that same look in those steel blue eyes many times in his past. The most memorable, the night his mother died.

When they rounded the first corner and tackled the second flight of stairs, Shane broke his silence. "Tell me again what happened."

Jonathon pressed his lips tightly together. He'd already relayed the story to Shane on the trip across town. "Mrs. Mitchell had a severe asthma attack."

The sharp planes of the other man's face stiffened. "That's not what I meant. I need you to describe the events leading up to the attack."

Keeping his eyes straight ahead, Jonathon tapped into his remaining stores of patience. "Fanny and I were dining with her parents in the restaurant downstairs. Near the end of the meal Fanny became noticeably upset and left the table with some excuse about fixing her hair. She wouldn't allow me to escort her, though I tried, and made a point of insisting—"

"Hold on," Shane interrupted. "Was Mrs. Mitchell's breathing normal up to this point?"

Jonathon thought a moment, then nodded. "As far as I could tell, she was fine. Her breathing only started coming quicker when Fanny didn't return to the table right away. She expressed a desire to check on her daughter. Her husband offered to go with her, but she rejected his support."

This was when the story got a little fuzzy, primarily because Fanny had been vague in her retelling. Jonathon had a good idea why.

"Apparently, Mrs. Mitchell arrived at the ladies' washroom in time to catch an unpleasant exchange between Fanny and another woman. I don't know what was said." Fanny claimed the conversation didn't matter. Jonathon suspected otherwise. "But the incident was the catalyst for Mrs. Mitchell's attack."

Jonathon had never witnessed an asthma attack before, but he'd watched his own mother gasping for air on her deathbed.

The memory materialized despite his efforts to hold it at bay. She would suck in a labored breath, pause for endless seconds and then choke out a wheeze. Just as he gave up hope that she would manage another breath, the pattern would begin all over again.

Shane had called it the death rattle.

Jonathon shuddered. There'd been nothing he could do. Tonight, he'd struggled with a similar sense of powerlessness.

"All right." Shane's voice came at him as if from a great distance. "That gives me a good idea what I'm dealing with."

"Will she survive?"

"I'll know more once I examine the patient."

Not the answer Jonathon wanted to hear, but he didn't press for more information. They'd arrived at the fifth floor. Reaching around Shane, he opened the door and motioned the other man into the hallway ahead of him.

Shane glanced back at him over his shoulder. "Which room is she in?"

"503."

He checked numbers on the closest doors, then set out down the long corridor. Jonathon fell in step beside him.

At their destination, Shane paused. "You'll want to wait here."

Not sure what he saw in the other man's eyes, Jonathon nodded. "Of course."

"I'll bring news as soon as I can."

"Appreciate that."

Features twisted in a frown, Shane entered the room and then shouldered the door closed.

Alone with nothing but his thoughts, Jonathon paced.

The sound of his breathing filled the empty hallway, a mockery of what he'd witnessed tonight. He flexed his neck to relieve the knots that had formed there, then checked the time on his watch.

He'd felt this sense of helplessness during his mother's final hours. So many years had come and gone since that terrible night. Yet here he was, once again unable to ease a woman's suffering. When he'd watched Mrs. Mitchell struggling for air, when he'd felt Fanny's stark terror, it had become personal for him.

He stopped abruptly, leaned a shoulder against the wall and lowered his head in prayer. *Lord, heal Mrs. Mitchell. Give her relief from the pain. Please, help her find her breath again.*

The door to room 503 swung open.

Shane joined Jonathon in the hallway. His dark, rumpled hair had a wild look, as though he'd run his fingers through it so many times that the ends now stuck out permanently.

A lump rose in Jonathon's throat. He pushed it down with a hard, silent swallow. "How is she?"

Rubbing a hand over his face, Shane rolled tired eyes to him. "She's resting."

"Will…" Vicious fear clogged in his throat, stealing the words out of his mouth. He swallowed again, started over. "Will she recover?"

Shane speared splayed fingers through his hair. "She's had a life-threatening attack. I believe the worst is over, but I'm afraid she still has a long, agonizing night ahead."

Memories of his mother's long, agonizing nights swam in Jonathon's head. Amelia Hawkins had died of tuberculosis, another terrible lung disease. Her final days had been excruciating and painful.

But that had been years ago. Surely modern medicine had made strides since then. "Is there no medication you can give her? Don't you have something in that black bag of yours that will relieve the pressure in her lungs?"

"I've done what I can." A line of consternation drew Shane's eyebrows together. "There's no cure for asthma. I can only relieve the symptoms as best I can."

That wasn't the answer Jonathon wanted. "Tell me what I can do to help avoid another one of these attacks."

Shane studied his face for an endless moment. The look in his eyes warned Jonathon he wasn't going to like what he heard.

"I've known you for some time, since you were a boy living at Charity House, so I'm going to be frank."

Jonathon waited for the rest.

"Tonight's attack was triggered by stress. Mrs. Mitchell is the kind of mother who loves her children and worries about their welfare, at the expense of her own. If you truly want to prevent another episode, then do whatever you must to shut down the gossip concerning her daughter."

"Understood." Conviction sounded in his voice, spread deep into his soul. The situation between him and Fanny had become a matter of life and death.

"I trust you'll make the right decision." Shane gripped him on the shoulder. "You're a good man, Johnny."

Johnny. No one had called him that since childhood.

Giving him a tight smile, Shane dropped his hand. "I need to get back to my patient now."

After watching the doctor return to the room and shut

the door behind him, Jonathon went back to pacing and praying, praying and pacing.

Ten minutes later, the door swung open again. This time, Fanny stepped out into the hallway.

Jonathon strode over to her. Taking note of the worry creasing her brow, he opened his arms in silent invitation.

She launched herself into his embrace.

"Oh, Jonathon." She said his name in a low, aching tone. "I've never been so scared in all my life."

"I know, baby." He tightened his hold.

"She's breathing easier now."

"Praise God for that." Watching Mrs. Mitchell struggling to breathe earlier tonight had been living torture.

Fanny shifted in his arms and glanced up.

At the look of sorrow in her eyes, a dozen simultaneous thoughts shuffled through his mind, pinpointing to one clear course of action. Ease this woman's pain.

This wasn't the way he wanted to propose to her again. He'd had plans of courting her properly, with flowers, unexpected gifts, gentle kisses, the whole romantic package. There would be time for all that later.

For now, he started with a simple apology. "I'm sorry, Fanny. I'm sorry your mother suffered because of something I did."

"You mean something *we* did together. Oh, Jonathon." She pressed her cheek to his shoulder. "You realize what this means, don't you?"

"I do." He ran his hand over her hair. "We'll make it work. I promise we'll figure out a way that will benefit all parties involved."

As if she didn't hear him, she continued speaking into his shirt. "San Francisco isn't so very far away. I can come home several times a year."

"No, Fanny, you don't need to leave Denver." He set her away from him, looked her straight in the eye. "You can stay in town, if you marry me."

She blinked. "You…you're proposing again?"

"I am, and by the shock in your eyes, I'm making a terrible hash of it. Let's try this again." He took her hand, brought it to his lips, then pressed her palm to his chest. "Fanny Mitchell, will you marry me?"

"You don't have to do this." She swiped at her eyes. "I know how you feel about marriage, and I—"

"Will you marry me?"

She dragged her bottom lip between her teeth. "You are sure this is what you want?"

More sure than he'd been about anything in his life, he repeated the question a third time. "Will you marry me?"

He saw her mind working, saw the moment when she quit fighting the inevitable. For the rest of his life, he would remember the look in her gaze when she became his wife, all but for the ceremony.

"Yes, Jonathon." She rose on her toes and placed a soft, tender kiss to his lips. "I will marry you."

Over the course of the following week, Fanny's life changed dramatically. Her brothers and their families left Denver and returned to their lives, while her parents remained in town, primarily so Dr. Shane could monitor her mother's health.

Fanny liked having her parents close by. It was a pleasure planning her wedding with their input.

Sitting behind her desk, she opened the writing tablet beneath her hand, then reached for the stack of RSVPs. One by one, she checked the responses against the master list of wedding guests.

The news of her impending marriage had not brought a complete end to the gossip, but enough that Fanny no longer worried about her mother's health. In fact, Mary Mitchell hadn't suffered a single relapse since Fanny's engagement became public. Physical proof she'd done the right thing by accepting Jonathon's proposal.

In one short week, she would recite wedding vows with him and become his wife. A little jolt of excitement raced through her. In the days since she'd accepted Jonathon's proposal, he'd made no mention of conditions on their marriage.

Dare she hope he'd changed his mind? Dare she hope he wanted true love and, maybe, one day…children?

It would be foolish to allow her mind to chase down that rabbit trail. One step at a time, she told herself.

She would enjoy being engaged to Jonathon. She had faith the rest would work itself out in time.

Claiming a key role in their romance, Mrs. Singletary was enjoying many accolades for her continued success as a matchmaker. Tomorrow evening, when she hosted Fanny and Jonathon's engagement party, the widow would remind everyone in attendance of her skillful maneuverings on their behalf.

Checking the time on the clock perched above her small fireplace, Fanny yelped. Five minutes past three.

She was late for tea with her mother and sister.

After a quick check of her hair, she hurried through the lobby. She passed a familiar woman and her two teenage daughters. All three were dressed in various shades of blue, their beautiful, expensive gowns cut in a popular style, with the requisite form-fitting bodices and A-line skirts.

The three halted when they saw her.

Fanny smiled. Only one returned the gesture, the youngest.

Fanny refused to be daunted. "Good morning, Mrs. Wainwright." She glanced from mother to daughters. "Sylvia, Carly, lovely to see you both."

The older woman sniffed in disdain. "Girls, do not respond." She herded her daughters away from Fanny, giving her a ridiculously wide berth. "We do not speak to women *like her*."

Mortified at the implication of the words, Fanny found her footsteps faltering.

Did Mrs. Wainwright think she had no feelings? Did she not care that it hurt to be snubbed so profoundly? Of course it hurt. But after facing the very real prospect of losing her mother, Fanny recognized the value of putting moments such as these in perspective.

Once she married Jonathon, much of the censure would disappear, but some would never go away. There wasn't much she could do about that, except hold her head high and pray her mother didn't suffer because of the gossip.

Shaking her head, Fanny continued on to her destination.

The maître d'hôtel welcomed her with a large smile. "Miss Mitchell. Your sister and mother are already at the table you reserved for the afternoon."

"Thank you, Mr. Griffin. I'll find them."

With a critical eye, she took a quick inventory of the restaurant. She noted the details others would miss. The white table linens were clean and pressed, with perfectly placed pleats hanging down the sides. The silverware was dainty and feminine, specifically purchased to use solely at afternoon tea.

Fanny's gaze landed on her mother and sister, who sat at a table near the fireplace. Beneath the golden light, Callie glowed. Her mother looked equally healthy and happy.

Callie caught sight of her first and gave a quick, jaunty wave above her head. Returning the gesture, Fanny hurried to the table.

"Hello, Mother." She leaned over and kissed the beloved cheek. "How are you feeling this afternoon?"

"Like my old self. The daily breathing treatments Dr. Shane is administering are working wonders. I haven't wheezed in nearly a week."

Fanny's heart soared. "Are you certain? You're not—"

"Now, Fanny. We are here to celebrate your engagement to a kind, wonderful man I am growing more and more fond of by the day."

"I like him, too." Beaming at her, Callie poured Fanny a cup of tea. "He makes you happy, which makes him pretty wonderful in my eyes."

Laughing, Fanny took a sip of tea while she eyed her sister over the cup's rim. Speaking of happy...

"Marriage suits you, Cal."

Her sister laughed, clearly delighted by the compliment. "Oh, Fanny, I never expected to find such joy in my life. But Reese is the best thing that ever happened to me. I fall in love with him more every day."

"It shows."

"While we're celebrating, your sister has news," her mother said, smiling at Callie. "Tell her, dear."

A delicate frown marred Callie's pretty face. "Now's not the time, Mother."

"Of course it's the time."

Wondering at the odd mood that had descended over the table, Fanny looked from one woman to the other. "Tell me what? What's going on with you, Callie?"

"Nothing that can't wait." Callie lowered her head, looking incredibly uncomfortable and far too much like the old Callie, the one who didn't like to be the center of attention.

"Tell me your news." Fanny reached over and touched her sister's hand. "Please."

"All right, I…we…" Her cheeks turned a becoming shade of pink. "Reese and I are going to have a baby."

A baby. Fanny stared at her sister. *A baby.* Callie and Reese were officially starting their family. No wonder Callie glowed. She was with child.

Fanny blinked as the news settled over her, as reality gripped her heart and squeezed. Hard.

I will never have news such as this to share.

For a terrible, awful moment, she didn't know what to say, how to feel.

Happy. She was supposed to be happy for her sister. *Of course* she was happy for Callie.

"Oh, Callie, that's marvelous news."

Will that ever be me? Will I ever know that joy?

She squeezed her sister's hand. "You're going to make a wonderful mother."

Happy tears sprang into Callie's eyes.

Fanny's filled as well, and she had a moment, a brief, terrifying moment, when she felt a surge of crippling jealousy. She wanted what Callie had. She wanted a husband who adored her, who wanted her to bear his children.

If only Jonathon would…

No. She would not allow her mind to formulate the rest of that thought. She'd made her choices and would live with them. "How did Reese take the news?"

"He picked me up and twirled me around and around until we were both dizzy. Then—" she giggled "—he called his father into the room and told him the news. A lot of hugs with me and backslapping between the men followed."

Laughing softly, she shook her head, her expression filling with fond affection over the memory. It was the same look Callie got in her eyes whenever she spoke of her husband.

A happy ending to what could have been a disaster. Fanny had been right to jilt Reese. She'd also been right to leave town. Her absence had given her sister the opportunity to fall in love with the man she was meant to be with for all eternity.

"I'm so happy for you, Cal." Her vision blurred, her eyes turned misty. "You and Reese belong together."

As if sensing her shift in mood, Fanny's mother reached over and patted her hand. "I'm confident your marriage will bring you equal happiness and joy."

"You're right, of course." She said the words for her mother's benefit. But, oh, the mess she'd created. One impulsive kiss under the moonlight, and she'd changed several lives forever, Jonathon's most of all.

Thinking of him now, of the situation she'd put them both in, Fanny could barely hold back her grief. One rogue tear wiggled to the edge of her lashes and slipped down the side of her face.

No. No more crying. She would not regret her decision. She only regretted that her behavior had affected others.

"We've already discussed baby names," Callie said, blissfully unaware of Fanny's battle to contain her rioting emotions.

Happy for the distraction, Fanny focused once again on her sister. "Any you'd like to share?"

"If it's a boy, Reese, of course."

"Of course," she said, then laughingly added, "Reese Bennett III is a most regal name, indeed."

"And if it's a girl?" her mother asked.

"We plan to name her Fanny," Callie said, her eyes shining with quiet affection, "after the best sister a woman ever had."

Fanny could hold back the tears no longer. She let them fall freely down her cheeks.

Over sandwiches and cookies, they discussed her future namesake because, according to Callie, she was surely carrying a girl.

Fanny allowed herself to get swept away in her sister's joy. By the time she returned to work, her mood was restored.

She was helping behind the registration desk when Jonathon appeared by her side. He'd been doing that a lot, showing up unexpectedly, taking her on long walks, where they discussed themselves, their childhoods, their likes and dislikes.

"Did you have a nice visit with your mother and sister?"

She smiled. "I did."

"I'm glad." Their gazes stayed connected for longer than usual.

Jonathon looked especially handsome this afternoon, his blue-gray eyes full of masculine interest. It was then that Fanny realized what he was doing. He was officially courting her, attempting to win her affection.

What he didn't seem to know was that the battle had been decided long ago.

Her heart already belonged to him.

Chapter Thirteen

The night of their engagement party, Jonathon settled on the cushioned seat across from Fanny in their hired coach. Due to a last-minute issue with the kitchen equipment, they'd left the hotel a half hour later than planned. He'd sent Fanny's parents ahead so they could alert Mrs. Singletary of the delay.

Now, as their carriage bounced over ruts and divots in the Denver streets, Jonathon took the opportunity to study his fiancée. His heart pounded with uneasiness. Something was wrong.

Fanny wasn't herself.

In truth, she hadn't been herself for several days. Nothing was amiss at the hotel. That meant whatever was bothering her was personal. He studied her a moment longer in the semidarkness.

A sliver of moon provided him enough light to see that her lips were tilted at a worried angle and her gloved fingers were threaded together primly in her lap. He'd seen her adopt the pose before. That, coupled with her unnatural silence, convinced Jonathon she was upset.

He leaned forward. "What's troubling you, Fanny? Is it your mother's health?"

Not quite meeting his eyes, she readjusted her position so that their knees wouldn't touch. "No, she's quite well."

He felt a moment of relief.

"Then what's wrong?" He sat back and employed a relaxed posture, hoping to put her at ease. "Whatever it is, you know you can tell me."

She lifted her chin at that stubborn angle he was growing to recognize as a precursor to trouble. "If you must know, I've been thinking about us."

Several responses came to mind, none of which he voiced aloud. "In what way?"

"It's…we need to…" She lowered her head and stared at her lap. "We need to make our engagement look real."

"It *is* real."

Head still bent, she muttered something that sounded suspiciously like *not real enough*. Whatever that meant.

"Fanny." He placed a knuckle beneath her chin and applied gentle pressure until her gaze met his. "What's happened to make you so distraught?"

She closed her eyes and gave a slight, shuddering sigh before opening them again. "Since the official announcement of our engagement ran in the *Denver Chronicle*, my mother's health has shown rapid improvement."

"That's a good thing."

"Yes, but I fear it won't last."

"What makes you convinced she'll have a relapse?"

"I discovered recently that the gossip about us hasn't actually faded. It's merely shifted in a new direction." Gaze troubled, Fanny glanced out the small carriage window. "If what people are saying gets back to my mother,

I'm afraid she'll suffer another life-threatening asthma attack."

"The talk about us is still that significant?"

Not quite meeting his eyes, Fanny lifted a shoulder.

He said her name again, softer this time, wishing he could soothe away her concerns with nothing but his voice. "Once we are married, the gossip will go away, if not completely, then nearly so."

"You can't know that for certain."

No, he supposed not. "You have evidence to the contrary?"

She snapped her gaze back to his. "Don't you know what they're saying about us?"

Her frustration filled the tiny, enclosed space of the carriage, wrapping around Jonathon as if it were a living, breathing thing. "Has someone said something to you? Did they approach you in the hotel? If that's the case, I'll make sure they are denied permanent access. Give me a name."

Sighing again, she gave a weary shake of her head. "It doesn't matter who started the rumors. The point is that people are openly questioning our motives for marrying. Some claim it's a desperate attempt to quash gossip."

Two simultaneous reactions shot through him, one of impatience, the other of fury. "If you tell me who started this latest rumor, then I'll—"

"What? What will you do, Jonathon? Tell them to stop?"

"If it'll make a difference, yes."

"You know it won't."

He frowned. She was probably right, but he wasn't willing to concede fully. "You are proposing that we combat this latest spin of the gossip mill by making our engagement look real?"

"I know how it sounds," she admitted, twisting her hands over and over again in her lap. "As though I'm asking you to put on a show for the benefit of others."

For all intents and purposes, that was exactly what she was asking of him. She'd clearly put a lot of thought into this, but she'd missed a key element in the argument.

"Our engagement is real, Fanny." He moved to her side of the carriage. The seat dipped and squeaked under his added weight. "In less than a week, we will pledge our lives to one another before God."

"I realize that." And yet she worried her bottom lip between her teeth, as if she feared their wedding wouldn't come to pass.

The carriage hit a bump and she lurched forward. Jonathon pulled her against him to prevent her from falling to the floor.

With her wrapped in his arms, and the pleasing scent of her hair in his nose, he set his chin atop her head and spoke the truth from his heart. "I will honor our wedding vows, always, and will remain loyal to you until the day I die."

Her shoulders rose and fell with a wordless sigh. "I will do the same."

"But you would feel better if the skeptics believed that ours is a love match."

Misery rolled off her in waves. "Don't you see, Jonathon? It's the surest way to end the speculation for good."

Setting her away from him, he returned to his side of the carriage and considered her request. There were a dozen reasons why showing the world how much he cared for this woman was a bad idea. The most powerful one being he was already half in love with her. Allowing his affection free rein might very well send him over the edge.

Then where would they be?

Headed straight for heartbreak, both of them.

As if sensing where his thoughts had gone, Fanny smiled at him. It was a lovely display of fortitude. However, it fell flat enough for him to see past the false bravado.

"You only have to pretend you are in love with me when we are in public. I wouldn't expect you to continue the pretense when we are alone."

Her voice sounded as tormented as she looked. Jonathon's heart lurched in his chest. He'd hurt her. They weren't even married and he'd already let her down.

The thought barely had time to settle over him when the carriage pulled to a grinding stop outside of Mrs. Singletary's house.

Jonathon did not reach for the door handle.

He continued staring at Fanny, consumed with an emotion he couldn't name. The sensation reminded him of grief, as if he'd just lost something very precious before he'd ever fully had it in his grasp.

"Say something," she whispered.

"I'll do it. I will play the besotted suitor tonight, and every night until our wedding." The promise had disaster written all over it. Jonathon would be in love with Fanny before the week was out, and then it would be that much harder to keep their marriage in name only. Especially if she looked at him the way she was now, with a mixture of adoration and tempered hope.

"You...you will? You will pretend to be in love with me?"

Lord, help us both. "Consider it done."

Happiness bloomed in her eyes, then immediately vanished behind a scowl. Even in the muted light, he could see her mind working at double its normal rate.

"Don't look so worried, sweetheart." He took her hand and dragged it to his heart. "Tonight is supposed to be a celebration. We're going to have a grand time at our party."

Without waiting for her response, and praying he was right, he wrenched open the door and helped her out of the carriage.

They entered Mrs. Singletary's house just as a large grandfather clock struck the bottom of the hour.

The widow's butler met them in the foyer.

Threads of silver encroached on the few strands of red left in the bushy head of hair. But the broad, welcoming smile erased at least ten years from the heavily lined face.

"Mr. Hawkins, Miss Mitchell." Back ramrod straight, he took their coats with the efficient movements that came from decades of practice. "The other guests are gathered in the blue parlor on the second floor."

"Thank you, Winston, we know the way."

Taking Fanny's arm, Jonathon guided her toward the sweeping stairwell that wound along the southern wall of the cavernous foyer.

Fanny paused at the foot of the steps to study a portrait of Mrs. Singletary and her now deceased husband.

Jonathon considered the painting, as well.

"My sister discovered in her time as Mrs. Singletary's companion that the widow's marriage was one for the ages," Fanny murmured.

Jonathon didn't doubt this. The people in the portrait were the picture of happiness. "I heard they married young."

A wistful smile played at the corner of Fanny's lips. "She was barely seventeen, he but nineteen. Sadly, Mr. Singletary died fifteen years later."

Jonathon did a quick calculation in his head. Mrs. Singletary had been a widow for nearly thirteen years. That was a long time to grow comfortable in her circumstances. Yet was she? She seemed to still believe in fairy-tale endings, as evidenced by her penchant for matchmaking.

"Perhaps," he mused aloud, "it's time the widow quit meddling in other people's lives and made a match for herself."

Fanny smiled at the suggestion. "Callie recently intimated that Reese's father is campaigning to win Mrs. Singletary's heart, but the widow is proving most stubborn on the matter."

Chuckling softly, Jonathon shook his head at the image of Mrs. Singletary and Reese Bennett Sr. as a couple. "Your sister is an endless source of information."

Fanny joined in his laughter. "So it would seem, at least where Mrs. Singletary is concerned."

Appreciating the light mood between them, Jonathon took Fanny's hand and guided her up the stairs. At the second floor landing, they worked their way toward the blue parlor.

The sound of laughter spilled out into the corridor, a clear indication that nearly all forty invited guests had arrived.

As if by silent agreement, Fanny and Jonathon both halted several feet away from the room. Practicing his role as besotted suitor, he dropped a look of adoration onto his lovely fiancée.

Her answering smile sent his pulse roaring in his ears. "Are you ready?"

She nodded, the gesture loosening several curls from their pins. Unable to resist, he reached up and tamed the stray wisps of hair. At the feel of the silken strands between his fingers, resolve filled him. After tonight, everyone in Mrs. Singletary's home would know his engagement to Fanny was real, including Fanny herself.

Caught by Jonathon's stare, Fanny couldn't take a single easy breath. He was looking at her with such open affection her heart tripped over itself. She wanted to bask in the moment, but they were already late to their own party. After several failed attempts, she managed to tear her gaze free and then leaned forward just enough to get a glimpse inside the blue parlor.

None of the occupants had noticed their arrival.

Fanny took a quick inventory of the guests already in attendance. Her eyes landed on one in particular, a lone gentleman who'd evidently come without his wife. Something hot and ugly filled her. "What is *he* doing here?"

Jonathon followed the direction of her gaze. His shoulders visibly stiffened. "I'd like to know that, myself."

Judge Greene had not been included on the guest list for tonight. Yet there he was, conversing with—of all people—Fanny's parents.

The rush of fury had a growl slipping past her tight lips. The one consolation was that her mother looked beyond bored, and her father seemed terribly unimpressed with whatever the judge was saying.

Fanny moved closer to the doorway, wishing she could hear what the odious man was saying to her parents.

Looking at that superior smile on his face, she felt rage burn beneath her skin.

Judge Greene might claim he wanted a relationship with Jonathon, but Fanny suspected ulterior motives. She would never forget he'd once considered his own son a mistake.

No child was a mistake, of course, but Jonathon truly believed his birth was an unwanted accident. The foul message had been given too often, with too much strength, when Jonathon had been too young to understand the nature of the lie.

To this day, regardless of proof to the contrary, he believed he wasn't capable of breaking free of his past, that he would always be…somehow…less.

The drive to prove otherwise had made him a huge success. At what cost?

How did she combat a lifetime of distorted thinking? How did she help Jonathon recognize he was a treasured child of God?

The answer blew through her mind like a stiff, unrelenting wind. *Love.*

Jonathon's healing started and ended with love. God's love reflected in her love for him. Yes, Fanny would lead Jonathon to the truth by loving him.

She would stand by his side, always, and do whatever she could to protect him from his father.

"Despicable, loathsome man," she growled under her breath. "I should have kicked him in the shin when I had the chance."

Jonathon laughed at her remark. The sound was strangled, and a bit rusty, but loud enough that several party guests took notice. Fanny ignored every one of them.

"He doesn't matter." Jonathon took one of her hands

and brought it to his lips. "Thank you for agreeing to be my wife."

A collective sigh fell over the room, a sure sign they were not only being watched but also overheard.

"There is nowhere else I'd rather be than right here, next to you," she replied. Happiness flared to life and she let it fill her. "I can't wait to become your wife."

He set her hand on his heart, a gesture she was coming to think of as his silent pledge of devotion. "You make me want to be a better man."

"I like you just the way you are."

Slowly, he released her hand. "People are staring."

"Are they?"

"Shall we give them something to talk about?"

She laughed. This was not the way she'd planned to prove their engagement was real, and yet it was the most perfect moment of the night. "What did you have in mind?"

"Nothing too terribly shameless."

By the look in his eyes, she expected him to do something sweet. He did not disappoint. He kissed her hand again, this time lingering a moment beyond polite.

If only this was *real*, she thought. The familiar ache clutching at her throat was immediately followed by a jolt of rebellion.

Why can't it be real? If only for tonight?

Why not revel in the joy of knowing this man would soon be her husband? Decision made, she smiled up at him and let her feelings show in her eyes.

Mrs. Singletary chose that moment to insinuate herself into their private moment. "Our guests of honor have arrived at last."

The announcement was all it took to send the rest of

the room into a flurry of activity. One minute, people were staring at them, watching them enjoy one another. The next, Fanny and Jonathon were surrounded by family and friends.

Everyone talked at once, creating a cacophony of congratulations and thoughtful well-wishes.

Almost immediately, Fanny lost track of Jonathon.

She circled her gaze around the room, found him conversing with Callie, Reese and Reese's father at a spot near the fireplace.

Jonathon's father had moved away from Fanny's parents and now held court on the opposite end of the room with one of Denver's most prominent couples, Alexander and Polly Ferguson.

Their daughters Penelope and Phoebe completed the group. It seemed fitting somehow that the women who'd started the gossip that had led to tonight's celebration would be in attendance.

They wore matching dresses in blue, with silver trim. One of them—did it matter which?—turned her big blue eyes toward Fanny and smiled at her as if they were dear, dear friends.

Fanny pointedly looked away.

Jonathon caught her eye and motioned her over. She moved in his direction, but then found herself being pulled into a pair of willowy, female arms. "Congratulations, my dear."

Another tight squeeze and then Laney Dupree stepped back to smile into Fanny's eyes. "You and Johnny make a wonderful couple."

Dressed in a pretty bronze-and-gold dress that complemented her mahogany hair, the woman who'd started Charity House looked serene, elegant and incredibly beautiful. "I can't think of anyone I'd rather Johnny marry than you."

Fanny's heart fluttered with pure happiness. She liked this woman and knew how important she was to Jonathon. "That's so very kind of you to say."

"Not kindness, truth. You make him happy, Fanny. I can't tell you how much relief that brings me."

Overcome with too many emotions to sort through at once, Fanny reached up and wiped at her eyes. "He makes me happy, too, more than I can put into words."

"I'm glad." Laney hugged her a second time.

The moment she let go, her husband swooped in for his turn. His embrace was briefer than his wife's, but no less special. Marc Dupree had been more of a father to Jonathon than Judge Greene had. For that reason alone, Fanny adored the man.

Dark-haired, clean-shaven, he wore a red brocade vest and matching tie made of the finest material available, the kind a successful banker might choose for his clothing.

"As my wife so eloquently said, we couldn't be happier with Johnny's choice of brides. Welcome to the family, Fanny."

"Thank you," she choked out, pleased for Jonathon that these two considered him one of their own.

Though Fanny didn't know all the particulars, she knew that Marc had been a strong influence in her fiancé's life.

"I believe you'll make Johnny a fine wife," Marc added with a smile. "A very fine wife, indeed."

"Far better than I deserve." The familiar voice came from behind her. Before Fanny could look over her shoulder, Jonathon's arm came around her waist, securing her to his side.

Tucked in close, she swiveled her gaze up to his.

For reasons she didn't want to explore too deeply, Fanny could do nothing but stare in muted wonder at the expression in his eyes. The warmth looked real, not pretend real, but *real*.

Her stomach rolled. Her throat burned. Her heart pounded. And still she continued staring up at Jonathon. Even when he turned his attention to Marc and Laney, Fanny continued watching him. She adored his profile.

So strong.

So handsome.

She should not be this aware of her fiancé, not if she wanted to survive their marriage in name only.

Perhaps, she could convince Jonathon to change his mind on the matter.

But how?

The answer came to her again.

Love him.

Could it be that simple? Yes. *Her* love would conquer *his* doubts.

All she needed to do was trust God to heal Jonathon's heart. Enough to give him the courage to take a leap of faith, to trust that he could break free of his past.

If in the process Jonathon chose to make Fanny truly his wife, well, she would know that it all started here, now. With love.

Her love.

Chapter Fourteen

Even as Jonathon carried on a conversation with Marc and Laney—something to do with the renovations under way at Charity House—he was highly attuned to the woman next to him. He kept his arm wrapped around her waist, at one point pulling Fanny closer.

She didn't protest.

In fact, she settled against him as if she was determined to stay by his side the rest of the night. He felt Fanny's eyes on him, felt the warmth of her smile wash over him.

He tried not to betray his pleasure. Nonetheless, his lips lifted in secret satisfaction. Tonight was a glimpse into what his future would be like with Fanny as his wife.

Jonathon liked what lay ahead.

The evening was turning out to be surprisingly enjoyable, partly because he hadn't spoken to Judge Greene once all night, but also because of Fanny herself. He liked her, admired her, valued nearly everything about her.

An absurd notion encroached on his thoughts, one he couldn't seem to ignore no matter how hard he focused on the conversation with his friends. Jonathon's entire life, every mistake, every wrong turn, every good and wise decision, had led him to this one woman. Fanny Mitchell was his destiny, his future.

It felt as natural as breathing to pretend he had deep feelings for her. Probably, he realized, because he actually had deep feelings for Fanny.

This is going to be a problem.

He was a man, after all, and Fanny was a beautiful, mesmerizing woman. Soon, they would be married in the eyes of God. How was Jonathon supposed to spend a lifetime with Fanny without making her his wife the way the Lord intended?

You are not a mistake, Fanny had once said to him.

If Jonathon wasn't a mistake, if the Bible verse from Jeremiah was accurate, and the Lord had known him before he was formed in his mother's womb, then perhaps he *could* break free of his past. Perhaps future generations wouldn't suffer because of who Jonathon was and where he came from.

The thought barely had a chance to slide through his mind when the conversation shifted to the newest arrivals at Charity House, two brothers and a sister.

Not long after that, Fanny's parents joined their group and the discussion turned once again, this time to the exciting topic of the weather. Seizing the opportunity to move on, Jonathon pulled his fiancée away with the excuse of needing a moment alone with her.

It was true. He wanted to be alone with Fanny, if only for a few minutes.

"Jonathon," she said, laughing as she broke into a trot to keep up with his long strides. "Where are we going in such a rush?"

"Somewhere private." He slowed his pace to match hers, then leaned down so only she heard his words. "You have a problem with that?"

"Not at all." She laughed again. "It sounds quite promising."

"I like that you think so."

Her eyes sparkled with delight. "Well, then, take me away. I'm all yours, Mr. Hawkins."

She was wrong, of course. She would never be completely his, not really, not unless he reconsidered the parameters of their marriage.

Did he dare take the risk?

It was something he needed to ponder seriously before their wedding night.

Hand clasped with Fanny's, he drew her into the darkened hallway. They'd taken several steps when a masculine voice spoke his name.

Jonathon's footsteps came to an abrupt halt and a deep unease sliced through him. He didn't need to look over his shoulder to know it was Joshua Greene who spoke his name.

"You cannot avoid me all evening," the man added.

At the familiar sound of icy disapproval, knots formed at the back of Jonathon's neck. He was transported to another time, to the night he'd first confronted his father. Jonathon had laid his heart bare in the hope of saving his mother's life. He'd actually *begged* for Greene's help.

Jonathon attempted to release Fanny's hand. With a little hum of rebellion, she held on tight. Together they faced his father. Jonathon eyed the older man without an ounce of emotion in his heart.

Dressed in a hand-tailored suit, Joshua Greene looked every bit the distinguished Denver citizen most of the world thought him to be. The disguise was so well done that Jonathon nearly believed the pretense himself.

"Must we do this out here?" His posture stiff, his arrogance evident in every inch of his pinched face, Greene looked around them in disapproval. "I dislike lurking in darkened hallways."

"Then I shall make a habit of lurking in darkened hallways."

"There's no need to be snide, son."

Son. For half his life, Jonathon had waited to hear that word come out of this man's mouth. He'd spent the other half forging his place in the world on his own terms.

He'd endured loss and suffering, had survived poverty and the humiliation of illegitimacy. He no longer needed, or wanted, this man's acknowledgment. Not now. Not ever.

Aware that Fanny still held tightly to his hand, all but vibrating with suppressed emotion, Jonathon kept his response curt. "We already had this conversation in my office last week. We have nothing more to say to one another."

"Now see, that's where you're wrong." Something calculated flashed in Greene's eyes. "While I confess I have not handled matters well in the past, you must admit that I have recently shown my willingness to mend our relationship—"

"We have no relationship."

"An oversight I wish to rectify. I am fully prepared to accept my duty as your father."

Jonathon leaned forward and addressed the real reason for the judge's sudden interest in *duty*. "We both know this is about your run for the Senate. How do you think the truth of what you did to my mother will go over with the voters?"

With a snort and a flick of his wrist, Greene dismissed the question. "They will sympathize with my decisions, once they hear my side of the story."

"What will they think when they hear mine?"

The question seemed to give the man pause, but only briefly. "Who will they believe?" he asked. "Me, a law-abiding, God-fearing member of the judicial community? Or you, a former pickpocket and by-blow of a prostitute?"

Jonathon stood very still, in full control of every inch of his body, knowing the importance of revealing not one ounce of weakness to this man. "Tell your story to the world. But be prepared for me to tell mine."

"Very well." Greene spun around and moved toward the doorway of the blue parlor with quick, clipped strides. "There is no time like the present."

A bolt of alarm shot through Jonathon. "Do not do this here. Not tonight." *Not in front of Fanny.*

Greene ignored the request. "May I have everyone's attention?" Playing to his audience as if he were a seasoned stage actor, he swept his hands in a wide, dramatic arc. "I have a very important announcement to make."

Conversations came to a stuttering halt and a roomful of curious stares turned in their direction.

Time seemed to shift, transporting Jonathon back to his childhood, to the boy who'd shivered and quaked in back alleys, who'd witnessed his mother's fall into despair, then illness, then ultimately death.

Anger and hurt, regret and desperation, so many ugly emotions warred within him. For a dangerous moment, those memories paralyzed him.

"Jonathon." He felt more than heard Fanny's voice,

but he couldn't respond. His gaze was riveted on Judge Greene.

The man shot a benevolent smile over the crowd. "It is my honor to announce to everyone present that…" he paused for dramatic effect "…Jonathon Hawkins is my—"

"No!" Fanny rushed in front of the judge, her swift, unexpected move rendering him momentarily speechless. "Judge Greene is only offering up a joke no one will find funny. Carry on with your conversations."

She glanced briefly at Jonathon. A tactical error.

With the swift, deadly movements of a jungle cat, Greene regained the room's attention.

"I wish to announce that Jonathon Hawkins is my son."

A blast of murmurs and gasps followed the statement, then came a highly palpable lurch of silence.

"I only recently discovered my connection to this successful man, whose rags-to-riches story I greatly admire. His mother, I'm afraid, kept his existence from me a secret."

And so began a bevy of lies as the esteemed judge wove his fictional tale of the past.

This was Jonathon's legacy, he realized, as his father blatantly revised history. Lies, half truths, rationalizations when they suited the moment. Jonathon himself had used similar methods in the past, at first to survive, then in a desperate attempt to run from his past, to separate himself from this man.

He'd come full circle. There was no more escaping the truth. He was this despicable man's son down to the bone.

Perhaps it was for the best that everyone knew.

But what of Fanny? How would this affect her? Icy

numbness crept into Jonathon's veins. He could still protect her from suffering the repercussions of the judge's announcement.

He pulled her close, spoke words in her ear no one else could hear. "You may break our engagement, if you wish. I will not hold it against you."

"I will *not* abandon you," she said in a low, ferocious tone. "As you have stood by me, so I shall stand by you."

Her conviction was a golden, glimmering keepsake. "Fanny—"

"Jonathon. My loyalty is nothing if not total."

Greene smiled over at him. "I am unspeakably proud to publicly ally myself with this man, my son."

The easy charm was to be expected, of course. Joshua Greene was a natural politician. He knew how to impress an audience.

However, he'd misread the room.

The horrified silence coming from the wide-eyed guests wasn't directed at Jonathon, but at Greene.

Fanny tightened her grip on Jonathon's hand.

He glanced down at her, an apology on his tongue, but she wasn't looking at him. She was glaring at his father.

Before Jonathon knew what she was about, she suddenly yanked her hand free and marched over to Judge Greene.

"Quiet," she snapped, fists jammed on her hips.

Greene blinked in mute astonishment.

"Judge Greene is shamelessly retelling the past. Do not be fooled. He has known about Jonathon since the day he was born."

Laney confirmed this to be true, as did Marc.

The expected outrage on Jonathon's behalf erupted like a spark to dynamite.

Greene attempted to explain himself, using phrases such as *youthful indiscretion* and *deep regret* and *mistakes that can still be corrected*. Once again, he miscalculated his audience.

The more he tried to rationalize away his behavior, the angrier the crowd grew. Jonathon half expected pitchforks and torches to materialize inside clenched fists.

Mrs. Singletary ended the spectacle by stepping firmly into the fray. "Enough."

In her no-nonsense tone, she asked the judge to leave her home at once.

Smart enough to recognize the need for retreat, he did as she requested. Before exiting the room, however, he stopped beside Fanny. "I find your interference in this matter most distressing."

She gave him her sweetest smile. "I cannot tell you how much it pleases me to hear that."

Greene left in a huff.

In the silence that followed his father's departure, Jonathon ran a hand across his brow, left it there for several seconds. Saying nothing, Fanny simply touched his arm. Her silent show of support was exactly what he needed.

He momentarily closed his hand over hers. "Thank you."

To his surprise, the party guests made the pilgrimage to where they stood. One by one, they expressed their support and their hope that his marriage to Fanny would erase the pain of his past. Even the Ferguson sisters had kind words for him.

Jonathon did not doubt their sincerity or that of the others. Yet his father's words continued echoing in his mind. *Jonathon Hawkins is my son.*

No matter how much he tried to distance himself from

the man, one truth remained. Jonathon would be forever connected to Joshua Greene by blood.

Depressing thought.

The room eventually emptied out, leaving only Fanny's parents and the Duprees.

"It's going to be all right, Johnny." Laney made the promise in much the same voice she'd used when he was a boy. "In time, everyone will know the truth. They will have every reason to side with you."

There was no way of knowing how the rest of Denver would take Greene's announcement. Unlike the people here tonight, mostly family and friends, many in town would believe the judge's version. *His word against mine.*

"Jonathon." Mrs. Mitchell gripped his forearm.

Fearing how the drama of the evening might have affected her, he swiveled his gaze to hers. Her brow was creased in concern, but her breathing appeared normal.

"Take heart," she said. "You are not alone in this."

"That's right, my boy." Cyrus Mitchell clapped him on the back. "By marrying Fanny, you inherit the entire brood. That's a total of nine Mitchells, their assorted spouses and various herds of children, all for the price of one slip of a girl."

He winked at his daughter.

The comment had the intended effect. Jonathon laughed.

He appreciated knowing that these good, solid people considered him part of their family. But right now all he wanted was to be alone with Fanny.

He endured another ten minutes, then made his and Fanny's excuses.

"We have an early morning" was all he said. It was enough. Not a single argument prevented their departure.

Minutes later, and with great relief, he climbed inside the hired coach with Fanny and closed the door behind them.

He made an attempt to sit across from her.

She shook her head. "Oh, no, you don't."

With great deliberation, she settled on the seat beside him and leaned her head against his shoulder. In the calm following the dramatic events of the evening, he liked having her close. He braided their fingers together and breathed in the scent of her. They sat that way for nearly twenty minutes.

Only when the carriage pulled to a stop outside the hotel did she smile up at him with a mischievous light in her eyes. "Well, I'd say tonight went quite well. Wouldn't you agree, Jonathon?"

Like an echo from the past, his responding bark of laughter was equal parts pain and tempered hope. "I adore you."

Still smiling up at Jonathon, Fanny let his beautiful words settle over her. He'd been quiet during the carriage ride back to the hotel. She'd honored as long as humanly possible his wish to remain silent.

Now, with their gazes locked and their fingers entwined, she felt his sorrow as though it were her own.

He reached for the door handle. She stopped him with a tug on their joined hands.

"Before we head inside, I want to say—"

She broke off, suddenly at a loss for words. What could she say that would make his pain disappear?

Her heart broke for this wonderful, giving man. Tonight had been difficult for him. Joshua Greene had claimed Jonathon as his son and in the process killed whatever chance there'd been for reconciliation.

Any hope his father would prove himself an honorable man was dead. Now, Jonathon clearly grieved. Fanny saw the sense of loss in his eyes.

"You can't pretend you're not hurting over what happened tonight, and I can't pretend not to hurt for you."

The smile he gave her was full of sadness, the depth of which she'd never seen in him before. "Fanny, you realize tonight was merely a trial run for the days ahead."

"I'm not sure what you mean."

"The truth is out, if somewhat skewed. By tomorrow morning everyone will know I am Joshua Greene's son and that my mother never told him about me."

"That's a lie. Not everyone will accept his word as truth." But she knew that wasn't entirely possible. Though she'd like to think the whole of Denver would believe Jonathon's version over his father's lies, Fanny wasn't that naive.

As if reading her mind, Jonathon voiced her concerns aloud. "Some will believe his tale, Fanny. They may even think I conspired with my mother for years and am now extorting Greene with this information for my own purposes."

"That's absurd."

"The gossip will turn toward you. Your reputation will suffer yet another blow. I can't let that happen."

Something in the way he spoke, with such resolve and a complete lack of emotion, terrified her. "What…what are you saying?"

"You don't have to go through with our wedding. I'd understand if you are having second thoughts."

"Are *you* having second thoughts?"

"Yes, I am," he admitted. "I won't marry you if a connection to me further jeopardizes your reputation. That would defeat the entire purpose."

Fanny thought she'd been afraid before. But now, at the determination she heard in Jonathon's words, she grew terrified he would break off their engagement.

She could not lose him, not like this.

Words tumbled quickly out of her mouth. "Judge Greene might be arrogant enough to think people will believe he is without fault. But he shamelessly committed adultery. That point cannot be denied. The people in this city will not be as forgiving as he claims."

For a long, tense moment Jonathon stared at her. Then finally, thankfully, his mouth lifted in a smile. "Is that your way of saying I'm stuck with you?"

Relief made her shoulders slump forward. "That's absolutely what I'm saying. In one week from today, in front of a hundred witnesses and God Himself, I will proudly become your wife."

Jonathon's eyebrows lifted. "Proudly?"

She leaned toward him. "You caught that part, did you?"

"You're the finest woman I know, Fanny Mitchell." He cupped her face in his hand.

"We'll get through this, Jonathon." She placed a kiss on his palm. "With all the practice we've had lately, we're masters at facing down gossip. We could teach classes on the subject."

He angled his head, searched her face as if looking for a hint of remorse or doubt. He would find none.

Being the good man that he was, he gave her one last chance to change her mind. "You can still back out."

"Yes, yes, so you've said. Can we be through with the discussion now?"

He moved his head close to hers, paused when their faces were inches from touching. A shift on either of their parts and their mouths would unite. "I'll take the full blame, Fanny. Your reputation won't have to suffer, and would perhaps be enhanced if you—"

"Are you going to continue blathering, or kiss me?"

One corner of his mouth lifted and a very masculine light shone in his eyes. "You want me to kiss you?"

"Yes, please."

He seemed to need no more encouragement, and pressed his lips to hers. Silent promises were made by each of them, promises Fanny prayed they both would keep.

Far too soon, he set her away from him.

This time when he reached for the door handle she didn't stop him. As he escorted her to her room, they spoke about nothing of substance, a nice change from all the emotion of the evening.

At her door, he paused. "Good night, Fanny."

"Good night, Jonathon."

He lightly kissed her forehead, her temple and then her nose. There was such tenderness in each brush of his lips. Her eyes filled with tears.

One last touch of his lips to hers and he stepped back. "I pray you have sweet dreams."

"I know I will." With the memory of his kisses warming every corner of her heart, how could she not?

Chapter Fifteen

Fanny woke the morning of her wedding to the pleasant sound of birdsong outside her window. She stretched
beneath the warm, downy comforter and looked around
the luxurious room Jonathon had insisted she move into
three days ago.

Snuggling deeper under the covers, she let out a jaw-
cracking yawn, the result of too little sleep. Callie had
spent the night with her, claiming it was one of her duties as the matron of honor. They'd stayed up late, giggling and sharing secrets as they'd so often done as young
girls on the ranch.

Fanny hadn't realized how much she'd missed her sister. Ever since Callie had married Reese, Fanny had intentionally avoided spending too much time with her. The
newlyweds deserved a chance to build their relationship
without any distractions. An ex-fiancée—who also happened to be the bride's younger sister—definitely quali-
fied as a distraction.

When Callie had announced she was going to have a
baby, Fanny had created even more distance, this time

for selfish reasons. She'd been fearful that her jealousy and yearning for her own child would put a permanent wedge between her and Callie.

She'd been wrong to worry. Last night, she'd felt only happiness for her sister.

Fanny attributed her change in perspective to her growing relationship with Jonathon. She'd never felt more treasured, more special, than when she was in his company. Not because of the few stolen kisses they'd shared under the stars, but because of Jonathon's tenderness toward her, his attentiveness and—all right, yes—his kisses.

More importantly, they'd faced down, as a couple, the gossip over his connection to Judge Greene, and had grown closer for the experience.

Society hadn't sided with Greene, or even Jonathon, but with the judge's poor, deceived wife. Fanny hadn't foreseen that particular result, but lauded the gossips for rallying around Mrs. Greene. Fanny almost felt sorry for Jonathon's father. *Almost*, but not quite, especially since he was still arrogantly sticking to his version of the story, as if *he* was the injured party.

Fanny banished all unpleasant thoughts from her mind. Today was a day for joy.

She stretched her arms overhead, and once again hooked her gaze on the ceiling. For this one moment, when Callie was off who-knew-where, and Fanny was completely alone, with no one watching her, no one asking her questions about the future, she let herself…dream.

In a matter of hours, she would become Mrs. Jonathon Hawkins. Anticipation hummed in her veins. They would have a good marriage, a happy, long—

Her door swung open with a bang.

Callie rushed into the room, jumped on the bed, then proceeded to bounce up and down on her knees. "You're getting married in a few hours."

"Oh." Fanny pretended to yawn. "Is that today?"

"You know it is." Still bouncing, eyes lit with a teasing light, Callie pointed a finger at her. "No begging off this time."

"Ha-ha, very funny."

Fanny scooted to her right, as much to avoid getting mauled by her sister's enthusiasm as to make room for Callie on the bed.

Still laughing at her own joke, Callie collapsed backward, wiggled around a bit, then set her head on the pillow and studied the ceiling with narrowed eyes. "Will you look at that? Even the plaster is beautiful in this hotel."

Fanny eyed the swirling rosettes set inside a four-by-four square pattern. "When it comes to his hotels, Jonathon is a stickler for detail."

"So I gathered." Her gaze running from the center of the ceiling to the crown molding, Callie laughed again. Then stopped abruptly and swiveled her head on the pillow. "Are you happy, Fanny? Truly?"

"Oh, Cal, yes, *yes*, I am." Fanny smiled over at her. "I am so very, very happy."

"I knew you would end up with Mr. Hawkins." Her sister's voice held a decidedly smug note. "In fact, I have known for some time now, almost a full year."

Fanny very much doubted that. "You can't possibly have known for that long. Besides, I was in Chicago a year ago."

"I stand by my assessment." Callie held her stare

without flinching. "I am very wise about these sorts of things."

"Are you?" Fanny rolled her eyes. "Might I remind you, oh wise one, how for weeks after I broke my engagement with Reese you pushed me to change my mind? And when I left town, you all but threatened to bodily drag me back to Denver so I could make amends?"

Callie opened her mouth, closed it, sighed heavily. "I find in cases such as these that a dreadful memory is most helpful, as is a swift change in subject."

"Indeed."

"Back to what I was saying." She lifted up on one elbow. "I've known Mr. Hawkins has had feelings for you ever since I worked as Mrs. Singletary's companion."

How could Callie possibly have known such a thing? Fanny and Jonathon had been veritable strangers at the time Callie had lived under Mrs. Singletary's roof.

"I detect your doubt, but remember, Mr. Hawkins was a frequent guest at the widow's house," Callie told her. "Whenever your name came up, he sang your praises."

Something warm and wonderful spread through Fanny. "Truly?"

"Oh, yes. He made a point of telling me that you were *thriving* in Chicago. At the time, I was very upset with him, so the news didn't sit well." Callie sank back onto the pillow. "I blamed him for helping you leave town."

"If he hadn't given me a job, I would have found another route of escape."

Callie sighed. "I know that now."

"Come on, Cal, you must admit." Fanny nudged her sister's shoulder. "Things worked out pretty well for you. You are married to a wonderful man and have a baby on the way."

Callie turned her head, her gaze full of gratitude. "If I haven't said it enough already, thank you, Fanny, thank you for breaking your engagement to Reese."

"You're most welcome."

They fell silent, each lost in her own thoughts.

Callie shifted, rose up on her elbow again. "I confess, I didn't know for certain that Mr. Hawkins was besotted with you until Mrs. Singletary's charity ball."

Fanny thought of the moment on the hotel terrace when she'd kissed Jonathon. "I have a confession of my own to make."

"That sounds interesting." Callie poked her in the ribs. "Do tell."

"I…" Fanny sighed. "I was the one who initiated our first kiss. If I'd known the Ferguson sisters were watching, I would have never—"

"Wait, stop, go back. I wasn't talking about Mrs. Singletary's charity ball this year. I was talking about the one she held last year."

"*Last* year?"

"I saw the way he looked at you. It's the same way Reese looks at me. But what really gave Mr. Hawkins away was how he capitulated to your every request for your current position. He adores you, Fanny, and has for some time."

Could it be true? Fanny barely dared to hope.

If Jonathon had feelings for her, feelings that had been building for over a year now, surely he would want to have a real marriage with her.

"Enough lazing about." Callie hopped off the bed and dragged Fanny with her. "It is my duty to ensure the bride has a hearty breakfast. I will not shirk my responsibilities."

Fanny hugged her sister. "I love you."

"Love you, too. Now," Callie clapped her hands together in a gesture that reminded Fanny of Beatrix Singletary. "You require sustenance and I shall see you get some."

"I think…" Fanny pressed a hand to her churning stomach. "I'm too nervous to eat."

"There's nothing to be nervous about." Callie presented her best big-sister smile. "It's going to be a good day, Fanny."

A ridiculously pleasant flutter went through her heart. "No, Callie, it's going to be a *great* day."

Later that same morning, huddled inside his heavy coat, Jonathon made the journey to Charity House on foot. In just over an hour, he would pledge his life to Fanny's at the church connected with the orphanage. It was one of the many things they'd agreed upon about their wedding.

He'd enjoyed the planning process. He and Fanny made a good team. Their easy working relationship at the hotel had seamlessly translated into a personal one.

Fanny was purity and light, so little of life's tragedies had truly touched her. Jonathon didn't want that to change because of him. He wanted to be a good husband, but he was a little fuzzy on what that actually entailed.

Surely Marc Dupree would have pearls of wisdom to share on the matter. The man had been happily married for over sixteen years.

Jonathon would like to think he'd played a role, albeit small, in Marc and Laney's romance. Had he not picked Marc's pocket that fine spring day, been caught in the act and then been marched back home to Charity House, the two may never have met.

Smiling at the memory, Jonathon unlatched the gate and sauntered up the front walkway, his gaze on Charity House. Not much had changed since he'd lived here. The three-story structure was as regal and imposing as he remembered.

The red bricks, black shutters and whitewashed porch rail fit in with every other mansion on the street. The difference being, of course, that forty boys and girls slept under this roof, rather than one family and a host of servants.

The familiar sound of children at play wafted from the backyard. Smiling at last, Jonathon conquered the front steps two at a time and entered the house.

The front parlor was empty, as was expected. The children weren't allowed in this area of the house without adult supervision. "Anybody home?"

"We're in Marc's office." Laney's muffled response came from the back of the house.

Jonathon worked his way through the labyrinth of hallways and corridors, then pushed through the door that led to Marc's office.

Warmth. Acceptance. Unconditional love.

They were all here for him, in this room, with these two people, the man and woman who'd taken on the role of his parents for four years.

"There's the groom." Laney rushed over and yanked him into a motherly hug. After nearly squeezing all the breath out of him, she stepped back and straightened the lapels of his morning suit. "Aren't you handsome? Your bride is going to swoon when she sees you."

He grinned at the absurd image her words created. "Keep complimenting me like that, Laney Dupree, and I might have to steal you away from your husband."

He winked at Marc, then swooped the petite woman into his arms and dipped her low to the ground.

She came up gasping and laughing.

"Oh, you." She playfully slapped his arm. "You always did have quick moves and too much charm for your own good."

"Which," Marc said, "if I remember correctly—and of course, I do—those quick moves got our boy into more than a few scuffles. One in particular comes to mind, involving my wallet."

"If *I* remember correctly," Jonathon countered, "had I not picked your pocket, you would have never found out about Charity House. The way I see it, you owe me a debt of gratitude."

"No argument there." Chuckling, Marc circled around his desk and, ignoring Jonathon's offered hand, pulled him into a quick, back-slapping hug. "You ready for today?"

He nodded. "Thank you, again, for agreeing to stand up with me."

"It's my honor and privilege." Sincerity sounded in Marc's words and shone in his eyes.

Jonathon's throat tightened.

This was the man he'd spent his entire adult life attempting to emulate.

"We have a while before we're due at the church. I thought you and I might take a few minutes to talk before we head over."

"That's my husband's polite way of telling me to leave

the room." Laney rose onto her toes and kissed Jonathon's cheek. "I'm proud of you, Johnny. You're going to make your lovely bride a superior husband."

Jonathon wanted to agree with her, but found he could only manage a noncommittal shrug.

"Talk to Marc. You'll feel better once you do." She patted his arm, then quit the room without another word.

Typical Laney, he thought, as he stared at her retreating back. The woman was both perceptive and kind.

Still, dread slid down Jonathon's spine. He would never hurt Fanny, that was a given. He would provide for her and protect her from harm. Would it be enough?

The world she came from was vastly different from the world he'd once inhabited. They certainly didn't have the same definition of family. Misunderstandings were sure to arise. Would they navigate them well, or would seemingly small matters grow into issues too big to overcome?

"Take a seat, Johnny, before you fall over."

"I'm good standing." But he wasn't. So he did as Marc suggested and sank in an overstuffed chair covered in brown leather worn to a fine patina.

Marc sat in the chair beside him. "I know that look in your eyes. It's called panic."

Not bothering to argue about the accurate assessment, Jonathon rubbed a hand over his face. "I don't want to hurt Fanny."

"Then don't."

"It's not that simple."

"It should be."

Too agitated to sit, Jonathon hopped to his feet and paced over to the bookshelf, ran his hand across several of the bindings. "My situation with Fanny isn't conventional."

"Perhaps your engagement didn't start out like most, but that's not to say your marriage won't bring you both great joy. I've seen you two together. You're good for each other."

Jonathon wasn't nearly as confident as his mentor. "You know where I come from, *who* I come from."

For several long seconds, Marc eyed him in stone-cold silence. "The question isn't if I know who you are. It's whether or not you do."

The look in Marc's eyes gave Jonathon pause. If he didn't know better he'd think he'd insulted the man. That hadn't been his intention. "I'm the product of an alliance between a woman of questionable virtue and an adulterer. *That's* where I come from. My blood is forever tainted."

"Your background is no different than my wife's." Marc leaned his elbows on his knees. "Is Laney's blood tainted?"

"You're missing my point."

"Am I?"

Heart grim, Jonathon told Marc about his half brother's recent antics, about the money he'd given Josh to set up his latest mistress in her own house, where she would raise their illegitimate child in secret. "The sins of my father have carried over into one of his sons."

Marc pressed the tips of his fingers together, brought them to rest beneath his chin. "You believe you'll turn out like your father and brother."

Unable to deny it, Jonathon merely nodded.

"What about my influence in your life?" Marc asked, his tone giving away nothing of his thoughts.

And yet Jonathon knew exactly what his mentor was

thinking. By hanging on to his connection to Joshua Greene, Jonathon was denying his link to this man.

Breaking eye contract, Marc stood, stepped around his desk and rummaged through the top drawer. He pulled out what looked to be a faded photograph, and handed it to Jonathon.

The image of the first Hotel Dupree stared back at him. The brick building had boasted nine impressive stories, and large, wrought-iron balconies on every floor. Jonathon had copied Marc's original design, all the way down to the blue-and-white striped awning over the entrance.

"You once told me," Marc began, "that you kept my name on your hotels because you wanted your legacy tied directly with mine."

Jonathon continued staring at the photograph, the word *legacy* ratcheting around in his mind. "I remember."

Marc laid a hand on his shoulder. "Not only did you go into the hotel business because of me, but you have carried on my tradition of hiring employees who need a second chance. Men and women with little skill or talent, who may have made mistakes in the past but want to change their lives for good."

Jonathon looked up from the picture.

"The future stands before you, Johnny. You can either continue focusing on the fact that you are the son of an adulterer and a prostitute, or you can accept that you've overcome a difficult past to make something more of yourself. It's up to you."

Jonathon lowered his head and studied the image of the original Hotel Dupree, built by the man he most admired in this world. The backs of his eyes stung.

He swallowed hard, attempted to return the picture.

"Keep it," Marc told him. "As a reminder of where you really come from."

Unable to speak, he tucked the picture in an inner pocket of his jacket. "Thank you."

"I've had the privilege of watching you grow from a troubled youth to a good, solid, godly man. You'll make Fanny a proper husband. Don't let anyone ever tell you otherwise, including yourself."

If there was any good in him, it was because of this man's influence. The Lord had blessed Jonathon with a surrogate father a thousand times better than his real one. Part of him would always be defined by his past, but he didn't have to make the same mistakes the men who shared his blood had made.

Marc squeezed his shoulder. "Let's get you married."

They made the trek out to the backyard, which spilled onto the church's property. With plenty of time before the ceremony, Jonathon took a few minutes to toss a ball around with a couple of the older boys. The activity was simple, a game he'd played hundreds of times in this yard.

A reminder of where you really come from.

A half hour later, with Marc standing on his left and Laney perched in the front pew beside Fanny's mother, Jonathon took his place at the front of the church.

Reverend Beauregard O'Toole moved in on his right. The rebel preacher opened his church to the lost, the broken and the hurting. Jonathon had found God thanks to Beau's guidance. It mattered that he was the one to officiate this next step in his life.

Beau nodded to the woman at the piano and the short processional began.

Fanny's sister entered the church first and made the

brief journey down the aisle. Callie's gaze was stuck on her husband sitting in the second pew. Reese Bennett Jr. winked at her. She blushed. He winked again.

Feeling as if he was intruding on their private moment, Jonathon looked away.

Still smiling, Callie drew to a stop on the other side of Beau, then turned to face the back of the church.

The music changed.

The wedding guests collectively rose to their feet.

And then…

Fanny appeared at the end of the aisle, her arm linked through her father's.

Jonathon's breath caught in his throat and all he could do was stare in wonder at the vision she made.

Dressed in cream-colored lace from head to toe, Fanny was the very picture of a beautiful bride. She'd pulled her blond curls into a fancy, complicated style atop her head. Little sprigs of wildflowers were scattered throughout, giving her beauty an ethereal quality.

His heart pounding with rib-cracking intensity, Jonathon knew he would forever treasure this moment when his bride stood in the doorway, arm in arm with her father, poised to begin her march down the aisle.

She was too far away for him to read her expression accurately, but he could feel her run her gaze over his face, each sweep a soft caress.

Minutes from now, she would be his wife.

She'd had little choice in the matter.

Jonathon braced his shoulders for the familiar guilt to slam through him. He experienced only a surge of joy.

His mind emptied of every thought but Fanny.

She was more than his business associate, more than his friend.

She was his future.

His bitter soul didn't deserve this woman, but now that he'd received her caring, experienced her generous spirit, he would never let her go.

Chapter Sixteen

Caught inside Jonathon's stare, Fanny's heart took a tumble. Now that the time had come to pledge her life to him, she couldn't be more ready.

She started down the aisle.

Her father pulled her to a stop. At the sight of the concentrated intensity on his face, she felt her stomach clutch. He had something important to say to her, something that he wasn't quite sure how to voice.

She waited, impatient for him to break his silence.

"Are you sure this is what you want?" he asked at last.

Fanny glanced to the front of the church, her gaze uniting with Jonathon's once again. His eyes were filled with promises, promises she knew he would do everything in his power to keep.

If she'd had any doubts before, they vanished beneath the silent assurances she caught pooled in his eyes.

There were no guarantees, Fanny knew, but she also knew that with her love, and God's guidance, Jonathon would one day give her his entire heart.

She had to believe he would fully commit to their

marriage, and make their union real, preferably one day very soon.

Fanny wouldn't force his hand on the matter. She would not nag or cajole, but she wouldn't remain completely docile, either. Some things were worth fighting for, and her marriage to Jonathon lived at the top of that list.

For now, Fanny would take whatever he was willing to give her, and hope for the rest. "Yes, Daddy, I'm absolutely, positively sure this is what I want."

He tilted his head to the side and regarded her with a long, searching look.

"Truly," she added.

He nodded, obvious relief flickering along the edges of his gaze. "Then I wish you the same happiness I have with your mother."

Fanny remembered what her mother had said to her just this morning during the carriage ride over. *Where there is life, my dear, there is always hope.*

Hope. All Fanny needed was hope, which started with faith. One small leap of faith.

She lifted her foot to begin the march into her future with the man she loved. This time, her father didn't pull her back.

With a quick glance to the left, then to the right, Fanny took note of the people packed shoulder to shoulder in the pews. The majority of her family was here, Mrs. Singletary, of course, as well as friends and other close relatives.

She caught her mother's eye.

Mary Mitchell looked happy, healthy and—praise God—was breathing easily. Her asthma seemed to be improving by the day. For that reason alone, Fanny had been right to accept Jonathon's proposal.

Her gaze returned to the front of the church. Marc Dupree stood like a sentry by Jonathon's side.

Jonathon had gone through most of his life alone, save for the four years he'd spent at Charity House. Four blessed years that had helped mold him into the man she loved. As she closed the final distance between them, Fanny made a silent promise to herself, and to Jonathon. She would spend the rest of her days making sure he knew he was loved.

The next few minutes passed in a blur. Pastor Beau asked who gave this woman away. Her father answered without pause, "Her mother and I."

Eyes shining, he kissed her cheek and then joined his wife in the front pew.

Jonathon took her father's place, reaching out his hand to her. Fanny placed her palm against his and let him draw her forward.

"Ready?" he whispered in her ear.

She smiled up at him. "I am more than ready."

Pastor Beau opened his Bible and began the ceremony.

"Dearly beloved, Jonathon Marc Hawkins and Francine Mary Mitchell have invited us to share in the celebration of their marriage." He paused to smile at Fanny, then Jonathon. "We, your family and friends, come together not to mark the start of your relationship, but to recognize the bond that already exists."

As the preacher continued, Fanny swiped surreptitiously at her eyes. Conflicting emotions rolled through her—joy and excitement, restlessness and anxiety. The combination made her stomach churn. She wasn't afraid, precisely, but…all right, yes, she was afraid, a little. What if Jonathon didn't come around to her way of thinking?

She didn't regret agreeing to marry him. She loved

him. But what if she couldn't convince him to make their union real?

Fighting back a wave of panic, she swung her gaze up to meet his. Her breath caught in her throat. He was watching her with tender affection.

The sweet expression helped allay her fears.

She gave in to a smile. Something quite wonderful passed between them, something that nearly stole her breath again.

Biting back a sigh, she quickly focused her gaze again to the front of the church. She really needed to pay attention to the words of the ceremony. Both she and Jonathon were about to make lifelong promises to one another.

Per the pastor's direction, her groom took her hand and repeated the first of their marriage vows. "I, Jonathon Marc Hawkins, take thee, Francine Mary Mitchell, to be my wife, to have and to hold from this day forward, for better, for worse, for richer, for poorer, in sickness and in health, to love and to cherish till death do us part."

His voice was strong, each word spoken with perfect diction. Fanny nearly believed he could love her.

She knew it would be unwise to allow her mind to wander toward something that could very well end in heartache.

Where there is life, my dear, there is always hope.

The preacher directed Fanny to repeat after him.

She did so with her chin high and her eyes locked with her groom's. "I, Francine Mary Mitchell, take thee, Jonathon Marc Hawkins, to be my husband, to have and to hold from this day forward, for better, for worse, for richer, for poorer, in sickness and in health, to love and to cherish till death do us part."

As she made each pledge, Fanny knew she would keep

every word. She would stick by Jonathon through each and every trial, no matter what joy or suffering lay ahead. She would work through any challenge with him—even if they had a child together.

Pastor Beau's strong, steady voice broke through her thoughts. "Will you, Jonathon, have Fanny to be your wife? Will you love her, comfort and keep her, and forsaking all other, remain true to her as long as you both shall live?"

"I will."

Fanny detected the confidence in his voice, the seriousness behind his vows. She also noted how Jonathon's eyes gleamed with genuine affection. Surely, love was but a step away.

Pastor Beau shifted his stance and presented Fanny with the same questions he'd just asked of Jonathon.

She responded directly to her groom. "I will."

Jonathon clasped her hand and squeezed gently.

Her world instantly became brighter.

Only when he pulled his hand away did she become aware of the preacher's voice once again.

"Before this gathering, Jonathon and Fanny have professed their devotion. They will now give each other rings to wear as a sign of their deep commitment."

Jonathon stretched out his hand to Marc, who passed him a pretty gold band. Eyes dark and serious, Jonathon took her hand in his.

"Fanny, I give you this ring as a symbol of our vows, and with all that I am, and all that I have, I honor you." He slipped the gold band on her finger. "With this ring, I thee wed."

Fanny looked over her shoulder at Callie. At the sight of her sister's watery eyes, she felt her own fill. Firming her chin, she resolved to get through the rest of the ceremony without crying.

Callie handed over the ring Fanny had picked out for her groom weeks ago. She slipped it onto his finger and kept her hand over the band of gold.

"Jonathon, I give you this ring as a symbol of our vows, and with all that I am, and all that I have, I honor you. With this ring, I thee wed."

He smiled, then leaned so close to her she thought he was going to kiss her before given the go-ahead. Instead, he whispered in her ear. "I promise to do right by you, Fanny."

She treasured that final vow above all the others, because she knew he meant to keep his promise.

Everyone else faded away, leaving just the two of them.

"I'll never leave you," she whispered, not sure why she felt the need to say those words to him.

"Marriage is a gift from God," Pastor Beau said, straying slightly from the traditional service. "Fanny, Jonathon, through the sacredness of your vows you have become one with one another and God. I urge you to honor your commitment the way the Lord intended from the beginning. Be fruitful and multiply."

Be fruitful and multiply.

Prudent advice, straight out of the Word of God, and yet the words were like a dagger to Fanny's heart. Feeling like a fraud, she lowered her gaze. When she lifted her head again, Jonathon's eyes were different. He'd morphed into the stranger he'd once been, not the man she knew now.

The thought had barely materialized when the pastor continued with the ceremony.

"Let love rule your household," he said. "Hold fast to what is good and right and true. Outdo one another in showing love and mercy. And…" He paused, gave a self-deprecating laugh. "I think that's enough from this preacher for one day."

The gathered guests joined in his laughter.

Fanny and Jonathon simply stared at one another, neither moving, both caught in a suspended moment of shared consternation.

Unaware of the tension between them, the pastor placed his hands on their shoulders. "It is with great honor that I declare you husband and wife. Jonathon, you may kiss your bride."

Jonathon seemed to come back to himself at the pastor's instruction. Gaze somber, he placed a palm on Fanny's waist and drew her close.

Fanny wasn't sure what she saw in his dark, intense eyes. But when his lips pressed against hers, all her doubts and fears disappeared.

To Jonathon's way of thinking, this kiss with Fanny, their first as husband and wife, was filled with more emotion and feeling than all the others combined. He wanted to linger. Just a moment longer…

From a great distance, he heard Pastor Beau clear his throat, twice.

Slowly, reluctantly, Jonathon stepped back, away from Fanny, now his wife.

His wife.

By the sound of muffled snickering and actual hooting from a few of the Mitchell brothers, Jonathon figured he'd been a bit too enthusiastic with the obligatory kiss.

He gave Fanny an apologetic grimace.

She simply smiled. "Well done, Mr. Hawkins."

"Thank you, Mrs. Hawkins." He liked the sound of her new name rolling off his tongue.

Arm in arm, they turned and began their walk down the aisle.

Fanny's mother beamed at them from her perch on the front pew. Her father gave him a nod of approval.

Smiling at the people who were now his family, Jonathon continued guiding Fanny down the aisle. Each step pulled them toward an uncertain future, one they would face together as husband and wife.

Jonathon didn't know what awaited them in the days, weeks and years ahead, but he was determined to make their marriage a success.

At the back of the church, Fanny turned her face up to his.

She was so beautiful, so full of compassion and goodness. He wanted to believe all would turn out well.

But a sickening ball of dread knotted in the pit of his gut. He was going to let Fanny down, the truth of it as inevitable as snow falling in winter.

Smiling tenderly, Fanny touched his face. "I'm in this with you fully, Jonathon. I'm not walking away or letting you go, no matter what you say or do. I believe in you. I believe in us."

These were her real wedding vows, the ones that came straight from her heart. He had to blink to stop the tears in his eyes.

He wanted to be as confident as she, wanted to give her a similar pledge from the depth of his soul.

Overcome with emotion, and an unfamiliar surge of hope, he planted a tender kiss on the tip of her nose.

"I'll do everything in my power to be the husband you deserve."

"I can't ask for more."

She should. She should ask for much more from him.

After a moment of basking in her goodness, her purity of heart, Jonathon looked out over the church still full of family and friends. "Please, everyone, join us back at the hotel and celebrate our marriage with us."

Taking Fanny's hand, he escorted her to the carriage waiting for them outside the church. He climbed in behind her. The carriage dipped and swayed as he settled in the seat across from her.

He smiled at his beautiful bride. "And so begins our adventure as husband and wife."

"Not yet." She took his hand and yanked him onto the cushions beside her. Snuggling against him, she released a happy sigh. "*Now* the adventure begins."

Chapter Seventeen

The wedding reception lasted well into the evening hours. As they'd done for Mrs. Singletary's charity ball, many of the wedding guests had reserved rooms in the hotel. Jonathon predicted a long night.

He stood away from the main crowd gathered in the grand ballroom. Shoulder propped against the wall, he was content to watch the festivities from a distance.

His gaze followed Fanny as she wove from one group of guests to the next. She moved with natural grace, fresh and poised as a delicate flower that had found a way to bloom in the dead of winter. She'd worked her way past his defenses and had taken up residence in the darkest portions of his heart.

Despite their unconventional route to the altar, Jonathon couldn't say he was sorry to have Fanny for his wife. He felt more alive because of the vows he'd pledged to her, more awake, as if he were emerging from an unpleasant dream that had held him in its dark grip for far too long.

Already, after only a few hours with Fanny permanently united to him, the world made more sense. His footsteps were lighter, the air around him smelled sweeter and—

The air smelled sweeter?

Jonathon shook his head at the fanciful notion. Any more of this sappy introspection and he would find himself putting pen to paper in an effort to write verse in honor of his wife.

Him, a hardened street kid turned ruthless businessman, a worthy opponent in any fistfight, who'd maneuvered through every dark corner in the underbelly of Denver, had been reduced to poetic musings by a mere slip of a woman.

Then again, Fanny was no mere woman. She was confident and strong, bold and courageous, with a spine made of steel.

And now she was his wife.

Jonathon would share the rest of his life with Fanny Mitchell—no, Fanny *Hawkins*. By the grace of God, they would grow old together. An image of her in the distant future insinuated itself in his mind. She would be as beautiful to him in her dotage as she was to him now.

Jonathon would do anything—sacrifice everything— to make her happy. He adored her. He might even be in love with her.

Was he in love with Fanny?

It was too soon to tell. *Definitely* too soon.

Mouth tight, jaw clenched, he tried to calm his raging heartbeat. Sliding his gaze past Fanny helped.

The ballroom had a decidedly different feel for this party than the one hosted by Mrs. Singletary nearly a month ago. The atmosphere was more festive, while also being more relaxed.

Instead of elegantly dressed men and women twirling around the dance floor, people were gathered in small groups, talking, laughing and generally enjoying themselves.

But the most notable difference was the hordes of children in attendance. After a full day of being on their best behavior, many were growing tired of following the rules of decorum dictated by the adults. A few of the boys fidgeted, others tugged on their neck cloths. Some had already taken to poking each other.

Two of them began chasing a third boy in a circle; others soon joined them. A game of tag suddenly erupted in the center of the dance floor.

With a firm shake of his head, Jonathon alerted his hovering staff to let them play. The room was large enough to accommodate their antics without encroaching on the adult conversations.

Besides, the children's laughter was infectious. Jonathon would like nothing more than to join them. It had been far too long since he'd indulged in a rousing game of tag.

A smile tugged at his lips.

"Now that's the sight of a very happy groom. Does my heart good."

Mrs. Mitchell's pleased tone further improved his mood.

Smiling easier still, Jonathon pushed away from the wall. "How could I not be happy? I just married a woman nearly as beautiful as her mother."

Mrs. Mitchell's tinkle of laughter was its own reward.

"There is nothing I'd rather hear than flattery from a handsome young man, but my dear Mr. Hawkins—"

"Jonathon."

"Jonathon." She sent him a quick, lovely smile reminiscent of her daughter's. "Why are you hovering in the shadows instead of joining in the festivities?"

He decided to be truthful. "You have a large, extended family, Mrs. Mitchell, and I am bit—"

"Overwhelmed by the vast quantities of us?"

He laughed.

"It's not the numbers." He'd lived surrounded by hordes of boys and girls at Charity House. "It is more that I find myself besieged with too many people in one room who play very different roles in my life."

Her head tilted and she looked confused. "I'm not sure what you mean."

He expelled a breath. "I have known some of the people in this room since childhood. A few are new friends, many are old. And then there is…your family."

"Ah, now I understand."

"Do you?" He hardly understood himself what he was trying to say.

"But of course. You don't know where your new family fits into your very organized world. Everyone else has his or her place. The Mitchells do not. Adding to the confusion, there are…" she cast her gaze over the room "…quite a lot of us."

To his amazement she'd described the situation perfectly. "You are a very wise woman, Mrs. Mitchell. I have half a mind to put you in charge of my entire hotel empire."

"Tempting." She gave him a friendly nudge with her shoulder. "But keeping track of my grandchildren is more than enough work for me."

They shared a laugh, then turned as one to watch her grandchildren at play. One of Hunter's kids, the youngest boy—Christopher?—noticed them staring. He shot in their direction, a blur of shaggy blond hair and fast pumping legs in a tiny black suit.

Jonathon barely had time to scoop up the boy before he could slam into his grandmother. "Whoa, little man, what's the rush?"

Giggling, Christopher wiggled in his arms, then slapped Jonathon on the shoulder.

"Tag," the little boy shouted, loudly enough to be heard on the top floor of the hotel. "You're it."

Jonathon set him back on the ground, leaned over and tapped the boy's head. "Tag, *you're* it."

The kid blinked at him, once, twice, then a wide grin spread across his mouth.

"Okay." He sped off to find another victim, arms flaying, shouting, "I'm it. I'm it."

"You're good with children," Mrs. Mitchell noted.

Was he?

It'd been years since he'd spent any length of time around kids. Now that he thought about it, Jonathon decided he wasn't so much good with children as he understood them. They wanted very little from adults. A sense of safety. Authenticity. Honesty. Things Jonathon hadn't experienced himself until he'd moved into Charity House.

"You clearly like being around little ones."

Realizing he hadn't responded to Mrs. Mitchell's earlier comment, Jonathon nodded. "I suppose I do."

If he understood children, if he *liked* them, perhaps he wouldn't be such a terrible father, after all. Perhaps he might even make a decent one.

How would he ever know if he didn't take the risk?

"No frowning on your wedding day," Mrs. Mitchell scolded softly, patting his arm as Laney had done that morning. "The Mitchell brood isn't as daunting as we first appear. And for the record, we are pleased to call you one of us."

"Truly? But you hardly know me."

"You make Fanny happy. That goes a long way to softening even the most skeptical members of my family."

As if her words had the power to summon the "most skeptical," Fanny's brothers sauntered toward them. They each wore a version of the same stern, determined expression.

"Ah," Mrs. Mitchell said, spotting the men mere seconds after Jonathon had. "Here come my three handsome boys."

With a show of amused indulgence, Mrs. Mitchell greeted her sons by presenting her cheek to each of them. They each gave her a loud, smacking kiss. Then they swung their attention to Jonathon.

Deciding to take the first shot, er…lighten the mood, he lifted his hands in mock surrender. "No need to kiss my cheek. A handshake will do."

All three men went stock-still for the length of a single eye blink. Hunter cracked a smile first, followed a half beat later by Logan and Garrett. Soon all three men were giving Jonathon hearty backslaps.

"Welcome to the family, Hawkins." Hunter gave his shoulder a hard squeeze. "You already fit right in."

Jonathon was surprised at how intensely pleased he was by the statement. He now had five brothers. These oldest three, plus the other two who were attending university back East.

Knowing how these men worked, having watched them interact with one another, Jonathon adopted a dry, ironic tone, and said, "Lucky me."

Again, it was the exact right thing to say. All three Mitchell brothers laughed.

"Well done, Hawkins." Logan gripped his shoulder as his brother had just done. "You are officially my second-favorite brother-in-law, Reese only barely nudging you out because he's been around longer."

Shaking her head, Mrs. Mitchell looked from her sons to Jonathon and back again. "Yes, well, I'll leave you to your man talk."

Before she turned to go, she set her hand on Jonathon's shoulder and presented her cheek for him to kiss.

He did so without hesitation.

A whimsical smile crossed her lips as she wandered away.

The moment she was out of earshot, Hunter took on the role of family spokesman. "We actually came over for two reasons. The first is to welcome you into the family, the other to give you your wedding gift."

Wedding gift? The man couldn't have surprised Jonathon more if he'd called him out for a gunfight. "Fanny and I have everything we need."

"Everything you need, yes." Hunter gave him a meaningful look. "But not, I think, everything you want."

What Jonathon wanted was a wife he could not hurt, a wife he could not fail. Anything else, he could acquire on his own.

But then he remembered the land deal that had never come to pass. *Mitchell land stays in Mitchell hands.*

In the craziness of the day, he'd nearly forgotten his dream of creating a legacy for himself separate from his father.

The picture in his jacket pocket—*a reminder of where*

you really come from—told Jonathon he was already forging his own legacy.

"I have everything I need *and* everything I want." It was nothing short of the truth.

"Not yet." Hunter hitched his chin at the youngest Mitchell brother.

Garrett reached into his jacket pocket and pulled out a familiar pack of papers. The contract Jonathon had presented these three men the day before Mrs. Single-tary's charity ball.

"Go ahead," Logan urged. "Take it."

With the brothers staring at him expectantly, he in-stinctively reached out.

"I predict you'll be pleased with the terms."

He flipped through the agreement, skimming the fa-miliar words, taking in the changes, specifically the ri-diculous price of *one dollar*. On the final page, the three Mitchell names were scrolled across the bottom. All that was missing was Jonathon's signature.

"The land is yours," Hunter said, eyes glinting with good humor. "Assuming you can afford the asking price."

Before Jonathon could respond, Garrett added, "We'll support whatever you want to do with the property."

Carte blanche. The Mitchell brothers were giving him total freedom to develop the land however he wanted. Far more than he'd expected.

The victory felt hollow, but he couldn't think why.

He'd been planning this project for an entire year, ever since making the Denver Hotel Dupree his permanent residence. But it was as if he'd somehow lost something valuable, something he couldn't put a name to yet.

"I have a better idea." He thrust the contract back at Garrett. "Put the land in Fanny's name."

Surprise registered on two of the three faces. Hunter, however, simply nodded in approval. "Consider it done."

After the last guest left the ballroom, Fanny hid a yawn behind her hand. Given the late night giggling with Callie, coupled with the excitement of her wedding day, she was worn to the bone. If she didn't sit down soon she feared she would collapse in an embarrassing heap at her husband's feet.

Jonathon's soothing voice washed over her in a low, rumbling, masculine purr. "Tired?"

She shot a smile at him. "Exhausted, actually."

"It's been a long day for both of us." He took her hand and drew her out of the ballroom. "Time to head upstairs."

The warmth in his gaze brought a rush of anticipation. Dare she hope her husband would make their marriage real? On their wedding night?

Most brides didn't have to wonder about such matters. After all, the Lord had created marriage for intimacy between a husband and his wife. There was no shame in that, she told herself, even as her cheeks heated.

Ever the gentleman, Jonathon escorted her into the elevator and told the attendant to take them to the top floor. With their very avid audience of one, they kept a respectable distance from each other.

Oh, but Fanny was tired of being polite. She wanted to be Jonathon's wife, in every sense of the word.

Out of the corner of her eye, she cast a surreptitious glance in his direction. He looked so handsome in his formal wedding attire, the gray of his jacket nearly the same color as his eyes in the darkened elevator.

Always, Jonathon lived easily in his skin, no matter

what he was wearing or the situation in which he found himself. The impeccable clothing was merely drapery, elegant but inconsequential to the man beneath.

"Here we are," the attendant announced, releasing latches and sliding open the elevator door to the ninth floor, where Jonathon kept a suite of rooms.

Before exiting, Fanny made eye contact with the hotel employee. "Thank you, Harold."

"You're most welcome, Miss Mitchell, I mean..." he cleared his throat, slid a worried glance at Jonathon "... Mrs. Hawkins."

With Jonathon indicating she take the lead, Fanny stepped into the hallway. But not before she caught him handing Harold a bank note and then thanking him for his hard work on behalf of the hotel.

Fanny's heart swelled with affection. Her husband was such a generous man.

Her husband. She felt a rush of feminine pride that this man was hers.

Would she ever grow used to being married to him? She hoped not. She hoped she would always be full of this same sense of wonder whenever she looked at him.

"This way." Jonathon settled his hand on Fanny's lower back and escorted her to his—*their*—private suite on the top floor of the hotel.

He opened the door with his key and again directed her to take the lead.

She stepped inside the room.

For a moment, all she could do was blink in muted astonishment. This was her first glimpse into Jonathon's private world and it fell incredibly flat.

"I don't know what I expected but...*this*?" She stretched out her hand. "Isn't it."

Jonathon followed the direction of her gaze, narrowing his eyes as if trying to see his private domain from her perspective. "Would you like a tour?"

"I suppose." But what would be the point?

Though the space was certainly luxurious and spectacular, especially compared to the single-bed rooms, there was no sign of Jonathon anywhere. Gleaming woodwork adorned the walls. The dark grain contrasted perfectly with the rich burgundy and gold tones of the furniture and draperies. The elegant chairs and settees were upholstered with a swirling brocade pattern.

Tasteful restraint ruled the first bedroom he showed her, the muted ivory and green hues a pleasant divergence from the vibrant colors in the common areas.

The more Fanny followed Jonathon from room to room, the bleaker her heart grew. The cold, impersonal decor was clear evidence that her husband hovered on the fringes of life, not really connecting, but instead remaining cool and distant.

She remembered what her sister-in-law had said about him as a boy. *He kept a part of himself separate from the other children. He was friendly, but he didn't have a lot of friends.*

Nothing had changed for Jonathon, despite his financial wealth and business success.

Fanny longed to wrap her arms around him and chase away the memories of his childhood. She longed to show him he was not alone and that he was loved.

If only he would let her.

In strained silence, he led her into another bedroom, this one done in soothing tones of various blues.

"I thought you would claim this room for yourself. It's the largest and most comfortable." His lips curved in a gentle smile. "You may, of course, redecorate to your specifications. I'm thinking the colors are a bit masculine, however—"

"This is *my* room?" It appalled her to feel hot tears of disappointment gathering in her eyes.

"Unless you would prefer one of the others I have already shown you." He compelled her with only his eyes. "I want you to feel comfortable here, Fanny."

Didn't her husband realize that sharing his room would make her the happiest of all? That starting a family with him was what she wanted most in this world?

She'd seen him interacting with her nieces and nephews at various times throughout the day. He enjoyed children, more, she thought, than even he realized. He would be a good father. Fanny knew it. Annabeth knew it. It seemed everyone knew it except Jonathon himself.

Of course, now was not the time for that discussion.

"Where will you sleep?"

His eyebrows slammed together in masculine bafflement. "In my bedroom, of course."

"Which is where, precisely?" *Please don't say in another suite, or worse, on another floor.* Anything *but that.*

"My room is on the opposite side of the suite."

A moment of relief filled her. At least they would be living in close proximity. It was a start.

A very good start, indeed.

Summoning up her brightest smile, Fanny glanced around her new home and then back at her husband. "Thank you, Jonathon, this room will suit my needs perfectly."

For now.

Chapter Eighteen

Jonathon knew he was in trouble the moment Fanny turned docile and compliant. She was many things, but neither of those came to mind.

What was she up to?

He eyed her cautiously. "I'll have your belongings brought up from the other suite in the morning."

Her smile never wavered. "That'll be fine."

The overly polite response put him further on guard. "Is there anything else you'll want or need?"

"Not at the moment, no." She took a step toward him.

He took a step back and cleared his throat. "I thought we would share a late supper before we call it a night. I had room service deliver an assortment of cold meats and—"

"That sounds perfectly wonderful."

"I haven't finished telling you what I ordered for us."

Still smiling, she closed the distance between them and placed her hand on her chest. "I'm sure whatever the chef sent up will meet with my expectations."

Her low, accommodating voice poured warmth over the tense moment.

Jonathon quickly strode back to the main sitting area, where the staff had set up a small, intimate table for two.

An overabundance of meats, cheeses, breads and sugary confections were arranged in an artful display. Candlelight completed the romantic setting.

Fanny took her time examining the fare. She circled the table, running her fingertip along the edge of the pristine white linen cloth. Jonathon stood transfixed by her beauty. Her hair glimmered beneath the glow of the fire that snapped in the hearth.

"The setup is quite lovely, Jonathon."

Not nearly as lovely as Fanny was, swathed in golden firelight.

He cleared his throat again. "Would you prefer to eat here at the table? Or we could fill our plates and relax in the chairs over by the fireplace."

"I should think either option sufficient." The words sounded like cream in her soft, feminine voice.

Something inside him snapped. "Could you stop being so agreeable?"

Amusement entered her eyes. "You would wish me to be contrary instead?"

"Of course not." He drew in a sharp, impatient breath. "I wish…"

"You wish…?" she prompted, when he held his silence.

His breath stalled in his lungs.

What a picture she made, innocence and purity itself in her pretty wedding dress. He didn't regret marrying her, but he feared she would grow to regret marrying him. And that would be a tragic day, indeed. He felt as though he was seeing her for the first time, with the eyes of a husband.

He was in big trouble.

"Come here, Jonathon." With the faintest trace of nerves shadowing the move, she lifted her arms.

The emotion that swept through him when he pulled her into his embrace was like an unexpected thunderstorm that blew in out of nowhere, then was suddenly gone, leaving nothing but a sense of calm in its wake.

"Fanny." He buried his face in her hair, breathed in her scent of lilacs and mint.

Fanny belonged in his arms, in his life.

For a terrifying moment, he could hear nothing but the voice of his father on their first meeting. *You were a mistake never meant to happen.*

Jonathon knew it was a lie.

Fanny had taught him to see past the deception.

He kissed the top of her head, stroked her hair. When she pulled back to look at him, he lowered his mouth to hers.

The kiss started gentle, but it quickly got out of hand. He immediately set her away from him.

"Jonathon?" Confusion filled her eyes.

"Don't look at me like that."

"How am I looking at you?"

He put his back to her, speared a hand through his hair. It was easier to have this conversation without meeting her gaze. "You are looking at me as if you want the one thing I warned you I couldn't give."

"Oh, Jonathon, you're both right *and* wrong. I do want something from you." She threw her arms around his waist and pressed her cheek to his back. "I want you to know you aren't alone anymore. You'll *never* be alone again. I am here with you, always and forever."

Her words whipped through him like a balmy gust of wind. "I believe you."

He attempted to shift away from her.

Making a sound of protest deep in her throat, she worked her way around him until they were facing each other again.

No one had ever looked at him the way she regarded him now, as if she had every faith in him, as if he was the answer to all her hopes and dreams.

He had no armor against that look.

To keep from reaching out to her, he clenched his fists behind his back. He must not touch her. Not until they came to an understanding.

"You're tired." He saw the truth of it in the slight slump of her shoulders and the drooping of her eyelids. "Perhaps we should set aside any serious conversation until morning."

"No." She jammed her hands on her hips. "There's more to discuss."

She was quite spectacular glaring at him, her eyes full of purpose in the dazzling firelight.

He swallowed a grin. "All right, Fanny, have your say."

His agreement took all the iron out of her spine.

Sighing softly, she lowered her hands to her sides. "You are very good at keeping your distance from others, but it isn't necessary with me. One day you will know I speak the truth."

He knew it now and wondered why he continued fighting the inevitable. He could never have a marriage in name only with this woman.

As if coming to a similar conclusion, she whispered his name. "Will you do me the honor of making me your wife?"

His very soul wavered between battle and surrender.

If he did as she asked, if he made their marriage real, he feared he would eventually let her down. Maybe not today, or even tomorrow, but sometime in the future.

"Once we cross this line," he warned, "we can never go back."

"Jonathon, we crossed the proverbial line when we said our wedding vows. All that is left is making the commitment final."

A low rumble moved through his chest, sounded in his sharp intake of air.

"We have both had a long, tiring day," he said. One he didn't want to end anytime soon. But he needed to give her one last chance to retire to her own room. "You may still say good-night and I will let you alone."

In answer, she took his hand and smiled. "The tour of my new home is not yet complete. There is still one room you haven't shown me."

The only room he hadn't shown her was his bedroom. As the meaning of her words became clear, a slow grin spread across his lips.

Jonathon scooped his bride into his arms.

By morning, Fanny would be his wife in every sense of the word. For her sake, he prayed he wasn't making a terrible mistake.

The next three months were the happiest of Fanny's life. She was a blissfully married woman. Jonathon was turning out to be a very good husband. Their relationship grew stronger every day.

Now, as she sat behind her desk and reviewed next week's bookings at the hotel, Fanny allowed a smile to spread across her lips. She was completely, wonderfully in love with her husband.

She hadn't said the words out loud. Not yet, but soon, she told herself, when she felt Jonathon was ready to hear them. Perhaps once spring chased away the last of the winter chill Fanny would unveil the full contents of her heart.

For now, she showed her feelings for her husband in countless other ways. In the brush of her hand across his cheek before they fell asleep at night. In the notes she left on his desk beneath papers for him to find. Or simply wrapped in one of her smiles.

Though there were moments when she felt as though Jonathon still held a portion of himself back from her, she knew that tendency would go away in time.

Fanny had no doubt he cared for her. He might even love her. Like her, he displayed his affection in ways other than words. In the gentle way he spoke her name. In the unexpected moments he showed up at her office and whisked her away for one of their delightful walks.

There was one thing missing in her life with Jonathon, one thing that would make her joy complete. A child. Jonathon's child.

Fanny set down her pencil and placed her hand over her flat stomach. Would she ever feel a baby's kick against her palm?

Annabeth and Hunter had welcomed their newest family member three weeks after Fanny's wedding, a little boy named Sean, who had his mother's dark hair and his father's amber eyes.

Garrett and Molly's baby was due in another two months. Now that Mary Mitchell's asthma was under control, Fanny's parents planned to travel to Saint Louis for the birth. They would stay only two weeks, then head home in time to welcome Callie and Reese's child into the world.

It was baby season in the Mitchell clan. And Fanny couldn't help but yearn.

Her stomach performed a sickening roll. Suddenly, her office felt small and overly hot. This wasn't the first time she'd felt the sensation. Over the past week, Fanny had battled bouts of queasiness at the oddest moments. Perhaps she was coming down with something. The flu had been making its rounds through the hotel staff.

Her head grew light. She needed to breathe in fresh air. Maybe she could entice Jonathon to join her for a brief stroll.

Swallowing back a wave of dizziness, she stood, left her office and made her way to Jonathon's. She found his assistant standing in the doorway, nose buried in the notepad he kept with him always.

"Is he in?" she inquired.

Burke Galloway looked up. "I'm sorry, Mrs. Hawkins, you just missed him. He had a meeting at Mr. Bennett's office across town."

"Oh, that's right." Before they'd left their suite this morning, Jonathon had mentioned having an appointment with Reese concerning a recent land acquisition.

"Was there anything I could do for you?"

"No, thank you, Mr. Galloway. I'll come back later."

Still feeling a bit light-headed, Fanny decided to take a short walk, anyway. After retrieving her coat and gloves, she left the hotel through the front doors and breathed in the cool air. Lifting her face to the sky, she concentrated on the glorious blue overhead. Her nausea almost immediately disappeared.

Just as she lowered her gaze, a masculine voice reached her ears. "Miss Mitchell, may I join you on your walk?"

A prickle of unease navigated up her spine. "I am Mrs. Hawkins now."

"Of course, my apologies. May I join you on your stroll… Mrs. Hawkins?" As he made his request a second time, Jonathon's father stood unmoving. The air around him crackled with arrogance.

Lowering her lashes to cover her surprise at his sudden appearance, Fanny couldn't help but wonder what Judge Greene wanted with her. Even acknowledging him made her feel as though she was betraying Jonathon.

But when she looked more closely, she saw the signs of strain on the judge's face. He looked older and somehow less sure of himself, despite the arrogant tilt of his head. From what Fanny had heard, he was still holding to his story that he'd only recently learned that Jonathon was his son.

It was on the tip of her tongue to tell him what she truly thought of him. But then she remembered the portion of the Bible she'd read just this morning during her daily quiet time. The Lord commanded His children to love their enemies.

She should at least give it a try. But, truly, it was times such as these that Fanny wished she didn't know Scripture quite so well.

Jaw tight, she gave a short nod. "You may have five minutes of my time."

"Thank you, my dear."

Love thy enemy, she reminded herself.

Her clenched jaw began to ache.

The judge gestured with his hand for her to continue walking. When she did, he fell into step beside her.

She could not fault his manners.

Gaze locked on the mountains in the distance, she expected him to speak. Surprising her yet again, he seemed content to walk beside her in silence.

She was not so patient.

Fanny stopped, waited for him to do the same, before saying, "State your business, Judge Greene."

"I have a request to make of you, Mrs. Hawkins."

She pursed her lips into what she hoped was a bored expression. "I'm listening."

"I wish to make amends with my son."

"What does that have to do with me?"

Stuffing his hands in his pockets, he lifted an elegantly clad shoulder. "He refuses to speak with me, no matter how many overtures I make. I have come to ask you to intercede for me."

Shocked by his colossal nerve, she stared at him. "You cannot be serious."

"I assure you, I am." He crowded her as he spoke, moving around her like a hawk circling its prey.

She backed up a step, and another, and then several more, until she found herself against a brick wall.

"Even if I had the sort of influence on my husband you seem to think, I would never wield it in such a manner. I am sorry, Judge Greene, you are on your own."

"All I'm asking is that you drop a kind word on my behalf."

She dismissed his request with a delicate sniff. "You ask too much."

"It is but one small kindness."

Did he not recognize the hypocrisy in his words?

"Where was your kindness to my husband when he was a boy and came to you for help?"

The judge quirked an eyebrow at her. "I see my son has told you much."

"Jonathon has told me enough to know you showed him no compassion when he was in need. Yet you ask me for the very consideration you refused to give him." She realized that she could not love this particular enemy, no matter how hard she tried. "We are through here. I wish you a good day."

She started to push around him.

He stepped directly in her path. "I need an heir."

"You have an heir."

"Joshua is a disappointment. I have tried to contain his excesses. I have forbidden him to carry on with his mistress, yet he continues and has even produced an illegitimate child. I will not encourage his willful disobedience any longer." A muscle worked in the judge's jaw. "I have cut him off, once and for all."

Fanny blinked at the vast amount of information the man had supplied. One point seemed painfully clear. "So now that your legitimate son has disappointed you, you think to make Jonathon your heir?"

"Of course not." Outrage filled every hard plane of the older man's face. "Your husband is the by-blow of a prostitute and therefore unfit to carry my name."

Appalled, Fanny treated the judge to a withering glare. "He is your son."

"That is true. More to the point, he made the very wise decision to marry you, a woman of impeccable breeding from a prominent ranching family." His gaze dropped to her midsection. "I wish to name the first male child you bear as my official heir."

Fanny's hand instinctively covered her stomach. "You cannot claim my child as your heir over your own son."

The injustice horrified her. Just how many ways could this man hurt Jonathon?

"My hope is in the next generation. Josh's wife has proved barren. It is up to you, Mrs. Hawkins, to carry on my legacy."

Hand still on her stomach, she stumbled backward. Only once she caught her balance did she realize Judge Greene had somehow maneuvered her several feet down a darkened alley.

"Your child will be my grandson. He will carry my blood." The odious man leaned over her, his sense of entitlement easy to read in his eyes, even in the shadows.

Joshua Greene was truly a selfish man, clinging to a twisted logic that made sense only to him. He would go after what he wanted, regardless of the people he hurt in the process.

Fanny jerked her chin at him. "I am not afraid of you."

But she *was* afraid. She was afraid for her husband, afraid for what this would do to Jonathon. His father would deny him his birthright in favor of his own son.

Lord, may we only have girls.

"Will you help me, Mrs. Hawkins? Will you encourage your husband to meet with me about this matter?"

A gasp flew from her mouth. She had no doubt this man would do everything in his power to make his desire a reality.

Fear held a tight grip on her, paralyzing her in place.

Now she understood the depth of Jonathon's pain and why he was so determined never to father a child. Fanny closed her eyes, her heart squeezing in sorrow, because a part of her agreed with his decision.

"What if Jonathon and I choose not to have children? What will you do then?"

Momentary fury flashed in the judge's gaze. "You arrogant, self-righteous chit."

"Name-calling will not soften me to the idea of— Oh!"

Without warning, she was swept into the strong, familiar arms of her husband. Relief made her heart beat faster. She'd never been happier to see Jonathon. She barely had time to catch her breath before he maneuvered her against the brick wall, then stood in front of her, using his body to protect hers.

"Are you all right?" An edge of danger burned in his narrowed eyes, in his too-calm voice. "Did he hurt you?"

"No, no. Jonathon, I am completely unharmed."

He lowered his gaze over her, searching, measuring. When his eyes met hers again, her stomach filled with spears of ice. She hardly recognized the man standing before her. He had a quiet, lethal edge she'd never seen in him.

This was the man who'd survived on the harsh streets of Denver by any means possible.

Hand shaking, Fanny reached up to cup his face, hoping to soothe away the rage simmering in his gaze. His eyes burned hotter still and she dropped her hand, regretting ever leaving the hotel.

Instead of making the situation better, Jonathon's arrival had made matters much, much worse.

Chapter Nineteen

Jonathon struggled to calm his breathing. Rage ran cold as ice in his veins, leaving an empty vacuum in his soul dark as the alley in which they stood. He'd never felt this vicious, territorial emotion before. But no one had ever threatened Fanny like this, either.

He widened his stance, wishing he could be on all sides of her. He continued searching for injury, relieved to find none.

When he'd caught sight of Greene pulling his wife into the alley, Jonathon had been all the way across the street. Too far. He'd broken into a run, petrified for his wife's safety.

"Jonathon." Fanny's voice washed over him, soft and soothing, a warm, unexpected breeze in the cold, harsh air. "Our business is concluded here. We can head back to the hotel now."

She took his hand and tugged him toward the busy street ahead, away from the dark alleyway, from the past, from everything he wanted to forget. For several steps, he let Fanny guide him along, wanting the light that defined her, needing it more than air.

The bright sunlight beckoned, washing over Fanny, amplifying the blond streaks in her hair and displaying a dozen shades of gold.

"You are being overly dramatic." Greene's disapproving grunt hummed in the air. "The chit is perfectly fine."

With one fluid motion, Jonathon swung around, grabbed his father by the lapels and dragged him forward until their faces were inches apart. "Never come near my wife again. Do you understand?"

Greene's mouth went flat and hard, but he didn't struggle under Jonathon's hold. "There's no cause for violence. Your wife and I were having a pleasant conversation about the future."

"What did you say to her?"

"If you would unhand me, we could speak as civilized human beings rather than back-alley brutes."

The dig hit its mark, bringing up disturbing, dangerous images from his youth. Jonathon could feel his rage return, unraveling through him like a sticky spider web. But he was not the brute his father claimed. Not anymore. Violence was not a part of who he was now.

Filled with disgust for himself, as well as the man who'd sired him, he slowly, deliberately, released Green's coat and stepped back, palms raised in the air.

"Jonathon." Fanny's sweet, lyrical voice came from behind him. "Take me home. Please, I want to go home."

Over his shoulder, he looked at her, saw the plea in her gaze. But he wasn't through with his father.

"We will leave once the judge answers my question." He turned back around and repeated, "What did you say to my wife?"

He wanted to know, but sensed the truth would enrage him further. The only words he'd caught—*arrogant, self-righteous chit*—had been enough to unleash his fury.

Eyebrows lifted in condescension, Greene straightened his jacket, tugged his waistcoat in place, then finally deigned to give a response. "I merely told her my plans for your—"

"Jonathon, please." Fanny grabbed his arm. "It's not important what your father and I discussed. It means nothing."

The look of distress in her gaze told its own story. Now he *knew* he wasn't going to like what his father had said to Fanny.

Jonathon returned his attention to Greene. "Continue."

"I believe this conversation would be better served if we conduct it in a less unseemly environment. Let us follow your wife's suggestion." Green spoke in the tone of a man used to giving orders and having them obeyed. "And congregate inside the comfort of your hotel."

"We'll talk here."

"Very well, if that is what you wish."

"It is."

With a murmur of assent, Greene nodded. "I was hoping your wife would speak to you on my behalf."

"Why?"

For the first time the older man looked uneasy. "I wish to sit down and discuss the future of our family."

Feeling cold as ice and empty as a moonless night, Jonathon demanded, "What about it?"

His eyes shifting right, then left, Greene hesitated, as if to gather his thoughts. When he spoke, his voice came out smooth and confident. "It is my deepest desire to claim your firstborn son as my heir."

"No."

"I'm afraid it is already done. I had my will rewritten a month ago. Your son will carry on my legacy through future generations."

Legacy. The word ricocheted through Jonathon's mind like a stray bullet. His skin burned beneath his clothes. This bland, lifeless emotion rolling through him was grief, grief for the life he and Fanny might have had if only Joshua Greene wasn't his father.

Jonathon knew what he had to do, had always known it would come to this. He'd fooled himself into believing otherwise.

"I vow, this very day, that your immoral, godless legacy will die with you." He made the proclamation softly, his tone so low the judge had to lean in closer to hear him. "You will have no heir from me."

"No." Fanny rushed to him. "No, Jonathon, do not say such a thing. Nothing has to be decided today."

The decision had been made long before he'd met his beautiful wife.

"Let us be done with this conversation." With her face leached of color, her brow creased in worry, she reached across the small divide between them and grabbed his hand, squeezing hard. "Come away with me now."

Greene continued talking, spouting off the grand plans he had for Jonathon's future son. Jonathon tuned out the words and, hand in hand with Fanny, stepped out of the darkness.

The bright, afternoon sunlight brought no warmth to his cold soul. He felt hollow inside, a shell of a man sleepwalking through life.

They made their way down the street in silence, their

steps slow. People strolled past them, moving and living at a different speed.

Mind numb, Jonathon looked down at Fanny, then at their joined hands. His heart gave a quick, extra hard thump. Barely three months earlier he'd vowed to love, cherish and protect this woman. In the days since, she'd filled his life to completion. Her smiles, her voice, her laughter…he couldn't get enough of them.

In her presence, he'd come to believe he could overcome his past. But his past had caught up with him today. In the form of a selfish man who would do whatever necessary to forward his own agenda.

"Fanny." Hating that she'd witnessed the darker pieces of his soul, Jonathon released her hand. "What were you doing on the streets alone with my father?"

She lowered her head and sighed. "It was quite by accident, I assure you. I certainly never planned to run into him."

"I never thought otherwise."

She sighed again. "I wanted a bit of fresh air and so I went for a short walk. I'd barely left the hotel when he came up behind me." She lifted her gaze, her face pulled in a delicate frown. "He must have been waiting for me. Or you."

"I'm sorry he accosted you in public."

"It would have been equally reprehensible in private."

She released an unladylike sniff and increased her pace, all but stomping last night's snowfall into mush. "He looked rather terrible, as if he hasn't slept in weeks. Some dark part of my nature finds that quite heartening. But we won't discuss him anymore, at least not out here on the street."

Smoothly assuming control, Fanny gripped Jonathon's

hand again and pulled him through the entrance of the hotel.

A group of guests passed, looking curiously at their clasped hands. Neither of them broke stride.

Halfway through the lobby, Jonathon took over the lead. "We'll talk upstairs, where we won't be interrupted."

"I was just about to suggest the same thing."

They were stopped several times by staff with questions and concerns. Jonathon brushed the bulk of them off with a promise that he would be back in his office within the hour.

Neither he nor Fanny spoke again until they were alone in their suite.

While she discarded her coat, hat and gloves, Jonathon looked around the room. Fanny was everywhere, her personal touch apparent in the homey details she'd added to make the suite their home.

Fresh flowers spilled out of crystal vases. Light, airy watercolors by local artists covered the walls. A spattering of hairpins had been left on a side table. The novel Fanny had been reading last night before they'd retired for the evening sat open on the overstuffed settee.

He and Fanny had fallen into a happy rhythm that included work and laughter and joy.

Neither had realized they'd been living on borrowed time.

Heavyhearted, Jonathon walked slowly to the empty hearth, lowered himself to his haunches and began laying a fire.

"That can wait."

His hands stilled over the logs, but he didn't rise to his feet.

With the grace that defined her, Fanny settled on the hearth rug beside him. She filled the moment with her scent, her soft smile. Her very presence wrapped around him like a warm hug.

"Talk to me, Jonathon."

He worked his response around in his mind, considered each word carefully. "I think it's safe to say we will never be rid of my father. He is determined to tie his legacy into mine."

Jonathon held Fanny's stare, willing her to understand the meaning behind his words.

She simply blinked at him.

"That is something that must never come to pass. Joshua Greene will not have the opportunity to poison another generation. I won't allow it."

His bone-deep sorrow was mirrored on Fanny's face. "What…what are you saying?" she asked.

"I will not, under any inducement, father a child."

Alarm shot through Fanny, making her head grow dizzy and her stomach churn. She was helpless when confronted with Jonathon's determined reasoning.

Joshua Greene will not have the opportunity to poison another generation.

She searched desperately for a compelling argument to change her husband's mind. She couldn't think of one. It was an impossible situation, because a part of her understood—and sympathized—with Jonathon's decision.

But it was a decision made in the heat of the moment, after a very tense encounter.

"My father taught me that decisions must always be made from a place of strength, not emotion. Thus, we shall table this conversation until we are both feeling a little less emotional."

Giving him no chance to argue, she hopped to her feet and brushed off her skirt. She managed to take one step, two. By the third, Jonathon's voice stopped her.

"I won't change my mind, Fanny. It is a decision I made long before I met you."

She slowly pivoted around to meet his gaze. She found herself staring at his chest. When had he risen to his feet?

Craning her neck, she attempted her brightest smile. "Perhaps, one day, you will change your mind. I can be quite persuasive."

It was the wrong thing to say.

His guard went up, the invisible wall between them as impenetrable as if constructed out of granite.

"I meant what I said. Judge Greene's wickedness will not influence another generation."

"We will deny him access to our children."

"He will find a way. Take, for example, today's sequence of events. He managed to get to you."

She had no ready response.

Jonathon pounced on her momentary silence. "The only way to ensure he doesn't get to our children would be for us to move our main residence to another city. Are you willing to leave your home, your family, *your mother* so that we can have a family of our own?"

His voice sounded so empty, so devoid of emotion.

"We can find a way. With God all things are possible. We cannot let your father win. We can—"

"Can we?"

Fanny's heart dropped to her toes. Her husband had become an immovable force. What else could she say to sway him?

Nothing. There was nothing that would change his mind.

Her stomach took a sickening roll, the nausea so profound she had to take several breaths to keep from being sick. "Do you not want a child with me?"

He blew out a frustrated hiss of air.

Fanny used his brief silence to firm her own resolve. "Jonathon. Do you not want to see a child created from the both of us? Half you, half me, a human being uniquely made from our union?"

Such grief washed across his face Fanny thought he would capitulate rather than give in to the loss.

Any moment now, he would agree their child—the one only they could create together—was worth every risk, including the risk of his father's interference in their lives.

"You're right, Fanny. We should table this discussion. I have work waiting for me downstairs."

Looking as miserable as she felt, he walked around her and headed to the foyer.

"Jonathon, wait."

He paused, hand on the doorknob.

"Will you at least think about what I said?"

"My mind is made up." Turning around slowly, he studied her with eyes she could not read. It had been months since he'd given her that impenetrable look.

"I will sire no children," he said. "I told you this before we married."

This time, Fanny didn't need to read his expression to know he wouldn't budge on the matter. She heard the stubborn resolve in his voice.

Well, she was a Mitchell. Stubbornness was a hereditary trait that came part and parcel with the name. "How will you prevent me from conceiving a child? Will you—"

He never let her finish. Moving with lightning speed, he closed the distance between them. She scarcely had time to breathe before she found herself enfolded in her husband's arms.

"I want a child with you, Fanny. I want an entire houseful. I want a family and a lifetime of happiness, but I *cannot* risk the possibility of Greene's poisonous influence on another generation."

Hope burst in her heart.

She knew what to say. She *finally* knew exactly what to say. "You keep speaking of your father's influence. But he's had no bearing on who you've become. I have seen you in every situation imaginable. I know who you are when you're tired and pushed to the limit. I know who you are when you are feeling lighthearted and amused. I even know who you are when your family is threatened. I saw it today in that alley."

His arms tightened around her.

She pressed her advantage. "The only power your father holds over us is what we surrender to him. I beg you, do not let him win."

Jonathon set her away from him. His throat working, he swallowed several times. "I have to go."

"Will you at least think about what I said?" she asked again.

He tilted his head as if considering her words. "Yes."

Striding away from her, he didn't speak again. A heartbeat later, the door shut behind him with a firm click.

Just like that, he was gone. With nothing between them solved.

Fanny's mouth trembled and she sobbed, just once.

"I love you," she whispered to the empty room, wishing she'd had the courage to say the words to Jonathon's face.

Would it have made a difference?

She would never know.

Her husband must come around to her way of thinking on his own, or not at all, and certainly not because she'd manipulated him with tender words of love.

A wave of heat lifted up from her stomach, making her head spin. She had to reach out and steady herself on a nearby table, or else give in to the nausea that had plagued her on and off all week.

She and Jonathon were at an impasse, with each of them set on their own course for the future and no hope of changing the other's mind.

Could their marriage survive?

Could Fanny survive?

Jonathon's nearness, without his full commitment to their marriage, would tear her apart bit by bit. To see him, to speak to him, but never to be close to him again would prove torture.

And what would happen to him?

He would pull away from her and distance himself completely, first physically, then emotionally. Joshua Greene's legacy would live on in the worst possible way imaginable.

Fanny hurt for her husband. *Lord, what do I do?*

She sank to her knees and did the only thing she could. She prayed.

Chapter Twenty

Jonathon charged into his office and slammed the door behind him with a wood-splintering crack. He moved around his desk, his mind still upstairs with Fanny. If he were a less cynical man he would say his wife had looked at him moments ago with love in her eyes.

Maybe it was wrong, or even selfish of him to wish it were true, but if Fanny loved him, there must be more good in him than bad. More Marc Dupree than Joshua Greene.

Fanny had claimed his father had no bearing on who'd he become. Jonathon wanted to believe her. He wanted the promise of long, happy years as her husband. He wanted to love her with everything inside him, as a man loved his woman.

It was true, then. He loved Fanny. He loved his wife.

So many impulses flooded him. He wanted to rush back upstairs and profess his feelings.

He'd told her the truth just now. He desperately wanted to know the wonder of having a child with her, of staring into the face of a precious baby, equally comprised of them both. Which actually made his point for him.

Jonathon was the product of the people who'd made him, half his mother and half his father.

You are also the Lord's child.

The thought swept through him with such strength he collapsed onto the chair behind his desk.

He wasn't an accident. He wasn't a mistake. He'd come to grips with that, in his heart and in his head. But he couldn't run from his past, couldn't deny that any child he created with Fanny would also be Joshua Greene's grandchild.

Fanny claimed his father could wield only the power they surrendered to him. Perhaps she was right.

Perhaps it was time for Jonathon to put the past behind him once and for all. He needed to speak with Greene, set a few things straight. He would do so now.

Just as he stood, a knock came at his door.

"Enter."

His assistant quickly pushed into the room, a harried expression on his face. "An urgent telegram has arrived for you from San Francisco."

Jonathon read the short missive, felt his stomach drop. A main water pipe had broken, flooding the entire first floor. "I'll need to leave at once."

"I'll make the arrangements." Burke paused at the door, tilted his head as if studying a difficult puzzle. "Will you be traveling alone, Mr. Hawkins, or will your wife be accompanying you on the journey to California?"

The question took him by surprise. Jonathon hadn't thought to have Fanny accompany him. Now that idea was in his head, he rolled it around. Once they took care of the problem at the hotel, he and Fanny could stay a few extra days in the city.

Jonathon could show his wife San Francisco, the city

he'd found fascinating enough to build his fourth hotel there. He could take Fanny to all his favorite places. They could eat at five-star restaurants and walk hand in hand on the shores of the bay. He would fall in love with her all over again. When they retired for the evening, he wouldn't be able to keep his distance from the woman he loved with all his heart.

But the matter of children wasn't yet settled. There could be no more marital relations until final decisions were made.

Perhaps it was best to leave Fanny at home. Time away might actually help the situation.

"I will be traveling alone," he told his assistant, who stood patiently waiting for his response.

"Very good, Mr. Hawkins."

"Once you make the arrangements for my trip, alert Mrs. Singletary of the problem at the San Francisco Hotel Dupree." The widow owned one-quarter of his hotel empire. This situation affected her as much as Jonathon.

"I'll head to her house this afternoon and give her the news myself."

"I'm sure she'll appreciate that." Jonathon didn't need to give further instructions to his assistant. Burke Galloway already knew what to do in his absence.

When he was alone once more, Jonathon gathered the necessary papers and other accoutrements he would need to conduct business in San Francisco for the next several weeks.

All that was left was to go upstairs and pack his clothes.

Fanny was just coming out of the washroom when he stepped inside their suite. She'd restyled her hair and her features looked clean and bright, as if she'd recently splashed water on her face.

Jonathon had always thought his wife beautiful, but right now she glowed. In the way spring chased away winter, she'd chased away his loneliness and had brought light into his life. He didn't want to lose her.

"Oh, Jonathon." She ran to him and flung her arms around his waist. "I knew you'd come back."

She sounded as if he'd been gone for months, when in reality it had been just shy of a half hour.

"There's a problem at the San Francisco Hotel Dupree." He set her away from him and briefly explained the situation with the water pipe. "I have to leave town immediately."

"Of course you do. Something this major requires your personal attention."

She was so understanding, so calm, his love for her swelled in his chest. He wanted to hold her close, to make promises, to tell her that he could be the man she needed, and she could have the life she'd always dreamed of—with him. Only him.

But there was still too much uncertainty and darkness inside his bitter soul, none of which he could allow to spill onto her.

"Would you…" Studying the runner at her feet, she dug her toe into the swirling pattern. "Would you like me to help you pack?"

"No." Emotion coiled in his muscles, tightened in his stomach. He speared a hand through his hair, shocked at the raw, shattered tone of his own voice.

Her head lifted, revealing the hurt in her eyes.

"Oh." She looked away. "All right. I will leave you to it, then."

She turned toward the door, but he caught her by the

hand. "I don't need help packing, but I would very much like you to keep me company."

Her smile came lightning fast. "I would like that, too."

Fanny stood at the threshold of Jonathon's dressing room and silently watched him pack. His movements were stiff and impatient as he filled a medium-sized valise with various articles of clothing and personal items.

She knew he was still upset, but he'd erected a hard exterior to hide behind. The one he'd once worn as naturally as a medieval knight wore his suit of armor.

Was the cause of her husband's distance their conversation about children? Or was the problem with the San Francisco hotel the source?

Perhaps it was a little of both.

The thought of him leaving her with the tension still so strong between them was breaking her heart. She feared if he left Denver now, their marriage might never be able to recover.

Surely, he must be struggling with similar thoughts. And yet he hadn't asked her to join him on this trip. Fanny fought to remain outwardly calm, even as terror slid an icy chill down her spine.

"Why are you letting your father win?"

"I'm not leaving town because of my father. I told you why I have to go."

Her heart began to thump fast and hard and her stomach twisted in another sickening knot of dread. She thought she might be ill, right here, in her husband's dressing room.

She pulled in several tight breaths until the terrible sensation passed.

"Take me with you." She spoke so softly she wondered if he heard her.

Her doubts were dispelled when he looked up, his hand hovering over the contents of his luggage. "That wouldn't be wise."

"Why not?"

With a quick sweep of his hand, he shut the valise. "We need this time apart." Face expressionless, he secured the buckles. "To decide, individually, what we want from our marriage."

How could they decide such a thing individually? Marriage was a partnership, with two people making decisions together.

He was leaving her. Nothing else explained his refusal to take her with him.

Something bleak and angry rose up from her soul. The depths of the emotion would shock everyone who knew her, perhaps even Jonathon himself. It certainly shocked her. Enough that she again thought she might be sick.

She swallowed back the nausea. "You mean *you* need time away from *me* to decide what you want for your future. I already know what I want. Take me with you."

He moved past her and set the suitcase on the floor in the hallway. Then, eyes grim, he made the short trek back to where she stood. "There is only one thing that would induce me to ask you to join me."

"Name it."

"You come with me as my business associate, not my wife."

Sucking in a shocked breath, Fanny reared back. "You can't mean—"

But he did. She saw it in his cold, distant expression. Casting aside all pride, she lunged herself at her husband.

As if expecting the move, he caught her against his chest. Her pleasure at being near him trumped the terrible pain swirling in her stomach. She was all feeling at that moment, her emotions closer to the surface than she wished to show her husband.

Recklessly, she pressed her mouth to his. His hold tightened around her and he kissed her back.

I love you. I love you. I love you. Her mind silently screamed the words in her head, over and over and over again. Then came the more desperate plea. *Don't leave me.*

Did she have the courage to make the humiliating request?

It was some time before Jonathon eventually set her away from him. Heavy emotion weighed heavy between them.

They both gasped for breath and stared at one another, wide-eyed.

Fanny's heart was full of love for her husband and she knew he loved her in return. She saw it in his tortured expression, in the rapid rise and fall of his chest.

"Take me with you," she repeated, "as your wife."

"You know my terms."

She couldn't go with him as only a business associate. But she feared if he went to San Francisco without her, he might never return. Not the man she married, at any rate. A stranger would appear in his place, and then nothing would ever be the same. "And you know mine."

He nodded. "We'll talk more when I get back." He brushed a brief kiss to her forehead. "I'll return as quickly as I can, I promise you that."

She thought she might weep.

He picked up the valise and maneuvered around her.

"I will send a telegraph alerting you to the date of my return."

She made no sound, made no attempt to respond. She was too stunned that he would give up on her, *on them*, like this. She was cold to the bone. No amount of rubbing her arms warmed them.

Dimly, she heard Jonathon's footsteps move down the hallway, through the parlor, then into the foyer. The door opened and closed with a soft click. That was it.

Her husband was gone.

Only then, when she was completely alone, did Fanny acknowledge the nausea roiling in her stomach. She rushed into the washroom and gave in to the churning illness.

At least Jonathon wasn't here to see her brought low.

As the first week of Jonathon's absence turned into two, and he still didn't return or send a telegram, Fanny's sickness grew worse. She found herself wanting to sleep all the time. The sight of food made her ill. The only thing that seemed to settle her stomach was weak tea and a few bites of toast.

This is what grief feels like, she thought, wishing Jonathon would come home soon. They couldn't heal their rift if he wasn't here.

In the meantime, she put on a brave face. It proved quite a feat to swallow her nausea this morning, but Fanny eventually managed to get herself dressed for the day. She made it down to her office, and even managed to get some work done.

Not more than an hour into reviewing next month's employee schedules, she found the names and numbers beginning to blur. Though it was barely past ten o'clock,

Fanny decided she needed to retreat to her room for a quick lie down.

She'd barely set down her quill when Callie poked her head into the office. "I've come to unchain you from your desk."

Fanny sat back in her chair and studied her sister. "You have remarkable timing. I was just contemplating the wisdom of a short break."

"Then I'm not disturbing you."

"Not at all." She stood, but moved too fast and nearly lost her balance. Leaning on her desk, she calmed her spinning head with a few deep breaths.

She forced a smile for her sister.

Smiling back, Callie glided into the room, her tiny, slightly rounded belly tenting her dress in a most becoming way. She was nearly six months along, but didn't look more than three.

"You are looking quite well," Fanny told her sister, dropping her gaze over Callie's emerald-green dress with the pretty ivory trim.

"Oh, Fanny, I am feeling very well, indeed, especially now that the horrible morning sickness is behind me." She made a face that reminded Fanny of the time when they were children and she'd dared Callie to eat an entire lemon.

"Was it really so terrible, those first few months?" Fanny would give anything to experience morning sickness, knowing it heralded the reward of giving birth to Jonathon's child.

"Horrible doesn't begin to describe it. For months I could keep nothing down but weak tea and toast. But now..." She twirled in a happy, laughing circle, her joy as rich as if she'd just been freed from a prison. "I have more energy than ever before and the terrible bouts of dizziness are completely gone."

Fanny's mind latched on to several words, her heart filling with the ache of desperate fear. Weak tea and toast? Lack of energy? Dizziness?

Her hand flew to her stomach. Could she be...was it even possible...

Of course it was possible.

Fear, hope, anger, joy, too many emotions to count tumbled through her. She wanted to laugh. She wanted to cry. She wanted to give in to every emotion all at once, and then start over again.

She was carrying Jonathon's child.

Just for a moment, she let herself revel in the wonder of it. Her eyes filled with tears. She'd been doing that a lot lately, getting overly emotional over the tiniest things.

A baby is not a tiny thing.

No, a child was a blessing straight from God.

How would Jonathon take the news? Would he think she'd done this on purpose, to trap him?

The first tendril of anguish twined through her happiness.

"...and it's such a beautiful spring day." Callie's voice came at Fanny as if from a great distance. "Let's head outdoors and enjoy the living harmony of—"

She broke off and rushed to Fanny.

"What's wrong? You've grown pale as chalk."

"I... I need to sit down."

Callie guided her to the chair behind her desk. "I'll get you some water."

"No." Fanny stopped her. "I just need a moment to catch my breath. While I do, would you describe again what you experienced during the early months after you realized you were carrying Reese's child?"

"Are you…" Callie's hand flew to your mouth. "Fanny, do you think you're—"

"You said you were tired a lot? And could stomach only weak tea and toast."

Eyes wide with mounting excitement, Callie nodded. "There were other symptoms, as well."

"Such as…?"

Blushing furiously, she explained about the physical changes in her body, changes Fanny had experienced but had thought were due to the strain of her husband's extended absence.

"Oh, Callie. I… I think I'm going to have Jonathon's baby."

"Why, that's wonderful news." Her sister hopped to her feet and pulled her into a fierce hug.

Tears of joy, of fear, of wonder formed in Fanny's eyes and spilled over in a choking sob.

"Do you know what this means?" Callie twirled away from her. "Our children will grow up together. They will be as close as siblings."

"That…" Fanny snuffled into a handkerchief "… sounds perfectly delightful."

She only hoped Jonathon agreed.

Chapter Twenty-One

Jonathon arrived back at the Denver Hotel Dupree in the middle of the night. He'd been gone fifteen and a half days, which by his estimation was fifteen days too many. It had taken the cleanup crews longer to repair the damage to the hotel than he'd have liked. But construction was finally back on schedule, putting them only two weeks behind their original opening date.

The consequences of the water pipe bursting could have been worse, he knew, and could have kept him away from Fanny for months. But he was home now, home being wherever his beautiful wife laid her head. He'd meant to send her a wire warning of his arrival, just as he'd promised. But he'd been too eager to get home to stop at the telegraph office in San Francisco.

Jonathon let himself quietly into the suite, keeping his movements light, quick and methodical, so as not to wake Fanny.

Fanny.

His wife. His love.

His heart.

He needed her in his life. The days away from her had been torture.

Would he eventually destroy her? Or could he find a way to be a blessing in her life, as she was in his?

Unsure of the reception he would receive, especially at this hour, he went into his dressing room and took his time unpacking his valise. He could easily afford to hire someone to do these types of menial tasks, but he never wanted to forget his humble roots. Ironic, since he'd nearly allowed himself to forget the most important influences in his life.

Reaching inside his jacket, he pulled out the photograph of the original Hotel Dupree that Marc had given him on the morning of his wedding. *A reminder of where you really come from.*

Jonathon came from poverty. His mother had been a prostitute, his father an adulterer. But their influence had only partly made him into the man he was today. Marc Dupree had influenced him, as well. He'd taught him that character was the sum total of choices and habits.

Jonathon had a big choice before him. He could break the cycle of sin rampant in his family, or he could succumb to fear and live half a life.

He needed to see Fanny.

Assuming she'd been upset enough to separate herself from him, he checked the bedroom he'd given her on their wedding night. She wasn't there.

Lord, let this be a good sign. Let her be in the room we've shared since our wedding night.

His confidence grew, but was immediately replaced with dread. He'd boarded the train to San Francisco with matters between them unsettled. *Badly done, Hawkins.*

If Fanny had moved out of their home, he had only himself to blame.

He couldn't let her go. If she wasn't in this suite, he would find her and bring her back.

He moved to his bedroom, paused in the doorway and found himself struggling for every breath. He knew this sensation. It was the feeling of a narrow escape.

Bathed in a ribbon of moonlight, Fanny slept in his bed—*their* bed—in the spot Jonathon usually occupied, as if she wanted to be close to him even in his absence.

His heart swelled.

Barely able to move under the weight of pleasure that gripped him, he entered the room slowly and stepped to the end of the bed.

For several long breaths, he merely watched his wife slumber. Her long hair was fanned out across the pillow beneath her head. The golden waves appeared silver in the pale moonlight.

She was curled up like a cat, her hand resting protectively over her stomach.

This is what she will look like carrying my child.

The thought slipped through his mind with quiet ease.

In that moment, Jonathon admitted how deeply in love he was with his wife. Fanny had changed everything. He wondered what his life would be like without her in it. The thought was too dismal to contemplate.

After the wedding ceremony, her father had taken Jonathon aside for some friendly marital advice. Cyrus Mitchell had told him that the measure of a happy marriage is what a husband is willing to give up for his wife.

At the time, Jonathon hadn't fully understood what his father-in-law meant. Now, he knew. Love called for sacrifice. In San Francisco, Jonathon had come to the realization the he was willing to sacrifice anything, everything, for Fanny.

She wanted a child, the child only they could create together. Could Jonathon sacrifice his doubts and fears in order to give her what she wanted?

If love called for sacrifice, then faith called for surrender. Did Jonathon have the courage to surrender his fears, his very will and release the future into God's hands?

He didn't know.

Rubbing his palm across his tired, gritty eyes, he decided now was not the time for deep thinking. He needed sleep.

No, he needed his wife.

He sat on the bed and brushed her hair off her face. "Fanny, my love, I'm home."

Slowly, she came awake.

"Jonathon?" Her sooty eyelashes blinked in confusion. "Is it really you?"

He leaned over and kissed her cheek. "Shh, go back to sleep."

As if he hadn't spoke at all, she sat up, scrubbed the sleep from her eyes. "What time is it?"

"Just past midnight."

"Oh." She hid a yawn behind her hand. "I… Did I know you were coming home tonight?"

She yawned again. It was then he noticed the purple shadows beneath her eyes, shadows that came from too many sleepless nights.

"Lie down." He set his hand on her shoulder and gently pushed her back down on the bed. "We'll talk in the morning."

She didn't argue, but settled her head atop the pillow. A little hum of pleasure rumbled in her throat.

"If this is only a dream," she mumbled, "and you really aren't here with me…" her eyelashes fluttered closed "…then don't wake me again."

Within seconds her breathing evened out.

Jonathon leaned over and kissed her again, on her forehead, her cheek, her lips.

"I love you," he said to her sleeping form, promising himself he would say the words again when she was fully awake.

Fanny awoke to a cold, empty bed. Remembering the events of the night before, she propped herself up on her elbows and looked around.

Jonathon had come home.

Or had he?

She searched the room, looking for signs of his presence. Quickly donning her robe, she searched the bedroom, then Jonathon's dressing room.

The smell of strong coffee and the crisp sound of newspaper pages turning had her padding barefoot into the main living area of the suite. She drew in a quick, happy sigh at the familiar scene.

Jonathon sat behind the *Denver Chronicle*, completely hidden from her view. Before him, the table was laden with a large tray of eggs and bacon, buttered croissants and all manner of pastries.

The combination of scents made her stomach churn.

Bracing herself against the door frame, Fanny placed a hand over her mouth and willed her stomach to calm.

Once she had the nausea under control, she slowly, carefully, lowered her hand. "Good morning, Jonathon."

The newspaper immediately dropped to the table. "Good morning."

For a long moment, she drank in the sight of her husband, already dressed impeccably for the day. He looked so handsome, his gaze more approachable than when he'd left town. She'd missed him terribly and couldn't think why she shouldn't tell him so. "I'm glad you're home."

"I missed you, Fanny."

That was all it took. Desperate for her husband, she was across the room in a handful of steps. He was up on his feet in the time it took her to get to him.

And then they were embracing as if they'd been apart an entire year rather than a few weeks.

They talked over one another, alternating between apologies and kisses.

Laughing, they separated at last.

He cupped her face in his hands and simply gazed into her eyes. Love swelled in her heart and she felt her knees tremble. Then, to her horror, little spots played before her eyes.

She was going to faint. No, much worse, she was going to be sick. She swallowed, but the nauseating sensation only strengthened.

"Fanny. What's wrong?" Jonathon moved his hands to her shoulders. "Color is draining out of your face right before my eyes."

"I…feel…sick." She'd barely gotten the words out of her mouth before bile rose into her throat.

She rushed to the water basin.

Jonathon was by her side in an instant, rubbing her back and whispering soothing words. Her dignity hanging by a thread, she attempted to straighten.

"No, stay there a moment." Working quickly, as if he'd done this before, he dipped a linen napkin in a glass of water on the table and placed it over the back of her neck.

The cool relief brought tears to her eyes.

"There now," he soothed. "Let's get you seated."

With a gentle yet firm grip he guided her to a chair far too near the breakfast table. One inhalation and she was back at the basin again.

Again, Jonathon placed the cold, wet cloth on her neck.

"The food," she gasped. "Get it out of here. The smell is making me ill."

He gave her an odd look but did as she requested.

Once the room was empty of the offensive odors, Jonathon sat beside her and searched her face. "Are you still feeling sick?"

She nodded.

His expression filled with masculine concern.

"Don't worry." She tugged her bottom lip between her teeth. "It'll pass by early afternoon."

"How can you possibly know that?"

"I have been having bouts of queasiness every day since you left, but only in the mornings."

Her heart dropped as she watched understanding dawn on his face. "You are—"

"—with child. Yes, Jonathon, I am carrying your baby."

She saw the shock in his eyes, and then the fear. "You are certain?"

"Yes." She lowered her gaze and plucked at the lace trim on her sleeve. "Dr. Shane confirmed it last week."

"I have to go." Jonathon stood abruptly.

"Don't you want to discuss this? I just told you I'm with child, *your child*."

"Believe me, Fanny, I want to discuss this at great length. But I have something I must take care of first."

Risking another bout of nausea, she jumped to her feet and laid her head on his chest.

He smoothed his hand across her hair, the stroke as gentle as a whisper. She felt weak from her last bout of sickness and so terribly desperate. She wanted to fight for Jonathon, for the future of their marriage, but she feared she would somehow push him away if she said too much.

But what if she didn't say enough?

Clutching at his shirt, she whispered the truth in her heart. "I love you."

His chest tensed beneath her cheek, but he didn't say the words back. He didn't say anything at all.

Terrified of what she would find, she carefully stepped back and looked into Jonathon's face.

Fear rose up to choke her. A stranger stood before her.

"Are you not happy with the news?"

"Of course I'm happy."

His closed expression belied his words. From the start of their acquaintance, he'd warned Fanny he didn't want children.

She'd ignored his wishes, thinking she could one day change his mind, and now, *now*, she'd trapped him with the very thing he least wanted in this world.

Her hand instinctively covered her stomach in a protective gesture. Jonathon's gaze followed the movement.

After releasing a slow exhale, he said, "I'll be back shortly."

Dread burned in her throat. "Where…where are you going?"

Jonathon set out across the room, wrenched open the door and then looked at her over his shoulder. "To my father's."

His father's? "But…but why?"

"I must ensure our child is protected from my past." The steel of his determination was threaded in his voice. "There is only one way."

"What are you going to do?" She was talking to an empty room, with nothing but the slam of the door reverberating off the walls.

Chapter Twenty-Two

Too agitated to sit inside a closed carriage, Jonathon covered the five blocks between the hotel and his father's residence on foot. He moved with ground-eating strides, propelled by urgency and a need to settle the future—by way of the past.

A cold mist hung in the morning air, mimicking the gloom in his heart. He hunched his shoulders against the chill and rounded the bend, putting the Hotel Dupree at his back. The nine-story building was the crown jewel in Jonathon's hotel empire. An empire he'd created with sweat, perseverance and a determination to prove he was better than the man who'd fathered him.

He crossed the street and increased his pace. At the end of the block, he caught sight of his reflection in the shop window on his right. It was only the dimmest of images. But it was enough to send shock waves quivering through him.

He saw his father. He saw his half brother. He saw his future, if he chose to cling to past wounds and the darkness that came with them. Frowning at his image, he touched his jaw. The same shape as his father's and his brother's, the three of them similar on the outside.

But on the inside, thanks to God's mercy, Jonathon was a new creation. And he was going to be a father.

Fanny was carrying his child. Fascinated at the wonder of it, he felt a smile touch his lips. Then it instantly fell away. He'd responded to the news badly. He would make it up to his wife, *after* he reconciled with his past.

A light dusting of snow covered the ground. If Fanny was with him she'd point out the sound of the crystals crunching under their feet.

Just thinking about his wife brought him a moment of calm.

Fanny had accepted him without question. No condemnation. No judgment. She'd believed in him from the very beginning and had never let the knowledge of his past color her feelings for him. She'd shown him grace and mercy, and he'd failed her, by always holding a portion of himself back, afraid the ugliness of his past would somehow rub off on her.

He would spend the rest of his life showing her and their children the same unconditional love she'd always shown him.

But first, he had to deal with his father.

After being admitted into the house by the judge's impassive butler, Jonathon was left cooling his heels in the foyer.

He glanced around, remembering the last time he'd stood in this cavernous hall, when he'd been a boy full of anguish and desperation and lost hope. For a moment, he disappeared in the memory. He'd come seeking help for his mother, but also secretly hoping for acceptance from the man who'd fathered him.

He'd left empty-handed on both accounts.

Ever since that day, Jonathon had been trying to prove he was nothing like Joshua Greene, and in the process, had nearly condemned himself to a lonely, loveless life. But then Fanny had come along.

She'd brought warmth into his life. She'd brought love and chased away the aching loneliness that had always been a part of him.

He wanted to leave this cold house, to return to his wife and tell her he was blissfully happy with the news of their child. He couldn't allow himself that luxury. He had unfinished business with his father.

A shadow oscillated over the marble floor, elongated and then formed into a man. The butler had returned.

Posture erect, he directed Jonathon to follow him to a long, empty corridor. "He is waiting for you in his private study."

Jonathon lifted a questioning eyebrow.

"It is the room at the end of the hallway on the left."

"Thank you." Minutes later, Jonathon stood before a pair of gleaming ebony doors.

He nearly changed his mind. What he was about to do would tie him to this man until one of them died. The irony was that he would be tied to him, anyway. They shared the same blood.

But they didn't have to share the same legacy.

Reaching into the pocket of his coat, Jonathon pulled out the photograph of the original Hotel Dupree. *A reminder of where you really come from.*

A rush of—*something*—skittered though him. Guilt, maybe? Regret? For most of his childhood he'd dreamed of having a real home, with a mother *and* a father to care for him. He'd found those things at Charity House, but had turned his back on them after his fateful visit to this house.

It still amazed him that neither Marc nor Laney held his youthful rebellion against him. Today, he would do his best to honor them, as a child would honor his parents.

He entered Joshua Green's private sanctuary without knocking. The smell of expensive tobacco and freshly polished wood greeted him. His father did not.

The silver head bent over a stack of papers on the polished surface of the desk did not lift, not even when Jonathon cleared his throat.

"So you have decided to grace me with your presence." At last, Greene looked up, a sneer curling his lips. "Yet you stand there glaring at me in silence. Am I to guess at the reason for your visit?"

The question was typical Joshua Greene, part arrogant superiority, part condescension. If Jonathon hadn't been studying the hard planes of his father's face, he might have missed the wariness in the other man's eyes.

A part of him wanted to prolong this moment, to wield the power he held over a man who'd filled his youth with nothing but misery. He could even choose to leave, and prevent Greene from ever having what he most desired.

For years, Jonathon had carried the weight of his father's rejection inside him. But the Lord had gifted him with a remarkable woman as his wife. Because of Fanny, because of the child she would soon give him, Jonathon had surpassed the need for vengeance. All that was left was one final act of mercy.

"I have come to make a concession."

The judge's eyes narrowed. Clearly sensing a trick, he carefully pushed himself to his feet. "Very well, go ahead."

Now that the time had come, Jonathon needed a moment to gather the words in his head. He moved to stand by the stone hearth. A fire spit and snapped, spreading warmth and a pleasant, smoky aroma through the room.

He turned and looked once more at Judge Greene.

For his entire life, Jonathon had told himself he didn't care what this man thought of him. Finally, it was true. He *didn't* care. The past no longer held him captive.

He was free.

"I came to say I have no objection to you naming my firstborn son as your heir."

Proving the cold, cynical nature of his heart, Greene's eyes turned hard as flint. "I am assuming you have stipulations."

"No stipulations." Certainty laced Jonathon's words. "No conditions."

An invisible weight lifted from his heart.

The judge's grim expression did not change. "The last we spoke, you were determined to prevent this. Why the sudden change of heart?"

"I am not doing this for you, but for my wife." His marriage to Fanny would never be whole if Jonathon didn't release his anger and hatred for this man.

Forgiveness was hard, and came at a price, but the cost of bitterness was far steeper. "That's all I came to say."

With that, Jonathon left the room, strode down the empty hallway and out the front door.

Dressed for the day, and dreadfully worried for Jonathon's welfare, Fanny sat on the overstuffed settee, hugging her knees to her chest. She felt tears forming again. After an hour of crying she would have thought she was through, but obviously not. Weary in both mind and spirit, she felt sorrow tear through her.

She would never stop loving Jonathon, would never stop thinking of him as her husband and the great love of her life, but she would not force him to stay with her. She would rather let him go than trap him in a marriage he didn't want.

He'd said he was happy about the news of their child, but he hadn't acted happy. In truth, he hadn't been able to leave the suite fast enough.

She had no idea what he was doing at his father's, and that scared her. Sobbing, she buried her face in her hands.

The sound of a key twisting in the lock had her on her feet in an instant. Not wanting him to know she'd been crying, she swiped furiously at her face. But then she realized there was no reason to hide her emotions from her husband.

He'd married her. He'd agreed to love her and cherish her through sickness and in health and, she amended silently in her head, at the sight of messy, unpleasant tears.

The door swung open and—one breath, two—Jonathon entered the foyer. Their eyes met across the room.

Pocketing the key, he crossed to her.

"Jonathon," she breathed.

He cupped her chin in his hands and kissed her on the mouth. "I love you, Fanny. I should have said it to you on our wedding day and every day thereafter."

The words sank past her anguish and settled into the depths of her soul. The pain and fear in her heart vanished.

"I love you, too." She pressed her face into his shoulder. "I'll never stop loving you."

They clung to each other for several minutes, basking in the joy of simply being together. At last. Jonathon guided her to the settee and sat beside her.

"There's so much I want to say, starting with I'm sorry. I hurt you, Fanny, and there's no excuse for that. If you'll let me, I'll spend the rest of my life making it up to you. And our child."

Hope blossomed in her heart. "What are you saying?"

He kissed the palm of her hand. "I deeply regret how I handled your announcement earlier." He leaned closer, until his lips brushed her ear. "Tell me the news again."

The happy light in his eyes when he sat back gave her the courage to speak with a strong, confident voice. "Jonathon, my love, we're going to have a baby."

He let out a hoot of delight, and then yanked her into his arms. "Praise the Lord. You've made me a very happy man, Francine Mary Mitchell Hawkins."

"You…you are truly pleased about this child?"

"Overjoyed." He kissed her tenderly on the lips.

She wrapped her arms around him and kissed him back, fiercely, gleefully, this man she loved with all her heart.

He pulled away first, only far enough to whisper in her ear once again. "I am here to stay, my precious Fanny. I wish to raise an entire brood of children with you."

She believed him. But one thing still needed saying.

"You're not your father." Of all the things she wanted her husband to know, this was the most important. She would keep saying the words, keep reminding him, every day for the rest of their lives if necessary, until he was convinced he was his own man. "You're nothing like him."

"No, I'm not."

There was something different in his voice, something

she'd missed before this moment, a note she'd never heard before. He sounded freer, easier…liberated.

Fanny studied Jonathon's face. He looked as if a heavy burden had been lifted from his shoulders. "What exactly happened at Judge Greene's house this morning?"

"I'll tell you everything. But look outside—it's a beautiful, crisp morning with a light snowfall." He tugged her toward the door. "Come, my love, join me for a walk and I will reveal all."

Laughing, she grabbed her coat and hurried out of the suite with him.

They strolled through the morning streets of Denver as they had hundreds of times before. All around them, people went about their business. No one paid them any attention.

Jonathon directed her to the small park where he'd brought her the day after Mrs. Singletary's ball. That had been when he'd officially started courting her, though she hadn't realized it at the time.

As he'd done that day all those months ago, he brushed off the wrought-iron bench and then directed her to sit.

"I'm happy you came home, Jonathon. However—" she gave him her fiercest glower "—never, ever leave me behind like that again."

"No, never again. I'm sorry, Fanny."

The look of utter remorse turned her heart to mush. "You're forgiven."

"It's that simple?"

She quoted a portion of her favorite Bible verse. "'Love bears all things and endures all things.'" She smiled. "Of course I forgive you. I forgave you before you boarded the train to San Francisco."

"You're a good woman. You deserve a good man."

"I deserve *you*."

Chuckling, he settled in beside her, then pulled her back against his chest and rested his chin on the top of her head.

They sat that way for several minutes. Fanny broke the silence first. "Will you tell me what happened at Judge Greene's house this morning?"

Jonathon drew in a breath. "His power over me has been strong all my life, perhaps stronger than I ever knew. But you taught me that love is stronger."

She gave his hand an encouraging squeeze, but said nothing.

"When you told me you were with child, I knew there was only one way to release his hold over me, over us and our future generations."

"What did you do?"

"I didn't do anything, precisely. I told him…" Jonathon took a deep inhale, blew it out slowly. "I said if he wanted to name our firstborn son as his heir, he would get no objection from me."

She gasped at the implication of her husband's words. Pushing away from him, she twisted on the seat to stare at him. "You really told him that?"

"I realize I should have run it by you first." He gave her a repentant grimace. "I would understand if you are angry."

"Angry? I'm not angry. I'm proud of you. There are so many ways you could have handled your father's desire to name our son his heir. But instead of denying him, or threatening him, you gave him exactly what he wanted. You showed him grace."

"It was the only way I could break from the past."

Tears of happiness formed in her eyes. "Now you are free."

"I am free."

She threw herself at him.

He enfolded her in his arms.

"I love you, Jonathon, now and forever and always."

Smiling, he kissed her on the tip of her nose. "I love you, too, Fanny. More than I can ever put into words."

The sun chose that moment to split through a seam in the clouds. Fanny lifted her face toward the warmth before glancing once again at her husband. "What do you say we head back to the hotel and begin the rest of our lives as the happily married couple that we are?"

The corners of his mouth twitched. "We're going to have a full, sometimes frantic, mostly happy life together, with at least a half-dozen children underfoot."

"Only six?"

"All right, seven." He placed his palm flat on her stomach. "But we'll focus our love on this special blessing first."

"Oh yes." She covered his hand with hers. "This one first."

Epilogue

In a state of barely subdued terror, Jonathon paced outside Fanny's childhood bedroom on the Flying M ranch. Only moments before, he'd been banished by her mother and the other two women in the room, something to do with his tendency toward overreaction.

Admittedly, barking at the three women on more than one occasion to make his wife's pain stop—*now*—may have played a role in his expulsion.

He could only wonder what was happening inside that torture chamber disguised as an innocuous bedroom. The walls were thin enough that Jonathon could hear every sharp groan that came from Fanny, could feel every birthing pain that made her cry out in agony.

He'd never experienced this level of helplessness in his life.

Although he'd known the trip to her family's spread—their fifth in so many months—had seemed ill-timed this late in Fanny's confinement, there was something synergistic about her birthing their first child in the same room where she'd been born.

A screech of feminine anguish ripped into the unnatural stillness of the hallway. The last shreds of Jonathon's control snapped.

He lunged for the door.

A hand grabbed him by the shirt collar and bodily yanked him back. "That's it, you're done."

Jonathon strained against the inflexible grip at his neck.

Hunter pressed his face inches from his. "The expectant father needs to head outside and take a breath of fresh air."

Jonathon dug in his heels. "I'm not leaving my wife."

"She's in good hands." Reese Bennett Jr. spoke the words in his calm, lawyerly voice, which had defused many heated arguments at the negotiation table. "The women know what they're doing."

"That's a fact." Cyrus Mitchell agreed with his son-in-law, his shoulder carelessly propped against the wall.

Jonathon snarled at his father-in-law. "How can you be so calm?"

"The women have been through this countless times before. They haven't lost a mother or child yet."

It was the *yet* that sent Jonathon breaking free of Hunter's hold and sailing back toward the door.

"Enough." Fanny's father took charge. "You're coming with us."

He motioned to Hunter and Reese.

Giving Jonathon no chance to argue, the two men he'd come to think of as brothers dragged him down the stairs and tossed him out into the front yard.

Jonathon washed out his tight lungs with big, long gulps of air, then attempted to look around. The scenery was breathtaking. The barns were well maintained, the corral well tended. The roaming horses and cattle added to the picture of a large, successful Colorado ranch, as did the Rocky Mountains in the distance.

No matter how beautiful the setting was, abject terror remained alive inside him, nipping at him like tiny rodent teeth.

He strode back toward the house.

Cyrus barred his way. "Cool off, son. You're no help to your wife in your current state."

Shaking with pent-up frustration, Jonathon speared a hand through his hair. "I can't stand seeing Fanny in this kind of pain."

"Understandable." Fanny's father clasped a commiserating hand on his shoulder. "But as tough as this is to hear, what's happening inside that room upstairs is the natural way of things."

So everyone kept telling him.

Jonathon remembered silently scoffing at how the Mitchell brothers had hovered over their expectant wives. Turns out he was the hovering sort, as well.

Women didn't always survive pregnancy or childbirth.

Too overcome with a renewed surge of panic to stand by and helplessly wring his hands, he attempted to pray. But he couldn't focus his mind properly, so he sent up silent groans and wordless pleas.

Surely the Lord knew what was happening in that birthing room. Surely He was protecting Fanny and their child.

Another scream from the second floor sliced through the air. Jonathon broke out in a run.

Hunter tackled him to the ground, then hopped to his feet lightning quick and pressed his boot on Jonathon's chest. "Stay down or I'll make sure you're out cold for the rest of the day."

Rolling free, Jonathon scrambled to a standing position and glared at his brother-in-law, who was poised on the balls of his feet. Hunter's determined gaze communicated a silent message Jonathon fully understood.

He wasn't getting past Fanny's brother.

Grimacing, he glanced up at the second-floor window. *Please, Lord, let this be over for her soon.*

God answered his prayer a half hour later. Annabeth burst out the front door, a wide smile on her face.

Relief nearly brought Jonathon to his knees. "How is my wife?"

"Tired, but fine. May all the future births in this family go so well." The woman glided over to him and patted his cheek with affection. "Now, it's time you went upstairs and met your daughter."

"A daughter? I have a daughter?"

"She's beautiful. She has your dark hair and her mother's beautiful face and—"

Jonathon didn't need to hear the rest. He darted into the house and up the stairs three at a time.

He surged through the open doorway and froze a moment to take in the sight of his wife and brand-new daughter. He nearly wept in relief. Fanny was sitting up in bed, smiling one of her secret smiles that always managed to reach inside his heart and grip hard.

Someone had helped her bathe and change into a fresh nightgown. In her arms, she held a small bundle swaddled in soft cotton.

"We'll leave you three alone," Mrs. Mitchell said as she and Callie retreated from the room.

"Don't just stand there," Fanny said. "Come over here and say hello to your new daughter."

He gingerly moved to the bed and sat beside his wife. Eyes stinging, he kissed her softly on the lips, then glanced down at the child in her arms. The tears came then, tears of wonder and joy. Their daughter was perfectly formed, fair-skinned like her mother, with a remarkable quantity of coal-black hair.

"What should we name her?" Fanny asked.

He'd already given the question considerable thought. "Mary Amelia Hawkins, after your mother and mine."

Fanny gave a delighted laugh. "We are of one mind, except for a small variance. I'm thinking Amelia Mary Hawkins has a much nicer ring to it."

"Either version will do. I'll leave you the final decision, since bringing her into this world was completely up to you." He settled in beside her, ran a fingertip down the infant's cheek. "You did amazing, Mrs. Hawkins."

Fanny grinned up at him. "I did, didn't I?"

He smiled into his wife's eyes. She'd brought light into his life, and now the future stretched before them with endless possibilities.

"Are you happy, Jonathon?"

"Unashamedly so. I love you, Fanny." He dropped a tender kiss to her forehead. "May the Lord continue to favor our family with His many blessings, now and in the days to come."

"What a lovely prayer." Her eyelids drooped.

"Before you drift off to sleep, I have a gift for you."

"Oh, Jonathon, I have everything I need."

He reached inside his jacket and pulled out the document Reese had given him upon their arrival.

Her eyes widened. "What in the world is that?"

"It's a deed in your name to a piece of land just north of here."

"But what will I do with my own piece of land?"

"We'll talk more after you've rested a bit."

"I want to know now."

He smiled. He would give this woman anything she asked of him.

"There's a run-down train depot on the property." He explained his original reasons for wanting to build on the land. "I hope you'll join me in creating a train stop to rival all stops. It will be our legacy, together."

He paused, thought of his mother, of the desperation that had led her to make bad decisions out of terrible choices. "We'll pay our employees a fair wage, give them on-the-job training, as well as provide room and board for them *and* their children."

"You've put a lot of thought into this."

"We could name the stop Mitchellville."

"I like it." Her smile lit her face from within. "But I have just one question."

"Ask me anything."

"When can we break ground?"

The question signified what he'd already known. Fanny was his perfect match and of a like mind in nearly everything that mattered. They were going to have a good life together. "We'll start building as soon as possible."

"Nice." She snuggled against him.

He kissed her nose, moved to her cheek and then finally landed on her mouth, lingering there for several long heartbeats.

Fanny was the heart of him, his ideal mate, his savvy business partner and the mother of his precious daughter.

Jonathon hadn't wanted a wife, and definitely hadn't thought a baby would ever be in his future. Now, he had both.

He had the family he'd always wanted but never believed could be his. Not a happy ending, no, but a happy beginning.

A *very* happy beginning.

* * * * *

Danica Favorite loves the adventure of living a creative life. She loves to explore the depths of human nature and follow people on the journey to happily-ever-after. Though the journey is often bumpy, those bumps refine imperfect characters as they live the life God created them for. Oops, that just spoiled the ending of Danica's stories. Then again, getting there is all the fun. Find her at danicafavorite.com.

Visit the Author Profile page
at Harlequin.com for more titles.

SHOTGUN MARRIAGE

Danica Favorite

Love is patient, love is kind. It does not envy,
it does not boast, it is not proud. It does not dishonor
others, it is not self-seeking, it is not easily angered,
it keeps no record of wrongs. Love does not delight
in evil but rejoices with the truth. It always protects,
always trusts, always hopes, always perseveres.
—*1 Corinthians* 13:4–7

For Camy Tang and Cheryl Wyatt
thanks for being such great friends,
coconspirators (not that we admit to anything,
of course!), and for walking this road called life
with me, and all its ups and downs. I love you guys!

Chapter One

Leadville, CO, 1881

"Did you hear he spent their wedding night in a brothel..." The whispers came from one of the pews to Emma Jane Logan Jackson's left. But as she looked in the direction of the sound, all she saw were pious young women seemingly engrossed in their Bibles.

Jasper reached over and patted her hand. "Ignore them," he said quietly, clasping the fingers that rested in the crook of his arm and giving them a gentle squeeze. Odd to be receiving this small amount of comfort from the virtual stranger she'd just recently married. He'd barely talked to her, let alone touched her, since their wedding two weeks ago.

Ignoring the gossip was easy enough for him to say. He was Jasper Jackson, son of the richest man in Leadville. But Emma Jane? She'd spent her whole life the laughingstock of town.

Smoothing the delicate fabric of the pale blue silk dress her mother-in-law had purchased for her, Emma

Jane remembered all the times she'd wished for finer clothes to wear to church. She'd been wrong in thinking a new dress would keep the other women from talking about her. Whether it had been the poorly mended hand-me-downs, her father's drinking, her mother's antics in trying to make their family more respectable and even Emma Jane's own awkwardness, people always found a way to make fun of her.

All she'd ever wanted was to find respectability in the town's eyes, but even with marriage to Leadville's most eligible bachelor, it eluded her.

"I thought getting married was supposed to stop all the talk," Emma Jane whispered back.

Jasper squeezed her hand again. "It will be all right. Eventually some other scandal will hit town, and they'll forget all about the circumstances of our nuptials. Soon enough, they'll be begging to be invited to tea because they can't resist the Jackson fortune."

His emphasis on the words *the Jackson fortune* made Emma Jane stop and look at him. Her strikingly hand-some husband, with his dark good looks, seemed almost bitter, like he resented having so much wealth. Surely being well-to-do was a good thing. With her father's rising and falling fortunes, she knew both what it was like to be in plenty and in want, and frankly, she'd much rather have the plenty.

"What do you expect from a marriage practically forced on him by a scheming…"

Emma Jane turned in the direction of the voice, but all she saw was a group of women demurely peeking behind their fans. She squared her shoulders, straightened her back and gave them all a tight little smile. The only scheming going on was among the other women and their nasty gossip.

Jasper tugged at her hand again. "It's not worth it. They're just jealous because they aren't Mrs. Jasper Jackson."

More of the bitter tone as he emphasized *Mrs. Jasper Jackson*.

"You seem…" Emma Jane struggled for a descriptor that might induce her reticent husband to talk to her about it.

His lips turned upward in a smile that looked to be more painful than the effort was worth. "It's no secret that every woman in town wanted to marry me." He snorted. "Or, at least, they wanted to marry my fortune."

Then he looked down at her, his dark brow creasing. "I'm sorry. I know our marriage benefited your family financially. I didn't mean to insult you."

She couldn't give an answer to that, even if he'd wanted her to. The truth was, her family had insisted on the marriage, more for the funds it would bring to their coffers than any cares for Emma Jane's reputation. Her father had gambled away her sister Gracie's hand to settle a debt, and the only way to save Gracie from marriage to the town's most odious man had been for Emma Jane to marry into wealth. Her mother had come up with a scheme for Emma Jane to trap Jasper into marriage, but Emma Jane hadn't been able to go through with it.

Fortunately for the Logan family, Emma Jane's clumsiness took over where her conscience wouldn't let her act. She'd ended up trapped overnight in a mine with Jasper. Emma Jane's reputation at stake, marriage to Jasper was the only solution. Her family caused such a fuss that the Jacksons were glad to give them whatever funds necessary to avoid any further embarrassment. Emma Jane's family left town shortly after the wedding, pockets full of Jasper's money.

No wonder he was bitter.

Jasper cleared his throat. "It just would be nice, you know, if people cared about what I wanted to do with my life."

"Forgive me," Emma Jane said softly, pulling her hand out of his arm, then she tugged at the lace edging on the sleeve of her dress.

She hadn't considered what their marriage had cost Jasper. Nor had she thought about what he'd wanted. Her parents had browbeat her into the marriage, and because it was what Emma Jane had always done, she'd meekly agreed.

"No, forgive me." Jasper took her hand again and settled it back into the crook of his arm. "It was a thoughtless remark. You had as little choice in the matter as I did. Honestly, my frustration isn't even about that. I just can't stand the way everyone is so concerned with trivial matters."

Now *that* Emma Jane could understand. "We should find our seats," she said, tugging at her husband's arm.

"You go on. I see the sheriff has arrived."

Jasper's brow furrowed, and the line between his eyes had deepened. His thick, dark hair flopped over, seeming to have ignored the way he'd slicked it back earlier this morning.

"Is everything all right?" She followed his gaze and noticed Sheriff Calhoune standing on the other side of the church.

"We're tracking down some of the bandits who got away the night of the brothel fire. I'm hoping he has jumped in, and when they were found the next morning, her dress was in tatters."

"I did no such thing!" Emma Jane had gone for a walk to clear her head after listening to Flora's taunts. Well, all right, she'd run out of the barn crying. But Flora had been particularly cruel, telling the other girls that Emma Jane was going to be sold into a brothel. Not that Emma Jane would ever admit to Flora how those horrible rumors had affected her. For whatever reason, Flora had always picked on Emma Jane—had done so ever since they were in school together. Though Emma Jane had often wished she knew what she'd done to offend the other girl, mostly Emma Jane wished Flora would just leave her alone.

Emma Jane straightened her shoulders. "I'd gone for a walk and fallen into an abandoned mine. I had no idea Jasper was out there. He heard my cries for help and, in trying to rescue me, fell in, too."

She looked at Pamela, hoping she'd be sympathetic. "Truly, it was all just a terrible accident, and nothing untoward happened. Pastor Lassiter married us himself, and he would never have done so had any real harm been done."

The woman nodded slowly. But Flora wasn't finished yet. She gave Emma Jane a nasty smile, baring the points of her teeth before turning to the baby's mother. "I'm sure that's what Emma Jane would like people to believe. But Mrs. Jackson told me herself. The Logans would have ruined them. They told the sheriff that Jasper…" Flora lowered her voice. "Took liberties."

"Jasper would never do that!" Emma Jane stared at the other girl, horrified that she would spread such vicious lies about Jasper.

"Of course he wouldn't." Flora's voice lacked any kindness. "No man would even consider you in that way. You are, after all, most unfortunate in your appearance."

The pitying look Flora gave Emma Jane made her realize that not even the finest dress would ever make her pretty. After all, Flora was the very picture of everything a woman ought to be, with her golden blond curls and bright blue eyes. Emma Jane's hair was also blond, her eyes blue. But the blond was stringy and streaked with brown, and the girls used to tease her that it must be dirty. And her blue eyes had brown flecks in them that Flora had said came from being evil.

Even though Emma Jane knew in her head that Flora's accusations weren't true, it didn't make the cold lump in the pit of her stomach go away.

Flora was right about one thing, however. She had nothing to attract a man like Jasper into wanting to be her husband.

Still, the dig on Emma Jane's appearance was not enough for Flora, whose eyes glittered with a kind of blood lust.

"But what I don't understand is why you went along with the lies, unless, of course, you were telling them yourself."

A sickeningly sweet smile followed Flora's last statement, and she turned her attention back toward Pamela. "Jasper was so disappointed about being railroaded into the marriage that he spent the night…" Flora looked around, then lowered her voice. "In a place of ill repute."

The fact which every woman in church was still whispering about. But they didn't have the whole story.

"He was helping Will Lawson—a lawman—rescue an innocent young lady from the clutches of an outlaw."

Emma Jane spoke louder than was polite, but hopefully some of the other gossiping women would finally hear the truth.

"So you say." Flora flipped open her fan, then smiled at Pamela. "I just thought I'd warn you so you understood why none of the good families in Leadville are extending invitations to this woman. Bad company corrupting good character and all that."

With a final nasty grin, Flora flounced over to her seat in a pew a few rows up. Emma Jane gave the woman they'd been talking to a weak smile. "I'm sorry you were dragged into this. I sincerely appreciate your kindness to me, and I assure you that I've been nothing but honest with you."

The woman's noncommittal murmur spoke volumes. Flora's words had poisoned any hope Emma Jane had of even being able to delight in someone else's child.

Then Emma Jane spotted Mrs. Jackson heading in her direction.

"Stop dawdling." Jasper's mother took Emma Jane by the elbow. "We are to be an example for the rest of the church, and you're making a spectacle of yourself."

"Yes, Mrs. Jackson."

Face heated, she sat in the Jackson pew where Mrs. Jackson indicated, trying to enjoy the feel of the velvet cushions rather than the hard wooden benches the rest of the church endured. Mr. Jackson, Jasper's father, leaned into Emma Jane. "Where's Jasper?"

"He went to talk to the sheriff," she answered, further conversation being cut off by the sound of the organ's first chords.

After the hymns, Pastor Lassiter spoke, sharing the need for the church community to continue to rally around the women who'd been displaced in the brothel fire. While some of the women had moved on to other houses of ill repute, many had nowhere else to go.

Emma Jane tried to focus her attention back on the pastor's sermon, but she found herself unable to think beyond the poor women who'd been left homeless. Like Emma Jane, they were deemed unworthy and unlovable by the rest of society.

And yet, not one of them judged Emma Jane for the disgraced circumstances of being forced to marry. They all treated Emma Jane like she was a real lady, worthy of respect. Emma Jane had even become friends with a colorful woman named Nancy.

Emma Jane twisted around to see if Nancy had shown up at the church yet. The so-called fallen women often arrived after the service started, leaving before it ended to avoid ridicule.

Marriage hadn't brought Emma Jane any closer to finding respectability, but perhaps helping with the pastor's ministry, people would finally see her as a good Christian woman. Maybe then she would finally have the acceptance that had eluded her for most of her life.

Jasper Jackson stood at the back of the church, listening as Pastor Lassiter concluded his sermon. He hadn't intended to miss church, but he'd been caught up in talking to the sheriff to figure out their next move.

The newly acquired badge heavy in his pocket, Jasper couldn't help but touch it one more time. Him. A deputy. All his life, he'd wanted to do something important, but every time he tried to find his significance, his mother cited the need to carry on the Jackson legacy. She'd sob and tell him she'd been lucky to have even him, and he couldn't spoil it by…well, she'd have a fit of vapors for sure when he shared his news.

But this time, he would not be swayed.

A woman had died saving Jasper's life the night of the brothel fire. In the heat of an argument with the bandits, Jasper had acted foolishly, and the bandits started firing on them. Mel pushed him out of the way, getting shot in the process. Mel. A woman of the night. Not the kind of woman a man owed any kind of honor to, but she'd done the most honorable thing a person could do—she'd taken a bullet meant for him. He'd promised Mel that he'd find and rescue her sister, Daisy, from the gang of bandits that held her. The same gang who'd killed Mel.

No, his honor wasn't at stake. It was his very soul. Or at least it felt that way as church let out and his new bride, Emma Jane, approached, her delicate features unmarred by the thoughts that plagued him. He had to admit that she was a lovely woman. He'd done the honorable thing by marrying her, but until he completed his mission in keeping his promise to Mel, he would have no peace in his own heart.

"Hello, Jasper." Emma Jane gave him a weak smile. "Your mother—"

"There you are!" Before Emma Jane could finish her sentence, his mother stepped in between them. "Why didn't you sit with us?"

Jasper cringed. The Jacksons weren't typically confrontational, especially in public. But the only way he was going to be able to share his decision without encountering hysterics was to do it now.

"The sheriff was here, so I went to talk to him about the latest news on the bandits. I thought it would be a few days, but he decided to swear me in as a deputy today."

He never imagined that Emma Jane Logan's face would be the one to keep him calm. Until he realized that she wasn't Emma Jane Logan anymore. Jasper exhaled slowly, trying to let go of the inevitable tightness in his chest that always seemed to come at the reminder of his marriage. At least she didn't appear to be standing in the way of the one decision he'd gotten to make about his own life.

Of course, Emma Jane had what she wanted—his name and fortune. Though she'd insisted that the events leading to their marriage were not intentional, he couldn't forget the sound of her mother congratulating her on a job well-done. The woman had practically cackled with glee as she'd told Emma Jane that luring him to the abandoned mine had been masterful.

Marriage to Emma Jane would have been a whole lot easier had he continued to believe it was all an accident. He'd even thought, in their time at the church picnic, they'd become friends. But friends trusted each other, and Emma Jane should have trusted him when he'd told her that he'd find a way to save her family without her having to get married. Perhaps, in supporting his cause, Emma Jane could make up for taking away one of the most important choices a man had in life.

A stolen glance at his parents revealed they'd both turned odd shades of red—to be expected, of course—but part of him wished they'd have come forward to say they were proud of him.

No, it was Emma Jane who first spoke up.

"After everything that happened with the brothel burning down, I can understand your desire to bring justice." She gave a small smile. "I've been thinking I should do more to help Pastor Lassiter's ministry to the women rescued from the fire."

Her words shouldn't have surprised him. After all, aiding the less fortunate was what their church was about. Or, at least, that's what people said their church was about. He'd seen many of the young ladies pay lip service to helping others, but none ever seemed to put those words into action. Except Emma Jane. He didn't know her well, yet he could remember seeing her a number of times at other church events, helping out.

"Nonsense," his mother snapped. "We'll give the pastor some money, just as we always do, and that will be that."

Then she turned her attention to Jasper. "I hardly know what's gotten into you. Your unfortunate marriage, chasing bandits—I can't imagine what you'll do next."

He recoiled at his mother's description of his marriage. Especially when he noticed the pained look on Emma Jane's face. Why he was so concerned about his young wife's feelings, he didn't know, especially when the larger issue at stake was his ability to follow his dreams. No, his mission was bigger than a dream. Innocent lives were at stake.

Ignoring his mother, Jasper turned to his father. "I am alive today because of the noble sacrifice of a woman who only wanted her sister to be saved. If I don't help bring these men to justice, who will? If I continue to live with no other purpose than to entertain Mother's guests, then really, what was the point of a woman dying in my place?"

Then, taking another deep breath to dispel the inevitable lump that filled his throat when talking about Emma Jane, Jasper addressed his mother. "It would do you credit to remember that if it hadn't been for Emma Jane pushing me out of the way of the mine caving in, I'd be dead. She put her safety in jeopardy for mine, and I will always be grateful."

His life had been saved twice in a matter of weeks. By women. Perhaps, as much as he reminded his mother of his debt to Emma Jane, he needed to remind himself of it, as well. She risked her life for him. If marriage was the price he'd had to pay, so be it.

"Regardless of what happened in that mine, we both know you'd have had to have married her, anyway," Constance snapped.

Jasper swallowed. True, of course, but Emma Jane's sacrifice had somehow made his own more palatable. Even if the mine hadn't caved in, they would have both been gone long enough that their returning together—after being out alone in the pitch-dark—would have caused tongues to wag. But once they'd been trapped in the mine, marriage had been a foregone conclusion.

And as he watched Emma Jane's lower lip quiver, he couldn't help but wonder how much she regretted the cost of their marriage.

"What's done is done," Jasper said quietly, looking at Emma Jane. "And it's time we made the best of it."

His words didn't erase the sadness from her eyes, and while Jasper wished there was something else to be done, he knew that the distance between them wasn't going to be bridged by a few words.

As grateful as he was for Emma Jane saving his life, the sting of her betrayal was still too deep, the pain too fresh. When she'd approached him at the church picnic and told him that her mother wanted her to marry him to restore the money her father had lost in a poker game, he told her that he'd help her find a solution that didn't involve marriage. Emma Jane had said she was willing to trust him. But she'd lured him out to the abandoned mine, anyway. Obviously, she'd heard him say he needed to go clear his head, and gone out on her own. Of course he'd answer her cries for help. She couldn't have known how dangerous it would be, or that the rains would have weakened the ground to cause a cave-in. He wasn't even sure that she'd known the mine was there.

Regardless, Emma Jane had to have known that being alone with him, outside in the dark, was enough to compromise them both. For that, he blamed her.

So why, as tears shone in Emma Jane's eyes, could he not bring himself to hate her?

Maybe it was because, as he had just told his mother, they couldn't do anything about the past. All they could do was move on. Jasper was trying, he really was, and maybe someday he could hold more firmly to his resolve to look ahead rather than be afflicted by questions he would probably never find answers to.

"We should take this conversation somewhere more private," Jasper's father said, gesturing toward Pastor Lassiter's empty office.

Jasper looked around, realizing for the first time that while many of the churchgoers had exited, there were still enough people milling around that seeking privacy was a wise decision. He followed his father into the pastor's office, waiting until his mother and Emma Jane had entered the room before closing the door behind them. Pastor Lassiter wouldn't mind if they used his office while he was busy conversing with folks leaving the church.

"I meant what I said about making the best of our marriage," Jasper said slowly as he moved toward Emma

Jane, stepping in between her and his mother. "But you have to understand that my mission to save Daisy takes precedence right now. Her life is in danger, and every moment that I spend here is a moment closer to her demise."

Emotions he didn't understand flickered across Emma Jane's face as she straightened her shoulders and nodded. "You have my full support."

Then she hesitated, looking down at her Bible, as if she were hoping it would… Jasper shook his head. What could the Bible do for her? It wasn't going to save anyone's life.

Emma Jane sighed and looked up at him. "But… I'm tired of pretending that the whispers don't bother me. I'm tired of people thinking I've driven you away. I…"

"I'm sorry you're bothered by all the talk." Jasper cut her off, trying not to sound cold, but what else was he supposed to say? Everyone thought that being a Jackson was a wonderful thing, but all it did was put you in the limelight, where everyone always had something to say about your life. And by something, it never meant anything good.

Jasper took a step back. He'd intended for their marriage to ease Emma Jane's problems, not make them worse. The only reason he'd married her was because after being alone together overnight, her reputation would be ruined, and no decent man would have her. Apparently, their marriage hadn't had the desired effect.

"I'm sorry, Emma Jane." He held out his hand to her, then captured her gaze, ignoring his mother's indrawn breath. How had he never noticed before that Emma Jane's eyes were such an exquisite shade of blue, with little flecks of brown dancing within?

"I'd hoped that our marriage would be enough to keep

people from talking." He looked back at the ground, unable to face the way her wide-eyed expression asked questions of him he wasn't ready to answer.

"I don't know what to do about it right now. Even if I stay, people are going to find something to talk about."

He sent a glare in his mother's direction. "The best thing for Emma Jane right now is for everyone to stand beside her in my absence. You can support me, thereby supporting her, or…"

Or *what*? Jasper let out a long, frustrated sigh. His mother would do exactly as she pleased, which didn't do anything to help Emma Jane. Leaving him trapped in the conundrum of dealing with Emma Jane's hurt feelings or following his calling to rescue Daisy and bring the bandits to justice.

Why did doing the right thing have to put him in such a difficult position?

"It's all right, son." His father stepped forward, placing one hand on Jasper's shoulder, the other on Emma Jane's. "Your mother and I haven't done all we could in easing your wife's transition into our family."

He gave Jasper a squeeze, then moved back and addressed Emma Jane. "I apologize if we haven't been as welcoming as we could have been. Such a hasty marriage didn't give any of us time to properly prepare, and that's no excuse. I'll do what I can to address any talk."

Jasper couldn't help but notice his mother still remained near the door, her back stiff and unyielding, her mouth pursed tightly. There would be an argument between his parents later, and yet again, Jasper was responsible.

Why did so much have to rest on his shoulders? So many things for him to be held accountable for, and yet the one thing that mattered most—saving the life of an innocent woman—seemed to be directly at odds with it all.

He heaved another sigh, then took Emma Jane's hands in his, wishing her hands didn't feel like ice, like they needed him for warmth. "I don't know what you want from me."

"I just want you to talk to me," Emma Jane said quietly. Her shoulders rose and fell. "I know ours isn't a love match. But I at least thought we could be friends. That we *were* friends. Instead, I find that you have shut me out completely."

Her words weren't supposed to sting. All of this was her fault. They were once friends, and they could be friends still, but she had to trap him into marriage. So why was he the one who felt bad?

"I'm not sure what to talk to you about."

"You could have told me that you were leaving our wedding reception to help Will rescue Mary's sister Rose from the bandits. Mary knew, so why didn't you fill me in, as well? I understand you wanted to help them. Mary and Will are my friends, too. And now, trying to bring the rest of the gang to justice and find this Daisy person? Why can't I help?"

A whole list of reasons, starting with the fact that the only people who knew for certain that Rose had run away, and not been kidnapped, were Will, Jasper and Rose's family. Jasper had been asked not to apprise anyone of that fact.

Fortunately, there was one equally important reason. "These are dangerous people. The only reason Mary came along that night is because she followed me. She wasn't supposed to be there. These men are the kind to shoot first, ask questions later. I won't have you risking your life."

Emma Jane gave him a mournful look. One that almost made him feel bad for excluding her. But she didn't understand how dire the situation was.

"I just want you to let me in. To talk to me like we did before our marriage."

Jasper wanted that, too. But it seemed like there was too much at stake to waste effort on social niceties. They'd had good conversation, sure, but conversation did nothing when it came to saving lives.

"There's no time for that. The search party is leaving soon—with or without me. Once this business is settled, then we can talk."

The Emma Jane he'd always known was a little mouse. But when she straightened her shoulders, Emma Jane looked like a tiger.

"I can help."

With the ferocity in her eyes, Jasper almost believed her.

"Emma Jane, you're just a…"

He wanted to say "woman," but the truth was, his life had been saved by two women. He had no illusions about females being the weaker sex. But against these men, a person who didn't know how to fight, to survive and to kill if needed—that person was dead. Emma Jane could do none of those things.

"A woman who happens to be friends with the women rescued from the brothel. Women who were privy to the bandits' secrets. So do not condescend to me about what I can and cannot do."

She stepped aside, including his parents in the conversation. "I have tried to do what has been asked of me.

But I am tired of sitting and pretending that having insult upon insult heaped upon me does not bother me. I am Mrs. Jasper Jackson, for better or for worse. And as such, I will assist my husband in bringing these bandits to justice. And when that happens, I will walk through this town with my head held high, and not a soul will dare look down upon me."

A few tense moments ticked by. Then, with a steely look far more threatening than even his mother's fiercest glower, Emma Jane stared directly at his mother. "Including you, Mrs. Jackson."

Everything in him wanted to applaud Emma Jane at her words. As far as Jasper knew, no one had stood up to his mother before. At least, not with that level of vigor.

But Emma Jane was not finished, because then she turned her attention on him. "You will let me help you. If you do not include me in your plans, I will do my part, anyway. Even if it means going to the sheriff directly."

Jasper didn't doubt her words. No, this ferocious spitfire, a woman with whom he was entirely unacquainted, meant business. Just as Mary had snuck out and followed him to the brothel that night, he knew Emma Jane would do the same—and more.

They'd barely gotten Mary and her sister Rose out alive that night. How much more danger would Emma Jane face? It seemed an impossible choice—include Emma Jane in a potentially dangerous mission, or risk having her go behind his back and get mixed up in something potentially more precarious?

Chapter Two

"I need to go." Jasper had prolonged his leaving long enough. Almost too long. He'd only meant to tell everyone of his plans, not have the impassioned discussion that ensued.

"Hopefully, this lead takes us to where the bandits are hiding. Then it will be over and all will be well. I just wanted a chance to say goodbye, you know, in case. If all goes well, I'll be home by supper."

Emma Jane stepped forward and gave him an awkward hug. "Stay safe."

The rush of emotion in his chest came on harder than the force of the worst blizzard he'd endured. His wife's hug was all warmth and completely unexpected after Emma Jane's fervent speech about joining him.

"Promise me you won't try to help me with this case while I'm gone. We can talk when I get back."

He could see her hesitation as she shifted her weight and chewed on her lower lip. Those eyes looked at him in a way that made him believe that things would, in fact, be all right.

"I promise."

He wasn't supposed to care about Emma Jane Logan, er, Jackson. But he'd forgotten that underneath all that awkwardness lay a woman with deep compassion for others. If only she'd had compassion for the fact that he'd have liked to have chosen his own wife—a woman whom he actually loved.

In that, Jasper envied his friend, Will, falling head over heels for Mary. Their marriage would be a real marriage, full of happiness and love. What did Jasper have to look forward to?

Nights sitting by the fire and talking? That had been pleasant enough before he'd been forced to marry her. But what of the rest of their lives? And children? How were they supposed to have children when they didn't share the kind of feelings needed for the begetting of children?

Jasper jerked away. All this time, he'd remained in Emma Jane's embrace. How had he forgotten himself? Memories of their time trapped in the mine flooded back to him. Just before Emma Jane had shoved him out of the way of the rockslide, he'd kissed her. But then the rockslide hit, and while he'd been saved, Emma Jane's heroism had left her with a nasty bump on the head. Jasper had considered it a sign.

Kissing Emma Jane Logan had nearly killed them both.

Now that she was Emma Jane Jackson, Jasper had no intention of repeating the experience. He had more important things to think about than romance. Even if he couldn't get the memory of the soft press of her lips against his out of his mind.

"I should get going," he finally said, shifting awkwardly.

His father stepped forward and gave him a tight embrace. "Stay safe, son."

And then, almost as if his father feared the worst, he said slowly, "I can't pretend to like what you're doing, but I understand."

Henry's voice quavered slightly. "I don't want there to be any regrets between us. So know I love you and I'm proud of you."

Jasper should have been pleased to hear those words, but something in him ached, knowing he hadn't yet done anything to be proud of. He exhaled roughly. He'd save the joy in hearing the words for when he knew Daisy was safe.

His mother, though, held no such sentiment. Red-eyed, she stared past him at Emma Jane.

"If he dies, I will blame you. He never had such foolish notions about chasing bandits until after he met you. And I promise, you will rue the day…"

"Enough, Constance." His father took his mother by the arm.

After a glance at Emma Jane's stricken face, Jasper, too, had had enough.

"None of this is Emma Jane's fault. If you listened to me at all, you'd know that I've been wanting to do something meaningful with my life for a long time."

Jasper held out a hand to Emma Jane, and she took it, her gloved fingers seeming so small in his. He'd married her to protect her, and here, with his mother's hostility, he had to wonder for the second time today if it had done any good.

Was he wrong for trying to be more than what he was?

But could he live with himself if he didn't? Could he continue looking himself in the mirror if he were nothing more than a dandy, taking in social entertainments but contributing nothing but gossip to society?

Squeezing Emma Jane's hand gently, he gazed down at her. "Thank you for supporting me. I know this isn't the marriage either of us wanted for ourselves, but I'm grateful that you're standing by me and I promise to do the same for you."

The tears glimmering in her eyes were unexpected, and they stirred something in his gut he hadn't been prepared for. Was it sympathy? No, something deeper. Like maybe the friendship that had begun before he'd realized Emma Jane had set him up wasn't completely dead.

He swallowed the rising emotion and let go of Emma Jane's hand, turning to his mother. "Emma Jane is my wife. She is a Jackson and should be afforded every courtesy the name entails."

Henry coughed. "Jasper is right. What's done is done, and even if we could undo it, it would only bring more scandal to the family. We need to make the best of things."

Jasper noticed he gave Constance a slight squeeze before letting her go. The small affection between his father and mother made him even more grateful for his father's support.

Which made Jasper feel even worse. As difficult as his mother could be, he did love her. After all, he'd spent years playing her society games, entertaining the young ladies she deemed suitable and generally tolerating all of her misguided attempts at arranging his life. Perhaps he shouldn't have been so accommodating, then she might be more understanding of the desires of his heart.

At least his father appeared to be more understanding. He looked at Emma Jane with an expression of warmth that convinced Jasper that things would eventually work out. "Emma Jane is also right. We should be doing what we can to support Jasper. Doing everything we can to assist him will keep him much safer than if we're working against him."

Jasper's father held out his hand to Jasper. "I promise not to interfere. And if there are resources I can provide, say the word, and it's yours."

This time, the victory felt real as Jasper shook his father's hand. Even though Jasper could tell his mother was holding back tears. A Jackson did not cry in public, but he knew his mother would be home and in bed with a headache later, the acceptable excuse for sobbing her heart out.

He should feel bad, and part of him did, but he was used to his mother brandishing tears to manipulate people's feelings. More important, though, were the tears that needed to be shed for a woman who had no one to cry for her.

That had to be his focus. Not guilt over everyone else's overwrought emotions.

Jasper looked over at Emma Jane, then back at his father.

"Keep Emma Jane safe." Then he took another deep breath. "I'm sure everything will be fine, but if something should happen to me, take care of her."

"I will."

Two words, as solemn as the wedding vows he'd spoken. His father would keep the promise, just as Jasper would keep his.

"I don't need to be kept safe," Emma Jane huffed, but her tigress look faded as his father met her eyes.

An unspoken agreement seemed to pass between them

as his father turned his attention back to Jasper. "I'm going to get your mother home. I'll let you have a private moment to say goodbye to your bride."

His parents turned away, leaving Jasper alone with Emma Jane.

"I think we've said all we need to say," Jasper stated tersely.

"I meant what I said about helping you."

"You can't ride out with us."

Emma Jane nodded slowly. "I wasn't asking to. But I'll be talking to the women, and I will get information to assist you."

Her plan seemed harmless enough, but that was precisely the problem. Nothing about the people he pursued was harmless, and even if the women here knew something they could use, Emma Jane knowing could put her in danger.

"Please don't." He took her hands in his. "I know you mean well. But they will kill you, Emma Jane. If they think you know anything that can hurt them, they will kill you."

He hated being so blunt with her, but he didn't know any other way to put it.

"Don't you remember?" she said, too lightly to be anything than covering up her pain. "Everyone thinks I'm an idiot. The only perceived threat people see in me is that I've dashed the marital aspirations of every woman in this town. Instead of fearing that the bandits will kill me, you should be more fearful that one of your adoring fans will do it so they can take my place."

A little harsh, but as he remembered the vitriol aimed at Emma Jane since their wedding, she probably wasn't too far off the mark. Every woman in town wished them ill. No, not them. *Emma Jane*. She'd snatched the town's most eligible bachelor out from their noses. Despite their marriage, the rumors and innuendoes hadn't stopped.

"I'm sorry," Jasper said quietly. "I wish it were easier for you."

Oddly enough, he spoke the truth. Emma Jane hadn't been the first to try to trap him into marriage. Every girl in town had, at some point, contrived some scheme to attempt to compromise herself with him. Emma Jane had merely been the one to succeed. And they all hated her for it.

"It will be," Emma Jane reassured him with a small smile. "Once I help you bring down the bandits, everyone will see that I am a credit to you. A credit to this town. A woman worthy of respect."

"You don't need to put your life at risk for that. I promise you, Emma Jane, once this is all over, I will do everything I can to fix things. But for now, you have to trust me. Your respectability is not worth your life. Continue to occupy yourself with the pastor's ministry, but don't get involved with this case."

She appeared to consider his words, nodding slowly.

"I really do have to go." Then he locked eyes with her, squeezing her hand. "The most important part of marriage to me, the part ours is lacking, is trust. Trust me, and stay out of this. If you do this, our marriage will have the foundation it needs for us to have a future. Do you understand?"

Emma Jane's eyes filled with tears as she nodded again. Maybe there was hope for their relationship, after all.

As they started to turn to leave, Mary and Pastor Lassiter entered the office.

"I was just coming to find you," Emma Jane said, a happy smile finally filling her face.

As much as everyone talked about Emma Jane's unfortunate appearance, Jasper couldn't help but think that many of them had never seen Emma Jane smile. When she smiled, it lit up her whole face, and even her eyes sparkled. Jasper had escorted many of the town's beauties, and not one had a smile like Emma Jane's. Jasper shook his head. These thoughts had no business popping up. Not when he had so many more important matters to think of.

Pastor Lassiter returned her smile. "I'm glad to have run into the both of you. Your wedding was such a rushed affair, and then everything that happened with Rose, I fear that I haven't done my duty by the both of you."

"We understand, Pastor," Jasper said smoothly. "I've also been occupied. The remaining bandits still need to be caught, and I've accepted a deputy position to help make it happen."

Pastor Lassiter's brow furrowed. "You should be spending your time getting to know your bride. Emma Jane's a lovely woman, and she needs the support of her husband right now."

Why was everyone so worried about Emma Jane? She'd gotten what she wanted—the Jackson name. In the meantime, there were some very bad men on the loose, and another young woman potentially in danger.

"Emma Jane will be fine. We have the rest of our lives to get to know each other." Jasper didn't want to add that since there was no love between them, they'd need all that time—and more—to bridge the gap between them.

But if they could build the trust he asked for, perhaps,

as Pastor Lassiter had said the day of their wedding, love could grow.

"People are talking," the pastor said slowly. "I don't like to give credence to gossip, but in Emma Jane's case, the longer you remain absent from your wife, the worse it will be for her."

The pained expression on Emma Jane's face almost made him feel guilty. He'd been busy for most of the time in the days since their wedding, but he'd seen how people had treated her at the wedding and at their reception. None of the women from good families even spoke to Emma Jane, and all of the men had apologized to him for the behavior of their wives and daughters.

But it would blow over. Gossip always did. Soon enough, people would be clamoring for invitations for tea with Emma Jane, and they'd be looking for her sponsorship at their events. The Jackson name and fortune had that effect on people.

Ignoring the prickle at the back of his neck, Jasper replied, "No one ever died from gossip. The longer we delay in finding and rescuing Daisy, the more her life is at risk. As I said, my wife will be fine."

But something tugged at him as he remembered talking to Emma Jane when they were trapped in the mine, and how hurt she'd been by all the women mocking her dress, whispering about how her father had gambled away all their money, and worse—her sister's hand in marriage.

Maybe no one had ever died from gossip, but he'd seen how it had broken Emma Jane's heart.

"I'm sorry." He held out his hand to her. "I'm so used to people talking about me, I suppose I hadn't considered much about how it might be hurtful to you. But I have to go with the posse today. They're counting on me. I should be back by supper—we can talk then. I promise we'll figure something out."

The lines in Emma Jane's forehead disappeared, even though Pastor Lassiter still looked concerned. But it was the best he could do for now. If the bandits weren't stopped, how many others would be in danger? He'd do what he could to make more of an effort with Emma Jane. Maybe he'd talk to his friend Will about how to balance life as a lawman and making time for family. Of course, Will's engagement was as new as Jasper's marriage, but surely the other man would have some advice. He only hoped that Emma Jane had the wisdom to stay away from the case.

The humiliation of sitting and listening to the women mocking her in church was nothing compared to the fact that Jasper didn't seem to take the gossip she faced seriously. But of course it wasn't he who was called the names. A woman finds herself in a compromising position, and she is all sorts of evil. But what of the man? No one spews insults at him or tries to tell him that there is something wrong with him. Since their wedding, Jasper was perfectly able to carry on with his life with no ill effects.

Emma Jane watched as her husband justified his actions to the pastor. Jasper honestly didn't think he'd done anything wrong. But as Jasper pointed out that a woman's life was in jeopardy, how could Emma Jane argue? It seemed selfish to speak up and say that Pastor Lassiter was right—she did need him. Both in defense against the women at church and with his mother.

Jasper bowed his head slightly. "I'm sorry, Pastor. I

really am. But I do need to get going. The posse is leaving soon, and I need to be with them."

Then, without waiting for anyone's response, Jasper turned and walked away.

It shouldn't have hurt, since Emma Jane knew he was leaving, but the farther he went, the bigger the empty space in her heart became.

Mary came and put her arm around Emma Jane. "It will be all right. Hopefully, they catch the bandits soon and they won't have to keep rushing off. Will seemed confident that they were close to finding them. Their most recent lead was promising, he said."

Far more information than Jasper had given Emma Jane. Was it wrong to envy her friend and the open communication Mary and Will had?

"I hope so." She turned to Pastor Lassiter. "In the meantime, I believe you were saying that the church needed additional assistance with the women you're caring for right now. What can I do to help?"

Though the pastor's brow remained furrowed, he gave a smile. "It's as I keep telling everyone, Emma Jane. You have a good heart. Once the Jacksons figure that out, they'll be grateful to have you in their family. You've already done so much, and I'm proud to have you in our church. As for what you can do…"

Mary stopped him. "Oh, no, you don't. First, we haven't eaten. While I'm sure the Jackson chef is wonderful, you can't tell me that the food is nearly as good as the wholesome meals Maddie fixes. And then Emma Jane and I are going to sit down and catch up on everything that's gone on around here lately. After that, you can put Emma Jane to work. It'll be waiting."

Emma Jane had always admired Mary's take-charge

attitude. But now, faced with a friend who actually cared about her, Emma Jane couldn't help the tears that filled her eyes. She hadn't realized just how hard it had been on her own. Though she and Mary had only recently become close, Emma Jane couldn't imagine how she'd managed all these years without Mary's friendship. She'd thought she'd found that kind of confidant in Jasper, but since their marriage, he felt more like a stranger. No, worse than a stranger.

"None of that." Mary gave her a quick squeeze. "What did I tell you about tears ruining your complexion? You'll feel better once you've gotten some food in you."

Pastor Lassiter grinned. "And people wonder how *I* manage with all the people in my home. They should see how well the people in my home do all the managing for me."

They all chuckled together as they exited the church, then rounded the corner to the parsonage. Mary's younger brother and sisters were chasing one another in the backyard, playing some kind of game. The giggles filled Emma Jane's soul. She hadn't heard laughter at all since she'd been staying in the Jackson mansion. Even in her own home, laughter had often been missing. But here, at the Lassiter house, where Mary and her siblings were staying until their house could be built, merriment abounded. If Emma Jane could have one wish about her future with Jasper, it would be that their home would be more like this place than where they'd both grown up.

Emma Jane shook her head. She shouldn't be thinking such things. She had to believe that she and Jasper would find their way…somehow.

But how were they supposed to do that when he kept shutting her out? He said that it was for her safety, but that was what men always said to women. Jasper and Will had made Mary stay behind the night of the brothel fire for her safety, but Mary had followed them. And even though she had been in danger, Mary herself had told Emma Jane that it had been her quick thinking that had saved them. When the bandits had them all trapped, Mary distracted the bandits by throwing the lit lamps at them, giving Will, Jasper and herself time to get away.

Even now, word about Mary's bravery was getting out around town. She was a hero.

As they walked toward the parsonage, Emma Jane couldn't help but wonder if a heroic act of her own might make the town look at her differently.

So what could Emma do that wouldn't upset Jasper...?

"Mary!"

The youngest little girl came running up to them, and Mary swung her up in her arms. "How's my sweet little Nugget?"

"Hungry! You've been gone ever so long, and Maddie said we couldn't start eating until you and Uncle Frank got here."

Emma Jane couldn't help but smile at the child's honesty. She'd heard that the younger Stone children had taken to calling Pastor Lassiter "Uncle Frank," but experiencing it for herself warmed her heart. Just last winter, Pastor Lassiter's wife and all of his children but Annabelle had succumbed to the illness that had run rampant through their community. Many families had lost loved ones, and it had seemed horribly unfair to Emma Jane that the good pastor had suffered such a tragedy. Yet here, in the happy chaos of his yard, Emma Jane saw no evidence of loss, but of the joy of living.

If only she could capture some of that for herself.

"They're something else, aren't they?" Pastor Lassiter's voice came beside her.

"Yes, they are." She turned to him, noticing the happiness on his face. "Can I ask you what may be an impertinent question?"

"I'm not sure you're capable of asking an impertinent question." His eyes twinkled. "Ask away."

Emma Jane took a deep breath. "How did you do it? The past year, you've faced unimaginable losses, and yet here you are, still opening your heart and home with such joy?"

"That's a good question."

Emma Jane watched as he looked around the yard, seeming to take in every detail. "I think it's several things. The first is that the human capacity to love is limited by our humanness. But when we allow that love space within us to be filled with the Lord, our capacity to love is limitless."

Put that way, it was easy to understand as Emma Jane pictured the many folks who came through their church and their community, as well as the nearby communities Pastor Lassiter served so tirelessly. She'd wondered how one person could accomplish all of that.

"How do you get the Lord to fill that love space?" Immediately, Emma Jane thought of Mrs. Jackson. Perhaps relying on her own power to love her mother-in-law was where she was making the mistake. Could God give her the strength to love Mrs. Jackson?

"Ask Him. Read your Bible. And let Him work in you."

Then Pastor Jackson turned to her and looked at her intently. "The other thing that got me through was the realization that we must see everything that comes our way as an opportunity from the Lord. We remember to thank Him for the good things, but we also need to take the time to look at the bad and ask the Lord what He's trying to teach us through the situation." Clearing his throat, he waited a beat before saying, "For me, I learned that while it's easy to love the Lord during the good times, we must also cling to Him through the bad. Love Him just as much in the hard times, because the kind of the love that most honors God is the love that endures all things."

Still, Emma Jane couldn't imagine the strength it took to endure all of the loss in Pastor Lassiter's life. He took her hand.

"I know that your marriage, and the events surrounding it, are less than ideal. But don't think for a moment that the Lord has abandoned you. Draw near to Him, and I promise that you will make it through in a way far more profound than you could have imagined. He has good plans for you, Emma Jane, and I am praying you will cling to Him as He sees you through."

Tears pricked the backs of her eyes. No one had expressed such a deep belief in her before. And yet, as she thought back to the pastor's earlier words about the love of God, she realized that he wasn't just expressing his own personal belief about her, but God's belief in her.

"Thank you." Emma Jane squeezed his hand. "I appreciate you sharing your heart with me."

Pastor Lassiter gave a small smile. "If it makes you feel any better, I will also tell you that there are days I miss my sweet Catherine so much it hurts. It seems brutally unfair that I had to lose her. But as it says in Job, I can't accept only the good and not the bad from the Lord. It's all right to feel that way. Just keep giving it to God, and He will be faithful in standing beside you."

His openness touched Emma Jane deeper than any of his sermons ever had. She wanted that kind of relationship with the Lord. That depth of love and trust. She'd do as he said—when she got home, she'd spend as much time as she could reading her Bible. There wasn't that much else to do at the Jackson mansion, anyway. She might as well spend the time being productive.

However, before she could formulate a response, Nugget came barreling toward them.

"Uncle Frank! Let's eat! Maddie made fried chicken, and I've got my eye on one of the legs."

From matters of the heart to matters of the stomach. Emma Jane couldn't help the joy welling up in her at the absolute delight of being with this family. *Oh, Lord*, she prayed, *please let me find this joy in my own home.*

Chapter Three

Emma Jane's day with Mary had been exactly what she'd needed. Not only had she found incredible peace talking with Pastor Lassiter, but the afternoon spent visiting with Mary had given her a new strength. Their friend Polly, who was also staying at the parsonage with her family to help with the Stone children, had joined them, and Emma Jane could honestly not recall a more enjoyable afternoon. Then the three girls went to the barn, where the women from the fire were staying, and they were able to tend to some of the women's needs. Emma Jane hadn't had much of a chance to chat with her friend Nancy, so she'd promised to come back the following morning.

Which left her sitting in her luxurious bedroom in the Jackson mansion, Bible in front of her, and unable to sleep. The past several nights had been spent in misery, and now she felt so happy it seemed a sin to close her eyes.

Well, that and the fact that Jasper had not returned by suppertime as he'd promised.

Had he been hurt? Killed?

Or was it like all the promises she'd heard all her life from her father, the ones that consisted of "Things will be different this time, you'll see."

Nothing in her life had ever become different, not even when the one thing that was supposed to make a difference, marrying Jasper Jackson, had happened.

Floorboards creaked on the stairs, and Emma Jane jumped up. The Jacksons had already turned in for the evening, and surely by now the servants were already in bed. Which meant it had to be Jasper.

She opened the door and Jasper jumped.

"Emma Jane! What are you doing up?"

"Reading my Bible." She smiled and opened the door wider. "How was your expedition? Was it successful?"

Jasper shook his head. "Another dead end."

"Come in. Why don't you tell me about it?"

Jasper looked at her like she was crazy. "I can't come in your bedroom." He glanced at her nightgown. "You're not even properly dressed."

With a sigh, Emma Jane pulled her shawl more tightly around her. "My nightgown is much more modest than what half the women wear around town. Besides, we're married." She smiled up at him. "I've already been compromised, so it's not as though you can compromise me any worse."

But he glowered at her words. "That's not funny."

Emma Jane sighed. "I'm sorry. I was just trying to lighten up a bad situation. I didn't mean to hit a raw nerve. Can we pretend I didn't make a thoughtless comment, and then you come in and tell me about your progress? I'd like to work on our friendship, if that's all right with you."

When he didn't answer, Emma Jane continued. "Besides, I meant what I said about wanting to help. Since you won't let me *do* anything, at least let me listen. One of the women today said that having someone listen to her troubles was help enough for her."

For a moment, she thought he was going to snap at her or comment about how it wasn't time to work on their marriage, but then he sighed and took a step toward her door. "I suppose I can spare a few minutes."

What happened to the Jasper she used to like? The man who used to like her?

"The chair by the window is comfortable. You could sit there if you like." It sounded strange to her to be so formal with her own husband. Then again, it still sounded strange for her to refer to herself as having a husband.

"I'm glad you're comfortable here," Jasper said as he sat, settling against the soft velvety fabric.

"I'm still getting used to it all, to be honest. I've never had such luxuries, and having a staff is still intimidating."

He laughed. Not the fake laugh she'd heard from across the room at so many social functions where she'd stood in the corner, praying no one would notice her. Rather, it was the same warm sound she'd heard from him when they'd gotten to know each other during the mine cave-in. After their rescue, they'd recuperated at a nearby lake resort because it was closer than returning to town. A stay that had been extended to a week due to a snow storm making the roads impassable.

There, she'd thought they'd become friends. Stuck in a hotel with no one but the proprietors and Will and Mary for company, they'd formed a bond of sorts, and their easy camaraderie had made her wonder why they hadn't gotten to know each other sooner.

Emma Jane hadn't heard that laugh since their wedding.

"I've missed that sound," she said quietly, hoping it wasn't the wrong thing to say. She'd already blundered in mentioning their past, but hopefully this would be a happier reminder.

Fortunately, Jasper rewarded her with a smile. "I guess we haven't had much to laugh about. And I haven't exactly warmed to your attempts at trying to ease the situation. Sometimes I feel selfish for enjoying life when a woman is dead because of me and I've yet to make it up to her."

Back to sober Jasper. And yet, not. Because where he'd once shut her out, here he was opening up.

Could their relationship be turning a new corner as she'd hoped?

Emma Jane sat on her bed, pleased that at least Jasper had made himself comfortable on her chair.

"I don't think she saved your life so you would feel guilty for living." She gestured to the Bible she'd been reading. "I've been reading in John, where Jesus says that He's come so people can have abundant life. I know it's not an exact parallel, but Christ's sacrifice was meant for us to be able to do good with our lives. Surely Mel dying for you was similar."

Jasper stared at her for a moment, and Emma Jane felt silly for saying such things. Her mother and sister used to mock her for all of her "Bible nonsense," and even her father told her it wasn't seemly for a woman to be so familiar with Scriptures.

"I guess I hadn't thought of it that way," Jasper said slowly. "You used to say things like that in Sunday school, things that made me think. I'd forgotten until now."

Emma Jane felt her face warm, just as it had when

their Sunday school teacher had complimented her. The other girls in the class, however, had teased her mercilessly. On top of all of her other faults, she'd been too bold in showing off her knowledge.

"Why are you embarrassed?" Jasper looked at her with an intensity that made her feel even more unclothed than she already was. "You used to say such interesting things in Sunday school, then you stopped."

Then, with a note of what sounded like regret, he said, "And then you stopped coming at all."

"I was tired of being made fun of by the other girls." The words came out almost as a whisper, and her chest burned as she said them.

"I'm sorry. I never noticed."

He truly did sound as though he felt badly for not noticing. But no one noticed Emma Jane. Not unless they found something to tease her about. Except Jasper. He'd never teased her.

"It's all right. I stopped going to most of the church functions and took to reading the Bible on my own. I know it's not seemly for a woman to spend so much time reading the Bible, but sometimes it was all I had."

"Why did you come to the church picnic?"

Back to their shared history and events that they both seemed like they wanted to forget but couldn't.

"My mother made me. I didn't want to go. I knew word of my father's bad night at cards had gotten out. But my mother said it was our only hope."

"Marrying me." His voice came out raspy, like it hurt to say the words as much as it hurt Emma Jane to admit her shame.

"Yes." And then, because she couldn't help it, "I'm sorry. I never meant any of this to happen."

Flora's words at the church came back to her. "I heard some of the talk that's gotten around about what happened. I want you to know…"

"Stop. Please." He ran a hand over his face. "I thought I could do this. I thought I wanted to get through it, but…"

Jasper let out a long sigh. "I want to understand, Emma Jane. But there's still so much of me that thinks about what was taken away from me, and it's hard to let go. I need you to be patient with me."

Her chest was so tight it almost hurt to breathe. How she managed to get out the words, she didn't know. "Of course. I…"

The rest, she couldn't say. Because as much as she knew that Jasper resented not having a lot of choices in life, the choices he did have were a far sight better than anything Emma Jane had ever had. He acted as though she'd wanted to marry him. Not that she'd wanted to marry anyone else, of course, but just like Jasper had said he'd wanted to choose his own wife, she'd wanted to find her own husband.

Granted, what she wanted was probably a lot more than what Jasper wanted for himself. But for Emma Jane, she wanted a husband who wanted her. Who didn't marry her out of obligation. Who enjoyed spending time with her…and genuinely liked and loved her…

Didn't he realize that, in their marriage, all of her hopes and dreams had been dashed, as well?

She swallowed the lump in her throat. "I didn't mean for us to quarrel. Perhaps we can talk about something safe. Like what you're reading in your Bible."

Emma Jane forced a smile to her lips, hoping that, at least in this, they could find common ground.

Only, with the dark look that crossed Jasper's face, she knew she'd missed the mark—again.

"I don't read my Bible."

She'd hoped, in marrying a man active in their church, that their faith would eventually bring them together. Apparently, even that hope was to be dashed.

"Why not?"

Jasper shrugged. "I learn plenty from Pastor Lassiter's sermons. I know enough about God that I don't need to keep studying. After all, I've been attending church since I was a child."

Jasper might have grown up wealthy, but as Emma Jane recalled his mother's words earlier about giving money to the church in lieu of helping out, she wondered if he might have grown up poor indeed.

"But Pastor Lassiter talks about the importance of reading God's Word."

Jasper shrugged. "And he reads it to us every Sunday. Why should I do more?"

"Because it deepens your relationship with the Lord."

He looked thoughtful for a moment. "I suppose that's why you always made such insightful comments in Sunday school. How often do you read your Bible?"

"Every day." Emma Jane hoped her words didn't sound too prideful. When she'd made a similar comment to one of the girls at church, she'd chastised Emma Jane for being too full of herself.

Jasper didn't say anything for a long while, and as the silence began to grow uncomfortable, Emma Jane wondered what she could say that wouldn't cause more strife between them.

Fortunately, Jasper's stomach rumbled loudly, and it sent Emma Jane into motion.

"I just realized, the staff has all gone to bed, but if you're hungry, or you want some tea, I could get you something."

Finally. A small smile teased the corners of Jasper's lips. "Mother will be furious if she finds you in the kitchen." Then, in a mocking voice, he said, "Don't you know that is what the help is for? We do not belong in their domain, just as they do not belong in ours."

Emma Jane giggled. "That sounds exactly like her."

"I've heard it my whole life." Jasper yawned at the same time his stomach rumbled again.

"It would be no trouble to get you a sandwich. I spent all night working the night of the brothel fire to make sure everyone was taken care of. Cook and I became friends of sorts, and I think she'll be happy if I get you something without disturbing her."

Jasper sat up slightly. "I didn't realize you spent so much time helping that night."

"Of course. I couldn't sleep, knowing that you, Will and Mary were confronting a dangerous situation. Then, when Mary and Rose came here, telling us of the fire, I had to do what I could. Rose was with the doctor, and poor Mary was exhausted and famished. I had to make sure she had something, and then, with you and Will still out there, I knew that you'd need something, as well. I didn't sleep at all that night."

And then Jasper had been too busy talking to the authorities to talk to her. The only reason Emma Jane even knew the full story of what had happened in the brothel was because Mary had told her. Though that fact hurt, what wounded her even more was the surprised expression on Jasper's face. True, he had been too busy to notice Emma Jane's contributions, but the fact that it didn't occur to him that she'd want to help, well, that seemed like a far greater sin than Jasper's abandonment.

That was the trouble with marrying someone you barely knew. Jasper didn't know that for someone like Emma Jane, the easiest thing to do was to step in and work, because when you worked, you didn't have to talk. Because talking meant that people would notice her and make fun of her. No one ever seemed to pay any mind to the workers. Probably why Jasper had never noticed her, either.

"I'm sorry I never thanked you for your help," he said huskily.

"It was a busy night. Your mother rushed you into bed and had the doctor in there with you so quickly, I'm sure there were a lot of things you didn't notice."

The weariness on Jasper's face seemed to increase as the lamp flickered beside him. She hated continuing to make him talk, but they seemed to almost be getting along. Could they regain ground as friends?

"I think Pastor Lassiter has a point about us needing time together to get to know each other. I don't understand what's fueling your need to help this Daisy person, and you don't understand anything about me." Emma Jane pulled her shawl tighter around her. "Why don't I get you something to eat, and when I get back, you can tell me something you think I should know about you."

At least, with Jasper leading the conversation, it would keep her from making any more missteps that would drive them apart.

Hesitating before heading for the door, she watched the play of emotions on her husband's face. Could he see that she was offering him an olive branch? A chance to begin their marriage as it should have been? Asking him to love her was too much—Emma Jane knew that—but surely peaceful coexistence wasn't so far out of their reach.

After what seemed like ages, Jasper's lips turned upward into the grin that was rumored to melt every woman's heart this side of the Divide. Emma Jane had never been one of the girls to giggle and swoon over Jasper's famed good looks, but if he gave her many grins like that, she could easily find herself wanting to. However, a man's appearance faded over time, and Emma Jane hoped that what she found beneath was the same man she'd grown to like at the church picnic.

"All right. Don't put any pickles on my sandwich. Mother seems to think they're my favorite, but I really can't stand her pickles." He gave her a wink, then settled back into her chair.

No pickles. The simple request seemed to be the beginning of a friendship as Emma Jane went downstairs to the kitchen. There, she found Cook already at the stove, busying herself with the kettle.

"What are you doing up?" Emma Jane crossed the room and reached for a mug. Though Mrs. Jackson would probably disapprove of Jasper not being served on fine china, the mugs held more, and he seemed like he could use a larger cup of tea.

"I heard Mr. Jasper come home. He doesn't take good care of himself, so I thought I'd prepare some food for him."

In her short time at the Jackson mansion, Emma Jane had learned that everything was about catering to Jasper—when it wasn't about Mrs. Jackson, of course. But his mother's primary concern, other than reputation, was making sure that Jasper never wanted for anything.

"I should have known. I came down to do the very thing myself."

Cook pointed to a plate on the table. "Sandwiches for Mr. Jasper, just the way he likes."

Emma Jane couldn't help but notice the pickle hanging out the sides. She went over and removed it.

"What are you doing with Mrs. Jackson's prized pickles? Those are Mr. Jasper's favorite."

"When I asked him what he'd like, he mentioned that he'd prefer not to have pickles." Emma Jane hesitated, wondering if she should share his secret.

Cook nodded slowly. "I wondered who'd been leaving pickles in strange places in the dining room. Poor Mr. Jasper probably didn't want to hurt his mother's feelings. Mrs. Jackson prides herself on those pickles, though I don't know a single soul who can tolerate them. I'll keep that in mind for the future."

It was a simple conversation about pickles, but it told something about Jasper's character that Emma Jane hadn't been expecting. As much as he played the role of a carefree playboy, Jasper's compassion ran deep. Rather than hurt his mother's feelings, he'd gone along with the charade of liking her pickles.

As Emma Jane finished preparing Jasper's tea, she thought more about Jasper's compassion. At the church picnic, when everyone else mocked Emma Jane's outmoded dress and the ridiculous way her mother had painted her face to attract attention, Jasper had reprimanded the girls who'd mistreated her in front of him. He'd spoken to her with kindness and treated her with dignity even when everyone else was whispering about her father losing everything at the gambling halls. He'd even promised to help her find a way to get her family out of the mess.

Of course, he hadn't meant to marry her, and he'd said as much. Poor Jasper had only thought to do a good deed for Emma Jane, and she'd repaid him by forcing a marriage he didn't want.

She sighed and put the sandwich and tea on a tray. No, she hadn't forced the marriage. Her parents had. And when she'd tried telling everyone that it wasn't Jasper's fault they'd been trapped in a mine together and that nothing had happened requiring marriage, everyone ignored her.

When she arrived back in her room, Jasper lay sprawled in the chair, his mouth hanging open, snoring softly. His thick dark hair had fallen over closed eyes. The rugged lines had disappeared from his face, and he appeared so peaceful, full of calm and innocence. Looking at him like this, Emma Jane understood why his looks beguiled so many. He seemed so handsome and debonair. So…perfect. Everyone seemed to want that perfection, and yet, the more time Emma Jane spent with Jasper, the more she realized there was so much more to him. Which was strange, because she barely knew him at all.

After setting the tray down on a nearby table, Emma Jane took one of the blankets from her bed and tucked it around Jasper. She'd have liked to have moved him, but she wasn't that strong, and she didn't want to disturb him. He seemed to be sleeping comfortably enough, and because she'd napped on that very chair a time or two, Emma Jane knew he'd be fine.

Then, because it seemed like the right thing to do,

Emma Jane bent and kissed him on the forehead. "May God bless you and keep you."

She crossed the room, turned out the lights, then climbed back into her own bed and settled into sleep.

Jasper woke with a crick in his neck, feeling more rested than he had in days, yet not entirely comfortable. He opened his eyes, then realized where he was. Emma Jane's room. He must have fallen asleep when she'd gone to get him something to eat. He glanced around the room and noticed the tray sitting on a nearby table.

Dear, sweet girl. His stomach rumbled, so he went ahead and grabbed the sandwich. The tea was cold, but it quenched his thirst. He ate and drank, enjoying the meal she'd prepared for him. Even the lack of pickles on his sandwich warmed his heart. True, his mother would have done the same and brought him a tray. But something about the fact that Emma Jane had taken it upon herself to tend to him was endearing. She hadn't needed to go to all that trouble.

As if to remind him of her presence, Emma Jane gave a small sigh as she shifted in her bed. He looked over at her, noticing that she lay curled up in the blanket, almost like a child. Her hair lay spread out across the pillow, a deep honey shade that was neither brown nor blond, but a combination of the two. He'd heard people talk about how plain Emma Jane's looks were, but watching her sleep, he thought her quite lovely. True, she didn't have the classical beauty that seemed to be prized in society, but there was something genuinely attractive about her innocent face and lack of artifice.

Emma Jane sighed yet again and mumbled something

incoherent. Jasper turned away. He shouldn't be intruding on her private moments of rest.

She'd been kind to him the night before, trying to talk to him and find out what he was really like. For all her faults, Emma Jane was trying to be a good wife. But could she make up for the fact that she'd used him so badly?

He remembered how she'd made a point to tell him that she'd complied with his request, not investigating on her own and relying on him to share information.

Emma Jane was doing her part, and it was time he thought about doing his. Letting go of his resentment of the situation and giving her an honest chance. He'd told her last night that he was finding it difficult. But for as hard as he saw Emma Jane trying, he knew he owed her nothing less.

Jasper folded the blanket Emma Jane had put around him. Her consideration gave him pause. He hadn't known that she'd helped out the night of the brothel fire. Nor had he known that she'd been helping with the women displaced by the brothel fire. In some ways, it shamed Jasper to realize that as angry as he was about his marriage, he hadn't at all thought about what kind of woman he'd ended up with.

Somehow, in all of this mess, he'd found himself attached to a good woman.

As he placed the blanket on the chair, the bedroom door opened.

"Jasper! What are you doing in here?"

His mother's gasp jolted him and, from the startled sound in the bed, Emma Jane, as well.

"Good morning, Mother."

"Answer my question."

Jasper wanted to laugh at his mother's insistence. He was a married man, and still she concerned herself with the propriety of being in a woman's—no, his wife's—bedchamber.

"Emma Jane heard me come in late, and she wanted to be sure I was taken care of." He gestured to the empty plate. "I fell asleep in the chair, and she was kind enough to let me rest."

"She should have alerted the staff." His mother's face was pinched in an unpleasant expression. "Speaking of which, one of the maids says she saw Emma Jane leaving the kitchen last night. I cannot have her interfering with the staff's business."

He knew his marriage had been hard on his mother, who'd dreamed of a big society wedding with a woman of her choosing. But as he'd told her the day before, they had to come to terms with the fact that life had other plans for them.

"Emma Jane was being a good wife," Jasper said in a carefully modulated tone. "I was grateful for her kindness to me."

"I see." She turned her attention to Emma Jane, who'd just woken and now sat up in bed, pulling her covers around her. "In the future, please leave the care of my son to our staff."

Was his mother seriously telling Emma Jane not to take care of him? Did she truly expect that he and Emma Jane were going to continue to live in this house as strangers? But as he saw the tension in his mother's elegant figure, he knew that was exactly what she was thinking. His mother never thought that he and Emma Jane would have a real marriage.

Jasper swallowed. He'd never imagined it, either. But

he had hoped that, over time, he and Emma Jane could at least find a peaceful way to live together. Last night, she had reached out to him in an attempt to make that happen.

Constance's edict would only serve to drive a wedge between their already fragile marriage.

"I like Emma Jane's care, Mother. So if it's no trouble to her, then I see no need for her to rouse the servants on my behalf." Jasper looked directly at Emma Jane, hoping she understood that he was on her side.

"I see. However, I do want to stress that your *wife* should not be in the kitchen." His mother turned and sauntered out of the room, leaving the door open behind her.

Although Emma Jane's comment last night about her already being compromised had rubbed him the wrong way, he couldn't help but think it now. What did his mother think she was saving him from? They'd already been forced to marry.

"I'm sorry about that," Jasper said to her. "She'll warm up to you eventually."

"It's all right." Emma Jane stared at the blankets on the bed, not meeting his gaze. "I'm sure it must be hard for her to have you married to someone like me. I'm not exactly the society darling she'd hoped for."

Her words shamed him. Not because she was trying to, but because that's what Emma Jane seemed to truly believe. He thought back to the way the women had teased her at the church picnic, how Flora Montgomery had tried to persuade him not to speak to her because of the scandal surrounding her father's gambling losses. Even at their wedding, which was supposed to quiet all the talk about Emma Jane's fall from grace, he'd heard the whispers disparaging her character.

Jasper knew none of it was true. He'd assumed everyone else would figure out the truth sooner or later, as well. But it hadn't occurred to him that Emma Jane believed herself deserving of the censure.

"Any man would be honored to be married to someone like you," Jasper said gruffly.

Emma Jane finally met his eyes. "You aren't."

He'd forgotten how direct she could be. When they first spoke at the church picnic, he'd admired that about her. Even respected the fact that she'd come right out and said that if he married her, it would solve her problems. But that was before she'd tricked him into compromising her. Before she'd demonstrated her lack of trust in him.

"No man wants to be made a fool of."

He hated the way she shrank back at his words. Emma Jane wanted to be friends and recapture what they'd had before they'd been forced to marry. But how could they get past it, when she had no idea what she'd stolen from him?

A chance to fall in love. To have a loving home. A family of his own. Perhaps he and Emma Jane could get to a place where they could find a way to have children. But there'd never be the same loving glances he saw Will and Mary exchange. He'd never know what it was like to have someone see all the parts of him and love him, really love him, for who he was.

Maybe Jasper had been the fool. This whole mess had started because seeing Will again and meeting Emma Jane had made him want to be a better man. To be known for something other than the wealthy playboy who stole women's hearts. He'd thought he wanted a life of substance instead of playing to society's whims.

Yet here he was, stuck in a marriage of convenience because he'd tried to be the man of honor he wanted to be.

Tears rolled down Emma Jane's cheeks, and he knew he should be sorry for them. Part of him was, but the other part of him still mourned the life he could never have.

Chapter Four

When Jasper finally arrived downstairs, he found his mother in her sitting room, sorting through envelopes. She looked up at him and held out several in his direction.

"Do you see these?"

"Yes, Mother." He tried to sound as accommodating as possible, but he found it more difficult than usual. They often had this conversation about invitations. All the brides she'd hoped to snare for him. Now that he was married, he'd thought these conversations would end.

"All the best families in town, and not one invitation from them. We're supposed to be the pillars of society, and yet we seem to only be receiving correspondence from the lesser-known families."

"So what would you have me do? Throw her out on the street?"

Jasper gave his mother an icy look, then turned to go into the dining room. After the sandwich Emma Jane had so thoughtfully provided, he wasn't all that hungry. His encounter with his mother had stolen the rest of his appetite. But he could put together a few things to take with him on the trail.

Yesterday's dead end had him wondering. Everything seemed too convenient. The promising lead, and then it suddenly fizzling out. Something was off, and he couldn't put his finger on it. Trouble was, since this was Jasper's first foray into law enforcement, no one else in the sheriff's office took him seriously. Everyone assumed that his desire to take down the rest of the gang was a playboy's whim.

His father sat at the head of the table, and while he appeared to be reading his paper, as soon as Jasper entered the room, he looked up at him.

"Go easy on your mother. It's a rough transition."

"You don't think it's rough on me?" Jasper grumbled, pouring himself a cup of coffee as he sat. While he didn't want his father's lecture, he could use some advice on the case. Or at least in getting the other men to respect him.

The glare he got in response made Jasper feel about five years old. Henry folded the paper, then stared at his son. "Your mother has had one thing driving her all these years—her son marrying well so she could gain the daughter she never had. Your choice in wife is not exactly what she had imagined."

"I didn't choose to marry Emma Jane."

Silence rocked the room for several minutes before Jasper's father answered. "You would have left a girl ruined instead?"

Jasper squeezed his eyes shut, forcing himself not to say something he'd regret. Finally, he took a deep breath, then opened his eyes. "Nothing untoward happened. I told you. But society and honor dictated that we marry. I didn't make the rules, I just follow them. Now that we're married, I have to make the best of it."

"So why are you running away all the time? That

doesn't sound like making the *best of it* to me." His fa-ther's dark eyes bore deep into him, searching for the truth. Henry had been able to make Jasper come clean on even his worst deeds ever since he was a child.

This, however, was not like the entire plate of tea cakes he'd pilfered, eaten, then promptly became so sick he'd never had the urge to touch one of the dainty delicacies again. And yet, telling his father the truth about his in-tentions was even more important.

"I'm not running away." Jasper sighed. "If anything, my marriage is a complication getting in the way of what I want to do."

He took a long sip of the cooling coffee, then contin-ued. "Seeing Will again made me realize how little I'd done with my life. Everyone admires Jasper Jackson. But for what? My good looks, my last name, the money I'll inherit when you die? I want to do something meaning-ful with my life."

With everything that had happened over the past several days, Jasper hadn't been able to express those things. Finally getting it all out made the load feel so much lighter.

"When I helped Will rescue Mary's sister, I realized that in fighting for justice for those who can't fight for themselves, there was so much more to the world than just myself."

Emma Jane's image flashed before his eyes. When they'd been forced to marry, she'd told him the only rea-son she'd agreed to marry him was to protect her younger sister, Gracie. Had Emma Jane not married Jasper, Gra-cie would have been forced to marry one of the most execrable men in town. As part of their marriage agree-ment, Jasper's father had paid off Emma Jane's father's gambling debts. One of those debts was to a man who'd told Mr. Logan that he'd take Gracie as a wife in lieu of cash. Had Jasper had a sister, would he have done any differently to spare his loved one a miserable future?

Perhaps he and Emma Jane were not so dissimilar, after all.

He only wished he didn't feel so conflicted over his marriage.

One piece of his experiences of late continued to ring true, and that was the thing that drove him in his quest. "Even without my desire to be a better man, there's the fact that a woman gave her life for me. Mel didn't have to take the bullet meant for me, but she did. How do you ignore her dying wish to find and save her sister?"

All these days later, he could still smell the residue of gunpowder mixed with Mel's blood. Jasper had foolishly tried intimidating Ben Perry, leader of the gang he was now pursuing, and Ben's men had opened fire. Jasper should have died, but Mel shielded him. How does a man repay such a sacrifice?

Which was why he'd die before giving up on his quest for Mel. Everything in Mel's life had been about giving her sister a better life. He owed it to her to save Daisy. Married to Emma Jane, Jasper accepted that his other dreams of home and family would be denied. But he would make something meaningful of his life.

"Sounds like some powerful motivation," his father said slowly. "Just remember that when a man marries, his life is no longer his own."

Jasper gave him a long, hard look. He'd already spent time living the life his parents wanted. Just when he thought he'd figured out what he wanted with his life, it seemed life had other plans. How was he supposed to balance his dreams with being a husband?

Emma Jane's ears stung as she stood outside the dining room door. There was a reason for the saying that eavesdroppers never heard good about themselves. But this was more than just hearing bad about herself. Oh, Emma Jane knew that Jasper hadn't wanted to marry her, even without overhearing his conversation with his father. But realizing that Jasper felt like she'd taken away his chance to do something meaningful with his life…

Suddenly she felt very selfish for wanting him by her side to protect her reputation. Jasper wanted to do good in the world, and he wanted to help people. For the first time, she truly heard him as he explained to his father what it meant to save this Daisy person.

Taking a deep breath, Emma Jane stepped into the room. "Jasper's right," she said, not bothering to enter the conversation gracefully. "He's doing something important. Working to bring down a gang of criminals, and saving this woman, those things matter. I'll still be here when he's finished with his mission."

She gave what she hoped was a convincing smile as she turned to serve herself breakfast. While the words sounded like the right thing to say, her stomach churned. It certainly didn't feel right.

But what else was she supposed to do? Emma Jane couldn't argue any of Jasper's proclamations without being the worst kind of heartless, selfish woman there was. It already seemed wrong for her to have become his wife, even though she'd had good reason. Why add more selfishness to her sins?

Jasper and Mr. Jackson stared at her as she took her seat at the table.

"He might not come home," Mr. Jackson said slowly.

Emma Jane shrugged and speared a piece of sausage. "He came home last night. He came home from the fire. Perhaps we need to put our faith in God and pray for his continued safety."

It was a trite answer, but what else did Emma Jane have to give? She focused her attention back on her plate, methodically eating, though she had no appetite. It gave her something to do other than acknowledge the gazes focused on her.

Mr. Jackson coughed. "I suppose that's true. The Lord has protected our Jasper many a time or two."

Even without looking at him, Emma Jane knew Jasper was grinning.

"You remember that time I wanted to pet a bull?"

This got Emma Jane's attention. She looked up at her husband, and sure enough, his face was lit up brighter than the midday sun.

"Your mother still needs smelling salts when you tell that story." Mr. Jackson leaned in toward Emma Jane. "He wasn't more than six or seven years old, and we were visiting friends at a ranch. Jasper saw the bull in the pen and thought that red coat of his was the prettiest thing he ever saw, and he wanted to pet it. Trust me when I say, never attempt to pet a bull."

At this, the two men laughed heartily, and even though Emma Jane hadn't been there, she could imagine the anger of a bull at having a little boy chasing him around and trying to pet him.

More importantly, though, she couldn't help but feel a surge of warmth at Mr. Jackson's attempt at trying to include her. He'd defended their marriage in talking to Jasper, and even though he'd also defended his wife's cold attitude, Mr. Jackson seemed to be at least trying to be on Emma Jane's side.

Of course, marriage wasn't supposed to be about sides, but what else was Emma Jane supposed to think?

"It must have been something, Mr. Jackson." Emma Jane smiled warmly at him, trying to show that she, too, was trying to make the best of a difficult situation.

"You really should call me Henry. We're family now."

Emma Jane wasn't sure which warmed her the most, the genuine kindness on the older man's face, or his use of the word *family*. Perhaps things weren't going to be so bad, after all.

"Mrs. Jackson said..."

"Constance means well. It's just as I was telling Jasper. Give her time, and she'll warm up to you."

Another expression of understanding. Yes, Emma Jane had to have hope that things could get better.

At that moment, Mrs. Jackson entered the room. "What is all this tomfoolery I hear in here?"

Emma Jane tried not to shrink back in her chair, though she did remain silent. Nothing good ever came of opening her mouth in front of Mrs. Jackson.

"Jasper was just telling us of his intention to continue working as a lawman. I expressed my concern, but Emma Jane rightly reminded me that we need to put our trust in the Lord."

Being so endorsed made Emma Jane sit up a little straighter.

"How dare you!" Mrs. Jackson's voice jolted Emma Jane back to reality. "If it weren't for you driving him away by forcing him to marry you, my son wouldn't be leaving us. And you try to explain it away with faith?"

Mr. Jackson put a hand on her arm. "Now, Constance, you know that's not true. Jasper's involvement in the situation is because he feels obligated to repay the woman who saved his life."

"A woman of no consequence."

Jasper rose from his chair. "I would be dead without her. Surely she deserves to be given some consequence."

His dark eyes flashed as he looked from his mother to his father, then settled on Emma Jane.

She felt small under his scrutiny and, for a moment, hated herself for it. She had nothing to be ashamed of. Even if his mother seemed to think so.

"As for your comments about my wife…" Jasper swallowed as he glanced briefly at his father before bringing his full attention back on Emma Jane.

"She has not driven me away. On the contrary, I have not been the best of husbands by neglecting her of late. I only hope that she is willing to continue to be patient as I bring these bandits to justice and find Daisy."

Was that remorse she heard in his voice? Her heart fluttered in her chest. Perhaps his father's words had given him pause to think. To consider Emma Jane as his partner in all of this.

"Of course I can be patient," Emma Jane said softly. She smiled at him, then turned her gaze on his parents. "In fact, as I mentioned yesterday, I am greatly enjoying my work with Pastor Lassiter's ministry. It will occupy my time while Jasper assists Sheriff Calhoune."

Jasper's slow nod gave her the courage to look over at his parents. Mrs. Jackson still wore a pinched expression of someone who'd taken a bite of something most distasteful. But Mr. Jackson murmured approvingly.

"It seems you are both similarly matched in your pursuit of the greater good."

"Associating with people not of our kind." Mrs. Jackson glowered at Emma Jane.

"Who is not of our kind," Jasper asked, taking a step toward his parents. "The pastor? His family? Emma Jane is the model of Christian service."

"You know exactly of whom I am speaking."

Though Mrs. Jackson's glare intensified, Emma Jane found that she did not shrink under it as she normally did. Though her aim in helping Pastor Lassiter was not to receive praise, she could not help basking in the compliment Jasper had given.

"Constance, enough!" Mr. Jackson gave Emma Jane a kind smile. "Constance has always doted on Jasper. This has been a lot of change for her all at once. I hope you'll give her some grace as she learns to adjust to the situation."

Adjust to the situation? Emma Jane took a deep breath. More people asking of her, but not...well, it didn't matter. People didn't do things for the benefit of Emma Jane, anyway. It was always Emma Jane doing for others. But it would be nice sometimes if someone thought to do for her.

"There is nothing to adjust to." Jasper slammed his hand down on the table. "Emma Jane is smarter than any of the ninnies you've paraded through our parlor. If I had to choose between Emma Jane and any one of the girls you thought I should marry, I'd pick Emma Jane. Now if you'll excuse us, I believe my wife and I are going to visit the church so I can see for myself the good works she is engaged in."

After his discussion with his father earlier, Emma Jane wouldn't have expected his fierce defense. Especially the part about him preferring her to the other girls. He was most likely just being kind, but at least he knew what Emma Jane was up against. Perhaps he was more sympathetic to her plight than she'd first thought.

Emma Jane carefully dabbed her lips with her napkin, then looked up at Jasper.

"I'm sorry," he said, resting his hand on the back of her chair. "I didn't even ask if you were finished. Or if you had other plans for today."

"It's all right. I'm finished." Her cheeks warmed when his hand brushed her back as he pulled out her chair for her.

He was being polite, she knew, but it still felt good to have him give even that small consideration to her feelings. And while she'd always known Jasper to be a handsome man, it seemed the more he showed his kindness, the handsomer he became.

If he kept up such actions, Emma Jane might very well find herself one of the giggling girls fawning over their fans at him. Perhaps it was just as well Jasper was chasing after bandits rather than spending time getting to know her. It wouldn't do to find herself attracted to a man who couldn't possibly fall in love with her.

Chapter Five

❦

"You don't have to stay if you don't want to," Emma Jane said softly as they entered the barn that was serving as a makeshift shelter for the women displaced by the brothel fire.

Her permission for him to leave made it impossible for him to do so, even if he'd wanted to. The contrast between his father's chastisement for not doing more for his wife, and his mother's attacks on Emma Jane, as well as Pastor Lassiter's admonitions for him to get to know her better, made it apparent that this was exactly the place he needed to be right now.

Plus, he still needed to figure out his next move in pursuit of the bandits. It would be foolish to do anything without thinking it through. Yesterday's dead end had proven that.

"I want to." Jasper smiled and pulled her hand more firmly into the crook of his arm. "The voices of reason around us are right. I haven't spent the time I should have on getting to know you. Besides, didn't you tell me just yesterday that you thought your work here could help my case?"

Emma Jane's face lit up. Once again, he was struck by how pretty she was when she smiled. Why hadn't he taken more notice of her before?

"You should meet my friend Nancy. I'm sure she'll give us lots of useful information."

It pained him to see the eager expression on her face. Mostly because he absolutely could not get her mixed up in this case. But also because as quickly as he'd set the intention of spending time with Emma Jane, if he was to question the women, even if one was Emma Jane's friend, he would have to do it without her.

"Once you make the introductions, you'll have to occupy yourself elsewhere," he said quietly. "I can't have you involved with this."

Emma Jane's face darkened, like clouds covering the sun in an unexpected storm. He should have seen it coming, had, in fact, known it was coming. What he hadn't expected was how it twisted his gut and made him feel…

No. He was just doing his job.

"But I thought…" Emma Jane's eyes glistened.

"I know, and I'm sorry."

He took off his hat and ran his hand through his hair, then stared down at the hat. He'd chosen an older hat, one usually reserved for when he went out riding, and now as he stared into the rivulets that carried away his sweat, he wished he could disappear as easily.

But that would be doing Emma Jane an even greater disservice.

He finally looked back up at her, holding his hat in his hands. "Please understand. This gang is ruthless, and if they think you are helping me in any way, they won't hesitate to take you down."

Swallowing, he looked around to be sure no one was

listening to their conversation. "They made me a deputy because one of the other deputies quit. The gang had sent him a note, threatening to kill his wife if he kept poking his nose into their business."

What would they do to a woman actively working the investigation? Another deputy, Skeeter Ross, was recuperating from a gunshot wound he'd gotten while chasing them. If his horse hadn't tripped at that exact moment, Skeeter would be dead.

"I can't put you at risk," he said, hoping that beyond those tear-filled eyes lay some level of understanding.

"But they already know we're married. They could still come after me because of your work. What more harm could come if I helped you?"

"Do you know how to shoot a gun?"

"Don't be ridicu..." Emma Jane sighed. "I suppose that's your point. I don't know any of the things needed to be a lawman."

Then she looked up at him with those big, trusting eyes. So innocent. No way could he involve her in the case. "How do *you* know them? I can't see society's biggest dandy knowing how to shoot a gun or capture bandits."

"Will taught me. Back when my father and I first met him, my father thought it would be a good idea for Will to teach me in dealing with riffraff. Because of my father's wealth, I was a target for kidnappings, robberies and the like. My father wanted to be sure I knew how to keep myself safe."

Will had taught him a lot of things, and even though the practical lifesaving pieces were the ones he emphasized here, the biggest lessons Will had imparted to him were the ones that had more to do with the kind of man Jasper wanted to be.

The man Emma Jane had married was not the man everyone in society believed him to be. How was he supposed to be any kind of husband to her when she had no idea who he really was? When he was still trying to figure it out himself?

"More than that, though." Jasper looked at Emma Jane, who still carried an air of doubt about her. "Will taught me about being a man. About defending people who are weaker than you and fighting for what's right, even if others don't agree with you. I owe a lot to him, and I guess if you want to know about me, then those are the things you should know."

She'd asked that question of him last night, and here in the light of day, the answer was clearer than he'd expected. He hadn't been lying when he'd said those things to his mother this morning about the women she'd hoped he'd marry. Not one of them would respect the answer he'd just given Emma Jane, but he hoped, given what little he knew of his wife, that she would.

And if she didn't, well, he wasn't sure what he'd do. He knew her expectation in marrying him was all about the fortune that would save her family. She'd said she'd hoped to be friends, but what did that look like to a woman like Emma Jane?

Would she still want to be friends once she realized that being a good man, and being a society dandy, had nothing in common?

"Thank you," she finally murmured, her face unreadable. "I suppose that's a start. You said yesterday that you needed me to trust you if our marriage was going to have a chance. So I'll do my part. I'll introduce you to Nancy and a few other ladies, and I'll leave you to your work."

Her acquiescence should have been a victory. But like all of the victories he'd found lately, this one didn't sit well with him.

How was he supposed to balance it all? Will seemed to do just fine, balancing his work with keeping his fiancée happy, but Jasper seemed to flail at every turn. Apparently, his pal hadn't taught him all the lessons he needed. And now, with time running out to find the bandits, and a wife he couldn't please, Jasper was going to have to figure it out all on his own.

Emma Jane hated that her last sentence sounded so peevish, but she couldn't find a way to make herself take it back. Oh, she wanted desperately to leave Jasper to it, but she couldn't help but think of her friend Mary, and how Mary knew all the details of Will's work. Will shared with her, and bounced ideas off her, and even though she had no qualifications as a lawman, Will still respected her opinion.

Then again, Will adored his bride-to-be, so maybe being in love came with different rules than being married.

Fortunately, she spied Nancy sitting in a corner by herself, which gave her the perfect opportunity to help Jasper. Perhaps, if he saw how she could be an asset to him in what he allowed her to do, he would realize that she could lend a hand in other areas, as well.

He'd told her that she needed to earn his trust. She'd do all she could to make him see that he could count on her. That she was every bit as capable as Mary in helping Will. No, it wouldn't make him fall in love with her.

But at least, if they could find a way to work on this case together, they could find enough in common that Emma Jane wouldn't feel so alone.

"I believe I see my friend Nancy, if you'd like to meet her." Emma Jane hoped her smile looked more like she was being friendly than filled with her newfound determination. She'd been told in the past that her determined expression made her look cross.

"Thank you, Emma Jane." Jasper rewarded her with a smile of his own. Before the circumstances leading to their marriage, Jasper had hardly spoken to her, hardly noticed her, much less found cause to offer a smile. Surely this was to be considered progress.

After all, how could she blame him for resenting marriage to her? They'd been virtual strangers, caught together in circumstances beyond their control. And while it was easy to focus on the things they could not control, there was plenty Emma Jane could.

Starting with finding a way to get along with her husband.

Now, filled with newfound purpose, Emma Jane took Jasper's arm and brought him over to where Nancy sat.

"Hello, Nancy." She gave the other woman a smile, though she knew that Nancy would most likely not smile back.

"Emma Jane." Nancy looked up at her and, as Emma Jane predicted, did not return the friendly expression.

Nancy had never had cause for the niceties of society, being on the fringes on account of her occupation as a woman of the night. And though Mrs. Jackson would be scandalized by it, Emma Jane found it refreshing to be around someone who let her be herself.

"I would like to present to you my husband, Jasper

Jackson. He's expressed a particular interest in wanting to meet you."

"I'll bet he has," Nancy sneered. "I suppose you'll be warning me off about putting notions in your wife's head."

The smile that formed around Emma Jane's lips came of its own accord. She couldn't help but like the direct way Nancy spoke. Then, remembering to be agreeable to Jasper, she quickly replaced the mirth with a more solemn expression.

It wouldn't do to offend him so soon.

However, instead of being offended, Jasper chuckled. "I can see why Emma Jane likes you. A straight shooter. I like that myself."

Still, the hostile expression on Nancy's face remained.

"If you're a friend of Emma Jane's, then that's good enough for me," Jasper continued. "I was hoping to discuss another matter with you."

Nancy's eyebrows rose, but she didn't say a word.

"I've been recently deputized, and I was hoping you could give me information about the gang we've been chasing. Everything I've found has led to a dead end, and I was thinking, who knows these men better than the women who, um…"

Then Jasper turned beet red and turned his head away.

Nancy snickered. "We didn't exactly talk when I spent time with them, if that's what you're wondering."

"Be nice," Emma Jane said, giving Nancy an admonishing look. "It won't do you any good if you keep chasing folks away with your wild talk. Jasper needs your help."

Emma Jane had never spoken so boldly before, but as her heart thudded in her chest, it felt…well, it felt like the time her sister had dared her to use the rope to swing into the lake. Scary, but good. Jasper's earlier defense of her to his mother echoed in her head. He'd spoken up for her, and even though she knew he didn't fully accept her, she had to believe that if they kept speaking up for each other, then maybe…

She glanced at Jasper, who was still beet red. Surely they could at least become friends.

"I can't help him," Nancy said, looking around. "It's bad enough I'm associating with church folks. If word gets out that I was talking to the law…"

"We can protect you." Jasper looked fully recovered from the embarrassment over Nancy's frank talk.

"Dream on, rich boy. I'm sure it's all fun for you, playing with guns and chasing bandits. But it's not a game to the men you're after. They're ruthless killers, and it won't be just your body they leave in their dust."

Nancy looked at Emma Jane so hard it was almost like having a gun pointed right at her. Jasper seemed afraid that Emma Jane would be targeted by the gang, and Nancy confirmed it. Emma Jane swallowed. Perhaps she'd been too hasty in pushing her desire to work with Jasper on the case.

"And what about the innocent women they'll keep hurting if they're not stopped? What about…"

"If you're talking about Daisy, you need to let her go. I've heard talk that you're searching for her, and I can tell you right now that it's a lost cause. Forget about her and move on."

Emma Jane didn't know Jasper very well, but the emotions darkening his face told her that he'd do anything but forget about Daisy. In fact, she'd guess that Nan-

cy's words only served to make him more determined
to find her.

"And what if I can't?" His body was tense, his fists
balled at his sides. This was not the society dandy everyone admired. If any of the women who giggled over
their fans at him could see him now, Emma Jane wasn't
sure they'd recognize him.

If she had to choose, she'd say she liked this Jasper
better.

"Then I guess you'd better kiss that pretty wife of
yours goodbye."

Nancy turned to look at Emma Jane, then her face
softened. "No offense. But if he pursues this case, you're
going to be the one to suffer for it. I know you meant well
in coming to me, but you're putting every woman you
introduce your husband to in danger. And you're signing
your own death warrant."

A chill rattled through Emma Jane, and she pulled her
shawl tighter around her. Part of her wished she'd left well
enough alone and let Jasper go about his business. But
another part of her—something boiled deep within her.
Where an instant ago she felt cold, now she was on fire.

A gang so dangerous that anyone who tried to stop
them would be threatened like this? What would they
do if they weren't stopped? Who else would they hurt?

Frankly, they sounded like a bunch of bullies to Emma
Jane. The same kind of tormentors who'd mocked her
in church, whispering behind their fans, whether it be
about her family's debts, her father's gambling and public intoxication, her patched dresses or, now, her hasty
forced marriage.

"So you would let them continue to control you,"
Emma Jane said quietly, realizing as the words came

out that she needed to hear them just as much as Nancy. She had wasted far too much time cowering the way her friend was doing.

And nothing in her life had gotten better.

She looked over at Jasper, who gave her a slow nod. As if he…approved of her. Emma Jane swallowed. "I don't want to put you in danger, Nancy. I don't want to be in danger. But if we run in fear from this gang, these bullies, then we will always have to run."

She turned her attention to Jasper. "I'll do everything I can to help you stop them."

Emma Jane had spent her whole life trying to make herself agreeable enough to get people to like her. To get her mother to approve of her. And now, as she was encouraging Nancy to stand up to the bullies, she found that she could no longer do it.

She wanted Jasper to like her, to be her friend, so that somehow their marriage could have a reasonable sort of existence. But he needed to learn to like her for who she was, not the agreeable persona she tried to adopt.

Perhaps the biggest bully, the worst enemy, was not the threat of this gang plaguing the town. Rather, it was the ever-increasing pressure to fit in a mold that simply wasn't her.

So what did that mean for her marriage?

Chapter Six

"I'm sorry I couldn't have been of more help," Emma Jane said quietly as she slipped her hand into his arm.

"It's all right." He patted her arm softly, looking around the barn at all the women milling around.

Why, after all this time, had none of the other deputies come to talk to these women?

Then he spied Will in a corner, talking to a figure in the shadows. Of course his buddy would be here.

"No, it's not all right," Emma Jane huffed, pulling her hand away, then turning to stop in front of him and face him. "Why won't she help us? Doesn't she see that, either way, we're all in trouble?"

She looked so earnest, and in that innocent expression, he finally understood why all the lawmen in town didn't respect Jasper's intentions to rescue Daisy and stop the gang. The answers to her questions were not that simple. And, unfortunately, Emma Jane's passionate desire for justice meant that she was more apt to go into a situation hotheaded without thinking it through.

He glanced in Will's direction. Had his friend ever tried telling him those things? Would he have listened?

So how did he get Emma Jane to listen?

"You're right," he told her honestly. "It's not all right. But Nancy is also right. I don't want to needlessly put anyone else in danger. So what do I do?"

Emma Jane looked confused. She shifted her position slightly, glancing around before bringing her attention back to him. "I don't know. But I feel like I have to do something. I've just…"

She turned her attention to the ground, for all the fascination that dirt might hold.

"I've not had much experience in standing up to bullies before."

Which is when it hit him. Harder than any bullet that he feared.

He'd seen the way the other women in town picked on Emma Jane. Flora Montgomery in particular seemed to take great pleasure in tormenting his wife. How many times had he told the other woman to be nice?

This wasn't just about the gang that had Daisy in their clutches, but Emma Jane learning to stand up to people like Flora Montgomery.

She was using chasing down the gang as her line in the sand.

Except the two situations were not the same.

Flora Montgomery wasn't going to cause Emma Jane bodily harm. But this gang would.

"I'll help you stand up to the bullies." Jasper took both of her hands in his. "But I need you to help me, as well."

Those deep blue eyes of hers locked on to his. The little flecks of brown mesmerized him, as they always did when he took time to notice.

Hopefully, the expression meant that she'd trust him.

"I think we've already determined that I'm not cut out

for being a lawman," Emma Jane said, kicking at a small rock on the ground.

"Hey." He pulled one of his hands out of hers, then used it to lift her chin, forcing her to meet his eyes once again. "You may not make a great lawman. But you have many other fine qualities. And I look forward to discovering each and every one of them."

"But I want to help. And I feel completely powerless to do so."

"Then do as I asked you. Stay out of it, and if you see or hear something in your work, let me know, but don't try and do anything about it yourself."

Truthfully, he wasn't giving her any power. But he hoped that she knew that he saw…well, he didn't even know what he saw. Potential, maybe? He knew as little of Emma Jane as she knew of him.

Yet the more he learned of her, the more he realized that there was a greater level of goodness in her than he'd originally suspected. But how did he balance that with the questions he did have of her character? That was the trouble with trusting someone you barely knew. As much as he wanted to believe in Emma Jane wholeheartedly, he didn't know enough about her to know if he *could* trust her.

What was Emma Jane's true plan here?

The fear and uncertainty in her eyes, it looked a lot like she did the day she trapped him into marriage.

Wanting to trust him? He'd like to think so. But it was clear that she didn't. Did she lose faith in him after the church picnic somehow and decide to take matters into her own hands? Would justice in this situation not happen fast enough for Emma Jane, leading her to do something they'd all regret?

"I'm not a child," she fumed. "I know what's at stake. I've agreed to what you need from me. You don't need to patronize me."

"I'm sorry. I just don't know how to convey to you how dangerous this gang really is. There's so much you don't know."

"So tell me." Those luminous eyes of hers bore into him, and while he'd been noticing their beauty, he also couldn't help but notice their intelligence.

Every single society miss he'd ever courted all blushingly waved their fans at him and blithely agreed to whatever he wanted. Even Flora Montgomery, who sometimes made a show of standing up to him, mostly responded by pouting but always complying with what he asked.

And yet…he had more respect for Emma Jane than he had for all those other women put together.

Jasper hesitated before opening his mouth to speak. How did a man balance confidential work with talking about it with his wife? Will would know.

As if he knew the direction of Jasper's thoughts, the other man caught his eye, making a motion with his head. Whatever conversation he'd been engaged in now over, Will was indicating he needed to talk to Jasper.

"Will needs me." Jasper breathed out a long breath, hating the way Emma Jane looked at him—as if he was using Will as a convenient excuse to push her away. Mostly because she was mostly right to think it.

"Of course. You've spent a lot of time with me, and I appreciate it. I know you have work to do."

Dismissed. Polite, but with an undercurrent of pain that made him wince. Not because she was trying to hurt him, but because she was trying so hard not to sound like he'd hurt her.

Had it been any one of the simpering misses he'd courted, he'd have been able to walk away. But he was a husband now, and Pastor Lassiter's warnings about their relationship rang in his head. He had to make his wife a priority. Even though his duty lay elsewhere.

"I didn't mean…"

"I know what you meant. You don't have to dance attendance on me, there's plenty here to occupy my time."

If it weren't for the tone of her voice, he might have believed her. And then there was the flash of her eyes. The brown flecks dimmed the main blue color, and in them, he read…

Who was he kidding? He didn't know her well enough to be able to read her eyes. But he wasn't a fool.

"I know you're displeased with me right now, Emma Jane. We're supposed to be spending time together to get to know each other and build a foundation for our marriage. And yet, I have this case…"

Jasper glanced in Will's direction. Mary had joined him, and they appeared to be conversing while looking at the two of them.

"Well, it looks like Mary has joined Will, so why don't you come with me to say hello?"

Emma Jane appeared to relax slightly as she nodded, her face looking more peaceful than it had since they began this conversation. Had she been that upset by him leaving her?

So many things he still had to learn about being a husband. All men had to learn them, he supposed solemnly, but it seemed so much harder with a wife he didn't want. Swallowing the resentment that had once again risen up, Jasper offered Emma Jane his arm. He was trying so hard to forgive her and move on, to figure out a way to make their marriage work. But how could he rid himself of this bitterness once and for all?

As they approached Mary and Will, Mary smiled warmly. Though the couple were an appropriate distance from each other, and no one could accuse them of impropriety, the connection between them was obvious. A person only had to glance at them to know they deeply cared for one another. Their bodies were tilted in toward each other, and their attention never strayed far from one another for long.

And when they looked at each other, it was obvious they were in love.

If only Jasper could have had that for himself.

People once said he was the luckiest man in all of Leadville, with the ability to marry any of the beautiful women in town. But what none of them understood was that when he saw the love between Mary and Will, he hadn't wanted to settle for anything less.

Beside him, Emma Jane let out a sigh, one so soft it was barely discernible. A quick glance in her direction made the breath in his throat catch. The longing in her eyes was unmistakable.

He'd been the recipient of many a wistful glance in his day. But this was not the look of a woman in love. Rather, he immediately recognized it to be something else. Emma Jane wanted the same thing he did—to have the same kind of love Will and Mary shared.

They might want the same thing, but unfortunately, neither was going to get it from the other.

"Did you see how fast Jasper scrambled up the roof to get away from Emma Jane?"

The familiar twitter of Flora's voice burned Emma Jane's ears.

Oh, she knew Flora was just trying to make trouble, but what was the point in causing problems for a woman who was already married? It wasn't as though Jasper was going to wake up one morning, realize it had all been a terrible mistake, divorce Emma Jane and marry Flora.

But Flora didn't seem to understand that.

"I heard from Jasper's mother that they aren't even sharing a bedroom," Flora's companion said in a whisper too loud to be surreptitious.

"Of course not." Flora cackled, her voice carrying in Emma Jane's direction, almost as though she'd turned in Emma Jane's direction as she spoke.

But Emma Jane didn't look up from the shirt she was mending. As women of the night, none of the women in the barn owned anything proper, even if it hadn't all burned up in the fire. Church members had donated what they could, and she, along with others, worked to make them fit.

She held up the shirt to the light, examining her handiwork. In that, no one would find fault. Her stitches were tiny and even.

"I hope you're not thinking of taking that for yourself," Flora said, dropping a pile of clothes in front of her. "It is last season, but I'm sure it's finer than anything you've ever owned."

Emma Jane's face heated. Her throat constricted, preventing her from saying anything as she put the shirt into the pile of clothes she'd finished mending.

"Then again, you're used to cast offs, aren't you? I believe many of your school dresses came from the church, didn't they? I'm sure I've even seen you wearing one or two of mine."

She tossed her golden curls and looked down her nose at Emma Jane. "You're so fortunate that Mother insists I always wear the latest fashions. My clothes are always in perfect condition when we donate them, since I never wear them but more than a few times."

Flora turned to her companion and laughed in that high-pitched, fake way of hers.

"It is such a chore being fashionable."

As the other girl turned more into the light, Emma Jane recognized her. Sarah Crowley, who had often vied with Flora for Jasper's attention. Apparently, nothing united two rivals like a common enemy. Her.

"It's also a chore doing penance for so many of your crimes against humanity."

Emma Jane swiveled at the sound of Polly MacDonald's voice.

"Honestly, I don't know how you sleep at night." Polly glared at the other two women. "You should be ashamed of yourself for the way you're talking about Emma Jane."

Polly picked up the pile of clothes Emma Jane had been mending. "You did a fine job, Emma Jane. Sarah might need a lace machine to make such beautiful trim, but I declare this cuff is exquisite."

She held up one of the gowns Emma Jane had repaired.

"The old lace was torn too badly to fix, and it seemed wrong not to have lace on that dress. So I improvised."

Improvising was something Emma Jane had to be good at. Flora was right in that a lot of her clothes had been cast offs. Unfortunately, that meant clothes from girls who were taller, shorter, fatter and thinner than she was.

"And that is why Flora is so nasty to you." Polly glared at the other girl. "She knows that you're far cleverer than she is, and that rankles. You always got better marks in school, and every one of us was green with envy at all the times you were chosen as an example of excellence."

Flora snorted.

Then Polly leaned in toward the other girl. "Now that Emma Jane is married to Jasper, you're even more jealous. I saw how you tried to get him to kiss you at the church picnic. Even though you told everyone he stole a kiss, I saw him spurn you."

The image of Jasper sitting in the mine came back to Emma Jane. He'd looked so anguished at the mention of his romance with Flora. Everyone, including Emma Jane, had assumed they were a couple. Jasper had denied it, but everyone had heard Flora's bold declarations of stolen kisses.

Maybe Jasper deserved a little more credit than Emma Jane had been giving him.

Sarah nudged Flora. "Is that true?"

"Of course it's not. She's just making up lies to make that creature feel better."

"That creature is Mrs. Jasper Jackson," Polly declared hotly. "And she's a good woman, far more virtuous than the likes of you."

Flora tossed her head. "As if you'd know anything about womanly virtue. I don't know why you're taking up for her, but I'm sure when word gets out, your already meager invitations will dwindle down to nothing."

Polly looked down at Emma Jane. "As long as I'm on Emma Jane's invitation list, I couldn't care less."

Emma Jane closed her eyes and swallowed, willing herself to speak. Why, oh, why, could she never speak up against bullies? But Polly was speaking up for her, and she deserved Emma Jane's support.

She smiled weakly up at Polly. "Of course. You're always welcome in my home…"

"We'll see what the real Mrs. Jackson has to say about that." Flora turned on her heel and walked away, Sarah trailing behind her.

The *real* Mrs. Jackson. That was the real problem, wasn't it? Jasper's mother refused to accept Emma Jane, and based on what the gossips were saying, everyone knew it.

Polly shifted her weight. "I, um… I should probably apologize to you."

"For what?"

"For not taking up for you before. Even at the church picnic, when Mary stood up for you, I told her she was crazy for supporting you. I think we were all too afraid of Flora's pernicious tongue to do anything." Tears filled Polly's eyes. "The truth is, we've all been victims of Flora's treachery, and we weren't brave enough to defend ourselves. I think everyone was just relieved that she'd found you to pick on and was leaving us be."

Emma Jane's heart constricted. The pain she'd been suffering all these years…her own eyes filled with tears.

"I was so caught up in what she was doing to me, I hadn't realized that I wasn't alone," she said, more to herself than to Polly.

Would things have been different had Emma Jane reached out? Had she looked around at the other girls in her class and at church? Could Emma Jane have seen that she wasn't the only one suffering?

"We all should have stood up to her a long time ago,

and again, I'm sorry that it's taken me so long to do so on your behalf."

"I should have stood up for myself," Emma Jane whispered, knowing that, even now, she wasn't sure she had the courage.

Polly sighed. "None of us did, either. We all went along with whatever she wanted us to do, knowing that if we displeased her, we'd face her wrath."

"How does one person get so much power?"

Tears streamed down Emma Jane's face, not just for all the abuses she suffered at Flora's hands, but also for the pain streaked across Polly's face.

"What's going on here?" Jasper came up behind Polly, his brow furrowed. "Why are you crying?"

Emma Jane swiped at her face with her sleeve before remembering that she had a handkerchief. There hadn't been money for such finery in her home, but when she'd married Jasper, Mary had given her several with her initials. Where she'd found the time to embroider them, Emma Jane didn't know, but that small gift meant the world to her.

As Emma Jane used her handkerchief, Polly said glumly, "We had a run-in with Flora."

"Polly was good enough to stand up for me, but I'm afraid it only incensed her more."

Jasper's scowl deepened. "I wish I'd never paid a lick of attention to her. I know her father is my father's best friend, but the longer I know her, the more I wish I'd never courted her, even if it made my parents happy."

More of the bitterness she'd seen from Jasper made sense. And, as Emma Jane replayed the times she'd seen Jasper with Flora at local assemblies, she now understood his detachment.

Then Jasper looked down at her, a muscle ticking in his jaw. "I'm sorry she's still being cruel to you, Emma Jane. I've wished a thousand times that I'd paid more attention and done more to make her stop tormenting you."

Actually, Jasper had done a lot more than most in stopping Flora's nastiness. Whenever Flora had picked on her in front of Jasper, he had always chastised her. In fact, the more Emma Jane thought about it, the more she realized that any time someone gossiped or said a cross word about someone in front of Jasper, he was always quick to quiet the talk.

As much as Emma Jane had said she didn't really know him, she was finding that she knew him quite well, after all. The more she realized the finer points of Jasper's character, the more grateful she was indeed that he'd married her.

"It's all right," Emma Jane told him softly. "As I recall, you've always stopped any talk that you've heard."

"For all the good it's done." Jasper sighed, then gazed at her with what seemed to be real compassion. "Look, I know I seemed harsh yesterday when we talked about how much the talk bothers you. But I've had to deal with it my whole life. I do my best to stop people when they're gossiping about others, but they just keep right on when my back is turned."

He glanced in the direction of Flora, who'd been joined by a few more of her cronies. "My reputation as a playboy is not undeserved. But a lot of the stories about me are either grossly exaggerated, or simply untrue."

Then he looked back at Emma Jane. "I apologize for any of that talk as it applies to you. I regret kissing every single one of those girls, and I truly regret the way it makes everyone look sideways at you."

Emma Jane hadn't realized that Jasper, too, might have been the victim of malicious gossip. And even though his admission of kissing other girls would lower his value in some people's eyes, it gave her even more hope for their relationship. Jasper was the kind of man to admit to his mistakes.

Of course, his admission also pointed out one glaring fact about their relationship. Not once had Jasper even tried to kiss her. Sometimes she thought she had a memory of a kiss while they were in the mine, shortly before the rockslide hit. But Emma Jane knew it was mere foolishness. If such a kiss had happened, why hadn't Jasper mentioned it? And if it was as good of a kiss as had been in her dreams, why hadn't he repeated it?

No, kissing Jasper had only happened in her imagination.

Clearly, if the man liked to kiss as much as his reputation claimed, and even in his own admission, his failure to kiss his wife meant only one thing.

He had absolutely no interest in Emma Jane.

Chapter Seven

The trouble with Jasper's sweet apology was that when he excused himself a few moments later, Emma Jane found it hard to refuse. Building a bridge between her and her husband wasn't going to happen in a single afternoon. Polly, too, had left her, needing to check in with her mother and catch up on her duties at home.

Emma Jane looked around for Nancy. She hadn't realized that having Jasper talk to her friend would put her in a bad position. Even though Emma Jane wanted Nancy to do the right thing, she knew all too well the difficulty in standing up to bullies. What Nancy needed most of all, what had helped Emma Jane, was having a real friend.

She spied Jasper, huddled in a corner with Will. After catching his eye, she gave him a quick wave, and he nodded at her. A simple acknowledgment, but in some ways, it marked a step in a positive direction for their relationship. How many times had Emma Jane waved at him in the past only to have him not notice her?

Warmth filling her heart, Emma Jane went into the stable area, where she knew Nancy liked to spend time.

They'd discovered a mama cat and her kittens a few days ago, and knowing Nancy, she was probably checking on them.

The stable was quiet, deserted. No Nancy, but at least Emma Jane could check on the kittens and read a little in her Bible. She was grateful for the small book Pastor Lassiter had given them as a wedding gift. It was perfect for carrying around, and it gave her the opportunity to read to some of the women here in the barn. Though some objected to hearing about religion all the time, Emma Jane noticed how many appreciated the comforting words of the Psalms. She slipped into the stall where the cat had made a place for her little family to sleep. Mama cat was gone, probably in search of food. The soft straw she and Nancy had found to give the cats a comfortable bed would make a nice place to sit and read.

She pulled out her Bible and opened it to the Twenty-third Psalm. A well-worn page, but all the women seemed to come nearer when she read it. Just like Emma Jane, they were all probably in their own private valleys of the shadow of death. Everything in their lives had changed overnight, and many of them had no idea what would happen next. Only the solace of the Lord would get them through. One of the kittens mewed, and she looked to see it had fallen and was stuck in the hay. Just as she reached for it, one of the barn doors banged open.

"I saw you talking to the law, Nancy."

"I didn't tell them nothin', Ray. You know better than that. Haven't I kept all of your secrets? I've given you an alibi plenty of times, so you needn't fear me."

"What about that wife of his? You two seem awfully cozy to me. Betty said you've been spending a lot of time with that woman."

Emma Jane shrank against the walls of the stall. Nancy had warned her that their friendship might cause trouble for her. Had looked fearful when Jasper had tried speaking to her. A shiver coursed down Emma Jane's spine. Had she needlessly put her friend in danger in hopes of winning over her husband?

"So I listen to some do-gooder read me Bible stories. What's it to you? I'm just biding my time until a place at the Silver King Saloon opens up. If that means letting some poor woman think she's doing a charitable deed, it doesn't hurt a soul."

Some do-gooder? Poor woman? Emma Jane's heart sank as Nancy so callously denied their friendship.

But Nancy had been the one to ask Emma Jane to read from her Bible, and as Emma Jane recalled, she'd told her that she'd turned down the opportunity to work at the Silver King Saloon.

What was going on?

The voices came closer.

Emma Jane could see Nancy clearly now, as the young woman was nearly even with the stall door. Nancy glanced over, barely looking at Emma Jane, but she understood as Nancy closed the door. She was trying to protect Emma Jane.

"Well, I don't like it." Ray stepped in toward Nancy, so close their faces were almost touching. "That posse last night got a little too close for my liking, and I'm thinking we have a traitor in our midst."

"It's not me." Nancy started to move away from the stall, but Ray grabbed her arm.

"Betty says…"

"Maybe you ought to be asking Betty what she's

saying to that deputy she's had as a customer all these months," Nancy said.

Ray snorted. "Who do you think our inside man is?"

Jasper had told Emma Jane he suspected the bandits had someone in the sheriff's office working for them. Now she could confirm his suspicions. It felt good to know that she'd be able to help him *and* keep her promise to stay out of the case. After all, she would be doing exactly as he'd asked—reporting back to him on what she heard.

As much as she wanted to jump in and tell Ray that Nancy was telling the truth, that she hadn't told Emma Jane or Jasper anything, she remembered Nancy's warning about how dangerous these people were.

Nancy, though, didn't appear to be afraid. She lifted her chin and looked Ray in the eye. "Well, maybe he's working both sides. Wouldn't be the first time, you and I both know that."

Emma Jane heard a strange clicking sound.

"I know it all too well. Which is why I'm getting rid of any leaks."

"You can't think…" Nancy's face crumpled as she took a step back. "I would never…"

"I don't think. I know."

A gunshot rang out, and then a thud. Emma Jane squeezed her eyes shut. The image of what had happened burned against her eyelids. Even if she scrubbed with the strongest lye, nothing could ever remove the memory of Nancy's last moments.

The kitten she held in her arms mewed.

"Who's there?"

Emma Jane let the kitten go, encouraging it to scamper in the direction of the man who'd just killed Nancy.

He wouldn't harm a kitten, but if he looked in the stall, she knew he wouldn't hesitate in killing her.

The kitten cooperated, but the man didn't seem to notice. Instead, he kicked open the door to the stall next to her.

Emma Jane's heart thudded against her chest.

He would search her stall next.

Maybe if he thought she slept through the whole thing, and hadn't heard anything, he'd leave her alone. But if he knew she'd been conscious, he'd kill her for sure.

She curled up in a ball, arranging the straw around her, like she'd been using it as a makeshift bed, closed her eyes and prayed.

The stall door, which had been slightly ajar, banged as he opened it all the way. Even with her eyes closed, she could feel his gaze on her.

"What are you doing? We've got to get out of here." An unfamiliar male voice broke through the silence.

"Seems we've got a witness."

"Looks like she's asleep. We've got to get out of here. Folks in the street heard the gunshot and are trying to figure out where it came from."

"There's gunshots around these parts all the time. We've got to take care of her."

Emma Jane heard the strange click again. Now she knew. It was the sound a gun made just before someone shot it. She swallowed, saying one last prayer.

Please, don't let this be my final prayer.

"Then they'll be on to us for sure. Let's go."

A heavy boot nudged her. "It's that do-gooder."

Footsteps crunched the straw nearby. "Jasper Jackson's wife. We can't kill her. Not with the Jackson power and money."

Shouts came from the street. The voices grew closer.

"What if she heard? At the very least, she can finger me for Nancy."

"We'll take her with us. Maybe we can use her as leverage. That rich boy needs to learn he picked the wrong hobby in poking his nose into our business."

This time, the man kicked her. Hard. Emma Jane winced at the pain.

Quickly, she yawned, hoping she was convincing in pretending that she'd just woken up.

"What's happening?"

Dark eyes glinted against the sunlight streaming through the crack in the roof.

"You're coming with us."

The shiny barrel of a gun—the gun used to kill Nancy—pointed at her face.

Emma Jane stood slowly, her heart thudding so loud, it echoed in her ears. If she took her time, the voices she heard might make it. And then they could catch these evil men in action. Her throat was so dry, she couldn't have screamed for help even if there wasn't a gun pointed to her head.

"Hurry it up. I'm not afraid to use this. Just ask your friend." He pointed toward the open stall door. Nancy's lifeless body lay beyond.

Seeing Nancy dead somehow made the situation seem all the more dangerous. Jasper had warned her. Nancy had warned her. And now Nancy was dead.

Tears pricked her eyes at the senseless loss. As much as she wanted to cry for her friend, there was no time for that, not when she had to figure a way out.

Emma Jane scooted forward, letting her Bible settle in

the straw. Would they notice it when they found Nancy's body? Would they realize Emma Jane was in trouble?

Selfishly, she wanted to keep the Bible with her. Until now, she'd never had a Bible of her own. She always had to use the family Bible. It had brought her so much comfort already, and she had a feeling that, with these men, she'd need it.

But if it helped Jasper find her…

"Let's go!"

Ray grabbed her by the arm and jerked her to her feet. The Bible remained where she'd left it as Ray pulled her out of the stall.

His partner waved his gun at her.

"You don't have to die. But if you yell, fight or put up any kind of fuss to draw attention to us, we will kill you. Live or die, it's your choice."

Strangely, Emma Jane didn't fear dying—not in this moment. Oh, she knew without a doubt that these men would kill her if they thought she was a threat. But something in her told her that if she just went along with them, she would be safe. Let them think she was cooperative, and somehow, some way, she would find a way to escape. If only she could convince her trembling limbs to believe in that hope.

Jasper removed his hat and ran his free hand through his hair. It seemed most of today had been a waste. Neither he nor Will had any leads, and it seemed like the bandits were toying with them. Even the gunshots they'd heard earlier seemed to be nothing but hotheads coming out of the saloon. Jasper sighed. The trouble with the lawlessness running rampant was that one never could tell if a gunshot was something serious or was just idiots fooling around.

At least things with Emma Jane seemed to be improving. He looked around for his bride.

The women were gathered in the main room of the barn, waiting for the noon meal. Knowing Emma Jane, she was probably helping set up.

Except, as he glanced at the women carrying dishes to and fro, he didn't see her. Mary, Polly and several other women who helped with the ministry were all present. He walked over to where Mary had just set a platter of bread on the table.

"Have you seen Emma Jane?"

Mary looked up, her brow furrowed. "No. I thought…" She turned toward the barn door, where Polly was bringing in a large pot. "Where's Emma Jane?"

Polly groaned and Jasper rushed toward her. The pot looked much too heavy for the woman to be carrying it herself.

As he took the pot from her, Polly said, "I have no idea. She wandered off to the stalls a while ago. There's some kittens she likes to play with."

Then Polly frowned. "But that was ages ago, and I can't imagine why she's not helping us. That's not like Emma Jane."

"Oh. You're looking for Emma Jane?" Flora sidled up to him, a nasty smirk on her face. "I saw her ride off with two men earlier. Guess she's as loose as we all suspected."

It took every ounce of effort not to dump the contents of the entire pot, which smelled like a hearty stew, on the horrid girl. With Herculean control, Jasper set the pot on the table.

"I'm sick of your lies, Flora Montgomery. Emma Jane never did a thing to you. She's a good woman, with more kindness in her pinky than you have in your whole body. You might be jealous that I married her, but let me set the record straight. There is nothing on this earth that would have induced me to offer for you."

Flora blanched, and for a moment, Jasper felt awful for his cruelty. But when had she ever felt bad for her malicious words about anyone else?

"It's true," Flora insisted. "Sarah Crowley saw it, too, didn't you, Sarah?"

Sarah walked over, wiping her hands on her apron. "I'm afraid so. I'm sure there's a reasonable explanation why she'd ride off with two men who were not her husband, sitting on a horse with one of them, and her ankles bared for all to see."

The looks she and Flora exchanged said that they clearly believed that only Flora's theory could be true.

Will joined them. "What kind of horses were they?"

Flora made an unladylike noise. "As if I would pay attention to any such thing. I have work to do, so if you'll excuse me."

She flounced off, her head held high, and by the exasperated groans from Mary and Polly, it was clear that Flora hadn't been doing any work at all. Jasper knew all too well that Flora often showed up to make an appearance at charity work so people thought she was helping, but she often just stood around, completely useless.

"What about you, Sarah?" Jasper narrowed his eyes at her, taking over Will's investigation. Something wasn't right, even if no one else seemed to care.

Before answering, Sarah looked away, her gaze settling on Flora, who wore such a deep scowl Jasper could hardly fathom why the other girl was considered so beautiful. Disgust filled him once again at the reminder of how he used to flirt with her.

How could he have thought a woman with Flora's character held any value? An image of Emma Jane popped into his head. She might not have been considered one of the most beautiful women in town, but…

He shook his head. Dwelling on her characteristics wasn't going to help him find her.

Sarah leaned in and lowered her voice. "Flora thinks it's unladylike for me to have such admiration for horses, but the only reason we saw Emma Jane was because I'd been staring at what a beautifully matched pair of chestnut roans they were. I have not seen such fine horseflesh. I have to go."

Then she straightened and turned, rejoining Flora.

Will nudged Jasper. "Where have you heard talk of a matched pair of chestnut roans?"

A flash of memory hit. "Didn't Eric Abernathy come into the sheriff's office the other day, ranting about his brand-new horses being stolen?"

Will nodded. "That's right! I remember now. He'd just had them brought over from back east. He was madder than a newly woken bear that no one would form a search party to help find them. We just didn't have the manpower."

"I'm sure it's the gang." Jasper frowned. "But why would they take Emma Jane?"

A shout sounded from the stalls. "It's Nancy! She's dead!"

Jasper and Will ran in the direction of the voice. A woman stood by the door to the stables, sobbing. "I just told Ray… I didn't mean…"

"Ray? He was here? What did you tell him?" Jasper glowered at her, grabbing her by the elbow. How had he missed one of the gang members in town?

"He'll kill me, too." The woman jerked from his grasp, then ran off.

Jasper started to go after her, but Will's voice stopped him. "Don't waste your time. Come here. I found something."

As he stepped over the body, Jasper's gut clenched. Another woman. Dead. Nancy had warned him that talking to him would get her and Emma Jane killed. Was this the result of Jasper's actions?

Will held up a Bible. "Recognize this?"

Jasper pulled it out of Will's hands without even looking at it. He didn't need to. "Emma Jane hasn't gone anywhere without it since the wedding."

The memory of her sitting in her bed in her nightgown, reading that Bible, came back to him. So innocent. Emma Jane hadn't been part of this fight. All she'd wanted to do was the right thing, to help, and now she was in grave danger.

Why hadn't she listened to him and just stayed out of it? Knowing Emma Jane, she probably went to talk to Nancy on her own and somehow got caught up in this mess. Clearly, his wife hadn't realized how dangerous the people they were dealing with were. She should have trusted him.

"You think she saw the murder and they took her to keep her quiet?" Will motioned toward the body.

Jasper swallowed the lump in his throat. "Why didn't they just kill her?"

"A Jackson?" The tone in Will's voice reminded him of how Will had come into his life. After Will had saved

Henry's life, Henry had asked Will to teach Jasper how to protect himself. Growing up, there'd been a number of kidnapping threats.

He'd just never imagined that, as an adult, those threats would still be there. Despite everything Jasper had done to learn to protect himself, he'd forgotten one important lesson. Passing those lessons on to his wife. Especially a headstrong one who didn't trust him to do the right thing and took matters into her own hands.

"I never thought…" Jasper's head spun as he realized the danger Emma Jane was in.

"Emma Jane is tough. You told me yourself that, during the mine cave-in, she possessed an inner strength you admired. She'll get through this, too."

Jasper nodded slowly, his gaze drawn back to Nancy's body. What would they do to Emma Jane? His gut churned at the thought. Was this because she was a Jackson, or was this Nancy's warning coming true? Or had Emma Jane somehow become more involved in trying to solve the case?

He looked around for clues, for any signs of struggle, but other than the dead woman lying at the entrance to the stall, the barn looked exactly as it should.

Will walked over to the other side of the stall area, leading out to the street.

"Over here!"

Jasper quickly joined him, looking at the place Will indicated on the ground.

"There haven't been any horses staying in this barn since we put the women up in here. Two sets of horseshoe prints. That has to be the kidnappers."

The prints left a clear trail as far as Jasper could see. Fortunately, the barn was at the edge of town, and the trail went straight into the brush, where other horses weren't likely to tread on them. Easy enough to follow.

"I'll get the horses." Jasper started toward where he'd left his mount without waiting for Will's response.

"We should get the sheriff first."

Jasper didn't pause. "You get the sheriff. I'm going after my wife. I'll leave tracks so you can catch up."

Chapter Eight

"What were you thinking, bringing him here? Bad enough you brought the woman, now him?"

Emma Jane looked up from the fire, where she'd been heating up a soup she'd cobbled together from the meager ingredients she'd found in the cabin. She'd realized pretty quickly that fighting the men would drain her of any energy she'd need to survive and, eventually, escape. For now, she'd make the best of things, and if cooking supper was part of it, at least she wouldn't go to bed hungry.

Two men were dragging an unconscious Jasper into the cabin. His hands were tied behind his back, and a handkerchief had been tied around his mouth.

"Jasper!"

She started toward him, but the leader of the gang, the dark-haired man who'd objected to Jasper's presence, pointed his gun at her. "You get back to tending that meal. I've still got half a mind to kill you, but so long as you're useful, I might let you live."

Emma Jane tried swallowing the lump in her throat, but it remained lodged in place. How had Jasper come to be here? Her heart sank and turned over in her stomach as she realized that he'd probably come after her, putting himself in danger in the process.

The men dropped Jasper on the dirt floor, his body thudding on the ground. A trail of dried blood had clotted down the side of his face. For a moment, Emma Jane's breath caught. But then his chest rose and fell slightly. It was enough to let her take a breath, but not enough to ease the tightness in her chest.

"He's injured," Emma Jane said quietly but not moving. "Supper should be ready soon. Let me tend to him."

"He'll be fine. Just a knock on the head." Ray, one of the men who'd kidnapped her, nudged his partner. "Might have been a little harder than we intended, but we got the job done."

"What job?" Their leader walked over and smacked Ray on the side of the head. "Seems to me every job I give you gets messed up. You were supposed to go into town to take care of Nancy. You come back with *her*."

He pointed at Emma Jane, giving her a dark look. "I do not need another woman in this place."

As if to remind them of her existence, the other woman began coughing again. When Emma Jane had arrived, the woman had been coughing up a storm, delirious with fever. She'd felt so bad for the poor woman and had been doing what she could to make her more comfortable.

The woman also had a small baby boy, now sleeping inside an old crate near the fire. When Emma Jane had arrived, the baby was nestled in with his mother. With the woman's raging fever, Emma Jane worried that the baby might get sick. She'd put together a makeshift bottle from odds and ends she'd found in the cabin, and one of the men, Mack, had given her some goat's milk. Not the best solution, Emma Jane knew, but with the way the baby had gobbled up the milk, she'd probably saved the baby's life. Already color was returning to the baby's cheeks, and he had stopped whimpering. Mack commented that it was the first time the baby had quieted in days.

Emma Jane went to the fire to stir the soup. Tasting it, she deemed it fit to eat. Perhaps if the men had a little food in their bellies, they wouldn't be so cantankerous. Which meant that maybe they wouldn't be so eager with their guns.

A nearby shelf held some bowls, and as Emma Jane dished out the soup, the men continued arguing.

"I told you, she was there when I did it. I didn't want her talking. I'd have shot her then, but Jimmy said killing a Jackson was a bad idea."

"And you didn't think to check for witnesses before doing it?" The leader blew out an irate breath as Emma Jane handed him a bowl.

"You didn't put anything in this, did you?"

He eyed her warily, and for a moment, Emma Jane wished she had put poison in the soup. Of course, she had no idea what she could have used as one. It wasn't as though there were bottles labeled Poison lying around.

"No." She handed another bowl to the one called Jimmy. After all, she owed him her life. Were it not for him, Ray would have killed her.

"Prove it. Take a bite out of my bowl."

Emma Jane did as he asked, looking him in the eye as she took a spoonful of his soup.

Satisfied, the man grunted and waved her away. "As I was saying, Ray, you're a disgrace. I gave you a simple job, and you fouled that up. But that doesn't explain how you ended up bringing him here."

Ray pointed at Jimmy. "Ask him. He's the one who had that idea, too."

Jimmy set down his soup. "Same reason we grabbed the girl. There's no way we'd get away with killing a Jackson. We went back to clean up our tracks, and he had started tracking us. Figured it was easier to knock him out and take him prisoner than it was to spend the rest of our lives running. You kill someone with that much money and power, there's no way you'll ever stop running, even if you do make it to Mexico."

"I'm not afraid of no Jackson," Ray declared.

"You should be." Jimmy stood, then pointed at Jasper. "We might have the law around here handled, but his father has the money to buy more law than we can. I know a guy who tried robbing him once. Trust me when I say that you cross a man as powerful as Jackson, you'll wish you were dead."

His answer seemed to satisfy the leader, who stood. "We'll continue this conversation outside. No need for big ears to learn the rest of our plan."

He looked pointedly at Emma Jane, but she didn't care. If the men left the cabin, she could tend to Jasper's wounds.

Before she could reach Jasper, the baby let out a small cry. Emma Jane picked him up, noting immediately that he was wet. A good sign, considering how weak he'd appeared when she'd first begun tending him.

"I wish I knew your name, little fellow." Emma Jane stroked his head as she laid him down and changed him. Mack had given her some old shirts to cut up and use for diapers. For an outlaw, Mack seemed like a pretty decent guy.

Satisfied the baby was comfortable, Emma Jane set

him back in the crate, then moved it closer to where Jasper lay.

After untying him and removing the handkerchief from his mouth, she moistened one of the clean cloths. She wiped the dried blood on the side of his head. Fortunately, the wound itself seemed small, and as Emma Jane pressed the cloth to it, no fresh blood came out.

Jasper moaned. Emma Jane's heart jumped and her breath caught. Was he waking up?

"Jasper?"

His eyelids fluttered open. "What happened?"

He struggled to get up, but Emma Jane stopped him. "Slowly. You took a nasty hit to the head, so you might be dizzy standing up."

When they'd been trapped in the mine, some of it had caved in and knocked Emma Jane unconscious. From what she remembered of her recuperation, she'd been dizzy off and on for days afterward. Jasper would need to take it slowly, but from the gleam in his eyes, Emma Jane figured he wanted to do anything but.

"Where are we?" He looked around the cabin, almost frantic in his motions.

"Shh…calm down. We're in the bandits' cabin. You're safe."

"Safe?" Jasper's head jerked up, then he pulled himself into a sitting position. "We've got to get out of here."

Just as quickly as he'd gotten up, he put his hand to his head. "Everything's spinning."

"You need to lie down and rest. There's a pallet by the fire. Let me help you over there."

He stumbled as he tried to stand, and from the way he grunted, Jasper seemed to realize the futility of not fol-

Shotgun Marriage

lowing Emma Jane's instructions. She helped him balance, then led him to the pallet.

"I made some soup. We'll see how you do with the broth, but your stomach might be upset."

One more thing she remembered from her own head injury. As much as she'd wanted to eat, she'd struggled to keep things down for the first day or so.

"You made soup?" Jasper looked up at her as he sat on the pallet.

"It was all they had ingredients for."

He continued to look at her with incredulity.

"Oh. You didn't realize I could cook, did you?" Emma Jane smiled as she sat down beside him. "I suppose there isn't much use for my cooking skills with all your help at the house, but when Father was in a bad place and we had to let the servants go, I ended up doing all the cooking."

The infant began to fuss. "Let me get the baby, and we can finish talking."

"Baby?"

"Oh." Emma Jane continued toward the little boy. "I have much to catch you up on."

She picked up the infant and held him up for Jasper to see before making her way to the rocker. "When I got here, the woman who'd been taking care of things was quite ill. No one was taking care of her poor little baby. The bandits were quite put out by the situation, so I pitched in to help."

"You did *what*?" Jasper ran a hand over his face. "Emma Jane, these are bandits."

"Bandits who are in a foul mood because they haven't had a hot meal since their woman took sick. They said they were going to let me go as soon as they finished their last job. They're going to Mexico when this is all over. They just need me out of the way for a while so I don't go to the sheriff before they get the last job done."

It sounded so much simpler when she explained it. Some of it, Emma Jane took a lot of pride in having figured out for herself.

"They told you that?"

Leave it to Jasper to sound annoyed with her when she'd done quite a good job, if she did say so herself. She'd been taking care of a sick woman, a baby, gotten supper ready and had done a little tidying in the cabin. Not bad for an afternoon's work. And, while doing all that, she'd figured out what the bandits were up to.

"Of course not. But you'd be amazed at what people will say in front of you when they think you're stupid. And me being a woman, in their minds, I'm a complete idiot."

Jasper let out a long sigh. "Emma Jane, they are not going to let us live. You know their plan, and I know where their hideout is."

"No, you don't." Emma Jane stared at him. "They knocked you out. You were unconscious the whole way here."

"But I'm sure, from our surroundings, I can figure it out pretty quickly. Once we find our way back to town, it will be easy enough for me to gather a posse and return."

Now who was the simple one? Emma Jane shook her head. "And how do you propose we get back to town?"

She pointed out the window. "Do you know how many men are out there? You've seen three. I've counted at least a dozen, and all of them are armed. They told me that if I cooperate, they'll let me live. But if I try to escape, I'm dead. Even with you here, what chance do the two of us have with a sick woman and a baby against that many men?"

"What do the sick woman and baby have to do with us getting out of here?"

The infant fussed slightly, bringing Emma Jane's attention to him rather than the incorrigible man sitting on the pallet. Otherwise, she might have lost her temper. But this gave her the opportunity to collect her thoughts, take a deep breath and look him in the eye.

"We can't leave them here."

Jasper let out an exasperated sigh. "I know you like to help others, but this woman and her baby are with the bandits. They…"

"You don't know that. She could have been kidnapped, just like me. Didn't you say this woman you were looking for, Daisy, was being held by the bandits?"

Light filled Jasper's eyes, but then it dimmed. "She didn't have a baby." Then he stopped and exhaled sharply. "But she was with child."

Jasper sat quietly for a moment, and Emma Jane thought it wise to just let him be. It was a lot to take in. Besides, the baby had started fussing again.

"I'm just going to give him some milk. You rest."

Who was this woman, bossing him around? Emma Jane had always been so meek and mild mannered. Maybe he'd been hit on the head harder than he'd thought.

His wife had only been partially right about him not knowing where the gang's hideout was. When the men were arguing about what to do with him, he pretended to be injured worse than he was. The kicks to his side they'd given him were well worth the pain, given he now knew exactly how to get here. And how to get back to town. Sure, he'd blacked out a few times, but he knew enough.

It now made sense why they kept losing the gang's trail. With the various creek crossings and doubling back the men did to hide their trail, it was no wonder the posse couldn't find them. Especially with the way the cabin was hidden among some rock outcroppings.

He watched as Emma Jane cooed at the baby and fed him from some weird contraption.

"Where'd you come up with that?" Jasper pointed to the bottle.

"Oh. One of the men helped me fix it up. They have bottles for babies in the mercantile, and when I explained to him what I wanted, he helped me put a few odds and ends together to do it."

Emma Jane acted like this was simply one of her mission projects rather than the cold-blooded killers they'd been pursuing.

"One of the men?"

"His name is Mack," Emma Jane said with a smile as she lifted the baby to her shoulder to burp. "He's quite nice, considering his profession. Calls me 'ma'am,' and is always offering to help me."

The name didn't sound familiar, but that didn't mean anything to Jasper. They'd still been trying to figure out the exact makeup of the gang. With the brothel fire, many of the men they'd thought were the leaders had been arrested and put in jail. But the remnant seemed to be just as strong and powerful without their leaders.

"He's not your friend," Jasper bit out, struggling to sit up straighter to get a better look around the place. His head pounded harder now, and spots danced in front of his eyes. Maybe he'd been hit harder than he'd thought.

"Maybe not," Emma Jane said, returning to her spot in the rocking chair. "But I've learned that when dealing with your enemies, you have to give them as little ammunition as possible. It seems to me, that in the case of men who are equally torn between killing you and keeping you alive, the best thing a person can do is be as useful as possible."

She smiled down at the baby and made a little cooing noise at him. "And that's what we're doing, isn't it, my sweet?"

He'd always known that Emma Jane was smart, but as he watched her bond with the baby as though her life wasn't in danger, he realized that she was a lot smarter than he'd given her credit for. Even without the infant and the sick woman who may or may not be Daisy, the odds of the two of them surviving an escape with a dozen men on guard were slim at best.

His stomach rumbled, and he remembered the broth Emma Jane had promised. "Could I have some of that soup you made?"

She smiled. "Of course. But broth only until we know your stomach can tolerate it."

Then she stood and tried to hand him the baby. "Take him so I can make the soup."

Jasper stared at the baby. "You want me to do what?"

"Hold him. Don't tell me you've never held a baby before."

He continued staring awkwardly at the child. "Actually, I haven't."

"Then let me show you. Babies are such a delight, and when you have your own…" Her face clouded. "Oh. I suppose… Well, that is… We never really talked about…"

Emma Jane turned away, clutching the baby to her chest before setting him in an old crate.

She didn't have to finish any of those sentences. After all, when a man promises a woman a marriage in name only, children aren't a likely outcome of the union.

As he watched her prepare the soup, taking longer than a simple task should have, he wondered how much she regretted their current circumstances, as well. Clearly, she loved babies, and with the marriage they agreed to, there would be none.

In this, they had both lost.

Jasper cleared his throat. "I would have liked children of my own. But I don't suppose that's possible now."

Her eyes glistened as she handed him the soup, but she didn't say anything. And he didn't ask.

They still had too many bridges to cross before they were in a place where such a conversation would be possible. Too many hurts stood in the way.

He supposed he shouldn't have said anything about his own desire for children when it seemed so out of reach right now. But the ache inside him, seeing Emma Jane with the baby and her seeming innocence on the subject, prevented him from keeping silent.

His silence often seemed like a willingness to be complicit in everyone else's plans for him. Maybe he should have spoken up sooner. Perhaps, if everyone had known that he wanted to fall in love, find a wife of his own choosing and have a home full of laughter and children, he wouldn't be in this mess.

Sipping his soup, Jasper watched Emma Jane go to the sleeping woman and bathe her face with a cloth. He couldn't hear the words she murmured, but the kindness and poise emanating from Emma Jane made him regret being so hard on her.

After a few sips, his stomach felt sour. He set the bowl aside.

Immediately, Emma Jane turned to him. "Are you all right?"

"Fine. You were right in saying I should take it slow."

"I just remembered what it was like from my own experience." Emma Jane stood and straightened her skirts. "I do wish I knew more about nursing the sick. All I know is that I should mop her face with a cool cloth and try to get her to drink some broth. But what if there is more I can do?"

The lines etched in her forehead spoke louder than anything she could have said. How could she be so deeply concerned for a stranger?

"You did just fine taking care of me."

She gave a half smile, but the lines didn't leave her forehead. "But I've had an injury to my head. I know what that feels like, and I know what helps. With this poor woman, I don't know what's wrong or what to do for her."

Seeing this side of Emma Jane made him question how she would be capable of the deceit leading to their marriage. Surely someone who cared this much about others wouldn't want to ruin someone else's life.

But would Emma Jane have seen it as ruining his life?

The door banged open, and Rex McGee, whose face graced a number of wanted posters across the country, entered.

"I hear we got ourselves a special guest. Leadville royalty." Rex chortled at his own joke, then started toward Jasper. "What kind of ransom do you think you're worth?"

Emma Jane gasped, but Jasper looked at him as coldly as he could. "I think you know my father has a long-standing and vocal policy that he does not pay ransom."

Rex grinned. "So tell me why we shouldn't kill you, then. I don't run no charity cases, not like that pretty little wife of yours."

"I think you know. I die, and the ransom on your head would tempt even your most loyal guns to turn on you."

Jasper continued glaring at Rex, but Rex had turned his attention on Emma Jane.

"I hear you've been making yourself quite useful around here."

Demurely folding her hands in front of her, Emma Jane bobbed her head at him. "I like to be useful. This woman is sick, and she needs a doctor."

"We don't need anyone else sniffing around our business."

"So I've been told. Which is why I'm doing the best I can to ease her suffering. Do you know what's wrong with her?"

"Do I look like a doctor?"

Jasper clenched his jaw. What was Emma Jane thinking, going toe-to-toe with one of the country's most nefarious criminals?

She looked Rex in the eye, raised her chin and said, "I've learned not to judge people by their appearance."

He grinned. "Well, if that soup of yours is half as good as the other men are saying, I just might have to keep you around. Perhaps you'll earn the keep for that worthless husband of yours."

Jasper opened his mouth to speak, but Emma Jane shot him a look. Even if he could remember what he'd intended to say, he was too stunned at this mouse turned into a lioness to say anything.

Who *was* this woman?

"I'd be happy to get you some." Emma Jane smiled sweetly at Rex, then walked over to the fire, where she dished out the soup. "I don't suppose you'd be willing to tell me anything about the operation here? The other gentleman acted like he was in charge, but he wouldn't tell me anything."

She handed Rex a bowl of soup and beamed.

Clearly, Jasper had married a madwoman.

"You know I can't say anything." Rex nodded in Jasper's direction. "I hear tell that Leadville's newest deputy has a burr under his saddle about having my men in prison, so I'm not likely to help that cause."

"Actually," Emma Jane said quietly, "his main interest is finding and rescuing a woman named Daisy, so if you could just confirm our suspicions that the poor woman lying in the bed is she, then most of Jasper's motivation in pursuing your men would be gone."

Had he called her a madwoman yet?

"Emma Jane," he said through gritted teeth.

Rex waved a hand as if to tell Jasper to be quiet. "What would a married man want with Ben Perry's doxy?"

"Her sister saved Jasper's life. It was her dying wish that Jasper would save Daisy."

Rex had the gall to laugh. A full-out belly laugh that rang through the room, causing the baby to stir. Emma Jane immediately went to the infant and picked him up out of the crate.

"Shh…" She held the child close to her, then glared at Rex. "Do be mindful of the baby."

Jasper closed his eyes. She was going to get them all

killed, that's what she was going to do. He'd heard tales of men being shot for looking at Rex wrong, and here was Emma Jane, chastising him as though he were an errant child.

Opening his eyes, he watched Rex give Emma Jane a little pat before coming to stand over Jasper. "You are one stupid man, you know that?"

As much as he hated to admit it, Jasper was starting to figure that out.

"A word of advice—chivalry only gets a man killed. You want Daisy, you found her. 'Course, you may not live much past this, but you can die with the satisfaction of honoring your promise."

He hated the bandit's condescending tone. But worse, he detested the knowledge that Rex was probably right.

Jasper's head was starting to throb again, and his stomach hadn't settled after the soup. With Emma Jane's clear lack of understanding of just how serious the situation was, there was no way he was going to get them all out alive.

He'd found Daisy, just as he'd promised. But the smirk on Rex's face told him that succeeding beyond this point was going to take a miracle.

Chapter Nine

Emma Jane had never hit a person in all her life, but if she could smack Jasper right about now, she would. He was glaring furiously, mouth set in a hard line, but didn't he realize that antagonizing this man was only going to get them all killed?

Holding the baby closer to her, Emma Jane gave the man her best smile. "I'm sure we will be most cooperative, and you will have no reason for hurting us."

The man slurped down the rest of his soup. "We'll see."

He turned to leave, but as his hand was on the door, Emma Jane spoke up again.

"I realize that I'm imposing on you… However, might I trouble you for the baby's name? I appreciate knowing that I'm caring for Daisy, and I'd sure like to know who this little guy is."

The man didn't turn around. "We all just refer to him as Ben's brat." Then he slammed the door behind him as he exited.

At least she'd tried. Obviously, she couldn't expect the

bandits to warm up to her and have a friendly little chat over tea. But she was making progress, and soon enough, their ordeal would be over.

"What were you thinking, challenging a dangerous criminal like that?"

Jasper's scolding came as completely unexpected and, in Emma Jane's mind, completely inappropriate. Didn't he see that she was trying to keep them both alive?

"*Me?* You were the one who looked like you were trying to crucify him with your eyes. I was just trying to be sure he knew that we are not a threat."

"By telling him all about Daisy?"

"At least he confirmed her identity, which is more than any of the others have."

The baby started fussing again, so Emma Jane began rocking him slowly. Then she spoke in a soft voice.

"We can't quarrel. It upsets the baby. But you have to know that I am doing my very best to keep the peace to avoid any conflict with the bandits that would make them want to kill us. Is it so hard to try to be agreeable?"

The dark scowl on Jasper's face said that it was, indeed, a difficult task. In fact, he looked like he wanted to kill her almost as much as the bandits seemed to want to kill him.

"These men can't be reasoned with. They are cold-blooded murderers."

"So you keep saying." Emma Jane sat down in the rocking chair with the baby. "What proof do you have of this?"

"The man who was just in here? His name is Rex McGee. There are a number of wanted posters from several places with his name and face on it. Rumor has it that he's killed many a man just for giving him a cross look."

"I thought you didn't pay attention to rumors." Emma Jane couldn't help but glower at him. For all his talk about hating people saying bad things about him, he was awful quick to believe stories about the bandits.

"Wanted posters are not rumors." Jasper groaned and rubbed the sides of his head. "But you're right, I have no factual basis for the rest. I'm sorry."

And now Emma Jane was sorry. Clearly, Jasper's head was paining him, and here she was getting him all upset.

"You should rest. The men gave me some pain relieving powder to use on Daisy, but since I can't get her to take any of the broth, I could give it to you. I found it most helpful when my own head was hurting."

For a moment, she thought he'd refuse out of pure stubbornness.

But then he sighed. "Do you think it's safe?"

Emma Jane got up and showed him the packet. "It looks identical to the one I had when I was injured. I think you should try it."

Jasper nodded slowly and closed his eyes. "I suppose you're right."

She put the baby back in the crate, then mixed the powder. Part of her felt bad for using medicine intended for Daisy, but if the poor woman couldn't take it, then at least it was being put to good use.

Sitting next to Jasper, she handed him the concoction. "I would tell you to drink it slowly, but it tastes terrible, so you should drink quickly and get it over with."

He took the cup and did as she instructed. The lines around his eyes seemed deeper as he released a ragged breath.

"Why don't you lie down and rest? I'm sure your head

pains you more than you're letting on, and the rest will do you good."

Jasper examined her face, like he was seeing her for the first time. "I don't understand you."

"What's there to understand? You're in pain, and I'm trying to help you."

"And Daisy, a stranger."

He sounded so incredulous. Even after seeing her helping out with the pastor's mission, he seemed oblivious to the fact that helping others is what Emma Jane did.

"Why would I do any less?"

And then he looked at her with such intensity in his eyes. "But why haven't you ever helped yourself?"

His words thundered against her chest as she stood. How was she supposed to answer that question? Help herself? What did that even mean?

"I don't know what you're talking about."

She started to walk toward where she'd laid the baby down.

"Don't pick up that baby as an excuse to avoid the conversation."

Emma Jane turned to him. "What would you have me do instead?"

"I'm trying to figure you out. I have seen you take all kinds of abuse from others, but when it comes to taking care of someone else, you are like a tiger. No one gets in your way, and you stand up admirably to anyone who does. So why haven't you ever stood up for yourself?"

For a moment, it felt like Emma Jane couldn't breathe. And then she did. She took a breath, and another.

"Because standing up for myself seemed like an exercise in futility. It never did any good."

Tears pricked the backs of her eyes as she remembered

all the times she'd tried standing up for herself against people like Flora Montgomery.

"Who do you think you are?" Flora and her friends would taunt her and laugh.

But laughter wasn't the only thing Emma Jane remembered. Those darker memories, though, those she shoved down. No use in remembering when she could prevent them from happening again.

"If you're so brave in your defense of others, you should do the same for yourself."

Easy for him to say.

"I'll try." She started to go back to the baby, but once again, Jasper stopped her.

"Why are you so nice to the bandits?"

"Why shouldn't I be?"

"You don't owe them anything."

Emma Jane closed her eyes. Tried to shut down the thoughts of the past that had been threatening her ever since she was kidnapped.

"You're right. I don't. But I also know that the more cooperative I am, the less likely they are to harm me."

"Look at me."

She opened her eyes.

"You keep saying that, as if you know what it's like to be kidnapped. Have you been kidnapped before?"

Gentleness filled his voice, and compassion was in his brown eyes. They'd been at odds so much since his arrival at the cabin, and here was the reminder that underneath was a Jasper that she found she liked, quite a lot.

The truth was so far from his suspicions, and she found she couldn't give it voice. Yet how was she supposed to let him believe a lie?

"I've never been kidnapped."

Emma Jane swallowed, unable to tear her gaze from his. "But I know what it's like to live among people who make you afraid. Who will hurt you if you don't do as they ask."

"Who were you afraid of?"

She sighed, knowing that the only path out of this troubling conversation was the truth. Ignoring his previous request to not pick up the baby, she went to the baby and took him in her arms. Not as an excuse to avoid, but as comfort against the pain.

"My father got angry a lot. But I learned that if I just took care of things to make our household run smoothly, then he'd not be so angry."

Emma Jane sat in the rocking chair with the baby, snuggling him to her, and looking at him rather than Jasper's questioning eyes.

"Did he hurt you?"

The words pained her too much to come out. It somehow seemed disloyal to say such things about her father. He wasn't a bad man, not like these men.

Emma Jane didn't look up. "Everything was fine as long as I took care of everyone."

Then she brought her gaze to Jasper. "And that's what I'm doing here. Taking care of everyone so no one gets hurt."

"Your father…" A muscle pulsed in his jaw, and he rubbed his head again.

"I don't want to talk about it. Sometimes he drank too much. But everyone knows that. I learned to keep myself, and my sister, safe. And that's what I'm trying to do here. That's all that matters."

Standing, Emma Jane shifted the baby to another position as she grabbed a blanket from a nearby chair. "Now I must insist that you rest."

He looked at her, his eyes full of a fight, but his head clearly so weary that it was obvious what he needed. Fortunately, he lay down, and Emma Jane did her best to tuck the blanket around him.

"Thank you, Emma Jane," he said huskily, putting his hand over hers as she patted the blanket. "I appreciate what you've done, and I hope you get some rest, too."

"I will." She gave his hand a squeeze, noting the warmth that passed between them.

As cross as he'd been with her, he still had room in his heart for kind feelings toward her. For warmth. Perhaps even for friendship.

Then she got up and walked over to where Daisy lay. Her fever had gone down, and she seemed to be less restless than she'd been when Emma Jane had first arrived.

"Everything's going to be all right, Daisy," she told the sleeping woman. "Your baby is just fine, and I'm taking good care of him."

As if to confirm Emma Jane's words, the baby gurgled softly, a contented sound, giving her hope that things really were going to be okay.

Though she'd been firm in telling Jasper that being kind to the bandits was the best way to keep them alive, part of her feared that it wouldn't be enough. Because what she hadn't told Jasper was while her tactics worked to placate her father, nothing had ever seemed good enough for her mother. The only difference was that while her father used his hand, her mother always wounded Emma Jane with her words. And sometimes, Emma Jane thought she'd much rather have the bruises.

Marriage to Jasper hadn't been what she'd wanted. But

in all her days as his wife, she hadn't once been afraid he was going to hurt her. His mother might not be the warmest woman in the world, and yes, her insults did sting, but Jasper and his father had shown her more kindness and consideration than her own family had.

Which again felt disloyal, since she was supposed to honor her father and mother. They did the best they could, she supposed, considering her father's battle with the drink and gambling. And her mother, being forced to live in a rough place like Leadville, when she'd been the belle of society before the war. Of course, Emma Jane had just been a baby during the war, and she didn't remember any of it.

All she knew was that her mother said the war had changed her father, changed their family, and nothing had been the same since. But at least with Emma Jane's marriage to Jasper, her family could have their finances restored. Maybe then they would find the happiness that had eluded them all these years.

As for Emma Jane, she'd learned not to pursue happiness for herself. But in taking care of others, she at least found a place where she could have contentment of sorts.

The smell of sizzling bacon woke Jasper. He tried to lift his head, but it felt heavy, like it was full of lead. When he opened his eyes, he could see Emma Jane, serving the bandits breakfast. He watched her, noting the same polite demeanor she'd had the previous day. But now, knowing what she'd said about her father, he noticed something more.

While Emma Jane appeared pleasant enough, the light didn't reach her eyes. How had he missed it before? She played the role of the servant beautifully, but her heart wasn't there.

He'd been wrong to chastise her. He still didn't like her being friendly with the bandits, but he could see where she was coming from. His heart weighed heavy in his chest as he realized how hard her life had been, and how he'd never noticed before.

"I fixed you some eggs," Emma Jane said softly as she knelt beside him. "If you're up to it, that is."

He tried reading her. Was the kindness because she cared for him, or because she feared him? The answer shouldn't matter, but he found it did—very much.

"Thank you." He struggled to sit up. "You don't have to wait on me, you know. You're not my servant."

She smiled, and her blue eyes warmed. "I know. But you're hurt, and it's important for you to get your strength up. So eat."

Emma Jane set a plate in front of him, then went to pick the baby up.

Efficient as always, and focused on the child. He thought again about their discussion last night regarding children. Rather, his avoidance of the discussion. As he watched her sing softly to the baby, he realized that she, too, had given up all dreams of having children.

Could they find a compromise? No, not a compromise. One didn't have a baby out of compromise. But could they find enough common ground that would allow them to have the sort of feelings a man and woman needed to bring a child into the world?

Emma Jane would make an excellent mother.

And the more he watched her, with the sun streaming into the room through cracks in the window, the more he had to admit that she was quite lovely. Even now, with her hair falling out of its bun, her dress dirty and a smudge of something on her cheek, he couldn't help but think everyone had been mistaken in mocking her for being unattractive.

"Is something amiss?" Emma Jane looked directly at him. She'd caught him staring.

"No." Swallowing hard, he had to remind himself that there was still a lot unsettled between them. Any admiration or attempts at expressing such admiration was best left for later.

One of the men entered the room, carrying Jasper's saddlebag. "Thought you might find something useful in here, miss."

A genuine smile lit up Emma Jane's face. "Oh, thank you, Mack. You've been so helpful."

"It was nothing, miss. You've sure brightened this place up, and while I do regret that we can't let you go, the least I can do is make sure you're comfortable."

Jasper tried not to groan. Unfortunately, he wasn't successful, because Emma Jane looked right at him. "Is your head paining you again? I could make you some more headache powder."

He sighed, then nodded. As much as he'd like to say he was completely recovered, he'd be a liar. And he'd need all his strength to plan their next move. Emma Jane might have faith that the gang would let them live after it was all over, but he knew better.

They might be under heavy guard, yet there *had* to be a way to escape.

She prepared the powder, then gave it to him. He drank it quickly, then, to ease the taste, ate some of the eggs Emma Jane had given him.

While he ate, she opened his saddlebags. He hadn't

kept anything valuable in them, especially since he hadn't been preparing for a trip, but hopefully she'd happen upon something useful.

"Oh, my!" Emma Jane's eyes lit up. "You found my Bible!" Then she stopped and looked at him apologetically. "That is, *our* Bible. I was hoping you'd see it and realize I'd left you a clue."

Jasper couldn't help but grin back at her. "No, it's your Bible. I know it was a wedding gift to both of us, but it brings you such joy that I wouldn't dream of it being anything but yours."

He didn't have the heart to tell her that while the Bible was important to her, it was just a book to him. But it seemed to mean a lot to Emma Jane, and if it made her happy, then he was all for it.

"As for finding your Bible." He gave a shrug. "I may not know much about you, but I have noticed the way you always seem to have it with you."

Then he looked around—some of the bandits appeared to be huddled over some papers. Jasper could identify Rex, and he knew that several others remained outside. As he observed their interactions, it was becoming clearer how the gang's leadership had evolved with the arrest of Ben Perry and other key members of the gang. Of course, this meant that there was no way they were getting out alive.

No matter how optimistic Emma Jane sounded, the gang wasn't going to be willing to risk being so exposed. Ultimately, if Jasper didn't find means of escape, they had but days to live. The only question was why the bandits were keeping them alive in the first place. Jasper didn't buy for a minute that they were afraid that killing him would bring about more attention. Surely they had to know, that even with Jasper having been kidnapped, there would be more people looking for them.

So what was their game?

As if he could sense the direction of Jasper's thoughts, Rex turned toward Jasper. "I need you to write me a letter."

"For…?" Even without looking at Emma Jane, he could tell she was glaring at him over his sullen tone.

"To your father. Letting him know you're alive, and where he can bring the ransom."

"I believe I mentioned that my father doesn't pay ransom."

Rex gave him a long, calculated look. "Doesn't matter. The sheriff will still send men to the drop-off point, giving us the perfect distraction to take care of stuff. We just need you to oblige us with a letter proving you're alive and that we mean business."

Jasper shook his head. At least he got the answer to his unspoken question. They wanted to keep him alive long enough to use him as bait.

Which meant as soon as the bandits had their plan in motion, Jasper and Emma Jane were dead. Well, he wasn't going to make it that easy for them.

"And what if I don't write that letter?"

Rex turned his attention to Emma Jane, who clutched her Bible to her chest and was observing their interactions with wide eyes.

"It'd be a shame if anything happened to that pretty little wife of yours."

Emma Jane's face screwed into an expression he couldn't read. For a moment, he thought she might start crying, but instead, she just stood there, looking like…

Like she did on their wedding day.

She hadn't wanted to marry him any more than he'd wanted to marry her. And now she was a pawn in some sick criminal's game, when all she'd wanted was to help others.

"What do you want me to write?"

He shouldn't have caved so easily, but as Emma Jane's posture relaxed, he knew it was the right decision, at least for her peace of mind.

Rex handed him a piece of paper. "And don't think I won't know if you're trying to trick me. I can read and write just as well as any of those uppity teachers in the school."

He gave Jasper pen and ink. "The only thing keeping you alive is your cooperation. That and Jimmy's squeamishness. He might not want to leave a trail of dead bodies, but make no mistake. I will shoot you dead if I have to. And if that means killing Jimmy, I'll do that, too." Rex's smile as he spoke verified the rumors Jasper had heard.

Rex liked killing. Chills pricked the back of Jasper's neck.

Did Emma Jane understand now how lethal these men were?

He looked at her for signs of having understood the import of Rex's words, but she was seemingly unaware, having opened her Bible and was now engrossed in its pages. Hands flexing at his sides, he strained to keep his temper in check. Maybe it wasn't right to be mad at her for it, but it seemed wrong that while he was trying to keep them alive, she seemed more interested in her Bible.

What was the Bible going to do for them? It wasn't as though God was going to reach down from Heaven to save them from these evil men. No, it was up to Jasper to find a way to get them out of this situation—before the gang decided they were no longer useful.

He picked up the pen and began writing the words Rex dictated. For now, he'd play the game and pretend to be just as agreeable as Emma Jane. But he'd be watching—and waiting. And he would find a way to save them both.

Chapter Ten

Emma Jane tried focusing on the words of the Psalms. David knew what it was like to be pursued by an enemy with greater might and power than his own. Surely God would give them a way out. If Jasper's stubbornness didn't get them killed first.

The baby started to cry. Again. Emma Jane sighed. If only Daisy would wake up and give her some idea as to how to take care of her son. At first, giving him the milk and some love had seemed to turn a baby who never stopped crying into a peaceful little thing. But now, all he seemed to do was cry, with a few moments of respite here and there.

She put her Bible down and went to pick up the baby. Fortunately, he always calmed down a little in her arms. His wails turned into whimpers, and she cradled him close as she went back to her chair to focus on her Bible again.

The bandits had gone outside, but the occasional shadows passing the window told Emma Jane that they were still standing guard. Jasper had tried the door once but found it locked tight.

Now he was pacing, walking the length of the cabin and back again. She should be grateful he didn't appear to have any ill effects from the injury to his head, but right now, he was making her crazy.

His pacing, the baby's whimpering and Daisy's ragged breathing—it was enough to send a woman to Bedlam.

"Please, Jasper. Can you sit and rest? You don't want to have a relapse."

Selfishly, she'd admit that any concern over his health was secondary to her own need for peace.

"I don't like being locked up like an animal."

"We don't have much of a choice in the matter, so you might as well make the best of it."

She didn't mean to sound so shrewish, but really...

"You're good at that, aren't you?"

Jerking her chin in his direction, she gave him a defiant look. Jasper's words sounded almost like an insult. But he didn't understand that, for most people, it was the only way to survive.

"Yes, I am. I've found that most of the circumstances of my life have been foisted upon me and are not of my choosing. But I can choose how I respond to them."

Emma Jane took a deep breath. "In the past, I haven't always done such a good job of that. Sometimes I am almost ashamed of how badly I've reacted in difficult situations. But I've learned that such behavior never makes things better."

The baby had started to drift off to sleep. She looked down at him and wondered what choices he would have in this world. Born of a notorious criminal and a woman of the night, he would never live the kind of respectable life Emma Jane had. And her level of respectability had been marginal at best. All she'd ever wanted was respectability, and yet here she held an infant whose chances of attaining it were much more miniscule than her own.

"But don't you want things to be different?" Jasper's voice sounded almost hoarse, like he was trying to contain emotions and not quite succeeding.

He was referring, of course, to their marriage. Contrary to popular belief, Emma Jane wasn't stupid. He didn't want their marriage any more than she had. All right. He'd wanted their marriage even less than she had. After all, Emma Jane had already accepted that her fate would not involve a love match.

Still, she had hoped that, in some way, the man she married would at least want her.

"Of course I want things to be different. But they are what they are, so why would I waste my time wishing for things that aren't possible?"

"Or you could make them what you want to be." His words were quiet as he sank into a chair by the fire.

What was he saying? How did you make a marriage what you wanted it to be when neither of you wanted the marriage? Or was he suggesting they end it?

"Or you make the best of what you have." She looked at him squarely, challenging him. Making lemonade out of lemons was something Emma Jane had become quite good at. Not just in her life circumstances, but even in turning someone else's cast-off dress into something beautiful. Everyone had said her sister, Gracie, was one of the finest dressed young ladies in town.

No one realized that it had been Emma Jane's skill that had accomplished that goal.

Even now, as she cared for this tiny baby with few supplies, she'd made do, and while things weren't perfect, the baby seemed content enough.

She pulled her chair closer to Daisy. "Do you think she can hear us?"

"You're avoiding the conversation."

"What conversation?" Emma Jane didn't look at him, not wanting to see the expression on his face. Just as with the bandits, he seemed to be deliberately trying to bait her.

"About you."

"Me?" This time she did look at him. "Are you trying to provoke some sort of disagreement? I don't know what else you want to hear from me. I've told you that I believe in making the best of things. I'm not sure what else there is to discuss on the matter."

His eyes darkened, and his expression lay hidden by the shadows, which seemed to have deepened since he sat down.

"I'm trying to understand."

Though his words seemed to be in earnest, there seemed to be something else beneath the surface. Something Emma Jane wasn't sure she wanted to explore.

"Then please accept my need to make the best of things. We don't have a choice in being here. I could just as easily play the hysterical woman at being kidnapped. I've played that part before, and it did me no good. At least in this situation, I can feel like I'm doing something useful, and I have a distraction to keep my mind off the thing I fear the most."

"And what do you fear the most?"

Emma Jane swallowed. "Dying, of course. I have so much I want to do in my life, and I…"

She looked down at the baby. "I don't want to leave this earth without having experienced some of the joys I've been longing for."

Truthfully, as the infant snuggled against her, she had to admit that caring for this child was one of those joys. She'd always hoped for a baby of her own, yet the longer she had this precious little boy with her, the more he seemed like her own.

What was she going to do when Daisy got better?

"What joys?" Jasper's stare felt so heavy on her she couldn't bear to look up.

She didn't have an answer for him. After all, most of the things she wanted seemed too impossible to even give voice. Love, happiness—those were ideas she had to find a way to let go of. But the warm bundle in her arms forced one word out of her mouth.

"Family."

"I want that, too," Jasper said gruffly.

Her head snapped up and she stared at him. "You said ours would be a marriage in name only."

"We could discuss…"

Jasper shifted as though the idea made him just as uncomfortable as it made her. No, worse. It seemed as though he was suggesting something completely intolerable to him, but he'd be willing to do it for the greater good.

"No. I'm perfectly aware of what having a family would take. And I can't do…that…without love."

Emma Jane could feel the heat on her face rise. Proper ladies didn't speak of such things. But a gentleman would never suggest them, either. She closed her eyes. Except, of course, if they were husband and wife. Which she and Jasper technically were.

"I'm sorry. I didn't mean to offend you. I just thought, since we both wanted the same thing, we could find a way to compromise."

Finally finding the courage to look at him, Emma Jane opened her eyes. "I can't compromise on that."

She looked down at Daisy, whose breathing had grown more ragged. "It seems to me that a woman who compromises on those issues is no better than the women of her profession."

Smoothing Daisy's hair off her feverish brow, she examined the woman's features. Though probably younger than Emma Jane, Daisy's face was marked with years of rough living. "I mean no disrespect to Daisy, because I'm sure she did the best she could do."

Emma Jane brought her attention back to Jasper. "I've sacrificed enough in my life. There are some things I can cling to, and this is one of them. If you insist on fully being my husband, I won't fight you. But I hope you respect my desire to have at least that one choice belong to me."

"I would never force a woman in that regard. Like you, I believe such an act should be one of love." She couldn't read his expression in the firelight, but his tone was unmistakable. She'd offended him—deeply.

"I'm sorry… I didn't mean to suggest that you would. I was only trying…"

"Don't. I was wrong to bring it up," he said curtly. "We shouldn't be having this conversation. I'm sorry. Go back to your Bible, and I'll…" He shrugged. "Well, I'll do whatever I have to do. And we'll try not to infringe on each other's space too much."

Emma Jane didn't bother trying to respond. Jasper was right. It was the wrong conversation for them to be having, especially now in light of their current predicament. She sighed. Besides, talking about it only emphasized the fact that neither of them loved each other. Clearly, Jasper wasn't even attracted to her, given his penchant for kissing the other girls in town, and the fact that he hadn't even tried once with Emma Jane.

Oh, if only she hadn't had that silly dream of him kissing her in the mine. If only the feel of his lips against hers wasn't so deeply embedded in her memory.

But that wasn't love. Desire, maybe. Curiosity, certainly. But love? Love was an emotion she dared not even wish for, especially when it came to Jasper Jackson.

Daisy made a heaving sound, like she was struggling to breathe.

Her face was the color of day-old ashes, and as much as Emma Jane hated to admit it, there was little she could do for the other woman. She'd only seen one other person die, the Widow Sanders, who Emma Jane had briefly taken care of so her family could have extra money during one of her father's bad spells. Eugene Sanders had been a family friend, and he'd offered her father a goodly sum if only Emma Jane would sit with his elderly mother and make her last days peaceful.

Daisy had the look of Widow Sanders about her. So close to being claimed by death, yet desperately trying to cling to life. Fighting, not so much because she had it in her to live, but because she had so much unfinished business on earth.

Widow Sanders had been hanging on to the hope that her estranged daughter would come home. It was not until Emma Jane herself had whispered, "I love you. I forgive you," that she'd finally slipped into the beyond. Her words hadn't been a lie—she'd relied on the grace and peace of Christ to give a dying woman the comfort she'd needed. The daughter only came for the reading of the will, to take her thousand-dollar inheritance, then leave.

What comfort could Emma Jane give Daisy in these last hours? She'd been worshipping silently, but now, when she opened her Bible, she began to read aloud. Widow Sanders had taken great comfort in Emma Jane's Bible reading. During her brief awakenings, she'd told Emma Jane as such. She'd even confessed to Emma Jane her worries about God not wanting her after all she'd done in her life. But when Emma Jane spoke to her of God's forgiveness and love, Widow Sanders had appeared to take comfort.

Emma Jane read, noticing that the squeak of Jasper's footsteps against the floor had quieted. Even the baby had finally ceased fussing and had drifted off into a peaceful sleep.

She looked up at him, pausing in her recitation.

"Don't. I find your voice soothing." Jasper had settled into one of the chairs at the table and was watching her.

Emma Jane felt her face heat. "I'm not sure how to respond to that." She turned her attention back to her Bible.

"I was giving you a compliment. It's traditional to say thank-you when someone gives you a compliment."

His voice had taken on a teasing note, but Emma Jane found it unsettling. She'd seen him jest many a young lady, to be sure. He'd just never really done so with her. Why would he, when everyone knew that teasing was a form of flirting?

"Thank you," Emma Jane mumbled, not wanting to pursue the subject further.

She began to read again. Daisy's breathing caught, stopped, then just when Emma Jane thought it had been the other woman's last, she took another labored breath.

The poor woman was hanging on so tightly.

Lord, please, I've seen death before, and I know this

woman is close. If it is Your will to save her, then save her. But if she is to pass, tell me what I need to ease her transition into the hereafter.

The baby gave a small whimper. Of course! What mother would willingly leave this earth with such a small child with no one to care for him?

"I'll care for your baby like he was my own," whispered Emma Jane, squeezing Daisy's hand. As she made the promise, she felt the love swell up in her heart for the baby. Oh, she already loved him, there was no question of that, but this was an additional measure, the kind a mother felt for a child. And, as she recalled, the love Pastor Lassiter spoke of as the kind that came from the Lord. She'd sought this love for her mother-in-law, but as the infant lay in Emma Jane's arms, she knew the Lord had reserved it for her to give to this innocent child.

Daisy gave one last shuddering breath, then was still. A tear rolled down Emma Jane's cheek as she realized the other woman was gone.

Emma Jane looked down at the baby. "I still don't know your name, little one. But it seems to me with no one left to tell me, I'm going to have to give you one myself."

The baby looked up at her, his dark blue eyes warm and trusting. As the son of a fallen woman, he had no hope, no future. But as the son of Emma Jane Jackson, wife of one of the wealthiest men in Leadville, he would have everything.

She recalled the story of Moses, how his mother had given him up to be raised by the pharaoh's daughter. Her sacrifice had given him a chance at life.

"Moses," she said softly, stroking the boy's hair. "I will call you Moses. Because, like your namesake, you are being given a great opportunity at life, and I pray you will do great things with that opportunity."

Jasper wasn't surprised when Emma Jane informed him of Daisy's passing. The woman's labored breathing had told him she didn't have much time left. He'd tried telling himself otherwise, but he'd known.

What good had his mission to save her done?

He'd failed Mel. The woman had died, taking a bullet for him, and all she'd wanted, her whole reason for living, had been to give Daisy a good life.

And now her sister was dead.

He didn't even know what illness had befallen Daisy, but surely, had he gotten to her sooner, maybe she wouldn't have needed to die. If only he'd been able to get her to a doctor.

Jasper looked over at Emma Jane, who sat in the rocking chair, quietly reading her Bible to the baby. She'd pulled the blanket over Daisy's face, but having a dead woman in the room with them still felt wrong.

Frustration knotted his gut.

All of it was wrong. Daisy dying. Being locked in this old cabin. A baby who'd started wailing again. Emma Jane, trying to console the poor child.

The door opened, and Ace Perry, Ben's older brother, walked in. Now the pieces of the puzzle fit together.

"I thought you said that milk you got would shut the brat up."

Mack, who'd followed him in, shrugged. "Maybe babies don't like goat milk. Was the best I could do, getting a goat from that farm. Don't reckon I've seen any cows around."

Emma Jane started to approach them, and Jasper bit

back a groan. Was she ever going to learn? Why didn't she trust him to take care of things?

"I'm afraid I have bad news for you," she said quietly. "Daisy has passed away."

The mournful tone to his wife's voice almost made him want to cry. How could she be so tenderhearted toward a stranger she'd never really met? She truly sounded grieved over the loss.

"Well, that's one less problem we have to deal with." Ace grinned, then clapped Mack on the back. "See, now you won't have to worry about taking care of her."

"She was Ben's girl," Mack said, with an air of reverence that Jasper couldn't help but understand why Emma Jane liked him.

If you'd asked him why bandits were bad, he'd have just said because they were bad. But Mack had a sense of humanness, of gentility, that made Jasper wonder if there wasn't more to his original assumptions than he'd thought.

"And Ben's gone. Hanged by a bunch of vigilantes because he got sloppy."

There was no sadness in the other man's voice over the loss of his brother. Merely disgust at having been caught.

"Daisy was still a good woman, you know that." Mack walked over to the body. "We gotta do right by her."

Then Mack turned his attention to Emma Jane. "And the boy. He's your blood, Ace, you've got to…"

"I don't got to do anything. There's no proof, other than Daisy's word, that the brat was Ben's. Even Ben had his doubts."

"I'm going to take care of him," Emma Jane piped up. "I promised Daisy I'd love him like my own."

Ace grinned, his gold-capped teeth gleaming in the sunlight. "See there. It's already been settled."

Settled? Jasper shot a glance at Emma Jane, who stood proudly holding the baby. When had they discussed her taking care of the baby? Yes, while here in the cabin, it seemed like a reasonable thing to do. But moving forward? She hadn't even asked his opinion.

"If you've no objection, I'm calling him Moses." Again, Emma Jane looked at Ace for confirmation, completely ignoring Jasper. A baby wasn't like a stray puppy you could just bring home on a whim.

Ace snorted. "You can call him whatever you want. Like I said, not my problem."

Mack, though, turned to Emma Jane. "That sounds like a mighty nice name. The baby was born a couple of weeks before Ben was arrested, and Daisy wanted to wait until he could have a say in things before naming him. Now that the boy's daddy is gone, well…"

Ace walked over to Mack and smacked him on the side of the head. "What'd I say about being too free in your talk? Ben's big mouth and need to prove a point to that stupid lawman is what derailed our plans in the first place. We were this close to getting off to Mexico, and I'm not going to have it ruined a second time."

Jasper forced himself not to laugh at Ace's mistake. In chastising Mack, Ace confirmed what Emma Jane had already told him. They were planning something big, and then they were all headed to Mexico.

The question was, what was he plotting?

"Ain't no harm in being nice. This miss, here, she's been nothing but good to us," Mack said.

The door opened wider, and Ray and Jimmy strode in. "That's what I've been trying to tell Ray," Jimmy said. "She has no part in any of this, and with as much blood's on our hands, the last thing I want to do is take an innocent life."

Ray pulled out his gun and examined it. "I ain't got no problem with that." Then he pointed the gun at Jimmy. "I ain't got no problem with killing yellow-bellied cowards, either."

Jimmy slapped the gun away. "I'm not a coward, and you know it. Just ask Rex."

"Enough!" Ace's shout rang through the cabin. "No one is killing anyone."

Somehow, Jasper didn't find that comforting. He looked over at Emma Jane, who also didn't appear to be comforted by the bandit's words.

"Now." Ace turned his attention on Jimmy and Ray. "Did you or did you not go into town and deliver the letter, following my directions exactly?"

"Yes, sir," both men answered in unison.

"Good." Ace grinned at Jasper. "Your family has been informed of your status, as well as my demands. While it would be easier on my men to take care of business now, we may need to keep you around for a while, just in case things don't go according to plan." He spoke casually, but there was a dangerous glint in his eye. "I know I said I was going to let you live, but that depends on both your family's cooperation and your compliance. Am I understood?"

Jasper didn't blink. "Yes." Ace might talk a good game about possibly letting them live, but there was *no way*.

Ace turned his attention back to his men. "Mack, go dispose of the body."

"Dispose?" Emma Jane's voice squeaked as she interrupted. "Aren't you going to have a funeral?"

A funeral? Jasper gaped as Ace laughed.

"We're not the sort of people a preacher is going to visit."

Mack took a step forward. "That's a mighty fine idea. We don't need the preacher. Ray can sing us some songs on his guitar, and Jimmy can say a few words since he used to…"

"Enough!" Ace glared at Mack. "We can discuss this outside."

Jasper bit back his smile as the men left. The door had stuck as Jimmy closed it, and Jasper could see that it wasn't fully latched.

He crept toward the window and looked out. The men had gathered near a barn and were arguing, gesturing wildly. Five more men rode in, joining them. No one was watching the cabin.

At the door, Jasper noticed the simple lock mechanism. Now that the door was open and he had a chance to examine it, he could see how to disable it. This cabin wasn't equipped for keeping prisoners. Which was probably why some of the men were eager to kill them and get it over with.

The arguing ceased, and Mack started walking back to the cabin. Jasper stepped away and toward Emma Jane.

"They're coming back. Pretend you and I have been busy talking."

Emma Jane stared at him.

"I hope you can make more of those biscuits for dinner," Jasper said a little more loudly than he'd been speaking. "I had no idea you could cook so well."

"I'll see what I can…" Emma Jane still looked puzzled as the door flew open.

"I'd be obliged if you'd make those biscuits, too," Mack said, grinning as he strode in.

Emma Jane nodded slowly. The baby began to fuss again, reminding Jasper of the promise Emma Jane had no right in making.

But he couldn't mention it now. Not when Mack, Emma Jane's biggest supporter, was in the cabin. Mack had begun wrapping Daisy in the blanket Emma Jane had covered her with.

"I'll be taking the body for burial now," Mack said solemnly, looking Emma Jane in the eye. "We'll be having a short service and digging her a grave. I know you think we're a bunch of animals, but some of us were raised to do the right thing, even when it doesn't seem like it."

Jasper's gut churned as he saw the sympathy flicker across his wife's face.

"Then why *do* you live like this?"

Mack picked Daisy up as though she weighed no more than the baby in Emma Jane's arms.

"A lot of reasons. Mostly, a man does something he's not proud of, then there's no going back. I may not like everything Ace does, but he's been good to me. Might be hard to believe, but out of all the men I've worked for, Ace is the best."

He tipped his hat at Emma Jane. "I don't expect you to understand. But I do hope that when you say those prayers of yours, you find it in your heart to say a few for me."

Emma Jane gave him a smile. "I'm sure you know by now that I'd be happy to. And if you ever want to pray with me, I'd be glad to do so."

Her words made Jasper's heart do a funny thing. He wasn't sure what it meant, because part of him still thought she had to be the most naive woman on the planet for thinking she could befriend a gang of notorious criminals. But part of him marveled at the kind of woman she was to even try.

Mack didn't respond to Emma Jane as he exited the cabin. With his arms full, he didn't quite get the door closed behind him again.

Were they testing Jasper? To see if he'd try to escape, then shoot him in the act?

Once again, Jasper crept to the window. The bandits were off to the side, talking among themselves as Mack approached, carrying Daisy's body.

He took stock of the land, noting the clouds moving in. They were in for a big storm. By the smell of the wind, it carried a heavy snow that would leave them trapped for days. With the bandits distracted, this might be their only chance at escape.

Chapter Eleven

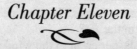

Emma Jane stared at Jasper as he announced his plan to make a run for it. "That's madness."

"Right now, their attention is on burying Daisy. With the wind picking up, they're going to start noticing the weather blowing in." Jasper pointed in the direction of the field. "They have livestock grazing there that they'll want to get in the barn before the storm hits. They're going to be so occupied that it'll be a while before they notice we're gone."

Two riders came in from the direction of the canyon opening leading to where the cabin lay.

"I'm pretty sure those are the lookouts. Right now, this place is unguarded and might be the only chance we have."

"Pretty sure?" The baby fussed against her.

Jasper gave her a hard look. "As sure as I am that if we don't escape, we're dead, anyway. If I'm going to die, I'd rather die trying."

"All right," Emma Jane said, trying not to sound as resigned as she felt. "Let me gather the baby's things."

"What things?" Jasper shook his head. "The baby's not coming with us."

Jasper might as well have shot her himself. "Wh-what do you mean?"

"Look, you made a promise to keep the baby without even consulting me. I didn't agree to care for a baby."

"You promised to save Daisy without consulting me." She snuggled Moses closer to her. "I am all he has in this world. You heard Ace. He wants nothing to do with the baby, and I'm pretty sure none of the other men do, either. They all call this sweet little boy a brat."

"Saving a person is different from taking a child into your home. You always act without thinking. I'm telling you, we are not taking this baby with us."

Emma Jane went and sat in the rocking chair. She'd never seen Jasper so angry, with his arms folded across his chest, and his eyes set so firm. She missed the twinkle they usually held. They'd both said they wanted children, and they'd both agreed that they did not have the kind of relationship people had to have children. He was the one who mentioned compromise. Surely taking in a child who needed a home was a sort of compromise.

Besides, he'd made a promise, too. "What about your promise to Mel about taking care of Daisy? Shouldn't that extend to taking care of her child?"

Jasper let out an exasperated huff. "I don't have time to argue with you about this. We have to make a run for it while we can. And taking a baby, especially one who won't stop fussing, is going to slow us down. We're barely going to make it out as it is. Bringing him will make it impossible."

Emma Jane didn't move. "Then I guess you're going alone. I won't leave Moses."

"Stop calling him that name! He's not your baby."

The door opened, and Jimmy walked in. "What's all this fuss about?"

The weight of Jasper's glare on her stung. What exactly did he think she was going to do? Tell a bandit they were arguing over escape plans?

"My husband doesn't approve of my plans to raise poor Moses as my own."

Jimmy snorted. "Don't blame you there. I wouldn't raise some other fellow's git. It ain't natural. And I got the scars from my stepdaddy's belt to prove it."

He grabbed a book off one of the shelves. "They want me to read a few words from the Bible."

Shrugging, he looked at Emma Jane. "'Course, I don't really know what to read, so if you'd like to come say a few words, I'm sure it would be welcome. The good Lord may not shine His face upon us, but it doesn't mean we don't have a little respect for doing the right thing by our dead."

For a moment, Jimmy looked sorrowful. "You may not like the kind of woman Daisy was, but she was a good woman. And we all respected her, no matter what Ace might say."

Emma Jane nodded slowly. "I'm sure she was. I'd be happy to suggest some passages to read, and if you'd like me to say a few words, I can do that, too."

Jasper's glare on her was so hard she didn't need to look at him. They were clearly at an impasse on the escape plan, so what harm did it do for her to say a few words at Moses's mother's funeral?

"I'd be obliged." Jimmy started for the door, then stopped. "Let me check with Ace first. He may not like me bringing you out of the cabin."

As soon as Jimmy shut the door behind him, Jasper stormed over toward her.

"What do you think you're doing?" His whisper was harsh, biting, unlike the man she'd thought she'd gotten to know.

"Cooperating."

"How are we supposed to escape if you're presiding over a funeral?"

Emma Jane took a deep breath. "We are not escaping unless Moses comes with us."

She emphasized the *we* as she gave him her most obstinate look. She'd promised to raise Moses as her own, and as far as she was concerned, she'd die to save her own child. So if staying here to take care of Moses while Jasper escaped meant sacrificing her own life, then so be it.

"He's just an innocent baby," Emma Jane said, using her most pleading voice. "A child of God…just like all of us. You were the one who stayed in a burning brothel to make sure everyone got out safely. If you were thinking clearly, you'd be doing anything to save him, too." Looking at him desperately, she asked, "Why aren't you?"

Jasper's face crumpled. "Because I'm not even sure I can save us."

He turned and walked toward the fire. "Bringing along a colicky baby only makes it that much more impossible."

Then he spun around, eyes blazing. "Fine. Bring the baby. But you're not keeping him."

Jasper's face was unreadable, and though she was resolute about keeping Moses, now was not the time to challenge him. He was right about the difficulty in surviving an escape. Which was why part of her brain screamed that it was suicide to even try.

However, the practical side knew that they'd never

survive if they stayed. She wasn't so naive as to believe anymore that the bandits intended to let them live. She'd seen too much of their bloodthirsty side. "I'll gather his things." Emma Jane filled Jasper's saddlebag with the makeshift bottles and scraps of cloth used to change the baby. It wasn't much, but hopefully they wouldn't need them long. As she recalled, it wasn't a very long trip back to town.

"Someone's coming."

Jasper moved back to the fire as Emma Jane set the saddlebag on the ground by the door. Near enough to grab easily, but not so near as to look suspicious.

Jimmy opened the door. "Sorry, miss. I appreciate your kind offer, but Ace isn't willing to take a chance on letting you out of the cabin. What do you suggest I read?"

He held out the Bible, and she turned it to the Twenty-third Psalm. "Try this one."

"Thank you." He tipped his hat at her and left.

Jasper immediately returned to his post by the window. "It looks like they're all gathered on the north side of the barn. I'm going out first. Look for me to the left, and when I signal, hurry out to meet me."

Emma Jane watched as Jasper fiddled with the door handle, then quietly slipped out, closing the door behind him. She watched as he ran to the side of the cabin, then stopped. The bandits still appeared to be oblivious to anything other than Daisy's services. Actually, they were still busy digging her grave, and it appeared the men watching were enjoying the spectacle of the other men digging.

She looked in the direction Jasper had gone, but he'd disappeared. Panic swept through her. Had the bandits gotten him?

Clutching Moses closer to her, she pulled a shawl she'd

found tight against her, tying the baby against her body. The shawl probably belonged to Daisy, and Emma Jane liked to think that it would be good for Moses to have something of his mother's.

Then Jasper gave the signal. The tightness in her chest eased momentarily as she realized he was safe—for now. Emma Jane grabbed the saddlebag, then exited the cabin, pulling the door tightly closed as she left. Hopefully, none of the men would return to the cabin for a while, and they'd have some time before they realized that Jasper and Emma Jane had taken off.

The wind whipped fiercely at her as she made her way to the small shed Jasper hid behind. Tiny pellets of ice pelted her, a hint of the storm to come.

Was it wise to leave now, or one more reason they were doomed?

Moses started to fuss, and Emma Jane put her little finger in his mouth, hoping he'd suckle and be quiet. Fortunately, that was all the comfort the tiny baby needed, and he nestled more closely to her body.

"They left a horse saddled over there." Jasper pointed at a horse several yards away. "I'm going to bring him over here. We'll have to ride double. It's too risky to try for two horses."

As Jasper went to get the horse, Emma Jane surveyed their surroundings. The bandits had chosen a good location for their ranch, with the natural protection of the mountains around them, and several rock formations to act as sentinels where the men could guard the place.

Jasper brought the horse over. "Give me the saddlebag."

She handed it to him.

"Why is this so heavy? We can't take much."

"Moses needs his milk and change of diapers and clothes." Selfishly, she'd also packed her Bible. It had come too far to be left behind now.

Jasper didn't respond but took the saddlebag and secured it to the horse.

"You'll have to ride astride," he told her solemnly. "It's not proper, but it's the only way we're going to make good time."

Emma Jane nodded slowly. "I can do it."

He helped her onto the horse, then mounted. The horse reared. Emma Jane clung to Jasper as he got the horse under control.

"Well, I guess we know why he was standing all alone with a saddle on him. He's barely saddle broke."

"I don't know what that means," she said.

"It's going to be a rough ride. Hang on as tight as you can, and if I tell you to do something, do it quickly, without questioning or arguing."

"All right."

"Now stay quiet."

Jasper led the horse into the clearing. They had several dozen yards of open space where the bandits could see them before they would find the protection of the rocks.

Once they got to the rocks, and out of sight of the bandits, Jasper made a clicking sound, and his legs scraped against hers as he urged the horse on.

The horse took off—faster than anything Emma Jane had ever been on, even faster than when the bandits had kidnapped her.

After the initial jolt, the horse settled into a rhythm, and as she squeezed Jasper tight, she found the warmth of his body in front of hers comforting. Her arms wrapped around his large, solid frame made her feel more secure than she'd imagined. Even little Moses seemed to be lulled into sleep as they barreled down the mountainside.

It seemed almost impossible to feel so sheltered with so much at stake. The farther they got from the cabin, the safer Emma Jane felt. At least until she looked down. The ground whizzed past them at an alarming speed.

"Don't," Jasper commanded. "If you look at the ground, you'll lose your orientation. Look out or close your eyes."

"How did you know?"

"I can feel your weight shift. Keep steady."

She pressed her head against his back, keeping enough space at her midsection so Moses had plenty of room. The wind was blowing harder now, and the little ice pellets had begun to turn to snow. Without her legs fully covered by her skirts, the air seemed even colder. Emma Jane shivered. The wind howled in response.

As she looked around, their surroundings became increasingly white. Though it would be almost impossible for the bandits to come searching for them in this weather, Emma Jane couldn't help but think that their chances of survival were almost as slim.

Saying a quick prayer, Emma Jane huddled closer to Jasper, grateful that Moses had the body heat of the two of them to keep him warm. Still, she feared that if they didn't find shelter soon, they would all freeze to death.

Jasper blinked against the decreasing visibility. The snow was almost blinding now, and even though he'd pointed the horse in the right direction toward town, he still feared they might be lost.

Escaping with a blizzard approaching had been a good idea in theory. However, he hadn't anticipated the weather would move in this fast. The wind screeching at his ears mocked him for daring to think he could predict Mother Nature.

He glanced behind him once again to be sure the bandits hadn't followed. The good news about the fast-moving storm was that their tracks were being erased by the snow and wind.

As for the bad news, well, Jasper just had to keep hoping they were indeed headed in the right direction.

Emma Jane's head rested on his back, but her body was not pressed as firmly against his as he would have liked. If the horse slipped on the ice, she would be jolted and easily fall off. But a tiny bundle lay between them— the baby.

On one hand, his wife was right. He couldn't leave a child behind to die. On the other hand, why hadn't she at least talked to him? Why hadn't she asked his opinion? One more decision about his life that was made for him without his consent.

Worse, Emma Jane had to have known that he wouldn't have said no to rescuing the baby, even if it did make escaping more difficult. Which meant he shouldn't be mad, except he felt as though she was taking advantage of his good nature and making assumptions about what he wanted without discussing it first.

And yet…how could he resist the warmth of the woman pressed against him, who would stand up to anyone who would harm an innocent child? He was mad, yes, but how could he stay mad knowing that Emma Jane was only acting in accordance with her good nature?

The snow started falling harder. No, *falling* wasn't the right word. It was as though the snow was coming at them like a train barreling down the mountain with no brakes. Faster, faster and still faster, with no end in sight.

He could feel Emma Jane shiver against him.

"We've got to be close," he shouted back at her. A half truth, because he really didn't know how close they were, and traveling against the wind, he'd had to slow the horse's pace to a walk.

The truth was, they could be miles from town yet. Worse, with the whiteout conditions, they could have veered far off course.

Why had he been such a fool as to think he could out-run both a gang of bandits and a storm?

"I hope so," Emma Jane shouted back. "I can't feel my legs."

A quick glance behind him reminded Jasper that, riding astride, Emma Jane's legs were partially exposed. Her thin stockings would yield little protection against the cold.

He gritted his teeth. Why hadn't he thought this plan through? He'd thought he had, and yet, the farther they went, the more he realized that Emma Jane might have been right to be more cautious.

"Let's pray we find shelter soon."

God had never bothered with such trivialities in Jasper's life. Why would He? After all, he had pretty much everything a body could want. Then again, Jasper had never asked.

But it seemed like Emma Jane's faith was different. She talked to God about these things and seemed to believe that God was real in His actions toward her.

He couldn't hear her words, but the soft murmur of her words echoed against his back. It was like all the time she'd spent reading her Bible to Daisy in the cabin. Emma

Jane had spoken quietly enough that Jasper couldn't hear the words, and yet he'd felt a greater peace than he imagined would be possible given the circumstances.

Even now, Emma Jane's hands around his waist felt warmer, even though he was pretty sure she was in danger of frostbite.

Frostbite.

One more thing he hadn't thought of in planning their escape. He could only hope that they'd both survive long enough for Emma Jane to forgive him for being so...

Wait. Were those lights in the distance?

At first it was hard to tell with the snow swirling around them, but then Emma Jane spoke.

"Is that what I think it is?"

Jasper nudged the horse to go faster. The animal also seemed to sense they were close to civilization as it lifted its head. Soon, he could smell smoke on the air, and the horse picked up its pace.

The lights weren't bright enough to be Leadville, or even one of the small neighboring towns. More than likely, they'd come upon a ranch or some other outpost.

"What if we've just gone in a circle and returned to the bandits?" Emma Jane's query chilled him far more than the swirling ice and snow.

Had they come all this way for nothing?

"We'd have seen the rock formations." But as soon as the words came out of his mouth, he knew that with such low visibility, they could have easily missed them.

Surely the answer to Emma Jane's prayer wasn't to return them to the bandits?

But even so, at least they'd be warm.

A gust of wind sent the snow swirling past them, revealing a sign up ahead. There were no signs in front of the gang's cabin. Which meant they were safe.

As long as the owners of the building ahead were friendly.

They got closer to the sign.

"I know where we are," Emma Jane shouted just as Jasper was able to read what it said.

Spruce Lakes Resort.

If there was a place worse than arriving back at the bandits' hideout, this would be it. Not because it wasn't a nice place, or the owners weren't welcoming and friendly, but because he wasn't ready to deal with the memories associated with the place.

After he and Emma Jane had been trapped in the mine together, they'd been brought here. The resort was closer to the mine than town and had the advantage of having a doctor there, who could tend their injuries. Emma Jane had been unconscious, and Jasper had feared for her life.

At the time, Jasper had said that he'd be willing to do anything, if only Emma Jane would survive. He'd made that promise before he knew that getting compromised by him had been Emma Jane's plan all along.

"It will be so good to see the Lewises again," Emma Jane said, her teeth chattering. "They were so helpful the last time we were here. I can't think of a better place to wait out a storm. I have so many pleasant memories of our time here."

Jasper swallowed the bile that rose up in his throat. He, too, had pleasant memories of their time here. At least until they'd been tainted by overhearing Emma Jane's mother congratulate her on finding such a masterful way of compromising herself.

Jasper snorted, then choked on the snow. Just how

much of the friendship they'd developed while at the resort had been real?

He'd like to think that they were starting to become friends again, but could he trust those feelings? What emotions could he trust when it came to Emma Jane?

As if to echo his tumultuous thoughts, the baby let out a small cry. Weak, thready, almost as if he, too, was cold and weary.

"It's all right, Moses, we're almost there," Emma Jane said gently, the wind having shifted so that it carried each and every word straight to Jasper's heart. So gentle and loving, the tenderness made him yearn for some of that directed towards him.

But how could they ever hope to find common ground when Emma Jane seemed determined to do everything her way? She hadn't even asked him what he'd thought of the baby's name. Jasper shivered, forcing his hands to maintain their grip on the reins. He had so many reasons to be angry with her, yet as he felt Emma Jane tremble against him, he found it easier to hold on to the icy reins than to count them.

They reached the hotel, and Jasper slid off the horse, his body half-frozen, then helped Emma Jane down. She landed, unsteady, but never losing her grip on the baby.

Jasper pounded on the door.

Stephen Lewis opened the door. "Jasper?"

"We got lost in the storm. Emma Jane is nearly frozen through."

Stephen ushered them in quickly as Mrs. Lewis came around the corner. "Olivia, put some water on."

"Oh, my!" Mrs. Lewis scurried off, and Stephen helped them get settled by the fire.

Emma Jane's lips had turned blue, and her normally

pale skin had turned such a deathly pallor that Jasper feared they'd gotten her inside too late.

Stephen handed her a thick buffalo robe.

But Emma Jane, fool that she was, said, "Wait, we need to be sure the baby is all right first. Help me untie this shawl."

Another woman scurried over and quickly helped Emma Jane with the bundle.

"It's a baby."

"Yes," Emma Jane said, the exhaustion in her voice obvious. "I've done everything I could for poor Moses, but I'm afraid…"

As much as Jasper resented Emma Jane taking on the baby without his consent, it didn't mean Jasper wished him ill. Just as he started to say a prayer that the baby would be all right, the woman took Moses in her arms.

"Oh, the little dear. He is chilled to the bone. But he'll be fine. Nothing a little of his mother's milk and a good cuddle won't fix."

The woman held the baby out to Emma Jane, and she shook her head.

"His mother is dead. I've been taking care of him." She turned to Jasper. "His bottles and milk are in the saddlebags. Hopefully, it's not too frozen for him to drink."

"Don't worry about it," the woman said, pulling the baby closer to her. "I've a baby of my own and plenty of milk. I'll just take him in the other room and feed him."

"Could I…" Emma Jane's fatigue was more visible now, and she closed her eyes for a moment before continuing. "That is, I know you need your privacy, but I've been caring for him like my own, and I just need to be sure he'll be all right."

"Of course. We'll sit by the stove in the kitchen, where

it's warm. Perhaps Mother will have some warm broth ready for you to drink."

Emma Jane seemed to gain more strength with the woman's words, and Jasper watched as the two women exited the room.

"Don't you worry none about the wee one. Abigail is my daughter, and a fine mother, if I do say so," Stephen said, smiling as his wife reentered the room, carrying a tray with a pot of tea and a bowl of steaming broth.

"Indeed she is." Mrs. Lewis smiled back at her husband. "I was thinking it was too early for the two of you to have a baby already, but knowing your generosity in taking in a foundling child, oh, how it does my heart good."

She handed Jasper the bowl. "This'll warm you right up. You're a good man, Jasper Jackson, and we are so pleased to once again be of service to you. The world needs more people like you."

He tried sipping the broth, but his throat was too clogged with emotion for it to go down. The Lewises might think he was a good man, but Jasper had his doubts. His desire to be a good man and bring justice to poor Mel was what had landed them in this situation. He'd nearly killed himself, Emma Jane and an innocent child.

As for his generosity in taking in the baby, how could it be considered generosity when it had been foisted upon him? He'd never agreed to raise the child, and despite what Emma Jane said on the matter, he wasn't sure he was going to. Jasper had done his duty by saving the baby, but now…now they could find the baby a real home, with a real family.

Chapter Twelve

The next morning, Emma Jane held Moses as the women sat near the fire, working on some embroidery. He hadn't fussed at all since coming to Spruce Lakes Resort. Abigail said that, most likely, the goat's milk had been upsetting the baby's stomach. She'd said she had plenty of milk for both her baby, who was nearly weaned, and Moses. And so, since their arrival, Abigail had been feeding the little boy.

"I declare, I haven't seen a baby fill out so fast in all my life," Olivia Lewis said with a smile as she handed Emma Jane an embroidered cloth. "Just look at those chubby cheeks."

"What's this?" She looked at the fine stitching and held it up to the light.

"Those rags you came with for him are disgraceful. I've made so many diapers for my babies and grandbabies that putting together a few things for little Moses was simple."

Emma Jane warmed at the older woman's generosity. For the second time, she felt so loved and well nurtured by this virtual stranger. And yet, Olivia felt dearer to her than her own mother.

"Thank you. Your kindness means the world to me. I know nothing about babies, just that they're darling little creatures. But I promised his mother I'd care for him as my own before she died, so I hope you'll teach me everything I need to know."

"You're a natural. Isn't she, Abigail?"

Abigail smiled as she reached forward and tickled Moses under his chin. "Indeed. You'd think he really was your own child. Had you not explained the circumstances of his birth, I wouldn't have known he wasn't yours."

The compliment gave Emma Jane more confidence than she thought it would. Until now, she hadn't realized her own fears in becoming a mother. Yes, she'd always loved babies, but her own mother had never done any of the motherly things she saw happening between Olivia and Abigail. The unmistakable affection between the two women sent a twinge to Emma Jane's heart.

Jasper and Stephen entered the room, flanked by Charles, Abigail's husband.

"Jasper!" Olivia smiled up at the men. "I was just telling Emma Jane what a fine boy you have. He'll be such a credit to you and your family."

A dark look crossed Jasper's face, and it pained Emma Jane to see that he was still resistant to the idea of taking in Moses.

"He's not my boy."

Stephen clapped him on the shoulder. "It's hard to form an attachment so soon, but mark my words, you'll love him like your own before you know it. Olivia and I have taken in more than our share of children needing homes—none as babies, mind you—but each and every one is as precious to us as if they were our own."

Jasper's scowl only deepened. Didn't he realize that this may be the solution to their problem? Both of them despaired of ever having children, so in taking in other children who needed homes, they could have a family of their own. Surely with all of Jasper's money, he could afford plenty. Perhaps he just needed a little time and the encouragement of how it had worked for the Lewises before he was sold on the idea.

Emma Jane turned to Olivia. "I had no idea that you'd done that. I'd love to hear more about how you were able to take in other children."

Jasper grunted, and the look he gave her made Emma Jane wonder if she'd made a mistake in asking the older woman to share her story. But the happy glow on Olivia's face was enough to convince Emma Jane that she'd made the right decision. After all, Olivia had been so good to them, it seemed only right to show support for Olivia's endeavors.

As Olivia talked about her joy in being able to give less fortunate children a home, Emma Jane couldn't help but watch the lines deepen between Jasper's brows. She hadn't meant to make him uncomfortable, but they also hadn't had much of a chance to speak privately since arriving. Last night, they'd both been so tired, and Emma Jane had fallen asleep as soon as her head hit the pillow. Since rising, they'd both been occupied by various members of the Lewis family.

Moses began to fuss, and before Emma Jane could ascertain what the problem was, Abigail reached for him. "I think this little one is due for another feeding."

She gave Emma Jane a smile. "I am so glad to be able

to help you with him. David is getting so big and independent that I miss these days of having a small one."

Abigail glanced fondly at the little boy who sat on his father's knee, tugging at his beard. Then she gave Charles such a deep look of love that it made Emma Jane's heart churn again. Oh, to have that for her own life. What would it be like to exchange such sweet, tender glances?

Emma Jane transferred the baby to Abigail's arms, then looked down at her own embroidery. Seeing her new initials stitched with her own neat hand seemed almost out of a dream or some other reality that couldn't possibly exist. Jasper glanced at her, then at her embroidery, then looked away.

Things were so different between them now. When they were last here, they'd built a friendship of sorts. During their time in the mine, they'd talked, really talked, and Emma Jane had thought they'd come to a level of mutual respect. Then here at the hotel, where Emma Jane recuperated from her injuries, they'd become even friendlier.

She looked out the window, covered by the swirling snow. The last time they'd been stuck here, they'd also been trapped by a snowstorm, but it was nothing like this one. Now that they were closer to winter, the snow lasted longer and was colder and thicker.

Spying the basket of yarn near Jasper's chair, Emma Jane smiled. Perhaps all Jasper needed was a reminder of their previous bond.

"Do you remember how I tried teaching you how to knit?"

When they were trapped here before, Emma Jane and Mary had tried showing Jasper and Will how to knit. The men's hands were clumsy with the needles and yarn, and while they did not get any real knitting accomplished, they'd had great fun. And, as Emma Jane remembered with a pang, she'd felt a connection between her and Jasper.

A hint of a smile twitched at his lips. But his voice remained dull. "As I recall, it was not a successful endeavor."

"Well, maybe we can play checkers instead," Emma Jane said brightly, hoping to engage him in some way.

"I don't like checkers." Jasper turned to Stephen. "You wouldn't happen to have any good books in that study of yours, would you?"

Emma Jane's heart sank as her husband stood.

"Oh, yes, yes, I do!" Stephen jumped up, and the two men exited the room, Charles joining them.

"Don't mind them," Olivia said, patting Emma Jane as she walked over to the teapot. "Stephen and Charles were arguing politics earlier, and they know I only allow it in the gentlemen's room. They've been itching to continue their discussion. Would you care for some more tea?"

Emma Jane nodded as she stared into the empty space Jasper left. If only it were as simple as Jasper wanting to discuss politics. Unfortunately, she knew for a fact that Jasper found the subject distasteful. No, he wanted to get away from her.

Being forced to marry someone was one thing. In the Jackson mansion, avoiding one another was easy enough. But here, trapped at the Spruce Lakes Resort, they were forced to be together. Except that Jasper seemed to be doing everything in his power to avoid it.

Was it so wrong to wish they would rekindle the connection they'd once had? Emma Jane dreaded the thought of spending the rest of her life married to a man who was sullen whenever he was in her presence.

Friendship... It was all she wanted from him. The romance, yes, that would be nice, but clearly it wasn't going to happen. So why couldn't they at least settle on a good old-fashioned companionship?

Jasper groaned at the heated argument between the two men, wishing he could be anywhere else, yet because he couldn't handle the mix of emotions he felt being with Emma Jane, here he was. Stuck.

Stephen pointed to the bookcase. "Help yourself to anything that suits your fancy. You sure you don't want to share an opinion on the upcoming elections?"

Jasper shook his head. "Quite sure." He already knew how he'd be voting, and listening to the heated debates in his father's study had given him a distaste for participating in them himself.

He glanced at the book titles. Everything he'd already read, and nothing that struck his interest. Once again, his mind drifted to Emma Jane. She'd spent a lot of time reading her Bible, and it seemed to take the edge off the somber mood while they were in the bandits' cabin. In fact, it seemed to make even an unconscious Daisy more at peace.

"You wouldn't happen to have an extra Bible, would you?"

Stephen smiled. "Ah, a man of the Word. I am so pleased to see one of the pillars of society so dedicated, not only to doing good, but in immersing himself in the Bible."

Stephen's compliment, while sincerely meant, felt like empty praise. Jasper didn't want to do the good he was credited with, and his Bible reading, well, he didn't really even know what it was about. He hadn't spent much time studying the Bible on his own. Even now, he couldn't understand why he felt drawn to it.

Jasper remained silent.

"As it so happens, my good man, when we emptied your saddlebag, I found your Bible. I set it on the dresser in your room."

Of course Emma Jane would bring the Bible. He hadn't given it any thought during their escape. Even though he'd warned her about carrying any extra weight, he found he couldn't fault her for bringing the Bible. After all, when she'd gone missing, he'd even brought it along.

"Thank you. If you'll excuse me..." Jasper nodded at both men and went up to the room he and Emma Jane had been given.

The Bible was not on the dresser but on the small table beside a chair that sat in front of the window. Emma Jane had probably already been reading it today.

He picked up the book and examined it. What treasure did it hold that kept Emma Jane so enthralled? And if it was really as useful in a person's life as the pastor seemed to think, then why wasn't she more...reasonable?

Sitting down, he thumbed through the pages. The Psalms seemed to be more creased and worn than the others, and he remembered Emma Jane reading from them at the cabin. Would this give him the peace he needed?

It hadn't seemed like he'd been reading long when he heard footsteps on the stairs. Jasper quickly closed the Bible and put it back on the table. He couldn't explain it, but he wasn't ready for Emma Jane to know that her Bible reading had inspired something in him. Maybe because he wasn't quite sure yet exactly what had been inspired.

"There you are." Emma Jane peered into the room. "Are you all right?"

"I'm fine." He gave what he hoped was an acceptable smile.

But he should have known that Emma Jane wasn't going to simply accept such a short answer and leave it at that.

"Things are different between us," she said slowly, hesitantly, like she was almost afraid to say it.

The trouble was, he wasn't sure he wanted to have the conversation. Not when he was still trying to figure out the puzzle of his life—the one that had been put together all without his consent.

"I don't like having so many choices taken from me." There. He said it. The thing that stood between them, that they could never find a way through.

"You're still upset that I'm keeping Moses."

There it was again. Her decision. Not his. Not even theirs.

"We didn't discuss it."

Emma Jane sighed. "There are a lot of things we don't discuss. But the right decision in this case should be obvious. Moses needs a home. We both want children, but aren't going to have any of our own."

The longing on her face was obvious. And her argument made sense. Especially after the conversation he'd avoided having with her about children.

"This isn't what I meant by compromise."

"You don't want to adopt?" Emma Jane looked at him like she didn't understand what he was trying to say. And clearly, she didn't.

"Compromise means both people talking about a subject and coming to a decision together. Everything in our relationship has been about you making a decision without me."

His throat felt raw as the words came out. Burned. Oozed with the emotion he'd been holding in. He took a deep breath. Closed his eyes. Tried to steady himself.

But, of course, Emma Jane wouldn't allow him that space to even find a steady place.

"Me, making decisions without you?" she huffed. "Who skipped out on our wedding without telling me? Who made a promise to a dying woman to save her sister? Who signed up to be a deputy? I'm not sure if you think you're the pot or the kettle, but either way, you are not entitled to be angry with me for making a decision without you."

He opened his eyes, and she stood before him—head held high, cheeks flushed, chest heaving. Looking like an Amazon ready for battle. Funny how he'd chastised her for not standing up for herself, and now that she was doing it, Emma Jane was every bit as glorious as he'd imagined. Only he'd never thought it would be used against him.

"You started it," he said, knowing the words were childish but unable to help himself. If Emma Jane wanted to have this out, they were going to have it all out.

"I have done everything you have asked." Tears streamed down her face. "What more do you want from me?"

"You didn't trust me to find a solution for your family that didn't involve marriage," he said quietly. "You didn't trust me when I told you not to get involved with the bandits. I asked you to please trust me, and I told you that the very foundation of our marriage depended on it, but every time I turn around, you are doing what you think is best, without regard to what I may want."

He shook his head slowly. "I thought we could build something. But the longer I'm with you, the more I realize that I can't trust you, because you don't trust me."

Jasper knew what it looked like when a woman was shot. He'd seen the look on Mel's face when she died. The expression on Emma Jane's face was no different. He'd hurt her. Part of him was deeply sorry.

But the other part of him felt free. For the first time since he'd married her, he felt like everything he'd been stuffing inside finally came out.

Except that only made him hurt more.

Because he knew that what he'd said was true. He didn't trust Emma Jane, and she didn't trust him.

So what exactly did they have?

"I do trust you." Her voice shook slightly, echoes of the tears she'd been shedding. "But I don't know how to get you to understand that."

"When we leave, leave the baby here."

Her face registered shock, but she didn't say anything, so he continued. "Abigail loves him and has the ability to take care of him in ways you can't. The Lewises have said that they believe God brings them children who need homes. We've done our duty by the baby. We've found him a home with people who love him and will care for him like their own, which is what Daisy wanted."

"But I promised Daisy I would…"

"No." The word caught in his throat. "Every time I see that baby, I think about how you didn't trust me enough to talk to me about your decision. How every other important decision in my life was taken from me. And rather than working together as a couple to figure out what was best for the baby, you did what you wanted."

Even now, he could hear the baby fussing downstairs and saw that Emma Jane's attention was immediately drawn to the sound.

"We can't even talk about our marriage without that baby taking your attention away."

He regarded her solemnly, hating how cold he sounded but not knowing how else to get Emma Jane to understand. "I need my feelings to matter, too."

"Ordering me to leave the baby here doesn't sound like my feelings matter to you."

There it was again. The strong Emma Jane with a ferocity he couldn't help but admire. But as much as he admired it, he also couldn't live with the way she continually disregarded his feelings.

"You're right," he rasped. "Right now, it feels like no matter what we do, one of us has to lose. The very foundation of our relationship is broken, and I don't know how to fix it."

A knock sounded at the door, and Stephen poked his head in. "Sorry to disturb you, but Abigail was wanting Emma Jane."

He turned his attention to Emma Jane. "She was going to give the wee one his first bath and thought you'd enjoy being a part of it."

"Thank you." Emma Jane didn't spare Jasper a glance as she hurried from the room.

He should have expected it, given that he'd been so hard on her. Even now, his gut churned, and he wished he could have taken back some of his words. But which ones? Did he continue walking on eggshells and avoiding what was really bothering him? He'd been completely honest about his feelings, and yet…it felt wrong.

"Marriage is harder than it looks, isn't it?" Stephen said quietly.

Jasper didn't look at him. "How much did you hear?"

"You were talking pretty loud."

"I'm sorry, I didn't realize…"

Stephen stepped in and put a hand on Jasper's shoulder. "Seems to me you've been holding a lot in. Sometimes, when it comes out, the explosion is bigger than any dynamite could create."

The older man's touch was warm in a way Jasper hadn't expected. Like he could almost feel the love flowing into him.

"I just don't know what to do. I know my words hurt Emma Jane, but I can't keep pretending that everything is fine. How do I be honest about my feelings when it's going to hurt hers?"

Stephen didn't answer, but he stood there, looking at Jasper as if Jasper was supposed to know what to do. Keep bottling it up and pretending that he didn't mind having his life stolen?

Jasper closed his eyes for a moment. "I suppose what's done is done. No matter what I do, I'm not going to get my old life back."

"Once a man marries, his life isn't his own."

Jasper opened his eyes to stare at the other man. His father had told him the same thing.

"So I just let her make all of these decisions without me?"

Stephen shrugged. "You'll find a way to make decisions that you both can live with. It takes time, son. But that can only happen if you move on past your anger."

"How do you move on when you feel like you can't trust the other person? When everything you dreamed of has been taken from you?"

"Well," Stephen said slowly. "You can keep looking back on shaky ground, expecting it to change when you can't change the past. Or you can look forward, finding something new and stable to build on."

"Again...*how*?" From Jasper's vantage point, it seemed impossible.

"Pretend you just met her. How would you court a woman, who, for all intents and purposes, you've just met?"

Court Emma Jane? "You want me to court my wife? Doesn't that end when a couple gets married?"

Stephen grinned, shaking his head. "Once a couple gets married, that's the most important time for folks to court. Otherwise, you run the risk of taking each other for granted and missing out on the really beautiful parts of being husband and wife."

There had been no beautiful parts about being married to Emma Jane. And with the way he'd just talked to her, he imagined there probably weren't any beautiful parts about being married to him.

Maybe he had set an impossible standard, asking her to trust him before they even knew each other.

Could he do as Stephen advised and court Emma Jane? Would a courtship help them find common ground?

At this point, Jasper wasn't sure he had anything else to lose. Stuck in the hotel, with nowhere to go and nothing else to do, he could at least try.

Otherwise, he might as well resign himself to a lifetime of marital misery.

Chapter Thirteen

Emma Jane smiled as Moses cooed up at her from the bucket they were using to wash him. She was beginning to see signs of dimples in his cheeks, and now that his dark hair was clean, it laid on his head in tiny little curls.

Abigail handed her a warm towel. "Usually I wouldn't give anyone a bath in this weather, but he seemed particularly grimy, and I wanted you to have Mother and me here for the first one in case you had questions."

Moses fussed as she lifted him out of the water, but once she had him securely wrapped in the towel, he quieted, staring up at her with his dark eyes.

"I appreciate having your assistance. So much. I didn't know anything about taking care of babies. How do women manage with their own?"

Abigail smiled at Olivia, and the two women exchanged the kind of loving glance that made Emma Jane wish once again that she'd had that sort of relationship with her own mother. Even her mother-in-law would never possess that level of warmth toward her.

"They have wonderful mothers who take care of

them." Abigail gave her mother a squeeze as she passed. "Speaking of mothers, I need to check on my own brood. Charles tries, bless him, but I'm sure they're driving him crazy about now."

As Emma Jane dried Moses, Olivia came beside her and rested her hand on Emma Jane's shoulder. "I know you must be thinking how hard it is, given that your mother isn't the warmest of women."

Emma Jane glanced up at her. She'd forgotten that Olivia had met her mother. Emma Jane's stay here last time had ended when her parents arrived, full of fire over their daughter being "compromised" by Jasper. Her mother had *not* been kind.

"But don't worry." Olivia reached for Moses. "May I?"

Emma Jane handed her the baby, smiling as the older woman made baby noises at him.

"Becoming a grandmother changes a woman. I can't explain it, but I am convinced that a grandchild makes a woman's heart grow even bigger. I love my children, but my grandchildren…" She looked up at Emma Jane and smiled. "That love is so much deeper."

Olivia planted a kiss on top of Moses's head and handed him back to Emma Jane. "And this little one is so darling I can't imagine not falling in love with him. You'll see."

"My mother went back east," Emma Jane said, adjusting Moses in her arms. "She's not likely to return."

Actually, it had been a condition of Jasper's father paying off her father's gambling debts. The family was sent back to Charleston to live with relatives. Jasper's father had some connections there, and her father was given a job. The Jacksons had made it clear that the Logans were not to return to Leadville or cause any scandal that would reflect back on them.

Emma Jane didn't miss her parents much—at all, really—but she often thought about her sister, Gracie. How would Gracie do without Emma Jane to protect her? The only reason Emma Jane had chosen this life, marrying Jasper, was to protect Gracie. Would someone be willing to teach Gracie the way Olivia was her?

"Well," Emma Jane said, looking down at the baby. "I think someone has fallen asleep. I'm going to put him down for his nap."

Olivia touched Emma Jane's arm as she passed. "You know, just because your mother wasn't warm, it doesn't mean you won't be a good mother. You're doing an excellent job of taking care of Moses."

Funny, that idea had never occurred to Emma Jane. As she carried Moses to the cradle the Lewises had so thoughtfully put in her room, she realized that caring for the baby had brought out a strength in her she hadn't realized she possessed. Defending her sister against her parents was one thing, but something about this innocent child made Emma Jane feel even more empowered.

Still, deep down she knew she shouldn't have said all those things to Jasper. But he'd just made her so mad! She was tired of him acting like he was the victim of all the bad circumstances of his life. Didn't he realize how lucky he was? Emma Jane had to make a life out of so much worse.

She smoothed Moses's hair as she set him in the cradle. People shouldn't fear their parents the way Emma Jane and Gracie had.

The only reason Emma Jane had agreed to Gracie

leaving as well was that Mrs. Jackson had enrolled Gracie in a private girls' boarding school, where Gracie could get an education and be away from their parents.

"Hello," Jasper said, causing her to jump.

Emma Jane didn't turn around. "If you're here to continue our argument, I'd prefer you just leave. Moses is sleeping."

"No. I came to apologize. I shouldn't have taken all of my anger and hurt out on you."

She stood and whirled around to face him. "So what's the truth, Jasper? Do you resent me for taking away your choices, or is it something else?"

His Adam's apple bobbed. His broad shoulders rose and fell, then he spoke. "It's the truth. I am hurt. I imagined my life different than this. But I can either stay stuck in the past, angry that I didn't get my way, or I can find a way to make my life good in spite of those things."

Then his lips turned up slightly. "Like you did in the bandits' cabin. That's what you were trying to tell me back there, isn't it? We didn't have a choice in being there, but you were making the best of it."

"Yes."

He crossed the room to sit on the bed, then patted the spot next to him. "I don't know how deep your role in trapping me into marriage was, but I'm choosing to forgive you. The past hurts, and we need time to heal from that. But rather than dwelling in it, I'd like to start over."

His words tumbled around in her head. Even now, Jasper still believed that Emma Jane was complicit in her family's plan to force a marriage between them. She'd been honest with him and told him of their plan and that she didn't want to go through with it. Yet he still blamed her.

But he was right. There was no sense in dwelling on it. She could proclaim her innocence until the day she died, and he still wasn't going to believe it. So what did arguing about it accomplish?

"All right," she said, sitting beside him. "I'm willing to start over."

Moses made a noise in his sleep, and Emma Jane looked at him briefly, reminded that this was about more than just their marriage, but a little boy relying on her for his care.

"But you have to understand that I refuse to give up Moses. I love him, and somehow you're going to have to find a way to accept him."

Jasper followed her gaze to the sleeping baby. "What if I can't love him?"

Squaring her shoulders, Emma Jane lifted her chin and gave him a no-nonsense look. "You will be kind to him. I've lived with unkindness from a parent, and my son will not have that same existence."

In the silence, Emma Jane could hear Jasper swallow. "I've never been unkind to a child."

"I wouldn't know that." She looked at the ground. Had she been wrong to make the comparison between Jasper and her father? Jasper had been angry with her, but he hadn't been cruel. And while his words hurt, he hadn't made her feel worthless. Rather, in their argument, while they had disagreed, she realized that he'd done his best to treat her with respect.

"No. I don't suppose you know me well enough."

Jasper stood and held out his hand. "Ordinarily, I'd ask you to go for a ride with me in my carriage, but since the wind is still howling, I don't suppose you'd be willing to head down with me to the kitchen to see if Olivia has any cookies."

An olive branch. Jasper wanted to make peace, and that gave Emma Jane hope. Perhaps they could find a way to make a life together, after all.

She glanced over at Moses.

"He's asleep. He'll be fine." Then Jasper paused. "If you leave the door open, you'll hear him if he cries."

It wasn't a declaration that he would care for Moses as his own, but the fact that he was giving consideration to Emma Jane's feelings for Moses, well, it was a start.

Emma Jane smiled. "Then I'd be delighted."

She took Jasper's hand, and they walked down to the kitchen, where Olivia was pulling a batch of cookies out of the oven.

"You knew she was baking cookies," Emma Jane teased.

"I am motivated by many things," Jasper said with a grin. "And freshly baked cookies are one of them. Mother was always harping on me for being in the kitchen when Cook was trying to bake."

Emma Jane rolled her eyes. "I can imagine. And I can't imagine that Cook was put out at all by your presence."

"No. She even let me eat some of the unbaked cookie dough, which is my favorite."

He grabbed a cookie from the pan. "Ouch!"

"Patience," Olivia admonished with a smile. "Let them cool for a few minutes. I'll leave you two alone, but please, save some of the cookies for the others. Stephen and Charles went to go check on the livestock, and they'll be mighty disappointed if you ate them all."

The kitchen door opened, and Molly, one of Abigail's daughters, entered. "Grammy? Is dem cookies ready?"

Jasper handed her the cookie that had been cooling in his hand. "Here's one for you, sweetheart." He patted her light blond hair and gave her a smile.

Molly grinned, then scampered away.

"Well, I did hear you have a reputation for the ladies," Olivia said with a grin, putting some cookies on a plate.

"What can I say? I can't resist a pretty face."

Jasper winked at her, but Emma Jane turned away. Why did he have to rub in the fact that she was so plain and unattractive? Especially now, dressed in a dress borrowed from Abigail that was too loose and slightly too long. Her hair had been pulled back into a serviceable braid, and she hardly looked the picture of any of the society debutantes Jasper had courted.

He reached for her hand. "Hey. I'm married to one of the prettiest faces in all of Leadville, so no need to be hurt that I'd admire someone so sweet."

"Please don't." Emma Jane pulled her hand away.

"I'm just going to bring some of these cookies in to the others, so we don't have any more cookie thieves in the kitchen," Olivia said, excusing herself.

"Don't what?" Jasper asked with a furrowed brow, pivoting around to face her. "I was trying to pay you a compliment."

"I don't want your charming lies. Flattery may work on the other girls in town, but I won't be trifled with. I know I'm not the prettiest girl in Leadville, so why perjure yourself?"

Jasper's face fell. "I wasn't lying."

Then he reached for the pan of cookies. "Do you want one?"

"No, thank you," Emma Jane said, wishing she could take her words back and wondering why it was so hard to get along with Jasper. Even if he had been lying, he was just trying to be nice.

"Well," he said, biting into a cookie. "We can't talk about the past, and I can't compliment your looks, so what would you like to talk about?"

Emma Jane shook her head in exasperation. "You mean to tell me that when you take a girl for a ride in your carriage, all you talk about is how pretty she is?"

Jasper shrugged. "And the weather, but..." He pointed to the window, where the snow still swirled. "I think that says it all."

"So, looks and the weather. That's all you have to say, and you're the town's most eligible bachelor?"

"Was." Jasper finished the cookie. "They prattled on about the goings-on around town, but truthfully, I don't think I paid any of it much mind. I couldn't care less about who was having what dance, and what they planned on wearing. I'm not sure we ever talked about things that mattered."

He grabbed another cookie. "You sure you don't want one?"

Emma Jane shook her head. She'd seen signs of this Jasper in some of their earlier conversations. Thoughtful, charming and well...enjoyable to be around. Especially during their time in the mine, and then when they were here, recuperating and waiting out the storm.

The truth was, she liked this Jasper. And that scared her. They'd become friends, and yet, once they were married, he seemed to have forgotten all about that friendship.

"So what do you think we should talk about, then?"

A dangerous question, and Emma Jane almost regretted asking it. But Jasper was right. They couldn't keep fearing the future based on their turbulent past.

"Um…" He stared at his cookie. "What do you like to do for fun? Besides read the Bible, of course."

"I like to knit, and sew, and do needlepoint." Emma Jane frowned. Those were all hobbies of women who needed the results of those hobbies to keep her family clothed. How would Mrs. Jackson feel about Emma Jane continuing those passions?

"Your attempts at teaching me to knit the last time we were here didn't work out so well." Jasper grinned. "I was all thumbs."

Then he looked at Emma Jane. "You know, my mother likes to do those things. She's made a number of blankets for the church. I know she hasn't warmed up to you, so perhaps that might be a way for you to find common ground."

Emma Jane shook her head. "I'm not sure she'd want to find common ground with the woman who stole her precious son."

She didn't mean for her words to sound so harsh, especially when Jasper frowned.

"You have to understand. My mother means well. According to my father, she tried for years to have a baby. Before I was born, they had a little girl. But she died as a baby. When they finally had me, my mother was so protective. So fierce. She was just so scared of losing me, too."

He smiled wryly. "It wasn't until Will came into our lives that she let me do anything she didn't think was too dangerous."

"I remember you telling me how Will taught you about

defending yourself and all the things involved with being a lawman."

The small connection warmed Emma Jane's heart. Somehow it made Jasper seem all the more human to her.

"Anyway, Mother likes having control more than I do. You think I'm upset at losing control of my life? I think, for her, it's even worse."

Then he regarded her in a way Emma Jane didn't understand. Like he was puzzling her out.

"I know it bothers you to see the way my father and I defend her. But deep down, she's a good person. She's just lost so much, and being in control is the only thing that's kept her going over the years."

Emma Jane reached out and took his hand. "Thank you for telling me. It makes her seem more human. I was praying about my relationship with her the other day and that God would give me a way to love her. Your words are an answered prayer."

And indeed they were. Even now, for as little time as Emma Jane had Moses, she couldn't imagine the heartbreak of losing him. That was the hard part about Jasper's lack of compassion for her wanting to raise the boy. He didn't understand how deeply she already loved him.

What would it have been like for Mrs. Jackson to have lost a child?

It didn't excuse her behavior toward Emma Jane, but she did find that knowing the depths of Mrs. Jackson's pain gave her compassion for the other woman.

"You talk a lot about answered prayers," Jasper said slowly. "I know the pastor talks about it, but I don't understand. We're just ordinary people—not pastors. We have no special connection to God. Why does He listen to you?"

Those words gave Emma Jane more compassion for Jasper. He'd made a lot of comments, here and there, that made her wonder how deep his relationship with the Lord was, and now she understood.

He didn't have one. Jasper Jackson, pillar of society, and one of the leading members of their church, didn't know the Lord.

"God listens to all of us," Emma Jane said, squeezing his hand. "We don't need anyone to speak for us. No qualifications, no special learning. He just wants us to talk to Him. To read His Word, and to seek His voice."

"But why would He listen to me?"

"Why would He listen to *me*?" Emma Jane smiled gently. "That's the wonderful thing about the Lord. He doesn't distinguish people between social standing, ability, goodness, any of that. He loves us, each and every one of us, just as we are."

She could tell that Jasper was struggling to process her words. How had he gone to church all these years and not realized this about the Lord? Then she thought about the other girls in church and her own family. Not all of them seemed to be living in the truth they'd been taught. And, if she was honest with herself, it was only her recent friendship with Mary that taught her that the Lord loved her just as she was. Emma Jane had always tried to be good enough to win the Lord's approval.

"I struggled with that idea myself," Emma Jane confessed, noting that Jasper still appeared to be befuddled by what she was saying. "I used to try my best to be good and follow all the rules, thinking that if I were good enough, I would be worthy. But Mary loved me in my darkest moment, when I was probably the least worthy of love. If a person could do that for me, how much more so could God?"

Jasper nodded slowly, but his furrowed brow and pursed lips told her that he still didn't fully comprehend her words. It would be easy to wonder why, but instead, she focused on her gratitude that her husband was finally trying to understand.

With the Lord's help, perhaps they could find their way.

"Well," Emma Jane said, giving Jasper's hand a final squeeze before going over to the cookies. "I suppose I should try one of these cookies before you eat them all."

She gave him a soft smile, hoping he understood that she was giving him space to work out his own relationship with God. When she first began helping Pastor Lassiter with his mission to the less fortunate in Leadville, he'd cautioned her not to push too hard in encouraging others to follow Christ. If a person pushed too hard, it had the opposite effect.

"They're good cookies," Jasper said, reaching for another as Emma Jane sat down next to him.

Emma Jane took a bite, then gave him a sly look. "Not as good as mine."

Jasper snatched the cookie out of her hand. "You don't deserve it if you can't appreciate it."

"Hey!" She gave him a stern look and retrieved her prize. "Just because mine are better doesn't mean I can't eat someone else's."

A wide grin filled Jasper's face, and the jovial man everyone liked, the one she wished would make an appearance more often, returned.

"I suppose. But you know this means you're going to have to bake me some when we get home."

She gave him a look of what she hoped to be mock horror. "And intrude on the servants' domain?"

"I'll distract Mother." Jasper winked, but something in his eyes dimmed.

He looked away from her, and she followed his gaze to the snow pelting the window.

"You're worried about getting home, aren't you?" Emma Jane said quietly, reaching for his free hand.

He let her take it, though his fingers remained limp, not participating in the gesture.

For a few moments, the only sounds in the room were the crackling fire and the wind's mournful cry.

Then Jasper spoke. "Getting home isn't the problem. Making sure the bandits don't get there first is."

Jasper wished he could have taken back his words to Emma Jane the second he noticed the lines furrowing her forehead.

"I'm sorry, I shouldn't have said that," Jasper said, staring at the cookie still in his hand. Suddenly, it seemed as unpalatable as a rock.

"Why?" Emma Jane lowered her gaze to meet his, drawing him away from his cookie and into the swirling blue depths, the brown flecks mesmerizing him.

Jasper shook his head. "I don't want you to be worried about what's going to happen to us."

He was doing enough worrying for both of them. And now that the baby was in the picture, he had one more life counting on him to get them through safely.

Which made this situation even more difficult. Trapped in this place, there was nothing he could do to keep them safe but hope the bandits would remain snowed in longer than they were. Emma Jane would probably say that he should pray, but he wasn't sure what good it would do.

Once again, Emma Jane squeezed his hand, the one he'd left carelessly on the table, not realizing how easy it would be for Emma Jane to touch him. And how desperately he wanted her to.

One more distraction he hoped wouldn't interfere with his ability to keep them safe.

"Everything will be all right." Her voice was low and gentle, and if there weren't so many facts that said otherwise, he might have believed her.

Jasper gave a noncommittal murmur, wishing he had something to say that wouldn't provoke an argument.

"It will be," Emma Jane said, her voice filled with a passion he'd never seen in her before. "You mustn't lose hope. Think of all the hopeless situations we've been in together over the past few weeks—being trapped in the mine, kidnapped by bandits... And here we are, safe."

He looked over at her, unable to fathom the optimism coming from her. "I seem to remember a girl sobbing her eyes out at the church picnic because her life seemed so hopeless."

And then she did a remarkable thing. Emma Jane smiled. "That's true. I did. And Mary encouraged me, telling me not to lose hope because it would be all right. And it has been. Which is why I can have hope now."

They had one of the most notorious gangs in the region wanting them dead. Emma Jane might believe that the bandits wouldn't hurt them, but at this point, they knew too much for the bandits to be willing to keep them alive.

As much as Jasper wanted to believe that everything

would be all right, he wouldn't put much stock in that belief until justice had been done.

He had valuable information about the gang, and when he returned to town, he'd be able to get the others in the sheriff's office to bring them to justice. Regardless of Daisy's outcome, the gang was still dangerous to the citizens of Leadville. Even if the gang made good on their plans to go to Mexico after their last job, not apprehending them would send a message to all of the other criminals in the country that Leadville was a place where they could get away with a life of crime.

He looked over at Emma Jane, who was staring at the remains of her cookie absently.

"Is everything all right? You're not upset, are you?" Jasper asked, looking for signs that he'd broken the fragile peace between them.

She shook her head. "No. I was just thinking about how my mother used to always spin her fantasies about what life must be like living in the Jackson mansion, having all the things you have and being at the pinnacle of society."

Jasper's stomach knotted. Everyone had their ideas of what his life must be like. Ladies used to beg for rides in their gold-leafed carriage. Jasper himself had never seen a need for such frippery, but his parents always thought it was good fun.

Then she let out a long, plaintive sigh. "But I wish I could go back and tell her that all those things are not what's important. It seems to me that no matter who you are, even with a life as wonderful as what people think yours must be, people wish their lives could have been different."

He couldn't speak. Couldn't feel his own heart beating in his chest. Everything he'd revealed to her, even the things that he'd only hinted at, she'd understood.

All this time, he'd been so angry at everyone not caring about his needs, his desires, and here she was, speaking to the fact that he felt so out of control. Not in so many words, perhaps, but at least she understood that the Jasper Jackson everyone so deeply admired was not the Jasper Jackson he wanted to be.

He took her hand as he moved closer to her. "Thank you. You've given me hope that you really do see me. You hear me. And I appreciate it."

Then he looked into her eyes. Those deep, mystifying blue eyes whose flecks of brown made it impossible for him to decipher what was going on inside her.

"I know our marriage started out rocky, but I promise you, I'll do my best to improve upon it."

"Thank you." She smiled and it lit up her whole face. A beautiful sight he hoped to see more of over the years. He truly hadn't understood the value of such a simple thing until now.

Then Emma Jane shifted her weight. "Does that mean you're more open to accepting Moses in your life, as well?"

His stomach dropped. Was that what all of this was about? Their connection? The seeming moments of hope in finding their way?

Every woman in his acquaintance was gifted at the pretty words, the lovely looks and the subtle manipulation used to get what they want. He hadn't seen it coming with Emma Jane—not when the words she'd used were all so…deep. So profound. She'd figured him out, all right. She'd known that he was tired of all the fluff and had been searching for substance.

Jasper coughed. "I'd hoped our conversation would be more about us. Without involving the child."

"I… I… I'm sorry." She looked away, but then turned her gaze back at him. "I didn't mean to offend you."

Then her shoulders rose and fell before she squared off with him. "But you must know that I'm different now. Emma Jane Logan did everything she could to please others and be as little trouble as possible. Emma Jane Jackson, she stands up for what she believes in, even if that's inconvenient to others."

She stood, her petite frame towering over him. "Moses is my son. He needs a mother, and I promised to be that mother. If you're looking to improve our relationship, then you need to accept that fact."

Perhaps she hadn't done such a good job of figuring him out, after all. No one backed Jasper Jackson into a corner. And clearly, she'd failed to understand that the one miserable thing in his life was his lack of choices. Because, yet again, she'd made it clear that she didn't care about what he wanted.

Telling her that meant rehashing the same argument they'd already been around. Clearly, she didn't respect his point of view in this matter. What other matters in their marriage would she fail to respect his wishes?

Jasper met her gaze with a steely look of his own. "And you need to accept that, in a marriage, a husband and wife make decisions like that *together*."

He didn't want to talk to her anymore. Couldn't, really. Taking care of an orphaned child, it was a noble decision. Daisy's child, yes, it made taking in the baby even more so. But he hadn't even been given the opportunity to think it through.

"You'll have to excuse me." He rose to his feet and exited the kitchen. Not his finest manners, he'd admit, but what was a man to do?

Jasper took the steps to their bedroom two at a time. Their bedroom. Ha! The Lewises had given them a room together, but the previous night, Jasper had slept in the chair while Emma Jane sprawled out on the bed. Not that he wanted to share the bed with her, but she'd been comfortable where he had not.

Childish of him to think that way now, because of course sleeping in the chair was the right thing to do. Just as raising Daisy's baby was the right thing to do. And eventually, he would tell Emma Jane that. But was it too much to ask for Emma Jane to… Jasper flopped on the bed. Pointless. He'd asked himself this question, asked Emma Jane that question, dozens of times with no answer.

It wasn't even that he wanted to say no. He just wanted to feel like he had some say in a life he felt like he had no control over.

He closed his eyes for a moment, thinking this might be a good time to catch up on the sleep he hadn't gotten the night before. While the chair by the window was pretty enough, it definitely wasn't suited for a man to spend the night in.

But immediately, Emma Jane's words about God, and how He was available to anyone who asked, came to mind. Did God care about Jasper? Would God be willing to help him see through the darkness of the situation?

He opened his eyes and looked over at the table where the Bible sat. Just a few pages. He could read a few pages, and maybe somewhere in there he could find an understanding like what Emma Jane had. Like what Pastor

Lassiter taught. Perhaps then he could pray to God, and He would hear him.

And then maybe, just maybe, he could see a way to a future where he and Emma Jane could peaceably spend their lives together.

Chapter Fourteen

Jasper had barely spoken to her at supper. In fact, the only thing he'd said to her was, "Could you please pass the peas?"

Why had she brought up Moses when they'd been getting along so well? Why couldn't he understand how important taking care of Moses was to her?

Emma Jane blew out a breath and set down the knitting project she'd began.

Abigail looked at her sympathetically. "That wool is a mess to work with. I think I should have spun it differently. At the time, I thought it would be good for socks."

"It's not the wool." Emma Jane sighed as she looked over at Jasper, who was reading the same newspaper he'd been reading since they'd arrived at the hotel.

"Marriage is hard, I'll give you that."

Abigail glanced in the direction of the men's study, where her husband and father were closeted. "Sometimes," she said in a low voice, "Charles makes me so angry I can hardly stand it. But as Mother always says, marriage is for better or for worse. Most of the time,

I'm pretty content with him, but, oh, how I wish he'd spend more time with the children and less time with his horses!"

Emma Jane couldn't help but smile at the other woman's expression. If only her marital woes were as simple as Jasper spending too much time with his horses. She understood that marriage was about the good times and the bad, but when would she and Jasper ever get to the good?

Though he was clearly trying to make an effort, his disdain for her was just as clear. He didn't want to be married to her, and no matter how hard she tried to make things better between them, they always ended up fighting. Or worse.

If Jasper had heard Abigail's comment, he gave no indication. Apparently, the same article he must have read several times over was far more interesting than anything the ladies were talking about. His brow was furrowed, as though that same article contained such monumental information that all of his careful rereads concerned him deeply. Emma Jane sighed yet again. It wasn't her place to judge his reading habits, but if the story was so important, why did he not attempt to discuss it with her?

He'd said he wanted to start over, to get to know each other as they should have done in the first place. Well, perhaps it was time they did so now. Emma Jane cleared her throat.

"Whatever is it in that article that has you so enthralled?" she asked.

Jasper didn't look up but he kept reading the newspaper. Was he deliberately ignoring her? Was he merely so engrossed in his reading that he simply didn't hear her?

"Jasper!"

Finally he glanced over at her. "Did you want something?"

"Why, yes, I did. I was wondering what you found so interesting in that paper that you keep reading?"

"This? You wouldn't be interested."

"Of course I would," she retorted. "Isn't the point of our time together that I learn about you? Even if you don't think I would be interested, I still would like to know what is engaging you."

Jasper sighed and put the paper down. Emma Jane noticed that he set it awkwardly under the table, as though he wasn't quite ready to put the paper away.

"I suppose you're right," he said. "It was an article on a boxing match coming to town. I was thinking about how very much I would enjoy taking Will to see it at the Tabor Opera House. However, with the bandits on the loose, I'm not sure it's wise to make plans."

Then his frown deepened. "It's so frustrating being stuck here knowing what I know about the bandits while everyone else is back in town coming up with a plan that probably won't work."

Immediately, Emma Jane felt guilty for pressing the issue. After all, it was selfish of her to focus on their relationship when very dangerous men were on the loose. But there was nothing they could do now. They were trapped until the snow let up. Since they were stuck here, why couldn't they make the most of their time?

"I can understand that," Emma Jane said, softening her tone. "However, it seems to me that worrying over something you can't change isn't going to make the situation better. So let's focus on what we can change."

He quirked a brow. "Is this more of your wisdom on making the best of things?"

"Yes, I suppose it is."

"Well," he said. "There you have it. There are many things I enjoy in life, but I'm finding that more pressing matters keep distracting me."

"Even though you can't do anything about them?"

A hint of a smile teased the corners of Jasper's lips. "Seems to me we just had this conversation."

"Then why are we having it again?" She kept her voice light at first but then looked at him with enough serious- ness that she hoped he'd understand. "Why aren't you letting God take control of your worries?"

"I suppose you're right," he said slowly, his brows fur- rowing back into the expression he'd worn while reading the paper. "I'd like to think that God is in control, but if that indeed is the case, how can He let these bandits con- tinue plaguing our town?"

"Have you tried asking Him? Have you prayed about the direction to take in pursuing the bandits?"

Abigail gave an approving murmur, and while it felt good to have her support, Emma Jane was grateful she stayed out of the conversation. This matter was some- thing that needed to be settled between Emma Jane and Jasper, and while it wasn't ideal to have this talk among other people, Jasper needed to know the importance of trusting God.

Jasper looked at her as though she were daft. "What good does that do? God doesn't give a person a battle plan."

Emma Jane frowned. "Maybe not literally, but it's amazing how God is present if only you just look."

Jasper didn't appear to hear her words, staring sul- lenly off into space, as though he wasn't even seeing her despite his face being turned toward her. "I've spent my whole life ignorant of the plight of others around me, and now that it's been brought to my attention, all of my attempts to do something about it seem to fail. I look, and I see nothing but problems."

Finally his gaze fixed on her. "I know you want me to make the best of being trapped here in the hotel, but I can't."

He gave Abigail a halfhearted smile. "No disrespect to you, ma'am. Your family's hospitality has been among the best I've ever experienced."

Once again, he frowned. "But what good is being a Jackson when I can't make a difference? What good is having all this information about the bandits when I'm stuck here and can't use it?"

"At least you can take heart in knowing that the bandits are also trapped in the storm. As for making a difference, you've made a difference to me," Emma Jane said softly. "Because of you, I have a home. My sister isn't married to Amos Burdette. And I'm able to do things that matter."

She should have known that Jasper's expression wouldn't lighten. Not when she knew what a burden she was to him.

"What kind of things?" A start. At least in that his curiosity was piqued. He wanted to see the impact his actions had for the good.

Emma Jane smiled. "Like helping with Pastor Lassiter's ministry. I'd always wanted to do more, but Mother was constantly harping on me for the time I spent at church. I'd have to sneak away, and then I felt guilty for disobeying her. Mary says I've been a great help to the ministry and that she has no idea how they'd have managed after the brothel fire without me."

Even now, with everyone else in town thinking Emma Jane worthless, she couldn't help the feeling of satisfaction in knowing her contribution to the community. She'd have also liked to have mentioned how Jasper's wealth would enable her to care for Moses, but given that they were finally communicating, it seemed wrong to bring up a topic that would only make him shut down again.

Jasper nodded slowly, like he was considering her words. And, if Emma Jane were to be so bold as to read his thoughts, like he was seeing her in a new light.

"Will said that Mary counts on you tremendously. You two weren't friends before?"

Emma Jane shook her head. "I would have never imagined I could be friends with someone as good as Mary. But when she reached out to me, and was kind to me, even when I least deserved it, something in me changed. I can't explain it. Because of Mary's kindness, I realized that all of the words in the Bible that I so cherished… they weren't just God's promises to the worthy. They were meant for someone like me."

"That is so beautiful," Abigail said, looking up from her knitting. "I don't mean to intrude on a somewhat-private conversation, but I cannot help but be thankful for what a marvelous work the Lord is doing in you."

Emma Jane smiled at her. "I'm thankful, too. I had no idea how miserable my life was, and while I knew how to bear through all things, I had no peace in my heart. Now I have nothing but joy, knowing that I can bear all things through the love of God."

Even as she spoke the words, all of her frustrations over her marriage to Jasper disappeared. The Lord had been with her through everything, and now, even with the future so uncertain, He would be with her still.

Moses gave a small cry, and Emma Jane started to get up to get him. She'd left him sleeping in the other room. Had she been wrong to leave him alone?

Abigail set a hand on her knee. "Give him a few moments. He needs to learn patience."

Patience? But he was just a baby. Moses began to wail.

"The baby's crying," Jasper said in the same dull voice he always used when mentioning Moses.

"Why don't you see what he needs, Jasper," Abigail suggested in a singsong voice.

The look on Jasper's face was almost worth all the trouble he'd been giving her. You'd have thought she'd asked him to pet a snake.

"Uh, I don't know anything about babies." He looked imploringly at Emma Jane, but Abigail set a hand on her knee.

"Sounds like the perfect time to learn," Abigail said in a matter-of-fact tone. "Every man needs to know how to take care of his children."

The weight of everyone's stares hung heavily on Emma Jane. She knew Jasper didn't want to have anything to do with Moses, and he certainly didn't consider the baby to be his son.

But maybe, if Jasper could just get to know Moses, he'd fall in love with him, just as Emma Jane had.

She'd just been praising God for taking care of her even when things looked bleak. Right now, Jasper's lack of interest in taking care of Moses was perhaps the most difficult thing she faced.

"It's all right, Jasper, he won't break." Emma Jane gave an encouraging smile. "Just pick him up and bring him in here. He might stop crying just because someone is holding him. But if he has other needs, we can help you figure them out."

"Just be mindful of his head," Abigail said. "You'll need to support it with your hand because he's not strong enough to hold it up himself."

Emma Jane was tempted to give him a few other cautions. After all, Jasper wouldn't know how Moses always managed to wiggle out of his blanket but preferred to be wrapped snugly. But too many instructions might be overwhelming for him, and it would give him an excuse not to try.

"Fine." Jasper turned and stalked out of the room.

Abigail patted Emma Jane's knee. "It will be all right. Every man needs to learn how to take care of a baby, and since Jasper has had no inclination to learn, this will be a good way for his feet to get wet."

Olivia entered the room from the kitchen, smiling as she said, "So true. Stephen was terrified of holding our children when they were babies. But a man has to get comfortable taking care of the little ones. There will come a time when you can't do it all yourself and he's going to need to help."

If only Jasper's hesitation at taking care of Moses was so simple. Were it his own child, Emma Jane had a feeling that Jasper would be much more hands-on and willing to take care of the baby. But Moses?

"What if he doesn't want the baby in the first place?"

The words slipped out of Emma Jane's mouth before she could take them back.

Olivia gave her a strange look. "I'm not sure what that has to do with anything. Babies come whether you want them or not."

Emma Jane sighed. "Not Moses."

"Who wouldn't want a sweet boy like Moses?" Abigail picked up her knitting and motioned for Emma Jane to do the same. "Why, if I thought Charles would let me, I'd be tempted to take him myself. He is such a dear boy. But Charles is upset because we already have too many mouths to feed, and he does so hate that we are dependent on my family providing work for him."

Abigail's long-suffering sigh made Emma Jane wonder if this wasn't part of the marital problems Abigail had alluded to earlier.

"Let's not vex poor Charles further," Olivia murmured. "We wouldn't want to give him one more thing to take responsibility for."

"Mother!" Abigail threw down her knitting. "Why must you make such remarks? You can't imagine how intimidating it is for a man to marry a woman whose parents can give her far more than he can. And then, to have to work for his father-in-law because there are no other jobs available to him."

Emma Jane thought she heard Olivia mutter something about him being too lazy, but she couldn't be certain. Regardless, it wasn't her fight, but clearly she wasn't the only one whose marriage made things awkward for the family.

Perhaps she'd expected too much out of her marriage so soon. When they returned to town, Emma Jane would make more of an effort with her mother-in-law.

Abigail looked over at Emma Jane. "You're never going to get anything accomplished if you don't pick up your needles. Now, show me what you're doing, so I can see where you've gone wrong."

Emma Jane complied, staring more at the door than at

her work. Moses had stopped crying, but Jasper hadn't returned.

"Well, that's where half of your mistake is. You're paying more attention to the door than you are to your knitting. Jasper and the baby are fine."

Emma Jane couldn't manage to find a way to take her eyes off the door to focus on her project. The wool would have ordinarily been a comfort to her, its softness a balm on her fingertips. Even the cheery yellow would have ordinarily brightened her mood, but she found that her thoughts of Jasper seemed to give everything a grayish hue.

"That's how I knew she was meant to be Moses's mother," Olivia said, her smile evident in her words. "She worries about him just as she would her own."

The words didn't comfort her, not when Jasper didn't want to accept that fact. How could others see it when he couldn't?

Abigail nudged Emma Jane again. "Now, let's get focused."

"How?" She looked down at the tangle of yarn and needles, and sighed. "How do you focus on something when the only thing on your mind is wondering if your baby is all right?"

"He's not crying anymore, is he?"

Acknowledging the silence was almost embarrassing, especially with the knowing look Abigail gave her.

"Oh, now." Olivia gave her daughter a sharp look. "As I recall, you were just as bad when Molly was born. You would hardly use the outhouse for fear something might happen to her."

"Mother!" Despite Abigail's rebuke, Emma Jane could hear the affection in the other girl's voice.

This was the sort of family life she'd always wished to have for herself. Was it too much to hope that it was still possible?

Jasper tried telling himself that this all had to be some crazy nightmare. Why would they want him to get the baby? Probably some bizarre test.

He entered the room where they baby lay in a small basket. The infant's hands were balled up at his red little face as big tears ran down his cheeks. If it weren't for all the trouble the little thing was causing in his life, he'd almost feel sorry for him.

Leaning over the basket, he muttered, "Don't cry."

The baby continued to wail.

"Look, baby," Jasper said as gently as he could. "I don't know anything about babies. They all seem to think I'm just going to pick you up and suddenly be able to take care of you, but listen…"

The baby had ceased his wailing and was looking up at him with dark eyes. Watching. Like he really was listening.

"I don't want to break you, all right? So if you could just stay settled down, then I won't have to pick you up and then I won't drop you. Because as mad as I am at Emma Jane for getting us into this situation, I don't want any harm to come to you."

The baby reached a hand toward Jasper, and Jasper couldn't help but reach in to touch the hand. So tiny. Fragile.

No, he couldn't possibly pick up the baby.

"Were you just lonely, little fella?"

The baby blinked up at him.

"You're probably missing all the pretty ladies fussing over you, aren't you?"

Jasper shifted his position slightly, so he was kneeling beside the cradle, and the baby's head seemed to move in the same direction, as if to follow him.

"I suppose they're taking good care of you. Emma Jane sure has taken a shine to you."

Jasper frowned. He had to admit, the baby was pretty cute, if you liked wrinkly faces, dark hair that didn't seem to go in any particular direction and big dark eyes that didn't seem able to stay focused on anything.

"What do I do about her, little guy?"

"You could try talking to her and working through the uncomfortable moments, instead of shutting down or walking away."

Jasper jumped at the sound of Emma Jane's sweet voice.

"I didn't hear you come in."

"Perhaps I should leave, so you could keep talking to Moses and I can hear more of what's in your heart." She knelt beside him. "He likes you."

Her words warmed him. They shouldn't have. After all, she'd gone and taken in this baby without his consent. Worse, he was starting to find that despite all of his frustrations in her lack of respect for his wishes, somehow Emma Jane was finding a way into his heart.

"Why do you want to know more of what's in my heart?" he asked, his voice catching as he spoke.

Emma Jane looked at him, the dark specks in her blue eyes mesmerizing him, as though they were a puzzle waiting for him to solve.

"You were the one who suggested we start over and get to know each other."

If she had been any other woman, he'd have complimented the beautiful smile lighting her face far better than the fire burning gently in the fireplace. But every time he told her of her beauty, it made her uncomfortable. She'd probably heard him compliment all the other ladies in town, and now it was probably difficult for her to ascertain his sincerity.

In truth, any compliment he'd want to pay her far outshone any he'd ever given. Emma Jane had a quiet loveliness, like an unexpected flower in... Jasper shook his head. He was known for that sort of compliment, and it clearly wouldn't work on Emma Jane. He'd need to think of another way to think about her.

"You're right," he said slowly. "Thank you. I appreciate you making the effort."

"Why did it take you so long to answer me?" Her words were gentle, not an accusation. But a deeper probing into the recesses of his heart.

He hadn't meant for their courtship to enter such troubled waters. Jasper was quite adept at maneuvering through all the small talk that occurred when courting a young lady. But Emma Jane... It was like diving into a place he'd never been.

"Because I don't know what to say."

"Whatever's in your heart." Her expression was guileless, and he hated how it immediately made him suspicious. Everyone always wanted something from him, and since Emma Jane knew his weakness, it almost made it harder to open up.

"I don't know how to do this." The words were hard to say, burning in his throat as they came out.

"It's all right." Emma Jane patted his knee and reached into the cradle, picking up the baby. "Just put your arm out, like mine, and I'm going to set his head in the crook of your elbow."

Jasper hadn't been talking about the baby. But as Emma Jane's soft hands placed the downy head against his arm, he had to wonder if it would have been safer to simply confess the longings and confusion in his heart. Having the baby in his arms, it made him feel...

"Please, Emma Jane, I know you mean well, but..."

"Look at him. He likes you."

Her voice was so soft and tender he couldn't help but obey. How could this baby look at him with so much... was it love?

"I don't understand." Jasper turned his gaze to Emma Jane. "He doesn't know me. Why would he?"

She looked down at the baby and smoothed the hairs on his head. "Because that's what babies do. All they ask is for someone to care for them and give them a loving touch."

Then she turned her face back up to Jasper, her eyes looking deep into his. "That's all any of us needs, really. But somehow we get it all mixed up as adults. Babies love automatically and unconditionally. We turn love into this complicated thing that seems to be unattainable. But it's not. We just have to be willing to trust as blindly as a baby."

Trust. He'd asked that from her, and she seemed to be asking that from him. Except Emma Jane was asking for trust on a different level. To jump into completely unknown territory and give her his heart, not just his fortune. Fortunes were easily gained and lost. But his heart...?

He'd never risked that before. Never even offered it.

Which was why, when he leaned in to kiss her, it

wasn't with the teasing look, flirtatious comments or flattery he'd given every other girl in town. He pressed his lips to hers with the gentle question, asking her to let him in. But more than that, it was an offering.

Every kiss he'd given had merely been to taste, to take, and had all been for pure amusement. As Emma Jane's lips moved against his, he knew that this kiss sealed something special between them. For Jasper, kissing Emma Jane was offering his first kiss, or at least the first sharing of all of him, asking for all of her.

When he pulled her closer to him, deepening the embrace, he felt the bundle in his other arm pressing between them. Emma Jane must have felt it, too, because she jerked away.

"What was that?" She sounded angry as she pressed her fingers to her lips.

"I'm sorry, I got caught in the moment."

Emma Jane backed away. "That wasn't supposed to happen."

No, it wasn't. "I'm sorry," he said simply. "I…"

He'd tried giving her a part of his heart and she'd…

She kept her fingers on her lips, like they were tingling the way his still were. Their kiss might not have been what was supposed to happen, but she'd felt it, too. Something intense had passed between them, and while he was trying to acknowledge it, Emma Jane seemed too afraid.

"I think I might be developing feelings for you," he said, hoping that his admission would put her at ease.

Emma Jane removed her fingertips from her lips. "You might?"

Then she shook her head. "I should have known. You know, at first I was offended that you hadn't tried to kiss me. I even imagined at one point that when we were trapped in the mine together, just before it caved in, you *had* kissed me. And now you've kissed me for real, and all you can say is that you *might* have feelings for me?"

She took the baby out of his arms and stood. "I am not one of your playthings to toy with."

Jasper quickly scrambled to his feet. "I know. And I wasn't. There is something between us, and I'm trying to make sense of it."

Then he stopped. Stared at her. Examined her flushed face, her flashing eyes and her heaving chest. She was angry. Truly angry. Confused. And hurt.

"Wait. You thought you imagined our kiss in the mine?"

Emma Jane nodded slowly.

"Why would you think you imagined it?"

A tear trickled down her cheek. "Who would want to kiss me? Why would you, a handsome, well-bred man who could have any girl he wanted, want to kiss me?"

So many reasons, and as they crossed his mind, he remembered all the compliments he'd paid her, and all the arguments she'd had against him. How could he tell her how very lovely she was? How desirable she was to him? How could he make her believe him?

All he had was the truth.

"That night, in the mine, I was attracted to you. When you approached me earlier in the barn and told me what was happening to your family and how you wanted me to help, I admired you."

Jasper took a deep breath as he remembered how he'd noticed her eyes and the way the dark flecks danced back then, just as they were doing now.

"I barely knew you, and I didn't want to marry any-one, let alone you, but I was so impressed that you came right out and told me that's what you wanted. No one had ever been honest with their intentions like that before."

She continued looking at him with that accusatory expression.

"Beauty isn't just about a person's outward appearance, you know." He returned her glare. "Your dress was the most awful thing I'd ever seen on a person, but I admired your honesty and courage. I'm sorry if you don't believe me, but I found that very attractive. And when we were stuck in the mine, and we were talking about real things, I felt a real connection to you. So I kissed you."

Jasper shrugged. "I'm sorry if that offends you, Emma Jane. It was wrong, I know. I shouldn't have taken the liberty. I acted impulsively in the moment, and I'm sorry if it caused you pain."

He'd tried to be sorry for kissing her, but even now, having kissed her a second time, he couldn't regret it.

"Why didn't you mention the kiss before?" Her eyes were still watery from her tears, but at least they were no longer trickling down her cheeks.

"Why didn't you?"

Emma Jane looked at the ground. "I told you. Why would anyone want to kiss me? I figured I must have imagined it."

He reached forward and lifted her chin, looking into her eyes. "No. But I felt like I'd taken advantage of your weakened state, and the honorable thing was to pretend like it had never happened."

"Is that why you so readily gave in to my family's demands that you marry me?"

"In a way," he admitted with a brusque nod. "I knew you'd been compromised, and the honorable thing to do was marry you. Plus, you'd saved my life. I felt like I owed it to you."

"And now?"

"Now what?" he murmured.

"Why did you kiss me?"

Jasper closed his eyes. Tried to come up with the right words when he had no explanation other than the one he'd already given.

He finally opened his eyes and looked down at her. "Things are changing inside me. My feelings for you are changing."

His answer didn't appear to be what she wanted to hear. Tears streamed down her cheeks. "You have told me over and over how much you do not want to be married to me. You've said that you don't believe me when I say that I did not trap you on purpose. You keep telling me that you don't trust me and that I have to earn your trust."

His own words hurt more when used against him. Especially because even though he'd tried offering himself to her, part of him knew they were still true. Yet they weren't. How could it be both?

"I can't explain it." He didn't even know what to tell himself. He wanted her, but he was still afraid. Something inside him had shifted, but he didn't know what or how. Was it the Bible reading he'd been doing when he thought Emma Jane wasn't looking? Or the wisdom from the Lewises? Or was it Emma Jane herself?

She stared at him, as if he owed her something more.

"It's like what you told me with Mary. How something inside you was different. I don't know why, but it's the same for me."

Her shoulders seemed to relax, and her posture seemed less tense. "I understand." Then she frowned. "And I suppose I also understand why you were hesitant to believe in me. Because I don't know if I believe you."

How quickly the tables turned. Jasper felt a new sympathy for Emma Jane and how his disbelief in her must have hurt. Yet this wound seemed to sting a little deeper. After all, he'd offered her something he'd offered no other—his heart—and she needed more proof.

"What do you want from me?"

Emma Jane held the baby out to him. "I want you to accept Moses as your son."

He looked at the baby, then he looked at her. "I've already held the baby."

"The baby." Emma Jane made a derisive noise. "You've not once mentioned him by name."

Jasper swallowed. He'd barely begun to accept the child, and now she wanted him to acknowledge a name he hadn't chosen and wasn't even sure he liked?

"I thought maybe we could discuss the baby's name."

"His name is Moses." She set her jaw stubbornly as she brought the baby back closer to her body.

"Moses," Jasper said slowly, feeling the word on his lips. He looked at the baby, then he looked back at her. "I'm really trying to make this work. But I give you all I have to offer, and you ask for more."

Emma Jane looked down at the baby and stroked his head. "A few days ago, that would have been enough. But now I have a child to think about, and I have to do what's best for him."

As he watched her retreat, Jasper suddenly felt weary. The room seemed emptier without her and the baby, but he didn't know how to make her stay. And if she stayed, would they continue hurting each other with their words?

The life he'd planned for himself was so much simpler.

Chasing bandits was easy enough. No, not easy, but at least he didn't have to sort through feelings only to find his effort had been for naught.

He'd offered a piece of himself to Emma Jane that he'd never offered anyone else. But she acted like he'd insulted her instead.

Exhaling wearily, Jasper shoved his hand through his hair. Obviously, he'd been wrong in following his heart and attempting to connect with her on a romantic level. He'd promised her a marriage of convenience, and tonight's kiss had violated that promise.

Emma Jane might have thought herself foolish to have imagined their kiss in the mine, but Jasper had been more foolish. He'd repeated what was clearly a mistake. One that wouldn't happen again.

Chapter Fifteen

Emma Jane slept poorly that night. Sometime around dawn, she gave up the fight for sleep and wandered into the kitchen. Jasper had never come to bed, not that they were sharing a bed, of course, but he hadn't even come to their room to keep up the appearance of being a married couple.

She heated a kettle of water and looked out the window, noticing that the snow had finally stopped falling. Moonlight glittered on the surface of the ground, blanketed in white. The drifts were almost to the base of the window, so that if she opened the window, she could touch the top of the snowbank.

Jasper would want to leave as soon as he realized the worst of the weather was over. How they'd make it to town through the deep snow, she didn't know, but knowing Jasper, he'd find a way.

As she'd found herself doing multiple times throughout the night, Emma Jane touched her fingertips to her lips again.

Why had he kissed her like that?

Jasper had said he'd been attracted to her. Which hardly seemed possible, considering how unattractive Emma Jane was. Everyone said so. Her mother used to tell her that only a blind man would be able to overlook her lack of beauty. Certainly all of the young ladies had far more to recommend them than Emma Jane.

Why then would he find *her* attractive?

Though Jasper had mentioned admiring pieces of her character, Emma Jane could hardly fathom such things would make up for her lack of looks.

Her eyes filled with tears. Why would he toy with her like that?

All this time, she'd been curious about what it would be like to kiss him, hurt because he'd kissed every girl in town except her, and now, she found it only to be more confusing than anything else.

She'd liked his kiss. Liked the way his big, strong arms felt around her. As if she was safe. And she could count on him.

For a moment, she even thought she might have felt a spark between them.

But for Jasper, he'd only thought he might be developing feelings. So what had the kiss been? A game? Just one more of his experiments in curiosity, like he'd had with every other girl in town?

He'd said it was different, but Emma Jane wasn't sure she could trust him. If he'd really changed, why was he still being so obstinate about Moses?

The water was finally ready, and Emma Jane began making her tea. Soon the sun would be up, and Olivia would be in to prepare breakfast. Emma Jane glanced at the closed door to the rooms off the kitchen. Abigail and her family occupied those rooms, and it was hard not to peek in and check on Moses. Because the baby was still too young to sleep through the night, Abigail had said it would be easier to keep him with her for his midnight feedings.

How was it possible to love someone so completely in such a short period of time? If only Jasper could understand that love and be more accepting of Moses.

Emma Jane sighed.

One more reason why it seemed hard to accept that Jasper's feelings were anything more than one of his passing fancies. His moods seemed to be up-and-down, not at all the steady emotion she felt for Moses.

Jasper's driving passion to find Daisy had been stronger than any of the emotion he'd expressed toward Emma Jane. And if she was to be completely honest about Jasper, well...

She sighed again.

The last time they'd been stuck here, she'd thought the two of them had developed a strong friendship. They'd talked and laughed, and Emma Jane was certain they'd have a good relationship once they returned to town. When her parents demanded they marry, she believed it wouldn't be so bad, considering she and Jasper had already bonded.

But this? The constant up-and-down and never knowing if Jasper was going to be friendly or antagonistic?

Which Jasper would she return home to?

The door creaked open, and Emma Jane turned, expecting to see Olivia but instead found Jasper, hair mussed and rubbing his eyes, walking through the door.

"I'm making tea," she told him, realizing that she'd oversteeped the leaves, but not sure she cared. Perhaps the stronger drink would help her gather her thoughts.

"I thought you'd still be asleep." He walked to the table and accepted the cup she offered him. "Thank you."

"What are you doing up so early?"

"I woke up when the wind stopped howling. Couldn't get back to sleep. Too much on my mind. I'm hoping to beat the bandits back to town."

That was the kind of devotion she'd hoped for him to feel toward her. The kind of devotion that should have backed up his kiss.

"I've been thinking," Emma Jane said slowly, even though the idea was just coming to her. "I'm going to stay here. You need to get back to deal with the bandits, but I need Abigail to feed Moses, so I'm going to stay with them."

Time seemed to stand still for a few moments as Jasper watched her. He had to know that she was right. Without Abigail, Moses wouldn't be able to eat. Why she hadn't thought of it sooner, she didn't know, but here, in the stillness of the morning with Jasper preparing to leave, it was all too clear. He'd have to go without her.

"Why do you think I asked you to leave Moses here?" His words were gentle, and while she'd expected some level of argument from him, she hadn't expected him to sound so...reasonable.

"I need to stay with my son."

"People will talk if I come home without you," he rasped.

"I thought you didn't care about what people said."

She watched as he flattened his lips, his jaw tightening. He didn't have an argument she couldn't counter, and she found, as he appeared to weigh her words, that she no longer cared.

What if people talked? She had done everything to

avoid people talking. And yet, it hadn't changed a thing. In fact, all the painstaking measures she'd taken to silence her critics had only made her miserable.

Well, she was done with that way of thinking. If people wanted to talk because she was doing what was best for her son, then so be it.

Jasper looked at her long and slow. "I don't like it, but that's the way of things. People talk, and while I try to ignore it, I know how it hurts people."

His expression softened. "Like you." He sighed and ran his fingers through his hair. "I know I haven't done my best by you to keep the talk down, but once this business with the bandits is done, I'll do what I can."

Yet again, Jasper was putting her off. Now that he was heading back to town, Emma Jane was no longer a priority. Just as she'd suspected, her husband had no interest in her other than being a passing fancy. He'd kissed her because she was convenient to him, not because he'd developed any special feelings for her.

She'd almost been fooled. For a moment, she'd almost thought that he'd developed a level of tenderness toward her. But no. He'd merely sought his amusement with her because there'd been little else to do.

Worse, Emma Jane had been the one to incite the action. Had she not taunted him into holding Moses, they'd have both remained content in their own worlds. The attachment she'd been forming to Jasper would never have happened, and then her brain wouldn't be so muddled by the kiss.

Spending time with Jasper was simply too dangerous to her heart. So prickly on the outside, he wasn't a man she wanted to know. But when he lowered his defenses…

Emma Jane sighed. Now that was a Jasper she liked.

Could perhaps feel something more for. Except that just as quickly as he let his guard down, the prickles came back up, and that was a man she couldn't live with.

Their marriage vows had been for better or for worse, but as Emma Jane watched her husband calmly sip his tea, she had to wonder if they really had a marriage at all. Technically, with their marriage not consummated, they weren't married. Emma Jane had heard that some people in those circumstances were able to get an annulment.

It seemed their reasons for getting married were no longer valid, at least not to Emma Jane. And after spending all this time trying to make things work with Jasper, to even establish a friendship, they'd gained no ground. He was still the same Jasper who refused to see anything other than his own interests.

Emma Jane cleared her throat. "All the same, I'd prefer to remain here. The talk doesn't bother me so much as the worry over what might happen to Moses."

Irritation flashed across Jasper's face. "And you don't think I care about what happens to the child? I'm not without feeling, you know. I can understand that you want what's best for the baby, but you seem to be forgetting that you lack the ability to feed him." Nostrils flaring, he drew several deep breaths, then bit out, "He was sick before we came here, Emma Jane, and now that he's well, it seems selfish to take him away."

Selfish? She glared at him. "It seems to me that, yet again, you're putting your motives right back on me. But you refuse to see any possibility other than my leaving him behind."

"And you refuse to see the fact that you may not be the best person to take care of that baby right now." Jasper's eyes flashed as his jaw tightened. "We're married, Emma

Jane. And while I'm trying to get to know you so we can find common ground, you keep hiding behind that baby and using him as an excuse to keep me at arm's length."

Every cell in Emma Jane's body heated. "I am merely doing what's right. Something I thought you would support, considering this is Daisy's child. You have just as many excuses keeping me at bay. As for using the baby as an excuse, you're the one who runs away every time the subject comes up."

Jasper took another swallow, then set his teacup down slowly. "Of course I do. Because no matter what I say or do, you refuse to see my side of things. So what's the point in sticking around and having the same argument over and over? Even now, what are we accomplishing?"

Emma Jane smoothed her skirts and straightened her shoulders as she gave him a long, steady look. "Precisely. Which is why it's time we both admit that what we hoped to accomplish with our marriage has failed. No matter what we do, people are going to talk. And you and I are never going to see eye to eye. So why would we spend the rest of our lives making each other miserable?"

"What are you saying?" Jasper's eyes narrowed.

She'd seen that expression on his face before. Her suggestion would have wounded the pride of any man, but since Jasper took such stock in his ability to help her, this wound probably cut deeper.

"You shouldn't have to give up your dreams because of my parents' greed. Because of my simple mistake. You deserve to have the life you want for yourself." She released a trembling breath. "So I'm setting you free, Jasper. Go back to town. Be a lawman. Find someone to fall in love with."

Emma Jane's throat tightened. Something in her heart

constricted at the thought of him finding someone else. But it was clear that she wasn't the one for him.

"Do you know the scandal a divorce would cause?" Jasper's voice was hoarse.

His response gave Emma Jane all the assurance she needed that ending their sham of a marriage was the right decision. If all he cared about was the gossip, well, that would blow over soon enough.

"I'm not asking for a divorce," she said quietly. "We have enough grounds for an annulment, given that we never had a real marriage to begin with. People might talk at first, but soon enough the Jackson fortune will be enough to smooth things over."

Even in the dim light, Emma Jane could see Jasper's face pale. He probably hadn't realized the extent to which she'd thought her idea through. There were still some details she hadn't figured out, like how she was going to support herself and her son, but she would find a way.

"I can't leave you with nothing. You're right, my reputation would be easily repaired, but you wouldn't fare so well. The only option available to you would be the same lifestyle as the women you're working so hard to help."

His blunt words were like being dumped into one of the snowbanks.

"Pastor Lassiter…" Emma Jane began, but the expression on Jasper's face told her all she needed to know.

The older man had been working so hard to help their marriage that he'd feel betrayed at Emma Jane giving up so quickly. He'd meant the words when he married the couple, and he'd expected them to mean something to them, as well. If there was anything to feel guilty about, it was the fact that she'd be breaking faith with the only person who'd truly believed in her.

"I could leave Leadville. Tell people I'm a widow. No one would question…"

"You'd make a liar of yourself?" His voice was quiet, but the accusation stung worse than it would have had he slapped her.

"I don't know. I hadn't thought…" Tears clogged her throat. Ending their marriage had seemed so simple, but Jasper's questions made it look more and more impossible.

But he was right. Of all the things Emma Jane valued most, it was her own integrity. She could sleep at night knowing she'd done nothing wrong, but how would she sleep if she built her future on a lie?

"Is being married to me truly that bad?" Jasper asked hoarsely.

"We want different things."

The expression on his face was tortured. "Is it because I kissed you?" His Adam's apple bobbed. "I am so sorry, Emma Jane. I acted without thinking. You were promised a marriage of convenience, and I crossed a line. I was wrong to have kissed you. I promise, I won't seek to impose on you ever again."

Tears escaped her eyes and rolled down her cheeks. "Don't you understand? That's precisely what I don't want. Being kissed was wonderful, and I can't imagine spending the rest of my life never having that again. You deserve a woman who will love you, just as much as I deserve a man who will do the same for me."

She took a breath, strengthened by finally being able to express the feelings deep in her heart. "I want to be kissed with the passion of a man who loves me. I want to be a man's choice, not a decision he was forced into."

Wiping the tears from her cheeks, Emma Jane looked

at him. "Isn't this what you told me you wanted for your own life? I care enough about you to want that for you, just as I hope you want that for me. Our happiness is between the two of us. So let's give that to each other as a final gift." She drew a bolstering breath, then went on. "I'll figure out what to do about caring for Moses, but I can't spend the rest of my life making us both miserable simply for the sake of living the good life."

Silence echoed through the room. She could almost hear Jasper's heart beating—or was that her own?

"All right," he finally gritted out. "If that's what you truly want, I'll see about getting an annulment. As for how you'll support yourself, I won't let you do without. My family won't like it, but I'll see that you get a house and a small amount of money to get you by each month." He rubbed a hand over his eyes. "I suppose I bear my own share of the blame for this mess, and I won't have you suffer for it."

His acquiescence should have been a victory, but the heaviness tearing at her heart felt like she'd just lost everything.

The words were harder to say than Jasper thought they'd be. But he'd been up all night, reading Emma Jane's Bible, unable to sleep. He'd been trying to figure out what to do about her and his growing feelings for the wife he hadn't been sure he wanted.

One section in particular, 1 Corinthians, talked about love. Had he shown patience to Emma Jane? Kindness? Long-suffering?

The desperation with which she made her arguments made it clear that Emma Jane found no joy in her marriage to him. And why would she? He'd never shown her any of the things the Bible said about love. Foolishly, he'd believed that giving her his name would be all she needed, but he could see now how he'd sold her short.

Miserable. That was the word she'd used to describe their marriage.

"Are you sure?" Emma Jane looked at him as though she wasn't confident she'd heard him right.

"Yes. I never meant you any harm, I hope you know that."

"I never meant you any harm, either," she whispered.

He knew that now, deep down in his soul, and he wished he'd been able to see it sooner, rather than thinking the worst of her. Of course her falling into the mine had been an accident. He didn't even need to ask to know.

"I know," he said thickly, watching her expression for any sign that she might believe him. "I'm sorry if I conveyed otherwise."

Emma Jane sat on a chair, her skirts whooshing with the movement. "For two people who never meant to hurt each other, we've sure caused a lot of damage, haven't we?"

He pulled up the chair next to her and sat beside her. "Nothing that can't be repaired. I'd still like us to be friends."

Friends. Actually, he wanted more. Much, much more. The memory of her kiss burned in his brain, and he knew he'd never again have the like. At least not from anyone but her. But for now, he knew what he had to do. Start over. Just like Stephen said. Court her. Be her friend.

"I'd like that, too." She smiled at him, one of the same smiles that had stirred something deep inside him, telling him that Emma Jane was a treasure he couldn't let go of.

Shotgun Marriage

The door on the side of the kitchen opened, and Abigail entered, carrying the baby.

"I thought I heard voices in here." She smiled, then yawned. "This happy little fellow has been up for a while now. He's fed, changed and gurgling happily."

Abigail handed the baby to Emma Jane, whose mood seemed to immediately lift just by having the baby in her arms.

Jasper should have paid more attention to the effect the baby had on her. He'd already known, he supposed, but he'd been too busy fighting the battle to really acknowledge how good Emma Jane was with the little guy.

"You look like you could go back to bed," Emma Jane said to Abigail, cuddling the baby. "Why don't you get some rest and I can help your mother prepare breakfast?"

"I couldn't do that." Abigail frowned. "I need to earn my keep."

"You've been doing that, and more. After all, without you, I don't know what I would have done for Moses."

The two women exchanged smiles that spoke of their bond shared over the baby.

"You know I'm delighted to care for him." Abigail looked at Emma Jane, then over at Jasper. "In fact, that's something I'd like to talk to you both about."

Jasper's stomach knotted. He'd known Emma Jane and Abigail had become close over the past couple of days, but this felt like an ambush. Had Emma Jane already been making plans to leave him?

"As you know, Charles and I have been living here with my parents, and as much as I love my family, it's not the best situation for Charles. I was hoping that we could return to town with you, and I could…" She hesitated, twisting her hands in front of her.

"That is, it's a pleasure to help with Moses, but if you could give me employment as his wet nurse, then Charles would have the opportunity to find a job in town and we could eventually have a home of our own."

The woman's unease only served to make the knots in Jasper's gut tighten. Why was his automatic response to question Emma Jane's integrity? Especially when he knew better.

He looked over at Emma Jane, whose face was downcast at Abigail's request. To say yes to Abigail meant that Emma Jane couldn't stay here. But to say no would be cruel to her friend, even if it gave Emma Jane what she wanted.

But at least it would help with Jasper's quest.

"We would be delighted to have you," he said smoothly, looking over at Emma Jane. "In fact, I would be willing to arrange an interview for Charles at my father's bank. Your husband is an amiable fellow, and if there's a position available, I'm sure he'd get on just fine."

Abigail's face lit up. "You would do that for us?"

"Of course I would. This is the second time your family has taken us in, and I can't tell you what it's meant to me."

Then he looked at Emma Jane, who was most likely put out that he'd spoiled her plans without discussing them with her first. Even now, that was still the trouble. They both acted, thinking it was in everyone's best interests, but never talked about it.

Which was where everything always went wrong.

"As far as helping Emma Jane with the baby, I have no objection, but I'm sure that's something she'll want to work out with you." He stole a glance at Emma Jane, whose attention remained fixed on the baby rather than the conversation.

Yes, she was angry. Using the baby as something to hide behind while she gathered her thoughts. Again.

"Although I will say, in case Emma Jane has any concern over finances, that she is fully authorized to pay whatever she feels is best. I trust her completely, and you have my word that I will pay whatever sum the two of you settle on."

He watched Emma Jane for any sign of acknowledgment that he was trying his best to give her what she wanted. That he would provide for her needs as well as the baby's.

Finally, Emma Jane looked up. Slowly. Her face shadowed, but not so much as to hide the tears forming in her eyes.

"I had hoped to remain here for a while longer."

"I'm afraid that isn't a good idea," Stephen's voice boomed across the kitchen. "I've been thinking a lot about your situation, and based on Jasper's description of the gang's hideout, it's not far from here. I wouldn't be surprised if they come here, looking for you."

The knot that had formed in Jasper's gut clenched, nearly ripping him in two. Why hadn't he considered the danger he might be putting others in?

"I am so sorry," he said slowly. "I hadn't thought of the fact that your family might be in danger. Please forgive me."

Stephen waved his arm. "Nonsense. Of course we would help you. But if the bandits come here looking for you and find Emma Jane here, there's no telling what danger she'd be in. I think the best move is to head back to town, where you can alert the sheriff, and everyone will be safe."

The older man's words made sense, if only they didn't cause such a look of despair on his wife's face.

His wife.

Jasper had finally gotten used to the word, and now it seemed, if Emma Jane had her way, it wouldn't be applicable at all.

But he would find a way to change her mind and win her back. Well, maybe not back, since he'd never had her to begin with.

"You're right," Jasper answered smoothly, then turned to look at Emma Jane, hoping to reassure her that he'd been on her side this whole time. "I'm sure the bandits are mighty angry that we got away, and if they manage to catch my wife alone, I don't even want to think about what they'd do."

He reached out and took her hand. "I'm sorry, Emma Jane, but you're going to have to come back to town with me."

Then Jasper looked back up at Stephen. "We'd just been talking to Abigail about the possibility of bringing her and her family with us to town. We still need a wet nurse, and I'm sure we can find a position for Charles. Would you be able to spare them?"

The older man nodded slowly.

But when Emma Jane squeezed Jasper's hand back, he had hope that things wouldn't be as bad as he feared.

"Please say yes," Emma Jane said, her voice steadier than it had been earlier. "I don't know what I would do without Abigail's help."

"They're both adults. If they want to go, they can go."

"Oh, thank you," Abigail said, tears filling her eyes

as she looked from her father to Emma Jane, then her gaze landing on Jasper.

"You have no idea how much this means to me." Then she looked up, past Jasper. "To us."

Jasper turned his head to see Charles standing in the doorway. The poor fellow had just had his entire life rearranged, and he hadn't been part of the conversation. Having been resentful of that type of managing his whole life, Jasper felt guilty.

"That is," Jasper said, removing his hand from Emma Jane's, then standing to face the other man. "If you're in agreement. I wouldn't want to force a man into a life he didn't want."

Emma Jane made a noise, and while Jasper didn't know for sure what it meant, once again he feared having said the wrong thing. While it was true he'd felt that way about his own life, this wasn't about him and Emma Jane.

"I appreciate it." Charles held out his hand to Jasper. "And I'm right honored that you'd be willing to help Abigail and me. I'd rather live in town, so this is an answer to prayer. So long as we're not putting you out, we gladly accept."

Jasper shook on their deal, grateful that, at least in this, he wasn't ruining someone else's life for his own convenience. It seemed as though all of the noble deeds he'd hoped to accomplish lately only turned out sour.

He glanced back at Emma Jane, who'd once again turned her attention back to the baby. Would his efforts to make amends actually work? Or was it too late?

Chapter Sixteen

As town loomed ahead, Emma Jane's uneasiness grew. Jasper had agreed to an annulment, but what would happen once they returned? He seemed to be just as eager as she to move on with his life. But would that change once they arrived at the Jackson mansion and Jasper faced pressure from his parents? Their biggest fear had been the scandal, which is why they'd sent her family away.

How would they react when they found out that Emma Jane was seeking an annulment?

The sleigh jostled as it hit another snowbank. Thankfully Stephen had a sleigh and had been willing to drive them back to town. Jasper had said that the roads were still impassable, which was one more advantage they'd have over the bandits.

Another bump sent Emma Jane closer into Jasper.

"Easy now," he said, putting an arm around her.

Jasper held her close, and though she'd steadied herself, it felt good to have his arm around her. She'd have liked to have said that it was because he offered more protection from the cold, but Emma Jane knew it was more than that.

She liked being in Jasper's arms. Their kiss might not have meant anything to him, since he so readily agreed to the annulment, but to Emma Jane, it had opened her eyes to a world where she could no longer exist.

No wonder all of the girls were crazy about Jasper. His kiss had been something like that out of a dream. And if all of them felt that way about his kisses, it was no surprise that every girl in town mooned over him.

Emma Jane had never thought that she'd be among the ones to succumb to his charm.

Even now, as her mind kept telling her she should pull away, she found herself snuggling closer. Despite all of her warnings to her heart that Jasper was not safe, a piece of her felt as though here was the safest place to be.

Nonsense. All of it. He'd agreed to the annulment, and even very generously agreed to provide support for her and Moses. Those weren't the words of a man who cared for her, but of a man who wanted to move on with his life as painlessly as possible.

Straightening her posture, blinking back a sudden stinging in her eyes, Emma Jane moved out of his embrace.

"I don't want to go back to your parents' house," she said, looking at him but avoiding his eyes.

His gaze landed firmly on her. "We've been over this. You're safer in town."

"I'd like to stay at a hotel."

The old Emma Jane would have never made such a bold suggestion. But she found, the more her ideas were accepted, the more it seemed like she was doing herself a disservice not to at least try.

Jasper didn't answer at first. Instead, his dark eyes bore into her like he was trying to puzzle her out.

"Father has a suite at the Rafferty. As long as it's not in use, I see no reason why you can't stay there."

The Rafferty. Leadville's finest hotel. She'd had tea there once, a prize for all the young ladies finishing school with top marks. Flora had been beastly to her about it, making snide remarks about it being the only way the likes of Emma Jane would be able to take tea in such a fine place.

She had vowed that, one day, she would have tea there again, and not one person would make fun of her for it.

Of course now, with her pending annulment and being a mother to Moses, there would be no stopping the talk. And yet, Emma Jane found that she didn't mind so much. In her heart, she knew she was doing the right thing, which was far better than nasty people like Flora Montgomery, who always seemed to do the wrong thing.

"Thank you," Emma Jane told Jasper, giving him a tremulous smile. "I appreciate how good you're being about all of this."

"It's the least I could do." He shrugged. "Plus, Father's suite will allow you to have more space than a regular hotel room. There's a sitting room and two bedrooms—one for you, and another for Abigail and Charles."

He sounded like he'd thought of everything. Worse, he sounded so accepting of the decision. Emma Jane sighed. She was right not to let her heart lead in this situation.

Jasper leaned forward and tapped Charles on the shoulder. "We'll be going to the Rafferty instead."

She couldn't hear Charles's response, but Abigail turned and gave Emma Jane a quizzical look. Emma Jane merely smiled tightly in response. With the wind, it was nearly impossible to hold a conversation with the occupants of the front seat. Besides, she hadn't told Abigail of her plans to have her marriage annulled.

As much as Emma Jane had told herself she didn't care what people thought anymore, people like Abigail were different. What if her friends disagreed with her decision? Worse, what if they refused to stand by her?

Abigail smiled back, then turned to face front again. She snuggled in closer to Charles, and for a moment, Emma Jane envied her. Even though Abigail hinted that things weren't perfect between her and Charles, they seemed happy. Abigail seemed to genuinely love her husband. Even their children, who'd stayed behind with Olivia until the weather cleared, since there wasn't enough room in the sleigh, were a part of that deep, abiding love.

Would Emma Jane have that for herself? The annulment would free her to marry again, but would a man be willing to love both her and Moses? She adjusted the blanket around the baby, cradling him closer to her. If only Jasper had been willing to accept the boy as his own.

She sighed. That wasn't their entire problem, but it sure had complicated matters.

"None of that," Jasper said, putting his arm around her again. "We're almost to town, and I've promised that I'll take care of everything. So have a little faith. Everything will work out all right."

For him, perhaps. He still had the Jackson fortune as inducement for someone to marry him.

Emma Jane's breath caught. Could she stand to see another marrying Jasper? She stole a glance at him. Would he be so easily trapped into marriage again? Or would he finally find someone to love?

Part of her wanted to see Jasper happy. Part of her…

Emma Jane told her aching heart to be quiet. The Jasper she loved was the Jasper who only seemed to be present part of the time. Too many parts, and not enough to make a whole.

"Are you cold?" Jasper rubbed her arm gently. "It's not far now. We're almost to Harrison Avenue."

"I'll be fine," she told him, wishing she had the strength to move out of his embrace but feeling proud that she hadn't snuggled any closer. At least it was progress.

As they pulled up in front of the hotel, Emma Jane's confidence sagged. Too many people were there, watching. Waiting to see who had arrived in such a spiffy sleigh.

Jasper alighted first, ignoring the crowd, and held a hand out for Emma Jane. She took it, careful to hold Moses against her as she stepped down.

As soon as she set foot on the sidewalk, she heard the familiar screech.

"Jasper, darling! Is that you? Everyone has been so worried since your disappearance after your unfortunate wife ran off on you."

Emma Jane took a deep breath, telling herself it didn't matter, yet straining to hear Jasper's response.

"Hello, Flora. My wife did not run off on me, as you can see by her standing beside me. I'm sure you're very eager to spread gossip about our return, and I won't waste your time with the truth. If you'll excuse us..."

He took Emma Jane by the arm and bustled her into the hotel.

"Is that a baby?" The words echoed behind Emma Jane, but Jasper did not stop to answer the question. He'd have to at some point, but she appreciated that they didn't have to deal with the confrontation so immediately.

He continued on to the front desk, where a brief discussion with the clerk confirmed that the Jackson suite was empty and Jasper was given a key.

"I'm sorry Flora was so ugly to you when we arrived," he said as they made their way to the room.

"It's not your fault. I'm glad you didn't turn it into a long conversation."

He stopped and looked at her. "Why would I? I thought you'd understand by now that I can't stand the woman. I owe her nothing, and given her penchant for gossip, I'm not telling her anything that would get to my parents before I have a chance to talk to them." Blowing out a sharp breath, he went on to say, "As it is, I can only hope the messenger I had the clerk send over gets to the house before she does."

He continued down the hall and stopped at a door, which he opened. "Here it is. Home sweet home."

The room, far larger than any of the modest rooms at the Spruce Lakes Resort, was a sitting room, as finely appointed as anything at the Jackson mansion. Emma Jane recognized the furniture as carved by the same hand that had done the intricate pieces she'd seen in Jasper's home. A crystal vase sat on a table, filled with delicate silk flowers. Even the wealthiest families couldn't get fresh flowers this time of year in Leadville, but the reproduction astounded her.

Abigail and Charles entered behind them.

"Oh, my," Abigail breathed, stepping inside.

"Mother decorated it," Jasper said with a sigh. "Father helped finance the hotel, and Mother asked that she be allowed to decorate our suite. It's not very practical, but it made her happy."

As Emma Jane's eyes swept the room, she couldn't

help but feel pity for her mother-in-law. Imported lace was draped over every surface, and she was certain that the crystal chandelier hanging from the center of the room had to have come from a far-off place.

But had any of this stuff really made the other woman happy?

They quickly sorted out the rooms, and Emma Jane insisted that Abigail and Charles take the larger of the two bedrooms. Jasper had thoughtfully gone to find a basket for Moses to sleep in, and when he returned, Emma Jane quite happily began filling it with the blankets Olivia had sent her home with.

"He's going to grow up well loved, isn't he?" Jasper's deep, masculine voice came from the doorway.

"I'd like to think so." Emma Jane stood and stretched out her back, stepping away from him. Even at a distance, he was too close.

Jasper stepped into the room, looking around. "I hope you have everything that will make you comfortable."

"It's far more than I would have expected." Emma Jane smiled at him. "I hope you know how much I appreciate all of this…"

He seemed to not hear her words, taking a step toward her, then reaching out and touching her cheek. "You are so beautiful when you smile. I know it makes you uncomfortable when I say it, but I wish you could accept how much I love your smile."

Emma Jane's face warmed. "I… I don't know what to say."

"*Thank you* would be a good start." He gave an impish grin, and for a moment, Emma Jane thought he might lean down to kiss her. Her heart fluttered at the prospect. Instead, he straightened, then took a step back.

A knock sounded at the main door, but before either of them could answer it, the door opened and Mrs. Jackson walked into the suite.

"I believe you owe me some answers."

Jasper winced. He should have known it wouldn't be enough to send a message to his father informing him of the circumstances. His father would wait, just as Jasper had requested. But his mother was an entirely different matter.

"Hello, Mother." He stepped forward and kissed her on the cheek. "I assume you read the note I sent Father."

"Note? What note?" She glared at him with enough ferocity to melt all of the snow in Leadville. "I was just at the dressmaker's, where I heard the most awful story from Flora Montgomery."

Jasper groaned. "Every story from Flora Montgomery is awful."

"How dare you speak of such a fine young lady in that manner? Her family is…"

"I don't want to hear it." Jasper shook his head, trying not to say exactly what he thought of Flora and her family. But he also wasn't going to allow the woman to continue maligning him and his wife. "Flora Montgomery has done nothing but spread vicious lies about me and Emma Jane, and I won't have it. And if you would ask me the truth rather than take her word on everything, you'd understand things a lot better."

The wounded expression on his mother's face gave him pause. "Sit. We'll order tea, and Emma Jane and I will tell you about everything that's transpired." He used a gentler tone with his request, and he was pleased to see that Emma Jane had already rang for service.

He'd asked her to try harder with his mother, and despite the fact that they were going to end their marriage, Emma Jane was still being kind to the difficult woman.

His mother sat on one of the gilt chairs, and Emma Jane sat across from her on the sofa. He took a seat next to his wife, then placed his hand over hers.

Then, calmly, as though being kidnapped by bandits and escaping through a snowstorm was an everyday occurrence, he relayed their story. Fortunately, his mother was too busy sniffling through her handkerchief to interrupt.

The tea service arrived, and Emma Jane immediately rose to serve them all tea. His hand grew cold without her warmth, and he found himself hoping she'd hurry so she could join him again.

Abigail entered the room carrying Moses. "He's been fed and changed, and I'm sure you're eager to have him back in your arms."

He watched as Emma Jane rushed over to her and immediately brought the baby against her. How could he have even suggested that she not raise this child? Her face glowed every time she held him.

"What is the meaning of this?" his mother demanded, looking at him rather than Emma Jane. "I know plenty of orphanages that can take the child. There's no sense in getting attached."

"Emma Jane is going to raise Moses," Jasper said quietly, looking at Emma Jane rather than his mother.

Did she understand what he was trying to say? What he couldn't say in front of his mother? He finally understood how Emma Jane felt about the baby, and hopefully, it wasn't too late.

"Why would she do such a foolish thing? Do you have any idea what people will say?"

He hated how his mother sounded, especially when he saw the way Emma Jane cringed.

"I would hope that they would say what I believe to be true. That Emma Jane is a fine woman, with a good heart and that she's doing a very noble thing by loving a child who needs a mother."

Continuing to keep his gaze on Emma Jane, he said quietly, "And I wish I'd realized that sooner, before pushing her away."

Then he looked at his mother. Taking a deep breath, he braced himself for his mother's reaction. "During our time away, we realized that our marriage was a mistake. Once things are settled with the bandits, I'll be speaking to Father's lawyers about getting an annulment. Emma Jane did nothing wrong, and she shouldn't be forced to marry me because of others' mistakes."

His mother turned a shade of scarlet that matched the lamp shade on the desk. "What kind of nonsense are you speaking? Have you any idea of the scandal it will cause?"

Jasper took a deep breath, then nodded. "I won't have Emma Jane be miserable for the rest of her life. Scandal will blow over. But…"

"Miserable?" His mother rose, turning her ire at Emma Jane. "You were taken from a low station in life, brought into my home and given everything a girl could have possibly wanted, yet you've somehow convinced my son that it makes you miserable?"

"How could it not? When you speak to her like that and treat her as though she were lower than a servant?"

Jasper moved to stand next to his wife. "Emma Jane

is the kindest woman I have ever known, and she's tried so hard to do the right thing by all of us, yet none of us have given her the respect she deserves."

Then he turned to her, blocking his mother from her view. "I am sorry. I've been blind to a lot of things concerning you, and selfishly only cared about how I was affected by it all. I have been the worst of husbands to you, and I deeply regret that I didn't do more to make our marriage work."

Tears rolled down Emma Jane's face, and he reached out to gently wipe them away. "I'm sorry for all the times I've made you cry. I do not deserve a wife of your character."

"A wife of her character?" His mother's voice clawed at his back.

Stepping so that Emma Jane was by his side, he regarded his mother coldly. "If you had taken the time to get to know her, you would have realized that for yourself."

"She is nothing but a gold digger. Need I remind you how much money your father spent to pay off her father's debt, send them away and put her sister in that fancy boarding school? There's nothing we can do about what we already spent, but if she thinks we'll continue supporting them…"

"Then she is absolutely right," he said smoothly. "I've already promised her as much, as well as a house and future support for her and Moses."

Jasper held out a hand to Emma Jane, and she took it. "Even if it means giving up everything I have, I will keep my promise to you."

More tears flowed down Emma Jane's cheeks. He hated putting her in the middle of his fight with his mother, because none of this was about her. No, this was about Constance's need to control everything. When he told Emma Jane about his mother's losses, he realized just how much of his world she controlled. He'd done so much to please his mother, but just like Emma Jane working tirelessly to please everyone else, he'd only made himself miserable.

He regretted the fact that this decision hurt his mother, but this was his life, and by continuing to fall in line with what she wanted, he was hurting someone even dearer to him—Emma Jane.

"You clearly are not right in the head. I'll be speaking to your father about this, and when you come home tonight, we'll discuss matters further."

"I'm not coming home." Actually, in his note to his father, he'd said he'd be home, but at his mother's words, he realized the Jackson mansion was no longer home to him.

Home was where Emma Jane was, and while he'd have to come to terms with her absence once they filed for the annulment, for now, he knew where he belonged.

"I'll send my apologies to Father. I know he was expecting me."

"You can't be serious," his mother said indignantly, looking from him to Emma Jane.

"I am. I won't stay anywhere where Emma Jane is not welcomed with open arms."

"Why have you turned him against me?" Tears filled the older woman's eyes as she looked at Emma Jane.

Before his wife had a chance to respond, Jasper did it for her. "She did nothing other than try to be agreeable in a place where everyone was unkind to her. I would suggest that you search your heart and find a way to make sure that Emma Jane is offered every kindness among those in your circle. I will not be kind to those who are not kind to her."

His words shamed him. They should have been uttered so long ago, and he should have done more to stand up for Emma Jane before they were even married.

Once again, he turned to her. "I'm sorry for not taking a stronger stand in your favor sooner."

"I…" Her lower lip quivered. "You don't need to do this. I've made my share of mistakes, and I can't bear…"

"We can talk about it later," he said, squeezing her hand, then releasing it.

Bringing his attention back to his mother, he said coolly, "You should leave now. I need to report in with the sheriff about everything that's happened, and I won't have you upsetting Emma Jane while I'm gone. When you feel that you are able to be kind, you may send us an invitation to dinner."

Her face turned as white as the scenery around them when they'd been lost in the blizzard. The anger replaced with the knowledge that Jasper was serious. She would probably go home and cry, and as much as he'd always hated making her cry, maybe her tears would serve a purpose.

Jasper walked her to the door and closed it gently behind her. His father would be angry, but hopefully once they sat down and talked, he would understand.

When Jasper returned to Emma Jane's side, she looked as though she was trying to find her way in that same blizzard.

"I don't understand what just happened."

"A lot of things you said to me finally sunk in. I'm sorry it took so long to see reason."

Then he looked around the room. "I hope it's all right

that I stay here. I can sleep on the sofa, and I'll try not to get in your way. We can settle things more firmly once the bandits are apprehended."

"Of course." Emma Jane frowned. She opened her mouth to say something, but then Moses began to fuss. After adjusting his blankets, she looked back at Jasper.

"I'm sorry. He needs to be changed."

"It's all right. I need to go talk to the sheriff, anyway."

Jasper turned toward the door, then paused. "I know it frustrates you that I've put you off in favor of pursuing this case. But I hope you understand the urgency of the situation."

"Yes." Emma Jane shifted the baby in her arms. "I suppose I owe you some apologies over that, as well. But as you've said, we can talk about everything later."

"Thank you for understanding." Jasper nodded goodbye, then left, torn between his duty to see the case through and his desire to make things right with Emma Jane.

Did she see enough sincerity in his words to his mother that she'd listen to what he had to say to her? Would she give him time to court her, to show her the true emotions in his heart?

Was there even room in her heart for him?

Chapter Seventeen

Jasper's absence created a void in the room that Emma Jane hadn't been prepared for. As much as she'd tried not to get attached to him, already the emptiness seemed as if it would swallow her whole.

What had he meant with all of his apologies and promises of talking later? Didn't he know it was only going to make their annulment that much harder? Leaving thoughtless Jasper was so much easier than leaving a man who seemed to genuinely care about her.

Moses had fallen asleep, and she'd laid him in his bed. Part of her yearned to pick him up and cuddle him close to have something to do, but Abigail had admonished her that if she held Moses too much, he'd be spoiled, and then when she needed to lay him down, he wouldn't let her.

At least she had her Bible. Since Moses had come into her life, she hadn't had as much time to read it as she'd have liked. The silence, with Abigail and Charles gone to bed and Moses asleep, was the perfect time to catch up.

Rummaging through her bag, she realized her Bible was missing. Emma Jane sighed. In her hurry to gather their things for their return to town, she must have left it at the resort.

She walked down to the front desk to see if they had one she could borrow, but as she neared the entrance to the saloon, she heard voices.

"Stupid rich boy. Thought he was so smart, telling them about the hideout. Little does he know the trap we've got rigged."

The man's cohort chuckled. "Thanks to you letting us know when the posse was leaving. Some of the men have doubted your loyalty, but they'll be mighty glad we have you after tonight."

"I'm just happy to be sitting here in the saloon, enjoying a drink and getting an alibi, instead of being near Mack and his explosives. I don't care what he says, he gets it wrong more often than not."

Emma Jane's heart seized. Of course Jasper would be with the posse. But for it to all be a trap? How had the bandits been able to put everything together so quickly? They'd only been back in town for a few hours.

Glasses clinked. "You're telling me. I was there when he blew up the outhouse. How'd you get out of posse duty?"

"At least one deputy has to stay behind in case there's trouble in town."

Deputy. Emma Jane could feel her pulse racing as she closed her eyes and leaned against the wall. Jasper had been saying that he suspected someone inside the sheriff's office had ties to the bandits. Now she knew for sure.

But that wasn't any help to her husband, who was walking blindly into a trap.

The men discussed the plan a few moments longer, but then their conversation moved to admiring one of the serving women. Hopefully, they'd given enough away for Emma Jane to be able to warn Jasper.

Slowly, quietly, Emma Jane made her way back to her room. After leaving a note for Abigail explaining her whereabouts, she went out the back door and ran down the road to the livery.

"Hello, I'm…"

"Mrs. Jackson. What a pleasure to have you here. It's a little late for a ride, isn't it?"

"It's an emergency," she told him breathlessly, looking about to be sure no one else was around. "I need your fastest horse."

Wes, the proprietor, scratched his chin. "Well, now. Most of my horses went out with the posse. What's the trouble? Maybe I can help."

Emma Jane hesitated, not sure who she could trust. If one of the town's deputies could be bought, who else might be on the bandits' side?

"I need to speak to Jasper. It won't wait. *Please.* It's a matter of life and death."

She hated sounding so melodramatic, but the posse already had a head start on her.

Wes frowned. "Will told me that Mary might try something like this, and I have strict orders not to let her have a mount."

His desire to protect Mary gave Emma Jane hope that this man could be trusted. "I overheard some of the bandits talking just now. The men are riding into an ambush!"

A long sigh escaped Wes's lips. "I knew it sounded too good to be true. All the best men went with the posse, but Deputy Jenks said that he'd remain behind. I figured the threat was to the town, not to the posse. We should let him know."

The back of Emma Jane's neck tingled. "I don't know the man's name, but he said that he was a deputy and deliberately stayed behind so he had an alibi."

"I should have known." Wes spat on the ground. "He always was too rough on his horse. Not so much as to hurt him, but just enough for me to question the man's character."

He straightened, then looked at Emma Jane. "I'll come with you. You can ride PB. He's one of my own, and he's fast."

"Thank you." Emma Jane watched as he got the horses ready, glad that he moved much more swiftly than she would have. Selfishly, she was also glad he'd volunteered to come along.

Will had been right to warn Wes that Mary might try to follow them and right in that Mary had no business being there. Though Emma Jane's time with the bandits had taught her that some of them were not so bad, their leaders possessed a ruthlessness and cunning that made any dealings with them dangerous.

One more thing Jasper had been right about. She'd acted much more bravely when she'd been in their cabin than she ordinarily would have. Mostly because she was so angry that he seemed to be so… She sighed. He'd been trying to protect her in his own way. But she'd wanted Jasper's love and protection on her own terms. She could see that now.

Wes helped her onto her horse, and she was too busy focusing on staying on the horse to continue thinking about all her missteps with Jasper. Fortunately, Wes knew what the posse's plan was, and he also knew a shortcut.

"We can head them off if we cut through Stumptown. The posse didn't want to go that way in case folks saw them ride through and suspected something was up."

Emma Jane couldn't answer for fear of losing her concentration and falling off. Once again, she couldn't help but be thankful for Wes's presence.

They rode hard, or at least as hard as the snow on the ground would allow. They finally rounded a bend, and Emma Jane could see the entrance to the canyon that had led to the bandits' hideout. The posse was gathered there, and from the looks of things, they were too late.

The bandits were in front of the canyon entrance, and the posse appeared to be surrounded.

Wes slowed their horses, but someone had caught sight of their movement. A shout came from the bandits, and some of them turned in Emma Jane's direction.

The momentary distraction seemed to give the posse the edge they needed, and before Emma Jane knew it, shots rang out. She started to put her hands over her ears, but as soon as she loosened her grip on the reins, PB took off toward the shooting.

Emma Jane grabbed the reins and pulled as hard as she could. Behind her, she could hear Wes yelling instructions, but she couldn't hear them.

Ahead of her, Emma Jane spied Jasper. He seemed to recognize her instantly, his eyes widening. If there was any cause for his disappointment, it was that she'd promised him not to get involved with the case. He'd told her that was the very foundation of trust in their relationship, and she'd gone and broken it.

Just when he'd finally started standing up for her, she'd ruined everything.

But there was nothing to be done. Hopefully, he'd be

willing to listen to her explanation afterward. She hadn't had a choice once she'd overheard the bandits talking about an ambush. Until they'd arrived, the posse had been surrounded, but Emma Jane and Wes had caused enough of a distraction to allow the posse to act.

Please, Emma Jane prayed. Let Jasper see it that way. But mostly, just let him come out of this alive.

He turned toward her, then a shot rang out. Jasper gave her a funny look as he fell off his horse.

"No!" Emma Jane screamed as she jumped off her horse, not waiting for it to slow down or stop. The force of hitting the ground jarred her, and she stumbled, then got back up. She ran toward Jasper, her heart thundering in her chest.

Why wasn't anyone else going to help him?

A bullet whizzed past her, and Emma Jane realized the bandits were shooting wildly at the posse now.

She reached Jasper, who lay on the ground at an odd angle.

"Jasper!"

He coughed. "I'm fine." His voice was raspy. "Just got the wind knocked out of me. Help me up."

Once he was sitting upright again, Jasper tugged at his great overcoat, fumbling with the buttons.

"Let me." Emma Jane brushed his hands aside and worked them open. Her Bible fell out of his coat.

She picked it up and examined it. A bullet was stuck right in the middle.

"Well, I'll be," he said, a smile teasing his lips. "I've been saying that a Bible couldn't save a man's life, but I guess I was wrong."

He took the Bible and kissed it, then he turned to Emma Jane and kissed her.

The kiss happened so fast Emma Jane didn't have time to react. She simply kissed him back. When it was over, she pressed her fingers to her lips and stared at Jasper. "I don't understand."

"I've been reading your Bible in secret. Things were happening inside me, and I needed to know. I wasn't ready to talk about it."

A bullet zinged the ground next to them. Emma Jane jumped, clinging tighter to him. Her heart thundered in her chest so loudly, she almost didn't hear his next words. "When I left today, I just had a feeling that I should bring the Bible with me. I'm not sure why, but I'm glad."

Then Jasper quickly scanned the area around them. "I need to get you someplace safe." Setting his gaze on her once again, he gave her a stern look. "What were you thinking, riding into the middle of this?"

"I was trying to warn you," she said. "I overheard one of the deputies telling someone in the saloon that it was a trap. They have explosives."

Emma Jane glanced around, trying to see how and where they'd use them, but Jasper pulled her close to him. "I should wring your neck for taking a chance like that. But I'm just so grateful that you're all right."

He kissed the top of her head, and once again, Emma Jane found his warmth coursing through her. For a moment, she couldn't even tell there was snow on the ground.

Had she made a mistake in giving up on her marriage so soon?

"Stay close." Jasper took her hand and, crouching low to the ground, moved toward a group of nearby boulders.

Another bullet whizzed past them.

Emma Jane looked behind them, noticing one of the bandits headed their way. "Jasper, watch out!"

He turned, and Emma Jane watched in horror as the bandit raised his pistol in their direction.

"Rich boy or no, I'm gonna git you. You done messed with the wrong man."

With all of her strength, Emma Jane shoved Jasper to the ground. Then a searing pain radiated through her back, like she was on fire. Which made no sense, since everyone knew you couldn't light a fire in the snow.

Which is when she hit Jasper as she fell to the ground.

The weight of Emma Jane's body slamming against him felt wrong. "Emma Jane? Are you all right?"

She didn't answer, and as he shifted his weight, he felt something sticky on her back. When he pulled his hand away, he saw blood.

"Emma Jane!"

She blinked. Mumbled something incoherent about a fire in the snow, then her eyelids closed and she went limp. Jasper held her tight against his chest so she wouldn't fall in the snow.

The crunch of boots on snow made him look up to see Will standing beside him.

"Emma Jane was shot." The words burned as they came out of his mouth. They were the correct words, but they felt so wrong.

Will's brow furrowed as he came closer. "Let me take a look at her. I saw the man take aim at you, but I thought I hit him before he managed to get a shot off. I'm sorry." The lines on his forehead deepend for a moment but relaxed as he squatted on the ground beside them, examining Emma Jane. "Fortunately, she appears to be breathing all right.

"I think we've finally got the upper hand against the bandits. They won't be bothering anyone else, that's for certain. Emma Jane and Wes coming when they did provided us the opening we needed. Let's see what we can do for her, and then we'll get her back to town."

Jasper watched as Will prodded at her wound. This was one area where Jasper had no idea what he was doing. A feeling of helplessness washed over him. The woman he loved had been shot, and he could do *nothing* to help her.

At least the moon gave off enough light that he could see the rise and fall of her chest.

"She's still unconscious," Jasper said, looking at Will for some reassurance.

"Her breathing's fine. She's had a shock, and it's probably best she's out. It won't be an easy trip back home."

One of the lawmen, Cam Higgins, joined them. "We got most of 'em, but we're sending a group of men to get the rest." Then he looked Jasper up and down. "You're the best rider we've got. Can you come with us?"

He glanced at Emma Jane, who murmured something incoherent as her eyelids fluttered. The old Jasper wouldn't have hesitated to go with Cam and the others. After all, what did he know about treating gunshot wounds? He'd be more useful chasing down the rest of the bandits.

Yet now, things were different. Leaving Emma Jane seemed almost inconceivable.

He turned to Cam. "My wife's been shot. I need to stay with her."

Shadows crossed the man's face. "Oh, no. I'm sorry. I didn't realize... Is she going to be all right?"

The question tore at Jasper's insides, biting in places so sensitive he wouldn't have known they existed otherwise.

"She'll be fine," Will said. "I just need something to press against the wound to stop the bleeding. My handkerchief and scarf are about soaked through."

Cam unwound the scarf from his neck. "Use this. Ugliest thing on earth, but it's made from good wool. A little blood can't make it any uglier."

Will took the scarf and pressed it to Emma Jane's back. Jasper adjusted Emma Jane's position to make it easier for Will to tend to her injury. If only he could do more than keep her out of the snow.

"I appreciate your help," Jasper told Cam. "I know you'll want to be with the posse going after the remaining bandits, but can you spare a rider to head to town to get a doctor?"

"Sure thing. You want him to meet you at your place?"

His place. Was there such a thing anymore? He couldn't imagine going back to his family home without Emma Jane, and she'd made it clear that it wasn't home to her.

"We're staying at the Rafferty."

If Jasper's change of address surprised Cam, he gave no indication. The other man gave a nod. "I'll get on it. That wife of yours saved a lot of men from being killed tonight. Wes told us about the trap with the explosives. Had she not come when she did, providing a distraction, we'd have all been slaughtered."

Jasper shivered at the thought. For a moment there, he'd honestly believed that there was no hope. But then he'd thought of Emma Jane and asked what she would do. Immediately, he had the instinct to say a prayer. All he'd said was, *"Lord, help us,"* and then Emma Jane had showed up.

Was she an answer to all of his prayers? He'd asked her about how God spoke to her and answered prayers, and she'd said it all happened in the way he'd just described. God didn't literally step out and give him an answer or do something for him, but it always seemed like He had exactly what he needed when he needed it.

Jasper stroked Emma Jane's silky blond hair. He'd been so blind about so many things, including how simple it was to follow God. And how God had brought them together.

Will said she'd be fine, but Jasper couldn't help but send up another prayer for Emma Jane's survival.

And when she was better, could they find a way to heal the rift between them? Now, more than ever, Jasper wanted to make their marriage work. He'd hoped to court her and get her to come around to seeing things his way. But maybe there wasn't time for that. Maybe he just needed to be honest with his feelings, exposing the rawest places of his heart, and risk being rejected.

"I love you, Emma Jane," he whispered hoarsely.

She murmured something incoherent, and Jasper hoped that, somehow, she'd understood.

"Don't worry," Will said, catching Jasper's eye. "You'll be able to tell her that when she's awake. Like I said, she's going to be fine."

Then Will stood. "Now, I'm going to get on my horse, and you're going to put Emma Jane in my arms. You need to keep pressure on the wound. She's still bleeding, and from what I can tell, the bullet's still lodged inside her.

We need to get her to the doctor and get the bullet out right away."

"I want to carry her." Jasper adjusted Emma Jane in his arms and stood. She was so light in his arms. How had he not noticed what a frail creature she was?

Probably because she was the strongest woman he knew.

Will looked at him like he wanted to argue, but then he shook his head. "Fine. But you need to keep her steady. Too much jostling is going to make the bullet move, and it could travel to her vital organs and kill her."

Jasper gave a quick nod. He'd already known what was at stake, but Will's reminder made it all the more important to be the one to carry Emma Jane into town. If these were to be her last moments, then he had so much he wanted to tell her.

Then Jasper stopped himself. No. He wouldn't let this be the end. Not for Emma Jane, not for them.

"You're going to live, Emma Jane," he rasped, kissing her on top of the head once more. "You're going to live and be my wife in all ways, and we're going to raise Moses…and whatever other children we may have."

Will and some of the other men helped Jasper mount his horse, and then helped get Emma Jane settled comfortably in his arms. Some of the posse had already ridden out in pursuit of the remaining bandits, while the rest were either gathering up the injured or keeping the ones they were apprehending together to send to jail.

They rode back to town, and Jasper was grateful for the buckskin's easy lope. When he'd bought the horse, he'd wondered if he was paying too much. But if it meant Emma Jane's survival, the gelding was worth every penny.

Doc Wallace was just getting off his horse when they arrived at the hotel. He helped Jasper get Emma Jane up to their room and settled in the bed.

"You did a good job of stopping the bleeding," the doc said as he examined her. "But I'm going to need to get the bullet out."

Emma Jane moaned, and her face was paler than he'd ever seen it. Too pale.

"It's going to be all right, sweetheart," Jasper told her. He looked at the doc for confirmation, and he nodded.

"I'm pretty sure the bullet didn't hit any vital organs. But she looks pretty torn up. It wasn't a clean shot."

Jasper closed his eyes. This was the second time a woman had taken a bullet for him. When they were in the brothel, Mel had died stepping in front of a bullet meant for Jasper. It had been that lifesaving action that had brought about Jasper's quest to find and rescue Daisy.

He'd failed to save Daisy, but the cry of a baby in the next room reminded him that he still had a promise to keep. Though he'd told Emma Jane finding a family for Moses would be enough, she'd been right in insisting on keeping him.

Seeing Emma Jane lying on the bed, wounded and in pain, he knew the debt he owed both women was far greater than he could ever repay.

In truth, this was the second time Emma Jane had kept Jasper from harm. When they were trapped in the mine, she'd shoved him out of the way of a rock slide, injuring herself in the process. Typical Emma Jane. Always thinking of helping others before herself.

How could he ever be a man worthy of such a woman?

The doctor's assistant arrived. A young man who

barely looked old enough to be shaving, let alone taking care of patients.

"This is my nephew, Augustus. He'll be assisting me in the surgery. I'm going to have to ask you to leave the room while we get out the bullet, as you'll only be in the way."

"Of course." Jasper pressed a gentle kiss to her forehead. "I'll be back soon," he said softly as he shut the door behind him and went into the sitting room to wait.

Abigail was already in there, rocking a fussy Moses and cooing to him softly.

"I think he knows something's happened to his mama," she said softly.

"Probably," Jasper said gruffly, reaching for the baby. "Let me try."

The knowing smile Abigail gave him made Jasper wonder why he'd spent so much time fighting the inevitable. He held Moses in his arms and gazed down at the little boy.

"Your mama is going to be just fine. But it doesn't hurt to ask God to make sure."

Jasper cradled Moses and began to pray.

Chapter Eighteen

Everything in Emma Jane's body ached. Well, not everything. But what didn't ache burned, and she felt like her entire head was stuffed with cotton. Nausea rolled in her stomach as she struggled to breathe normally. The best she could do was take a few shallow breaths, and even they hurt.

"Emma Jane?" Jasper's voice was soft, gentle and as welcoming as a fire after being out in the cold all day.

No, all night. The last thing she remembered was being cold. So cold. Yet her back had been on fire.

She opened her eyes and turned her head to look at him. Dark circles rimmed his eyes, and he was clearly in need of a shave, but she'd never seen a more welcome sight.

"Good. You're awake. The doctor gave you something for the pain, and he said it would help you sleep, but I'm glad to see you're all right."

Then his eyes examined her face in a funny way. "You *are* all right, aren't you?"

She closed her eyes. Then she remembered. After taking a deep breath, she looked at Jasper again. "I was shot."

The few words took so much effort it felt like she'd already done a day's work, even though she'd just woken up.

"But you're going to be fine," he assured her. "The doctor got the bullet out, and he said it didn't hit anything serious. Just tore up the muscles in your back and shoulder. You've lost a lot of blood, so you'll need to take it easy for a while, but you'll be fine."

Fine. He kept using that word, almost as though he didn't believe it. Emma Jane looked around the room.

"If you're looking for Moses, he's in with Abigail. He and I have been sitting here, waiting for you to wake up, but he was starting to get fussy and I didn't want him to disturb you."

Emma Jane blinked. Moses? Jasper had never willingly used the baby's name before.

"I can get him if you want." He jumped up before she could answer. Then, just as quickly as he left, he returned, carrying Moses as if holding the baby was the most natural thing in the world.

"There she is," Jasper said in a voice so sweet and tender, and clearly aimed at the baby, that Emma Jane hardly knew him. "See? I told you that your mama would be fine."

Her eyes filled with tears. Not only was Jasper calling her son by his name, but he referred to her as Moses's mama.

"Emma Jane? Are you all right? What's wrong? Is your shoulder paining you?"

The worry scattered across Jasper's face made her stomach flip-flop. Who *was* this man?

"I'm fine," she said, her throat scratchy. "I could use some water, though."

Keeping Moses cradled in one arm, Jasper poured her a glass of water. "You're supposed to sip it slowly. Doc Wallace says you may not tolerate much for a while, but it's good for you to drink as much as you can."

She sipped the water, marveling at how comfortable Jasper seemed to be with the baby. When she was finished, he took the glass. She'd only managed a few small sips, but at least her throat wasn't so dry.

"So you remember being shot?" Jasper studied her face intently, making her feel ill at ease. She'd never seen such concern in him before.

"Yes." Emma Jane took a breath. If only it didn't hurt so much to breathe, let alone talk. But so much needed to be said. "I'd gone to warn you that it was an ambush, but I got there too late. And then…they were shooting, and I pushed you, but something struck me. It must have been the bullet."

"It was," Jasper said, his voice solemn. "You saved my life."

Of course. Emma Jane closed her eyes. That's what all of this was about. Jasper had felt guilty when they were trapped in the mine and she'd saved him, which was one of the reasons why he'd married her. Then, when Mel saved him, he'd felt guilty again, thus propelling him on his quest to save Daisy.

Well, this was one act of gratitude Emma Jane wasn't about to accept.

She opened her eyes and stared at Jasper, drawing from all of her strength. "And now you can get on with it. I know you mean well, but living your life shouldn't be about repaying someone else."

Taking another breath hurt more than she'd expected it would. But this wasn't the pain of her wound. No, this was something deeper, and she didn't expect it to heal as quickly as the gunshot would.

"I want you to be happy," she choked out. "I know you feel responsible for what happened to me, and I'm telling you right now that this was my own choice. So go live the life you choose for yourself. You're not allowed to be beholden to me."

Jasper looked at her like she'd gone mad. And maybe she had. Who wouldn't want the town's handsomest, wealthiest man beholden to her?

Emma Jane Jackson, that's who. She deserved better than a man who felt only gratitude for her.

She wanted a man who loved her.

"I will be beholden to you for the rest of my life," Jasper said, looking at her with enough intensity that, if she'd been a block of ice, she'd have melted.

"But not for the reasons you think."

Then he looked down at Moses with such a loving expression, Emma Jane's heart felt like it was about to burst.

"You've taught me a lot of things. About God. About family. About selflessly giving to others."

Then he turned that same loving look on her. *Loving?* Emma Jane blinked. Surely…

"I had hoped that by agreeing to an annulment, it would soften your heart toward me, and eventually I would be able to court you and to convince you to share your life, your heart, with me."

His Adam's apple bobbed. "But that isn't what I want. If you want an annulment, I will give it to you because I love you. The Bible says that when you love someone, you are not selfish. You are not proud. You put the other person first."

Tears glimmered in his eyes. "The night I kissed you by the fire, I was too proud to say that I loved you, because I wasn't sure if you loved me back. And I was afraid I was giving my heart away to someone who would reject it."

Memories of that night flooded her mind, and her eyes also filled with tears. She'd wanted to say the same thing, but her fear of rejection, her comparison to others, it had been too strong, as well.

"I love you, Emma Jane Logan, and I hope will remain Jackson. I want a real marriage. I want to raise Moses together. And I want to raise whatever other children the Lord sees fit to give us—together—as a family."

His hand shook as he reached for her hand. "I said all these things when I thought I was going to lose you, and I don't know if you heard me or not. But I want you to hear me now. And I want you to understand."

Then he brought her hand to his lips, sending a tingle all the way down to her toes. "I'm asking you to be my wife in all ways. To share my life. I will give you everything you need to care for Moses, regardless of whether or not you accept my offer. I want you to say yes, not because of any of the reasons we were together before, but because you love me, too."

Her throat tightened, and she couldn't speak. Was this a dream brought on by her injury? She reached for Jasper with her other arm, ignoring the searing pain in her shoulder and chest.

"Is this real?"

Jasper leaned into her. "Yes."

"You love me?"

"Yes." And then he kissed her, gently pressing his lips to hers, spreading warmth throughout her body.

He was much more careful in this kiss, Emma Jane noted as she kissed him back. But when she tried bringing her arms around him, she understood why.

Pain ripped through her shoulder, and she couldn't help but wince.

"Careful," Jasper warned, pulling away. "I am convinced that you can do just about anything you set your mind to, but I won't have you tearing apart Doc Wallace's careful stitches when we have the rest of our lives for this."

Emma Jane let out a long, contented sigh. Despite the burning sensation in her shoulder, she'd never felt so light. Could she trust Jasper's words? Or were they merely a result of his concern over her condition?

So much in him had changed. He seemed to be every bit the Jasper she liked. *Loved.* When she'd found him last night, he'd told her that he'd been reading her Bible. He'd stood up for her against his mother.

"What happened with the bandits?" she asked carefully.

Jasper shrugged. "I was too busy taking care of you to pay much attention. From what I hear, though, most are either dead or in jail. Deputy Jenks had no idea you'd heard him and gone out to warn us, so they managed to capture him, too. They sent a posse after the couple who got away, but I haven't heard if they got them or not."

Emma Jane closed her eyes for a brief moment before opening them again. If only she didn't feel so weak. But she had to know.

"Why didn't you go with them?"

Jasper looked at her like she'd gone daft. "Why would

I leave my wife when she needed me the most? Why would I leave Moses when his mama is so ill?"

"But you've always wanted to be a lawman," she said quietly.

He shook his head. "No. I've always wanted to make a difference. I thought that meant being brave and being a lawman, but I'm learning that it also means being brave in the sense of standing up for what's right and taking care of those who need it the most."

Adjusting Moses in his arms, he set the baby at Emma Jane's side. She'd been longing to hold him but had been afraid that, with her lack of strength, she wouldn't be able to bear his weight. Having him lay at her side was a good compromise, and she wrapped her good arm around the baby as Jasper continued.

"There is so much good I can do with my money. Not just by donating it, as my family has always done, but also in the ways the Lord has shown me. Because of you, I know there are people in this world who need love and compassion, and that I need to keep my eyes open, serving where I am led."

Then Jasper smoothed Moses's hair. "Right now, that means being here for you and Moses and loving you the best I know how."

The door opened, and Emma Jane lifted her head to see Mrs. Jackson entering her room. She closed her eyes, not wanting another confrontation with the woman.

What would she blame Emma Jane for this time? She'd been the one shot, not Jasper. Surely no one had told the older woman of the near-misses Jasper had.

"I thought I heard voices," she said in a gentle tone that Emma Jane hadn't known the other woman was capable of. "Jasper, I'd like a moment with your wife, if that's all right. Perhaps you could go tell the doctor she's awake."

Emma Jane opened her eyes and gave Jasper a pleading look. She wouldn't ask him not to leave her alone with his mother, not in front of her, but surely he'd not set her to the wolf when she was so weak.

"Of course." Jasper stood. "I can't believe I didn't think of that."

Then he looked down at Emma Jane. "You'll be all right for a few minutes."

He exchanged a glance with his mother, one Emma Jane couldn't read. Mrs. Jackson took Jasper's place as he closed the door behind him.

"I realize this seems peculiar to you," Mrs. Jackson began, her brow furrowed. "I have never been in this situation before, and I hardly know what to say."

Emma Jane didn't respond and instead focused her attention on tucking the blanket around Moses.

"I don't know if you recall, but we had a rather difficult disagreement yesterday." Mrs. Jackson's voice shook, and her eyes were filled with tears.

"I do." Emma Jane kept her response short, not knowing where this conversation was going. She didn't have the strength to continue that argument or defend her choices.

"My son's words hurt me deeply," she said, a tear streaking down her cheek. "I was angry, and I'd thought for sure that I'd lost him to some gold digger."

The words didn't sting as much as Emma Jane thought they would. She'd heard them enough that they'd lost their power over her.

"But I spoke to my husband, and we prayed and I took a deeper look at everything Jasper said." Mrs. Jackson shook her head. "How was I so blind to everything? To the truth?"

She looked down at Emma Jane. "I misjudged you. I'm sorry." Jasper's mother reached down and took Emma Jane's hand. "I know that I have acted unforgivably toward you, but Jasper is all I have. I was scared, and I thought his life was ruined."

Emma Jane squeezed Mrs. Jackson's hand. "It's all right."

"No, it's not," the older woman said. "Jasper was right. Your behavior was without reproach, and I acted inexcusably."

Mrs. Jackson pulled a handkerchief out of her sleeve and dabbed at her eyes. "I pride myself on being a good Christian woman, and I denied you basic kindness. When Jasper read to me from 1 Corinthians about love and asked me if I'd displayed those characteristics of love, I've never been so ashamed of myself."

Emma Jane closed her eyes as she recalled Jasper's words to her about his treatment of her. Of not being selfish or proud. He'd mentioned reading the Bible, and now she understood. Jasper had changed. He'd allowed God into his heart.

Warmth surged through her as she turned to look at Mrs. Jackson. "I understand. I don't know why, but for some reason, we hear the words all our lives and we don't live them out. It took me a long time to learn that lesson."

She squeezed Mrs. Jackson's hand again. "I forgive you. So now you need to forgive yourself and move forward in the new knowledge God has given you."

At Emma Jane's movement, Moses started to fuss. She tried adjusting him, but it only seemed to make him angrier.

"Let me." Mrs. Jackson picked up the baby and cradled him in her arms. "There now, it's all right. I've got you now."

She adjusted his blankets. "You are a handsome little fellow, aren't you?"

If Emma Jane hadn't seen it for herself, she'd have never believed it. The stiff, formal woman who presided over Leadville society with a hawk-like expression had softened. She sat there, holding Moses, making cooing noises at him.

Then Mrs. Jackson turned her expression to Emma Jane. "I understand you call the boy Moses. I was wondering if you'd decided on a middle name."

Emma Jane looked at her blankly.

"Jasper says I'm not to interfere, but I was hoping you wouldn't mind if I made a suggestion. You see, we named Jasper after my father, who hated his given name, but I loved it, so we called him Jasper. My father, who went by his middle name, James, always thought we were trying to insult him. Even though my father has long passed, I thought perhaps you might consider James as a middle name."

The door opened, and Jasper walked in, carrying a tray. "Mother, I thought we'd agreed that you wouldn't interfere."

"It's all right," Emma Jane said, smiling at her mother-in-law. "The truth is, I didn't consider Jasper's wishes in naming Moses, and I know my lack of consideration hurt him deeply. I think we've all been guilty of not living out 1 Corinthians, and that's something I'm going to do better at, as well."

Then she turned her head toward Jasper. "I was hoping you'd be the one to give Moses a middle name." Then she hesitated. Was this enough of a compromise? Of working together. "That is, if you're agreeable to naming him Moses."

The sides of Jasper's lips twitched into a smile. "Does that mean you've accepted my proposal?"

"Oh, my! I didn't, did I?"

A grin so wide she thought it would split her face in two filled her. "Yes! I do love you, Jasper. So very much. And I want to be your wife and have children and spend the rest of our lives together."

Jasper set the tray on the table beside the bed. "Good." Then he set a hand on his mother's shoulder. "I'm sure my mother will rest easier knowing that the woman I love happens to love me back."

Mrs. Jackson smiled. "Indeed. I can't imagine wanting anything different for my son." Then she looked down at Moses. "Or my grandson."

If it were possible for a person's heart to burst from joy, surely Emma Jane's would. But it was the expression on Jasper's face that made Emma Jane's joy complete. She had never seen him looking so content, smiling down at his mother, holding his son, then catching her eye as if to say, "This is everything I always dreamed of."

Perhaps it was just fancy on her part, since in all of her biggest dreams, she'd never imagined it could be this good.

"Mrs. Jackson," Emma Jane said, turning her attention to her mother-in-law. "Would you mind taking Moses into the other room so I could have a moment alone with my husband?"

Gone was the expression of contented gentility on the older woman's face, replaced by the hawk-like version Emma Jane knew so well. "This will not do. I realize you have your own mother, but do you think you could at least call me Mother Jackson? Mrs. Jackson implies we have no relationship at all."

Mother Jackson's eyes softened. "And I do hope that we can have one. Jasper tells me that you knit. Perhaps when you're feeling up to it, we could make some things for my grandson."

A twinkle filled her eyes. "And perhaps any others who might come along?"

"I would like that," Emma Jane whispered, looking over at Jasper. He'd suggested that their shared love of knitting would bring them together, just as Olivia had said that a grandchild would change their relationship.

Jasper winked at Emma Jane, then turned to his mother. "Now that we've settled that matter, I do believe my wife has requested time alone with me."

He didn't wait for Mother Jackson to leave before bending down and kissing Emma Jane. For the first time, their kiss felt absolutely complete. He loved her, and she loved him. Which was all that mattered in the world.

Epilogue

Spring had brought a flurry of activity to Leadville Community Church. And not for tragic reasons. Emma Jane had no idea where so many flowers had come from, but as she gazed around the entrance to the church, she couldn't imagine it looking any more beautiful.

Though her silk dress was brand-new, it was already starting to feel tight. She rubbed the small of her back where it was starting to ache after spending all day helping her friends ready the church for today's ceremony.

"Tired already?" Jasper asked, putting an arm around her, then placing his hand over the tiny bump that was starting to form at her waist. They hadn't told anyone of the new addition soon to be joining their family, but tonight, at the celebration at the Jackson mansion, they would share their news.

"We don't have to go through this," he said, grinning. "After all, we've already been married once."

If she didn't know the twinkle in his eye so well, she'd have thought that he was concerned about her well-being. She pulled his head down for a kiss.

"Absolutely not," she chided when they were finished. "Guests are arriving, and your mother has been looking forward to this event for so long."

Mother Jackson approached, laughing as Moses reached for her diamond necklace and tried putting it in his mouth. "Jasper, do try to behave for at least one day. I know how you hate these things, but I am determined to show off your lovely wife and son."

She pulled the diamond out of Moses's hand. "As for you, young man, I think your father needs to teach you about the proper treatment of a lady's jewelry." In a swift motion, she handed the baby to Jasper.

Then she looked Emma Jane up and down. "Although I see he has neglected his own wife's collection, and that simply won't do."

Emma Jane tried not to groan. She'd made it clear that diamonds were not what she wanted from Jasper, and they'd both agreed their money would be better spent on their projects with the church.

Mother Jackson reached at the back of her neck, then took off her necklace. "Turn around, Emma Jane. This was a gift from Henry when we were married, and now I am giving it to you."

The diamond was heavy on her neck as she looked at Jasper, questioning. He merely shrugged.

"There." Mother Jackson turned around and examined her handiwork. "Absolutely breathtaking. Just watch your son's sticky little fingers on it."

She smiled as she turned to greet the guests who were arriving, but before she could take more than a step, an older matron with an oversize hat approached her.

"Whatever kind of celebration is this?"

"My son and his wife wanted to renew their wedding vows. Apparently, people have been saying it's not a love match. Which, as you can see, is simply not true. We are absolutely delighted to have Emma Jane as part of our family."

Mother Jackson turned and gestured toward Emma Jane and Jasper. "Aren't they the most beautiful couple?"

"Yes," the woman murmured. "But the baby looks nothing like them. So dark. And…"

"I do hope you're not disparaging my grandson." Mother Jackson looked down her regal nose at the woman. "I take insults to my family very seriously, and I would so hate for you to be left off all the good invitations, like the poor Montgomery family has."

Emma Jane felt a pang of regret at her mother-in-law's threat. The Jacksons had sat down with the Montgomerys and told them that Flora's behavior toward Emma Jane was unacceptable. Unfortunately, it had strained relations between the two families, and most people in Leadville had sided with the Jacksons. Apparently, Emma Jane wasn't the only person Flora's tongue had alienated.

The woman shrank back. "Not at all. I think they're a lovely family."

Mother Jackson snapped her fan open, and the woman scurried off. With the same impish look Emma Jane had learned to love about Jasper, Mother Jackson smiled at Emma Jane, then continued on her way.

Jasper leaned in and gave Emma Jane another kiss as voices swirled around them. It wasn't until she felt Moses tugging at her necklace that she pulled away.

"*Moses James Jackson*, that is enough! You mustn't touch Mama's pretty things."

His dark eyes filled with tears as he stuck out his lower lip. Jasper smiled and ruffled his hair. "I know, son. Sometimes she's a hard one, but you'll find, just as I have, that she's almost always right."

"Almost?" Emma Jane gave him a look of mock indignation.

"Yes, almost." Jasper placed a fleeting kiss on the tip of her nose. "And it's always worth it to work through the times when she's not."

"I can live with that."

She'd been right about many things and wrong about others, but Jasper's words about it being worth it to work through them were correct. In the end, none of those things had mattered, except the time and effort they'd both put into their relationship.

Her first wedding day had been one of the most miserable of her life, and while a person should never be forced to marry someone she didn't want to marry, she would never stop being grateful for her marriage to Jasper. It was just as Pastor Lassiter had said—by trusting in the Lord and allowing Him to work in their lives, they had found far greater happiness than Emma Jane could have ever imagined.

* * * * *

WE HOPE YOU ENJOYED
THIS BOOK FROM

LOVE INSPIRED
INSPIRATIONAL ROMANCE

Uplifting stories of faith, forgiveness and hope.

Fall in love with stories where faith helps
guide you through life's challenges, and discover
the promise of a new beginning.

6 NEW BOOKS AVAILABLE EVERY MONTH!

LOVE INSPIRED

Stories to uplift and inspire

Fall in love with Love Inspired—
inspirational and uplifting stories of faith
and hope. Find strength and comfort in
the bonds of friendship and community.
Revel in the warmth of possibility and the
promise of new beginnings.

Sign up for the Love Inspired newsletter
at **LoveInspired.com** to be the first
to find out about upcoming titles,
special promotions and exclusive content.

CONNECT WITH US AT:

 Facebook.com/LoveInspiredBooks

Twitter.com/LoveInspiredBks